Praise for
Kiss of the Rose

"Kate Pearce gives historical romance some serious fangs with *Kiss of the Rose*. Better plan on losing some sleep, because this is a guaranteed all-nighter!"
    —Jessica Andersen, author of the Nightkeepers novels

"A book you can really sink your teeth into! It has everything: adventure, romance, history, and Druids and Vampires too!"   —Brandy Purdy, author of *The Boleyn Wife*

"Wonderfully dark and intriguing . . . a fascinating, sensual world filled with adventure!"
                    —Colleen Gleason, author of the
                        Gardella Vampire Chronicles

"Pearce brings otherworldly passion, danger, and intrigue to life in her sensational new series . . . a wonderful, unique story penned by an amazingly talented author."
                    —Joyfully Reviewed

"Original and outstanding, *Kiss of the Rose* is a brand-new take on vampires. . . . I am really looking forward to Kate Pearce's next installment of this highly provocative series. Her ability to tell an awesome story with sensual and sinfully delicious love scenes is just one of the many reasons why I can't read enough from this amazing author! Five Ribbons."   —Romance Junkies

"Refreshingly imaginative and deliciously sensual . . . *Kiss of the Rose* is an exhilarating tale that will make you want to invest your time, your undivided attention, and maybe even a bit of your heart. This novel will seduce you with all its sensuality, passion, intrigue, danger, and magic. Five stars!"   —Book Soulmates

continued . . .

"A unique and thrilling series that will delight fans of vampire fiction and historical romance enthusiasts as well.... Combining history, the paranormal, and a whole lot of sensual excitement, author Kate Pearce deftly delivers...a distinctive tale that fans of both genres are sure to scoop up and enjoy." —Sharon's Garden of Book Reviews

Praise for the Other Novels of
Kate Pearce

"What an amazingly rich and engrossing story! I was hooked from the very beginning and absolutely did not stop reading until the very end. I hope to read more by this very talented author in the future."—The Romance Studio

"Intelligent characters, complex emotions, and a plot that engaged my emotions to a rare high. Very highly recommended." —TwoLips Reviews

"Can you say HOT?... From the first scorching page to the last, Kate Pearce takes you on a wild ride of sex and suspense, keeping you guessing until the very end." —Simply Romance Reviews

"This book has something for everyone: hot sex scenes, a sexy hero with a tragic past, a smart and compassionate heroine, intrigue, danger, and Regency London at its most decadent!" —*Romantic Times*

"Guaranteed to quicken the pulse." —Joyfully Reviewed

"One of the most arousing and enigmatic historical novels I have read this year." —Romance Junkies

"Hot and steamy ... with vividly imagined scenes." —Ecataromance

THE TUDOR VAMPIRE CHRONICLES BY KATE PEARCE

Kiss of the Rose

Blood of the Rose

THE TUDOR VAMPIRE CHRONICLES

KATE PEARCE

A SIGNET ECLIPSE BOOK

SIGNET ECLIPSE
Published by New American Library, a division of
Penguin Group (USA) Inc., 375 Hudson Street,
New York, New York 10014, USA
Penguin Group (Canada), 90 Eglinton Avenue East, Suite 700, Toronto,
Ontario M4P 2Y3, Canada (a division of Pearson Penguin Canada Inc.)
Penguin Books Ltd., 80 Strand, London WC2R 0RL, England
Penguin Ireland, 25 St. Stephen's Green, Dublin 2,
Ireland (a division of Penguin Books Ltd.)
Penguin Group (Australia), 250 Camberwell Road, Camberwell, Victoria 3124,
Australia (a division of Pearson Australia Group Pty. Ltd.)
Penguin Books India Pvt. Ltd., 11 Community Centre, Panchsheel Park,
New Delhi - 110 017, India
Penguin Group (NZ), 67 Apollo Drive, Rosedale, North Shore 0632,
New Zealand (a division of Pearson New Zealand Ltd.)
Penguin Books (South Africa) (Pty.) Ltd., 24 Sturdee Avenue,
Rosebank, Johannesburg 2196, South Africa

Penguin Books Ltd., Registered Offices:
80 Strand, London WC2R 0RL, England

First published by Signet Eclipse, an imprint of New American Library,
a division of Penguin Group (USA) Inc.

First Printing, February 2011
10 9 8 7 6 5 4 3 2 1

To Dana, Susan, and Amy. We've been writing together for many years, and even though you didn't get to read more than the synopsis of this one, it is still dedicated to you all, for your unwavering support, endless cups of tea, and sharp red pencils.

ACKNOWLEDGMENTS

Thanks again to my editor, Tracy Bernstein, and to my agent, Deidre Knight, for keeping me on track. Big thanks to my family for simply putting up with me when I disappear into "book world." Crystal Jordan and Dayna Hart had the doubtful privilege of reading the manuscript and get mega points for both pointing out the same mistakes, which actually makes it much easier to fix than if everyone disagrees.

On the research front, along with the usual suspects, I enjoyed Alison Weir's new book *The Lady in the Tower: The Fall of Anne Boleyn*. I also have to thank Chrissy Olinger for her knowledge about the correct herbs to use in a fertility potion, and April Morelock for creating a suitably Druidic fertility prayer. More research information can be found on my Web site at TheTudorVampireChronicles .com. Of course, this is primarily a paranormal romance, and I apologize in advance for any historical errors, which are entirely my own.

Chapter 1

Rosalind Llewellyn slid off her horse and immediately grabbed hold of the bridle. After a long day in the saddle, her legs seemed unable to meet the hardness of the ground and bowed like the branches of a willow tree. She glanced around the familiar royal stable yard and heaved a sigh. It was late evening, and everything was quiet. Despite her long absence, nothing had changed. Even the same horses' heads were framed in the half-open stalls and the same voices called out to one another.

She glanced at her companion, Rhys Williams, who was busy removing their belongings from the packs and simultaneously inquiring as to where he should stable the horses. Rhys looked the same as well—if she discounted a certain grim set to his features when he looked at her.

"Can I help, Rhys?"

"No, my lady. Why don't you just stand there in the way instead?"

Rosalind threw him a cross look. "I'm too tired to argue with you, Rhys. Just tell me what to do and I'll be glad to help."

He doffed his cap at her, revealing the dark auburn of his hair. "Then perhaps my lady might move the bags behind the safety of the wall? I'd hate for the horses to trip."

"Or for any of my belongings to be crushed," Rosalind muttered, as she gathered the first of the leather saddle-bags and hefted it over the wall. Rhys cocked an eyebrow at her as she continued her task.

"You seem a little out of sorts, my lady."

"Of course I am. I didn't expect to come back to court. My cousin Jasper is perfectly capable of guarding the king. I'm not sure why I had to return at all."

Rhys grinned at her as he led the first of the horses into one of the vacant stalls. "Coward."

The smell of fresh grain and horse dung drifted back to Rosalind. She waited for him to return, her task forgotten, her hands planted on her hips. "What exactly is that supposed to mean?"

He took her horse's bridle in his gloved hand. "You know."

"Are you saying I didn't want to return to court for a specific reason? You might remember that I almost died last time I was here."

"Oh, I remember." His smile faded. "I was right there beside you. You probably don't remember that part, being as you were too busy making cow eyes at Christopher Ellis."

"I was busy trying to kill the Vampire!"

He bowed. "As were we all. It didn't stop you becoming involved with that soul-sucking Druid slayer, though, did it?"

He stomped off again, and Rosalind could only stare helplessly at his broad back. It was true that she'd become intimately involved with Christopher, but Rhys knew perfectly well why that had happened. Between her Druid gods and the king, she had been caught very neatly in a sensual trap that she had still not managed to escape.

Rhys returned, his face severe. He picked up the heaviest of the bags and heaved it over the low stone wall. "The rest of your belongings should be here by the end of the week, if the carrier makes good time."

"Thank you. I believe I have enough to clothe myself decently for at least a few days." Rosalind touched his leather-clad arm. "Rhys, if you want to return to Wales, I would quite understand."

He looked down at her, his hazel eyes full of wry amusement, his lilting voice lowered to a soft murmur. "Are you trying to get rid of me?"

Rosalind sighed. "I'm trying to avoid hurting you."

"Because you plan on taking up with the newly elevated Lord Christopher Ellis?"

Rosalind raised her chin. "Officially and spiritually I *am* still betrothed to him." She frowned. "I can't quite believe my grandfather has allowed the betrothal to continue, but there it is. As Lord Christopher's betrothed, I am somewhat *obliged* to seek him out."

"Obliged, eh?" Rhys flicked her nose. "*Cariad*, you can call it what you like, but I know you want him and that you don't want me. I'll try not to let it interfere with my job of protecting you."

"I don't know what I want anymore," Rosalind groused and moved out of the way of an incoming horse and rider arrayed in the king's livery. "Christopher hasn't bothered to contact me and express an opinion as to our . . . situation."

Rhys helped her over the stable wall, his hands firm on her waist. "He could hardly come prancing into your father's stronghold, now, could he? He would've been killed on sight."

"That's true, I suppose, but . . . it would've been nice if he'd made the attempt. Or even just written me a letter!"

"And I thought you were deliberately lingering at home to avoid him and the king. Sometimes I'm glad I'm no longer one of your suitors. You have a somewhat bloodthirsty streak." Rhys handed her the lightest bag, which contained her jewelry, coins, and favorite silver dagger. "The position of your lover seems fraught with danger."

"I can't help that." Rosalind took the well-worn path that wound up from the stables to the main wing of the palace. She glanced across at the ruined Roman bathhouse where she'd met with Christopher and the others on her last visit to court. Was he even here? She had no sense of him yet. In the last year, she'd perfected her barriers against him in anticipation of having to see him again, especially if he turned up on the opposite side of a fight.

The last time she'd seen Christopher it had been spring. She and Rhys had fled the court, intent on making it back to Wales before the king's message about her betrothal to one of her family's worst enemies reached her grandfather. They hadn't made it in time, and Rosalind had endured her grandfather's wrath on the subject for several weeks until he'd finally gone quiet and left her alone. That had worried her even more.

She straightened her shoulders and focused on the welcoming lights streaming out of the palace. She would talk to her cousin Jasper tomorrow and see what calamity had arisen that had made him write to her grandfather and insist she return to court. Both she and Christopher had suspected another Vampire plot was in the offing. The urgency the Vampire Council felt about defeating the rogue Vampire, Lady Celia Del Alonso, had been quite out of character for them. It was almost as if Lady Celia had been seen as an obstacle. Or a distraction. As if there was a grander scheme afoot, or someone more powerful and likely to be even more successful in controlling or killing the king.

Rhys paused by the doorway into quarters for the maids of honor and deposited her bags on the ground. "Your grandfather wrote to Queen Katherine to ask for permission for you to return to court. But, from what the stable boy just told me, I'm not certain if she is still in residence here."

"Then where is she?"

"I'm not sure." He grimaced. "Apparently, the king does not wish to gaze upon her visage. She reminds him of his lack of an heir."

"That is so unfair."

"I can't help but agree. The queen is steadfast in her love for the king, but he seems to have moved onto other, more agreeable conquests. Life can be cruel sometimes."

Unwilling to delve into the thorny subject of love with Rhys yet again, Rosalind rose on tiptoe to pat his cheek. "I'm sure I can prevail on someone to give me a bed. Thank you for coming back with me."

His smile this time was definitely rueful. "I didn't have much of a choice, did I? Your grandfather was most insistent that I accompany you." He paused. "And I haven't quite given up hope that Lord Christopher Ellis might come to regret your betrothal and send you back into my arms."

"Rhys . . ."

He winked at her and disappeared into the darkness heading for the stable yard. Rosalind stared after him. Surely he hadn't meant it? She'd done everything she could over the last few months to convince him that she was a lost cause. Whether she was reunited with Christopher or not, she couldn't see herself turning to Rhys. He deserved more than that, deserved to be first with a woman rather than know he would always be second best.

And he would be second best. Rosalind closed her eyes and tried to imagine Christopher's expression when he saw her. Would he be pleased or horrified? She couldn't decide how she felt about seeing him again. All she knew was that he'd stolen her heart, her mind, and her body, and she would never be the same again.

*   *   *

Christopher Ellis slowly opened his eyes and gazed around the great hall. He'd fallen asleep over his ale again, his face cushioned on the trestle table, his boots digging into the musty rushes that covered the floor. Something had woken him up, some sense of danger or premonition. Since tangling with the ancient Spanish Vampire last year, he'd learned to pay close attention to his instincts.

"Lord Christopher."

He sat up, his dagger already in his hand, and found himself staring at Elias Warner, the Vampire Council's representative at court. Elias had the kind of golden looks that made the ladies of the court swoon over him. Christopher saw only the flatness of his silver eyes, the hint of the blood-sucking predator beneath the mask of humanity.

"Master Warner. Where have you been these past few months? Anyone might think you've been avoiding the court."

A small smile twitched on Elias's pale lips, displaying the tips of his fangs. "I've been busy, my lord."

"I'm sure you have." Christopher sat back and tried to look nonchalant. Elias wasn't one for idle chatter. If he openly sought Christopher's company, there was a reason. "How can I help you?"

Elias glanced around at the sleeping hordes and leaned closer. "I wish only to make a suggestion."

Christopher raised his eyebrows. "About what?"

"Your continued safety." Elias nodded. "The Vampire Council appreciates your recent actions toward those members of its community that it values most highly. The Council wishes you to continue to protect and value those individuals."

"I have no idea what you are talking about, Elias. Of course I protect your community. That has been my family's job for centuries."

Elias's smile was not pleasant. "Indeed, we value the Ellis family enormously." He hesitated. "And we would hate to have to dispense with the services of any single member of that family if he formed alliances that were not in our interest."

Christopher stood up and checked that his sword was in place. He stepped over his drinking companion's legs and headed toward the nearest door. "Are you talking about my 'alliance' with Rosalind Llewellyn?"

"I did not say that. But I understand that you are still betrothed to her."

"That is so."

"I do not understand why."

Christopher shrugged. "Because neither my uncle, nor the Llewellyn family, has succeeded in petitioning the king for our release. The king has been rather preoccupied recently."

"Indeed, he has." Elias's silver gaze flicked up to meet Christopher's. "But perhaps your families approve of the connection after all."

Christopher chuckled. "My uncle almost ran me through with his sword when he heard what had happened. I doubt he approves."

"And yet the Llewellyns have stayed their hand as well . . ." Elias sighed. "It seems as if you are tied to the Vampire slayer for good."

Christopher tried to keep his voice bland. "At least for a while, until one of the families comes up with something to entice the king to break the betrothal." A flicker of distaste crossed Elias's face. "You don't like her at all, do you?"

"On the contrary. But speaking from a practical standpoint, she is a dangerous woman."

"She is indeed." Christopher pictured Rosalind, her dark hair tangled in his fingers, her body and thoughts enmeshed with his as he made love to her again and again. Heat blossomed in his mind and in his groin, and he thrust her image away. Elias was far too perceptive for Christopher to drop his guard.

They'd reached the door of the great hall, and Christopher pushed it open. The rush of night air was warm and scented with flowers. He breathed in deeply, allowed the fragrance to settle him and remove the taste of Rosalind from his senses. Something was different. Everything looked the same, but everything had changed . . . He turned back to Elias.

"Now that you have delivered your cryptic message, is there anything else you wanted to say before you disappear again?"

"I think I made myself clear, my lord. I wish you good fortune." Elias bowed and was gone before Christopher had time to blink.

"Not clear at all," Christopher muttered. Something was afoot and he had no idea what. He hated that, hated the way it added to the frustration already raging through him. He was at odds with his family, his Vampire allies, and himself, and all because of Rosalind Llewellyn.

He looked around again. His mind was playing tricks on him. He could almost feel her in his arms, in his thoughts, even taste her . . . He shook his head to clear the strange sensation. Rosalind was safe in deepest Wales, surrounded by her family, and attended by Rhys Williams, who'd probably done his best to persuade her into his bed by now. Christopher slammed his hand against the oak door. And, more fool him, he had let her go, convinced she would return to him.

Christopher muttered an oath and decided to seek his bed. He had a demanding day filled with sporting activities planned for tomorrow, and needed to be up early to make the journey to Hampton Court to attend the king. He followed the ragged path that led along the side of the great hall, his dagger at the ready, his mind unsettled as he tried to puzzle through Elias's "message."

As he rounded the corner of the massive structure, a shadow leaped out at him and before he even realized it, he found himself in the midst of a fight. There were two men, and despite his best efforts, he couldn't withstand the attentions of them both. He was soon slammed face-first against the wall, his dagger hand wrenched up against his spine and a blade at his throat.

"Christopher Ellis."

He knew that voice, had trained alongside the man during his younger, more reckless years. "Sir Marcus Flavian." They were of a similar age and ability, which was probably why Marcus had the sense to bring reinforcements.

"You remember me. Good." Marcus shifted his stance and jerked Christopher's wrist higher. "Then you will no doubt understand why I am here."

Christopher said nothing as he focused on controlling the pain. Marcus laughed, the sound soft.

"You are required to present yourself at our next meeting and explain your actions."

The challenge and summons wasn't unexpected. Ever since his betrothal to Rosalind had become public, Christopher had been expecting the Cult of Mithras to command his appearance. The only surprise was that it had taken so long. He fought back a groan as Marcus twisted his arm again.

"You must have known we would want to question you about your association with the Llewellyn bitch."

Fury rose in Christopher's gut, and he kicked out, caught Marcus on the shin and off guard. He spun around and pushed away from the wall with all his strength. The other man made short work of helping Marcus recapture him, but Christopher didn't care. As he was thrown back against the wall, he glared into Marcus's calm gray eyes.

"I will answer to my superiors, not to you."

"As you wish, but you will answer." The blade of Marcus's dagger flicked out and nicked Christopher's cheek. "Someone will let you know when the meeting is."

Christopher didn't acknowledge either the blood now trickling down his face or the other man's statement. There was nothing he could do to avoid the summons, and in truth, he didn't want to. Thanks to his uncle, he'd had his fill of the Cult of Mithras years ago. Mayhap it was time for him to express his doubts in person.

He watched as Marcus bowed, his blond hair glinting in the moonlight, and then left with his companion. Christopher wiped absently at the blood trickling down his neck. He didn't want any Vampires scenting an easy victim and coming to feast on him. With a groan, he flexed his fingers and hoped he'd still be able to use his right hand come the morning.

Things were definitely getting interesting. He sighed and went to look for his dagger, which he assumed had landed somewhere in the scrubby foliage. Strange that both Elias and Marcus Flavian had reappeared on the same night to warn him of the consequences of his actions.

And a pity that the only way to leave the Cult of Mithras, without dying of natural causes, was by execution.

Chapteʀ 2

"The king is at Hampton Court today, my lady."

"And Queen Katherine?" Rosalind asked.

The maidservant Rosalind had accosted shrugged. "I don't know, my lady. Most of the court is with the king. She might be there."

"Thank you."

The servant's lack of knowledge and indifference as to the queen's whereabouts told Rosalind that things were indeed dire between the king and queen. Oblivious to her surroundings, she'd slept well and woken to find the queen's rooms deserted and only a few servants caring for the five or so elderly ladies who had remained behind.

Rosalind slid the smallest of her daggers into her hanging pocket and retraced her steps down to the stables. As she walked, the stiff, embroidered green skirts of her favorite riding habit brushed against the lush summer foliage. The thought of getting on a horse again didn't please her, but she had no choice. She needed to see King Henry and meet with Jasper, who had been watching over the king in her stead.

"Good morning, Rhys."

"Good morning, my lady." Rhys was already busy saddling her horse. "I assumed you'd want to follow the masses to Hampton Court this morning."

"Indeed." Rosalind made sure her headdress was securely fastened and pulled on her thick leather riding gloves. "You are going to accompany me, aren't you?"

"Of course. I wouldn't miss this for the world." His slow wink made her want to smack him.

"I'm *hoping* to see the king and Jasper."

"Jasper, eh? Not Lord Christopher Ellis?" Rhys tightened the girth on her horse and stood ready to help her into the saddle. "I wonder why Jasper wrote to your grandfather."

"So do I. He's always been convinced he would be far better at guarding the king than I would, so asking for my help must have been hard for him."

"Well nigh impossible, I should think, my lady. Things must indeed be bad." Rhys laced his hands together, waited until she placed her booted foot on his palms, and then threw her up into the saddle. She wanted to groan when her bottom hit the leather.

She waited until he mounted his horse with his usual easy grace and then set off after him. They passed through the great brick arch of the gatehouse. The clatter of the horses' hooves on the cobblestones made it impossible to speak or hear a thing.

As they emerged into the warm sunlight, Rhys glanced at her. "Are you still sore, my lady? If you'd asked me nicely I could've rubbed some horse liniment on your more tender parts."

"I'm quite well. Thank you, Rhys," Rosalind answered and forced a smile.

He nodded in the direction of the river. "If you prefer it, we could get a boat down to Hampton Court. We have enough coin to pay the ferryman."

Rosalind shuddered and gripped her reins more tightly. "You know I hate the water."

He shrugged, making his muscled shoulders bunch in his leather jerkin. "As you wish, my lady. It isn't that far, less than twelve miles, I gather." He slowed his horse to come alongside her. "I heard that Cardinal Wolsey made Hampton Court a palace fit for a king."

"That's why he couldn't keep it—the king obviously decided the same thing."

Rhys chuckled and eased his horse into a smooth trot. "You might be right. They say Wolsey gave it to the king in a last desperate attempt to win back his favor, but obviously it didn't work."

"I wonder why." Rosalind urged her horse into a trot. She could endure a short ride if it meant she was able to see Jasper and find out what was going on. Anticipation surged through her. After a year of almost no activity, she was anxious to return to fighting her Vampire foe. Excitement of another sort threaded through her as well. She might see Christopher again.

Eventually, Rhys pulled up his horse, and they both gazed down at the moat and gatehouse leading up to the newly renovated Hampton Court. The gleaming red brick still looked pristine, the scars of the new building not yet concealed by the parks and gardens encircling the vast house.

"It seems the cardinal did very well for himself—very well indeed, for the son of a butcher," Rhys said.

A cold shiver rippled through Rosalind. King Henry never liked to be shown up by anyone, and this imposing structure was far grander than most of the existing royal palaces. It wasn't surprising that Wolsey had handed it over. "Too well, I suspect."

"I won't argue with you. The king's favor is a fickle thing." Rhys nodded in the direction of the gate. "Shall we go in?"

Rosalind followed him down the treelined avenue and waited as he inquired at the gate. One of the king's guards seemed to recognize Rhys, and they passed through without incident into the Basse court and then through an imposing archway into another courtyard. Rosalind's gaze was caught by the large astrological clock that dominated the enclosed square.

Rhys turned in the saddle to survey the lines of windows. "The guard said the state apartments are in this area. After we stable the horses, we should find the king there."

Rosalind followed him through to the vast and busy stables and waited as he ascertained that the horses would be taken care of. She'd forgotten how good Rhys was at getting people to do his bidding with just a smile and a polite turn of phrase—far better than she would ever be. It was a quality he shared with Christopher, who could charm the birds from the trees when he put his mind to it.

As her ears adjusted to the noisy bustle, she heard cheering from somewhere in the grounds. "Is the king outside?"

A passing stable boy answered her, his freckled face ablaze with excitement. "Aye, my lady. He and some of his courtiers are playing real tennis in the pavilion."

Rosalind caught Rhys's attention and gestured toward the grounds. "Apparently, the king is playing tennis."

"Do you want me to go with you, or shall I concentrate on finding Jasper while you deal with the king?"

"Yes, please, find Jasper." Rosalind let out her breath. She'd much rather meet the king, and anyone else who happened to be included in the royal party, without Rhys at her shoulder. She picked up the skirts of her green riding habit and wished she was wearing something less heavy and concealing. It was hot in the sun, and she was sure she was red in the face. But it couldn't be helped. The king would have to take her as she was, as would everyone else.

She followed the roars and claps of the crowd, and came to a low covered building with one side open to the air. Galleys filled with courtiers lined three sides of the enclosed space as the king and a man she didn't know played a game of tennis on the court. Luckily for his opponent, it appeared that the king was winning. Rosalind squeezed into a small space and wiggled her way forward through the packed courtiers. The king made another shot and the crowd erupted.

By the time she reached the front, King Henry had finished his game and been replaced by another familiar figure, one that made Rosalind's heart beat faster. Christopher Ellis looked as lean and elegant as ever in his shirtsleeves and stockinged feet, his right hand gripping a racquet, his left holding the small ball in the air ready to serve.

He seemed quite familiar with his opponent, their laughing banter inaudible to Rosalind because of the crowd, but obviously not to each other. With a sigh, Rosalind sat back and watched Christopher. She'd missed him so badly, she'd cried for at least a month after leaving him.

She wrapped her arms around herself. Cowardly, too, when she thought about it. She'd been too afraid to stand up to her grandfather and demand that he allow her to marry her family's worst enemy. Instead, she'd skulked at home waiting for her grandfather to resolve matters for her like any silly woman. But he hadn't resolved anything and now she had to face Christopher again. In some part of her soul, it shamed her that she cared so much for Christopher that she was willing to abandon everything she had been brought up to believe in.

She nudged the man sitting next to her. "Excuse me, sir. Who is the man playing against Lord Christopher Ellis?"

"That is Lord George Boleyn, a gentleman of the king's privy chamber. Surely you must know of him."

"I've recently returned from the countryside, sir. I don't believe I've met him before."

The man gave a snort. "If you stay at court, you'll meet him soon enough. Thanks to the influence of his sister, the man rides high in the king's favor."

That gave Rosalind plenty to think about. The match drew to a close, and George Boleyn claimed victory as Christopher laughingly complained about his hand. Rosalind stood with the rest of the crowd, her gaze fixed on

Christopher as he headed for the exit. She stiffened as he and George Boleyn were surrounded by a bevy of beautiful court maidens. One of them even dared to mop Christopher's brow with her lace handkerchief. Not that he seemed to mind at all.

Rosalind set her jaw and stomped down from the viewing gallery to the ground floor, her intentions unclear. Part of her wished to find Christopher and ask him whether he'd missed her at all; the saner part of her knew that would be a mistake and urged her to use her common sense and go and find the king.

But it was too late; the group containing George Boleyn, the beauties, and Christopher was fast bearing down on her. Rosalind stiffened her spine and tried to look anywhere but at Christopher. A woman hung on each of his arms, and he was grinning like a fool who had not a care in the world.

Her smile died and she raised her chin. She would not cower before him. She had nothing to be ashamed of. Christopher's laughing blue gaze swept past her and then returned. Her heart beat uncomfortably against her bodice as he detached himself from his companions and walked over to her.

"My lady, I didn't realize that you had returned to court."

"Obviously."

His smile was a challenge. "Did you imagine I would hide in my room and mope without your presence?"

"That would have been nice, seeing as we are betrothed."

"Are we?" He took two hasty steps toward her, blocking out the light, his chest still heaving, either from his recent exertions or from his current fury. She inhaled the scent of his warm skin and yearned to place her mouth over his and just breathe him in. "I wasn't sure, seeing as you haven't bothered to communicate with me for an entire year."

"Why would I communicate with you? It was a matter for our families to deal with."

"Was it?" He stared into her eyes, and she swallowed uncomfortably at the fire in his gaze. She had no sense of him in her mind at all. Perhaps the connection had been lost. "How foolish of me to believe that it was a matter between *us*."

"Christopher? Are you coming?"

He glanced back over his shoulder, his charming smile suddenly much in evidence. "Yes, my lady."

Rosalind bit down on her lip. "Don't let me detain you from your ..."

"My what?"

"Your whatever it is you are doing."

"Don't worry. I know when I'm not wanted." His glare intensified as he looked over her shoulder. "Here comes your watchdog. I'm sure I'll see you again, my lady. Tell Rhys I sent him my greetings."

Christopher turned and stalked away, straight into the center of the laughing crowd of courtiers. The hint of the scent of fox drifted back to Rosalind, and she wondered which of the male courtiers was a Vampire, and whether Christopher had noticed it. He didn't look back, so Rosalind stayed where she was, her legs trembling and her heart racing so fast that she thought it might leap out of her chest. What right did he have to be so annoyed with her? What had he expected, a series of love letters?

She swung around and saw Rhys approaching her, his hand raised in a salute. Beside him walked her cousin Jasper, who wasn't smiling. Not that he ever smiled much. Unlike most men, he tended to keep his own counsel and only speak when he had something important to say. He bowed and kissed her hand. He was in his late twenties and unmarried, his hair as dark as Rosalind's, but his eyes slate gray to her brown.

"Cousin Rosalind. It is a pleasure to see you again."

"As it is you, cousin."

"I'm glad that you were able to return." Jasper grimaced. "But this is not the best place for us to talk. Perhaps I should meet you later tonight by the entrance to the maze. I doubt we will be disturbed there."

Rosalind glanced uncertainly up at Rhys. "I'm not sure if we are staying here for the night."

Rhys looked resigned. "It seems as if we are now. I'll go and seek some accommodation in the stables for the night. I suggest you find a member of the queen's household and do the same."

"Is the queen here, Jasper?" Rosalind asked.

"I believe she is on a local pilgrimage." Jasper lowered his voice. "She is not welcome here. King Henry, and the king's current companions, have made that very clear."

Jasper took her arm and continued to stroll back toward the main buildings. "For all intents and purposes, the Lady Anne Boleyn is behaving as if she is the queen."

"Anne Boleyn?" Rosalind frowned. "I don't believe I've met her, although I just saw her brother playing tennis."

"She and her brother are much together and their power over the king grows daily. Anne returned to court a year or so ago. She was raised mainly in France."

Rosalind lowered her voice. "Didn't the king have another mistress by the name of Boleyn?"

Jasper nodded. "Yes, her sister, Mary, who has since been married off. But don't make the mistake of assuming that the Lady Anne is the king's mistress. I believe she aims much higher."

"Is she here?"

"I believe so, although to keep the king's interest, she has been known to deliberately absent herself from court in a sulk." Jasper's smile wasn't pleasant. "I believe it is the first time in his life that the king has had to chase and woo a woman for more than a day or two. He seems invigorated by the prospect."

Even as she made the arrangements to meet Jasper that night, Rosalind's unease grew. It seemed that the rumors were true. Queen Katherine had indeed fallen far from the king's favor if he was openly parading his new love in her place. And if that news about the queen wasn't bad enough, what misgivings did Jasper have to reveal about their Vampire foes?

Rosalind didn't allow herself to think about Christopher's cool reception and obvious anger. It was far easier to focus on Jasper than to delve into the unpleasant swirl of emotions Christopher aroused in her. With a shake of her head, Rosalind went to find the controller of the queen's household and beg for a bed for the night. Whatever else happened, her mission to keep the king safe from the Vampire threat remained. She was determined that she—and Jasper—would protect the king at all costs.

Hampton Court was crammed full of the king's courtiers and, despite its size, the great hall seethed like an overcrowded anthill. Having nothing to change into, Rosalind arrived early for the evening meal and made her way to the trestle table where some of the queen's ladies had gathered. She was greeted warmly, although there was an undercurrent of unease among the women. Rosalind could only assume they were worried about their positions at court now that the queen was no longer in favor.

She glanced up at the high table where the king sat, surrounded by his favorites. Seated on his right was his chancellor, Thomas Cromwell, dressed in his black and gray robes, a thick gold chain around his neck. To the king's left was a woman Rosalind hadn't seen before, but assumed was the much-talked-about Lady Anne Boleyn.

Unlike her much-admired sister, Mary, Anne wasn't beautiful by current court standards. Her eyes were very dark, her chin pointed, and her body slender. As Rosalind considered her, Anne glanced at the king as if she owned him. Not beautiful at all, but she had something that drew the eye ...

Rosalind turned back to her dinner and tried not to look across the hall at the king's gentlemen. She'd already spotted Christopher's dark head next to George Boleyn, who was also one of the gentlemen of the privy chamber. The two men seemed close, sharing not only a trencher, but an equal interest in the women who constantly paraded before them.

Rosalind set her teeth. Christopher might think he had a right to amuse himself when she wasn't there, but she intended to set him right on a few matters before they were done. Much depended on what Jasper had to say to her about the Vampires. If Christopher was involved in any of that, she would be devastated.

She looked up to see that his dark blue gaze had fallen on her and found she couldn't look away. Part of her wanted to drop her guard and try to steal into his mind. Then at least she would know his true feelings. But she deserved the words, didn't she? If he was done with her, she deserved to hear it spoken to her face rather than steal the thought from his mind.

She dropped her gaze and made stilted conversation with the ladies around her, aware of the movement of the crowds, the fact that Christopher had turned to speak to a woman and had then disappeared. She could hardly expect him to remain celibate without her, could she? No woman should expect that from a man who wasn't bound by the ties of wedlock. Her fingers curled into fists. Except that if she ever caught Christopher in bed with another woman, she would have no hesitation in cutting off his . . .

"Lady Rosalind?"

With a start, Rosalind turned to find her cousin behind her, along with another man. "Cousin Jasper."

He smiled and indicated his companion. "I wish to present a friend of mine, Sir Reginald Fforde."

Rosalind held out her hand. "It is always a pleasure to meet a friend of yours, Jasper. How do you do, sir?"

Sir Reginald bowed, his fair skin flushing an unbecoming shade of red. "Lady Rosalind, a pleasure. Indeed, a rare and glorious pleasure."

A corner of Jasper's mouth twitched upward as he met

Rosalind's gaze. "Sir Reginald was most insistent on meeting you, cousin. He was— How did you put it, Reginald? 'Struck by your beauty.'"

"How flattering, sir." Behind Sir Reginald, Rosalind noticed the unmistakable looming presence of her betrothed. She smiled deeply into the stuttering young man's eyes. "If only all men were as poetic."

Sir Reginald turned quite puce. "I'll write you a beautiful sonnet to your fine eyes. If you permit, of course."

Rosalind gave a small, tinkling laugh and clasped her hands to her bosom. "Oh, my, Sir Reginald. That would be delightful."

Incoherent now, his mouth opening and closing like a stranded fish, Sir Reginald allowed Jasper to lead him away, leaving Rosalind facing Christopher. She made as if to move past him, but he grasped her firmly by the elbow.

"Where are you off to, my lady?"

Rosalind allowed her gaze to drop to the long fingers wrapped around her arm. "What is it you want?" Despite her best efforts to break free, he steered her toward the shadows at the end of the hall.

"If you wish poems written for you, ask me."

"With your surly and unpleasant attitude, sir, I would fear to read anything you had written about me."

"Obviously."

"What on earth do you mean?" He made no reply. She tried to shake off his grip, but he refused to release her. "Sir Reginald was only being pleasant."

His eyebrows rose. "I can be pleasant."

"I haven't seen any evidence of it so far."

He leaned in closer until his mouth brushed her ear. "My, my, you have a very short memory, don't you?"

She shivered and swallowed hard. "And you've an even shorter memory, judging by your ability to cavort around the court without a care in the world."

His soft laughter was far too intimate for such a crowded place. "Are you jealous?"

She opened her eyes wide at him. "Why would I be jealous? I have plenty of other suitors to choose from."

Christopher straightened, all expression removed from his face. "Ah, yes, and here comes another of them to rescue you."

"I do not need rescuing."

He shrugged. "*I* know that, but it appears the rest of your 'suitors' don't. Jasper is bearing down on us with a very determined expression on his face."

"Which is hardly my fault. I didn't ask him to."

"Why? Are you enjoying our little chat more than I anticipated?"

Christopher's anger was so glaringly obvious that for a moment Rosalind could only stare at him. His barbed comments hurt far more than she had anticipated and made even less sense.

"Why are you being like this?"

Instantly, she regretted her plea. She'd learned from an early age that it wasn't wise to show weakness. She was well trained in how to handle overbearing men, and she could usually overcome her opponents despite her smaller status.

Christopher's gaze softened. "Rosalind, I didn't mean . . ."

She wrenched free of his slackened grip and swung around to face her cousin. "Ah, there you are, Jasper. Have you come to take me to the king?"

Jasper bowed and took her hand, completely ignoring Christopher. Rosalind found she was clinging to his arm as he led her away and she tried to relax her grip.

"Actually, I've arranged for you to meet with the king tomorrow, but I sensed you needed rescuing." He hesitated and looked back over his shoulder, but Christopher had already gone. "Was Lord Christopher annoying you?"

"He always annoys me."

Jasper snorted. "He is an extremely irritating man. After you left, he actually tried to ingratiate himself with me.

I still can't understand why my uncle hasn't broken your betrothal."

"Neither can I." Rosalind kept moving and refrained from turning back to look for Christopher. His anger was puzzling. It was if he felt that she had let him down, but how could that be? She had done nothing to get out of the betrothal or to speak against him to her grandfather. She suddenly felt tired and squeezed Jasper's arm.

"I think I'll go and rest for a while."

"If you are sure you are all right." Jasper studied her for a long moment before releasing her hand. "I am more than willing to keep you company if you wish to avoid your betrothed."

Rosalind smiled at him. "Thank you, Jasper, but I'll retire for the night. I'll be quite safe." She curtsied, and he bowed, and she left the great hall. The clock in the courtyard struck eight times and Rosalind smothered a yawn. If she was to be alert and ready to hear Jasper's suspicions about the Vampires at midnight, a nap would be very welcome. She also needed time to ponder Christopher's behavior. Although, in truth, she was unlikely to understand him if she thought about him for a year and a day.

Chapter 3

As agreed, Rosalind met Rhys under the archway between Clock court and Basse court. The huge clock boomed twelve times, vibrating the wall at her back. She only wished she had brought her boy's clothes with her instead of having to wear her skirts. Running around in a riding habit and petticoats left much to be desired. But at least she had her dagger. It felt comforting in her hand.

"Are you ready, my lady?" Rhys whispered.

"I'm ready." Rosalind fell into step behind him as he skirted the archway and headed out into the formal gardens. He used the older, more established trees that had shaded the earlier church buildings as cover and Rosalind followed suit. After a little while, he paused to point out a dense line of bushes beyond the more formal knot garden.

"There's the maze. I understand the king intends to pull this one up and build a much grander version."

"Of course he does. Everything the king owns has to be bigger and better than it was before he glorified it with his attention." Rosalind considered the entrance to the maze. "At least it affords us some cover. A new maze would be very hard to hide in."

"True," said Rhys. "I'll go first. I'll call you over when I'm sure it is safe."

Rosalind always chafed at being left behind, but she had sense enough to realize Rhys was well trained to ensure their safety. After all, he had taught her all she knew about fighting Vampires. She studied the long shadows cast by the old yew trees to her left and drew her dagger. Someone was coming. She could only hope it was Jasper.

Rhys lifted his head and beckoned for her to join him at the entrance of the maze. Rosalind gathered her cumbersome skirts in one hand and ran to him.

"There is someone approaching from the right," she whispered.

"Aye." Rhys nodded. "I heard. We'll keep back until we're sure it's Jasper."

To Rosalind's relief, it was indeed Jasper who appeared, his sword drawn, his clothes a dull, serviceable brown that didn't attract notice. In the moonlight, he looked more alert and much harder. With a quick gesture he led them into the first passageway of the maze.

Keeping his voice low, he began to speak without preamble. "Lady Rosalind, I wrote to your grandfather because something is definitely wrong at court. I do not have your womanly skill for sniffing out Vampires, but even I've become aware that there are many more of our enemies gathering at court." He grimaced. "Despite my best efforts, I've had little success in getting any information from Elias Warner. He professes to know nothing, but I'm certain he lies. There is a gleam in his eye that convinces me he enjoys misleading me."

"That certainly sounds like Elias," Rosalind said. "He delights in being deliberately vague—except when he wants something for himself or information for his superiors."

"Perhaps you will have more luck with him, my lady," Jasper replied. "He seemed quite disappointed when you left court and he had to deal with me."

Rosalind shivered as she remembered the Vampire's

enigmatic silver gaze. Christopher had warned her that Elias had developed more than a friendly interest in her. And, when forced to share Elias's mind by the rogue Vampire, she'd realized it was true.

"I'll certainly try to get more information out of Elias, but surely the threat must be more specific for you to have requested my presence back at court."

"Oh, it's quite specific, my lady. Do you know the Boleyn family?"

Rosalind felt cold. "I met Mary Boleyn once, and just today I saw both the Lady Anne and her brother, George. But I'm not acquainted with them."

"It is whispered that the family has turned to the Dark Arts to ensure their rise to power. And it has certainly been spectacular."

"Witchcraft? That is what has you worried?"

Jasper hesitated. "I believe the Lady Anne is a Vampire out to win the king to the Vampire cause."

"But, by all accounts, she is just his latest mistress, one of his passing fancies. And he would never be influenced by a mere woman, in any case."

"He doesn't treat her like any other woman. He is determined to have her and she plays him like a fish on a hook. Surely you must have heard the rumors that the king is intending to annul his marriage to Queen Katherine on the grounds of their consanguinity?"

"Those rumors have swirled for years."

"But now the king has a reason to want to be free. Apparently, he has pledged Anne Boleyn a queen's crown and a place at his side as his wife."

Rosalind went still. "Are you sure?"

"Sure enough to write to your grandfather asking for your return. You are better able to detect a Vampire's scent than I am, and you are a maid of honor."

"To Queen Katherine."

"I'm sure if you asked the king, he would be happy for you to serve the Lady Anne instead."

Rosalind shivered and Rhys stepped up close behind her, shielding her body from the wind suddenly whipping through the channels of the maze. "How could I serve Anne Boleyn? I would feel as if I had betrayed and abandoned the queen when she needed me most."

Rhys squeezed her shoulder. "From what I understand, the queen has been forbidden to have more than a handful of followers with her. The king probably wouldn't allow you to go to her anyway."

Rosalind drew in a long breath. "Then I suppose my first task is to see the king and ask him if I might serve the very woman who wants to bring about his downfall." She glanced up at Rhys and then at Jasper. "At least if I can confirm that Anne Boleyn is indeed a Vampire I can inform the king."

Jasper nodded. "If he will listen to you. Many think him already bewitched and set on his course to end his first marriage and marry Lady Anne."

"We can only pray that is not the case and hope for a happy resolution," Rosalind said. "I will certainly do my best to talk to Elias and express our concerns."

"I pray you have more success than I did, my lady." Jasper bowed and smiled at Rhys. "Perhaps you can let me know what happens between the king and Rosalind."

"Of course, Jasper." Rhys bowed in return. "Now I suggest we return to our beds. It's a chilly night."

Jasper departed first, threading his way back through the yew trees. Rosalind turned toward the formal gardens, but Rhys suddenly blocked her path.

"There is someone else out here."

Rosalind tried to look around Rhys, but he shoved her back toward the maze. "Wait."

"There's no need to panic. It's only me."

Rhys didn't lower his weapon and neither did Rosalind.

"What do you want, Lord Christopher?" Rhys asked softly.

"Just to talk."

Rosalind finally succeeded in stepping around Rhys and saw Christopher, dressed in his habitual black, his hands open to display his lack of weapons, his expression somber.

"We have nothing to say to you, my lord."

Christopher smiled. "In truth, I have nothing to say to *you*, Rhys Williams. Only to Rosalind."

"Who has no wish to hear it."

Christopher glared at Rosalind. "Are you allowing Rhys to speak for you these days?"

"You know I am not."

Rhys grinned. "Mayhap you should, *cariad*."

A dagger appeared in Christopher's hand. "Did you just call her your 'love'?"

"I didn't realize you spoke Welsh, my lord."

"Never mind that. I don't appreciate you calling my betrothed your 'love.' "

Rhys pushed past Rosalind again and faced Christopher toe-to-toe. "You well know that your betrothal cannot last."

"And you think to take advantage of that fact and poach on another man's property?"

"I am not your property," Rosalind hissed.

Christopher gave her a quick glance. "My chattel, then."

Rosalind tried to get around Rhys, but he held her off with one muscled arm. "I can handle this, my lady."

She kicked him sharply in the shin and he yelped. "You two deserve each other. A pair of more mutton-headed fools I have never seen." To emphasize her point, Rosalind turned on her heel and walked back into the maze. She would wait them out. Perhaps she might even emerge to find they had killed each other, which would cheer her greatly.

The high hornbeam hedges closed in around her, but she kept walking until she could no longer hear their voices. She had an excellent sense of direction, so she reckoned the chances of getting lost in the maze were remote.

*   *   *

Christopher hardly heard Rosalind's cry of exasperation as he gazed at Rhys, a challenge in his eyes. "I have no intention of breaking the betrothal. You know that."

"It won't be up to you. Your family will find a way to release you, won't they?"

"I expect them to try. What is far more interesting to contemplate is why neither family has yet done so."

Rhys relaxed his fighting stance. "I've wondered that myself."

Christopher slid his dagger back into its sheath. "Perhaps someone wishes us to remain linked together. For what purpose I cannot yet fathom."

"I have no idea either." Rhys turned his head and then spun around in a slow circle. "Where did Rosalind go?"

Christopher smiled. "Into the maze to get away from us, I assume."

Rhys groaned. "I suppose I'll have to go in there and fetch her now."

"How about you let me do that?"

"She won't want to see you, my lord. She isn't happy with you at all."

"I noticed that, which is why I need to talk to her and set a few things straight." Rhys opened his mouth as if to object and Christopher kept talking. "Please, Rhys. Give me this one chance. If she tells me to go to the devil, or that she never wants to speak to me again, I'll gladly leave her alone."

"All right, then, but don't tell her it was my idea."

"I wouldn't dare." Christopher bowed. "I'll take care of her and get her back to bed safely."

"Her own bed." Rhys scowled. "Or I will be demanding a reckoning from you."

"I'll do whatever the lady wishes, I give you my word. Now let me go and find her before she is completely lost."

Christopher headed into the maze and placed his left hand on the left wall. There was no sign of Rosalind, but then she'd had a good start on him. As he walked he pondered the strange meeting he'd only witnessed from afar. Why had the Druids chosen to meet in secret and exactly why had Rosalind returned to court?

He had sensed a growing excitement in the Vampire community these last few months, but of course no one would tell him why. The stain of his mother's turning Vampire was enough to make his loyalty questionable to both his own family and the Vampires who despised impure bloodlines. It was even more apparent since he'd met Rosalind Llewellyn and become linked to her both physically and mentally.

Ahead of him he caught a whisper of sound and went still. Was that Rosalind cursing? A reluctant smile curved his lips. If he didn't find her quickly, she was likely to take her dagger and carve an exit all by herself.

Rosalind spun around in a fruitless circle. All the hedges looked the same now, and she was hopelessly lost. So much for her much-vaunted sense of direction. The maze stifled sound, so she had no sense of the outside, of the wind, of the direction of the huge main buildings. The hedges were over six feet tall and although dense, the branches were spindly and didn't offer the means to climb up and see where she was. Mayhap she would be better off trying to crawl in a straight line right through them.

Rosalind set off once again and found herself in yet another dead end. She kicked out at the hedge trunks and hurt her toe. Low laughter behind her made her spin around, her dagger drawn, her heart thumping.

Christopher swept her an elegant bow. "Are you lost, my lady?"

"Not at all." Rosalind continued to glare at him as he made no move to leave. "I'm just taking a quiet stroll and admiring the greenery."

"In the middle of a dark, cold night?"

"You are doing the same thing, sir."

He advanced a step toward her. "I am looking for you. Rhys and I were worried."

"You and Rhys were threatening each other not half an hour ago!"

"We came to an understanding."

"Men." Rosalind scoffed. "I was hoping you'd kill each other."

"I'm sorry to disappoint you, but I like Rhys."

"More than you like me, I warrant."

He regarded her seriously, his head to one side. "Sometimes. You bring out both the best and the worst in me."

"As you do me." Rosalind moved closer to the hedge and Christopher immediately copied her action. "I'm surprised you didn't let Rhys come after me."

"We fought over the honor of being your gallant knight."

Rosalind made a rude noise. "Did you lose?"

His smile flashed out. "Rosalind, it is very hard to be angry with you when you are so charming."

She clenched her hands into fists. "I'm not quite sure why you are angry with me at all."

His eyebrows rose. "I thought I'd made myself clear."

"As clear as most men."

"You've ignored me for a year and then you come skipping back to court and expect what? My instant attendance and adoration?"

"What brass! How have I ignored you?"

He advanced toward her. "You never wrote me a single note, not even to tell me you had reached home safely."

"That isn't true."

"Are you claiming you wrote to me?"

"I did!"

"I never received a letter from you." A muscle flicked in his cheek. He had an uncanny ability to slip from affability to anger in but a moment. "I had to take my cap in my hand and ask Elias Warner for news of you."

"But that is who I sent your letter to."

"He never gave me any letter!"

"Probably because it isn't in his best interests for us to be together."

He slapped a hand to his forehead. "And yet, fool that I am, I entrusted him with my letters for you. He promised me he would see them delivered. I should've asked him to whom."

"I never received anything from you." Rosalind stared at Christopher as she imagined him laboring over a letter for her. She found herself wanting to smile. "You truly wrote to me?"

"Of course I did! I even composed some terrible love songs in your honor." He groaned. "Elias must've enjoyed those. I wonder what he did with the letters. I can't wait to ask him."

"Me too." She licked her lips and looked up at him, warmth expanding in her chest. "It was kind of you to write."

"Kind of me?" He scowled at her. "I didn't do it out of kindness." The next moment she was in his arms. "I did it because of this."

He kissed her hard, his mouth taking possession of hers as if he had never left, as if he still had the right to command both her love and her obedience. Rosalind kissed him back, her tongue dueling with his, her hand tight in his crow black hair. When she pushed him away he was breathing as hard as she was.

It was far too easy for her to succumb to his body's demands. She wanted him, and had never forgotten the taste and smell of him. But the thought of her impending mission held her back from complete capitulation. Why did his mind remain as firmly locked against her as hers was to him? What secrets might he be keeping for his Vampire allies?

She stroked his bearded cheek, feathered her fingers over his fine curved lips and reluctantly pulled away. "We have to get out of the maze. Do you know how?"

He frowned. "That's all you have to say? What is amiss,

Rosalind, that you don't want to kiss me? Surely now that we have sorted out this muddle we can be at ease with each other?" His smile was a sensual invitation that made her long to wrap herself around him and drown in his kisses. If only it was as simple as a few stolen love letters . . .

She stepped out of his arms and smoothed down her skirts. "I simply wish to leave this maze. It has become quite oppressive."

He regarded her for a long moment and then held out his hand. "Hold on to me, and I'll have you out of here in the twitch of a lamb's tail."

She took his hand and his long fingers entwined with hers. It felt like coming home. He sheathed his dagger and placed his right hand on the prickly green wall. "It's easy. When exiting, you keep your hand on the right side of the hedge and follow it, even into the dead ends."

"That sounds far too straightforward," Rosalind muttered, but she kept hold of him and they were soon back at the beginning of the maze. "Thank you."

He released her, but didn't move away. "What's wrong, Rosalind?"

She tried to smile. "Nothing at all, my lord."

His eyes narrowed and his hand fell to his sword. "Then what were you doing out here in the first place?"

"That is none of your concern."

"Because it was Druid business?"

She shrugged, aware of a chill emanating not just from the breeze, but from Christopher's frosty blue eyes. It seemed the year apart had changed him, made his expression harder and his gaze more wary.

"As you may recall, my lady, Druid business often concerns the Vampires, which makes it my business."

"Is that why you were out here, spying on me?"

"I have a perfect right to protect my own."

"To protect the Vampires? You consider those monsters your own kind, then?"

He bowed and stepped back. "Verily, I was thinking of you, rather than the Vampires."

"I am not yours to protect."

"You are my betrothed."

Rosalind wanted to scream at his obstinate tone. "A temporary aberration, we both know that."

He took her hand and planted a kiss on it. "There's nothing temporary about this betrothal for me." He spun around and stalked off before coming to a halt. "By the rood, I promised Rhys I'd see you back to your bed."

For some reason, Rosalind felt close to tears. "I'm quite capable—"

He turned back and advanced upon her, the threat of retribution gleaming in his eyes. "Rosalind, by all that is holy, accept my escort, or I'll put you over my shoulder and carry you like the carcass of a pig!"

Without speaking, she marched off in the direction of the Clock court, Christopher muttering behind her. How could she trust him when she didn't know his relationship to the Boleyns? He'd seemed on familiar terms with George, but she had yet to see him with the Lady Anne. Whatever he said, and despite his kisses, she couldn't afford to relax with him yet. For all intents and purposes, he was clearly allied with her enemies once more.

Chapter 4

"Ah, Lady Rosalind, have you returned to court to prepare for your wedding?" King Henry asked, as he extended his beringed hand for Rosalind to kiss.

"My betrothal was certainly part of my desire to return to court, Your Majesty." Rosalind inhaled the king's over-perfumed scent and could detect no hint of a male Vampire's animal stench. As a rare female Vampire slayer, she had an ability to sniff out Vampires purely by scent that was highly valued. To her, the males tended to smell like animals, the females like flowers.

She breathed a silent prayer of relief. Although a faint hint of flowery fragrance hung around the king, he hadn't been turned by a Vampire—yet.

The king raised her to her feet and then sat in his ornate gold chair. Apart from the quiet presence of Sir Henry Norris, the king's groom of the stool, who remained at the door out of earshot, they were alone in the king's most private chamber. In the year of her absence, King Henry had gained several pounds and the chair creaked ominously when he shifted his weight.

"As your grandfather's ill health makes him unable to

attend court, I would be more than happy to stand up for you in his place at your wedding."

"That is very kind of you, sire. I hardly deserve such a great honor."

King Henry leaned toward her. "Indeed, you do, my dear. I believe I owe you my life."

Rosalind bit her lip. "As to that, Your Majesty. There are fears that another Vampire plot is in the offing, so I would urge you to be careful."

"Another plot? Is that another of those reasons for your return to court that you spoke of?" The king scowled. "I had hoped that by putting my wife away from me and distancing myself from her foul Spanish servants, I would be safe."

With great difficulty, Rosalind bit back her instinctive desire to defend Queen Katherine. "There are Vampires in every country of the known world."

"Even *English* Vampires?"

Rosalind thought of Elias Warner's perfect English complexion and cold smile. "Indeed, sire, you should never discount anyone, even those who are closest to you." She had no evidence to bring against the Boleyns yet, and she wasn't foolish enough to blurt out her suspicions to the king before she was prepared. Many had died for much less.

The king narrowed his eyes. "A year ago, I wouldn't even have entertained the thought that these creatures existed. The idea that my father made a pact with the Druids to win the crown of England still befuddles me."

"But remember, sire, my family also made a pact to protect yours, and we will do *anything* to stop the Vampires taking power."

"As you proved last year, my lady." The king sat back. "I know better now, and I can assure you that I will be wary."

Rosalind sank into another deep curtsy. "I am glad to hear it, Your Majesty. I would hate for harm to befall you."

"In the meantime, you will stay at court to guard my person, Lady Rosalind."

"Yes, sire." Rosalind hesitated. "Do you wish me to resume my service with Queen Katherine?"

The good humor drained from the king's face. "No, you can serve the Lady Anne Boleyn. She is much in my presence and she keeps a godly and pious state. You will do well with her."

Rosalind doubted that, but at least it would give her the opportunity to find out if Jasper's guess was correct and that Anne Boleyn was indeed a Vampire.

The king nodded to Sir Henry to open the door. "Let me know when your wedding is due to take place."

"I will, Your Majesty." Rosalind offered the king one last smile and escaped from his presence. It was unnerving to deceive her monarch, a man so powerful that he could have her killed with a single word. And she had much to conceal from him—not only her sham wedding preparations, but her need to gather evidence against the very woman he had raised above the queen.

Rosalind took a deep, steadying breath and straightened out the skirts of her crumpled riding habit. If she was to meet the Lady Anne, she needed to look her best and be prepared for anything.

Christopher finally cornered Elias Warner in the great hall and maneuvered him into a more private area near one of the massive fireplaces. Despite his ability to disappear at will, Elias allowed himself to be gathered up, his smile affable, his gaze amused. That alone was enough to rouse Christopher's suspicions. Elias was an old Vampire who had been the liaison between the Ellis family and the Vampire Council for centuries.

"What's going on, Elias?" Christopher demanded.

Elias blinked slowly like a cat. "I'm not quite sure what you mean, my lord. Is there something in particular that is worrying you?"

"You know why I'm worried. Why has Rosalind Llewellyn returned to court?"

"She has?" Elias sighed. "I was expecting that Welsh clodpole Rhys Williams would have married her by now, and got her with child."

"Lady Rosalind is betrothed to me."

"Ah, yes, so she is." Elias stared into Christopher's eyes. "And you wonder why I am reluctant to reveal anything about Vampire politics to you."

"When Rosalind was here before I didn't betray the Vampires. In truth, we helped you destroy a rogue who threatened the king."

Elias waved a careless hand. "You did help, that is true, but you are still suspect."

Christopher set his jaw. "The fact that Rosalind has returned indicates that the Druids are aware of the Vampires gathering around the king again. They obviously believe there is another threat, and I agree with them. If you do not keep me informed, how am I supposed to counteract the Druids?"

"That is an excellent point, Lord Christopher. Why don't you ask Lady Rosalind?"

"Because she won't talk to me either! And you know why."

Elias looked politely puzzled. "I'm not quite sure what you mean, my lord."

"The letters I gave you to send on to Rosalind. The letter she wrote to me."

"Ah, that." Elias shrugged. "I was quite willing to help you, but unfortunately, those above me, whose power I fear, ordered me not to send the letters anywhere."

"What did you do with them?"

Elias met Christopher's gaze. "I read them, as I was instructed to do, and then I burned them. There was nothing of interest in the letters—apart from your inability to construct a good rhyming couplet."

Christopher ignored the provocative comment. "How can I be certain that you burned the letters?"

"I do have some scruples, my lord."

"Not that I've noticed." Christopher knew he would get no further with Elias, and in truth, there was little he could do about the letters now. He steered the conversation back to other important issues. "Don't you understand that because you refuse to cooperate with me, I'm unable to do the job I was brought to court for—to protect the Vampires?"

"I can see that must be frustrating for you."

"And yet you don't intend to do anything about it, do you?"

Elias's smile died. "Be at ease, sir. We don't need your help."

Christopher stiffened. "My uncle will be most surprised to hear it. The Ellis family has been your right hand for more than a thousand years."

"And we will not forget your service when we rule this land. We'll allow you to live."

Christopher studied the other man's inscrutable face. As usual, he found it impossible to know whether Elias was telling him the truth. "You believe you are in a position to take over the whole kingdom?"

"We will be presently." Elias looked over Christopher's shoulder. "And now I must go. I believe your uncle is lodged in the Clock court. I suggest you speak to him about your concerns."

"I most certainly shall." Christopher bowed. "You have been your usual unhelpful self."

"I strive to please." Elias inclined his head. "Give Lady Rosalind my best, won't you?"

Protected by Christopher's broader form, he disappeared before Christopher could frame a reply.

Christopher punched the stone wall and took a moment to gather his thoughts. Elias's confident prediction of Vampire domination unsettled Christopher deeply. Like most Druid slayers, he only wished to live in peace with the Vampires; they were, after all, allies in their defense of Christendom from what he'd been taught to believe was a dangerous cult. Only the most fanatical members of the Mithras Cult dreamed of the Vampires turning every human in the land.

And he was unable to do anything, because no one was talking to him. Sometimes he cursed his mother for leaving him between two worlds, neither a Vampire nor completely human. Christopher let out a frustrated breath. There was nothing else to do but brave his uncle Edward in his chamber. He would probably find out little, but at least he would have tried all avenues open to him.

Rosalind followed the king's servant into the suite of rooms that the queen would usually have occupied. Laughter and music rose from the many groups of courtiers scattered around the large, sunny chamber. Rosalind recognized many familiar faces, but there were also a disturbing number of new ones. Younger folk with an avaricious gleam in their eyes, their desire to be seen and noticed by the woman seated in the center of the room far too obvious to ignore.

Although the chamber was large and well aired, Rosalind detected at least fifteen different Vampire scents blending with the more usual human smells. If the Boleyns weren't Vampires, they seemed to attract them like flies. Rosalind waited as the servant delivered the king's note to Anne Boleyn.

"Ah, Lady Rosalind."

Rosalind took a deep breath and stepped forward to curtsy. The sickly smell of honeysuckle assailed her nostrils, and she fought the urge to clap a hand to her mouth and retch. Either Anne Boleyn was a young Vampire who had no ability to mask her scent, or she was flaunting it. Rosalind guessed the latter. A woman who had come this close to entrapping a king would not be afraid of much.

"The king tells me I should add you to my ladies." Anne looked down at the note. Her light voice still held traces of her French upbringing. "He says he holds your family in high esteem."

"Yes, my lady. The king has been most generous to us." Reluctantly, Rosalind rose from her curtsy and fixed her gaze on Anne Boleyn's long white fingers and the black and silver roses embroidered on her elaborate bodice. For some reason, Rosalind was reluctant to look into the Vampire's face. She felt naked without her weapons. It was highly likely that Anne had heard of the Llewellyn family. They were hardly unknown in Vampire circles.

"The king also says that you are betrothed to a gentleman of the court and that you are preparing for your wedding."

"I am betrothed to Lord Christopher Ellis, my lady."

"Kit Ellis?" Anne's musical laugh forced Rosalind to look up into her dark, almost black eyes. Rosalind detected interest, curiosity, and a hint of hostility. "Why did he not mention it? I wonder."

Rosalind kept smiling and tried not to breathe in too deeply. The cloying scent of honeysuckle made her feel ill.

"If you are betrothed to dear Kit, of course you are welcome among my ladies." Anne clapped her hands as if she were indeed the queen. "Lady Wilkinson will make provision for you."

Rosalind curtsied again and turned away, glad to escape both that piercing black gaze and the tainted aroma of Vampire. As she followed a chattering Lady Wilkinson from the room, a heavy feeling settled in Rosalind's stomach. Lady Anne Boleyn was indeed a Vampire, and probably an old one at that, and the king was in love with her. How on earth was she going to tell King Henry? She wasn't sure if she dared.

*   *   *

"Ah, Christopher."

"Good morning, sir." Christopher shut the door and walked toward his uncle Edward, who sat by the fire. Since his last illness, Edward never seemed to feel warm. It made the small room stiflingly hot, and Christopher wished he could take off his doublet. He studied his uncle's smooth, waxen face and, as usual, was unable to gauge his feelings at all.

"What is the matter?"

Without being asked, Christopher took the seat opposite his uncle. "I was just speaking to Elias Warner. He gave me some worrying news."

Edward raised his eyebrows. "Master Warner likes to imagine he knows far more than he actually does. What scandal broth is he brewing now?"

"He suggested that the Vampires are close to ruling the king."

"In truth, I *have* noticed a new influx of Vampires to court."

Christopher clasped his hands together between his knees. "He also said the Vampires didn't need any assistance from our family."

"That seems unlikely. We have aided them for centuries." Edward paused. "Unless he meant you, specifically. The Vampires have no reason to trust you now, do they?"

The old familiar sense of being unworthy washed over Christopher, but he shoved it away. "Because of my betrothal to Rosalind Llewellyn?"

"Of course."

"Yet, as far as I can tell, you have made no effort to dismantle that betrothal. Why is that?"

"Because it might still prove useful to us." Edward closed the book of sermons on his lap with a snap. "In a way, having you locked together with the Vampire slayer nullifies you both. Her family doesn't quite trust her anymore, and—"

"And you've never trusted me anyway."

His uncle's smile confirmed Christopher's worst fears. "So you refuse to tell me what is going on either."

"Actually, I'd prefer it if you used your influence to find out what your betrothed knows."

"You want me to spy on Rosalind."

"That is your duty to your family. It's hardly a problem for you, is it? From all accounts, you are besotted with the wench." Edward's gaze sharpened. "Women tend to grow very confiding after a tumble in the hay."

Christopher stood up so abruptly his chair rocked back on its legs. "I am loyal to the Ellis family, but I resent being excluded from your confidence. If aught befalls me or anyone I care for because you have kept me in ignorance, I will not let it go unchallenged."

"Brave words from a man who already faces a death sentence."

"You are right." He gazed steadily at his uncle. "I regret my decision to join the Cult of Mithras more than you could know."

"And yet you begged and pleaded with me to be inducted. *Begged*, Christopher."

"Because in my youth, I wanted your approval. I realize now that I would never have gained it whatever I did. I will always remain suspect, firstly because of my tainted blood and now because of Rosalind Llewellyn."

His uncle stood up. "Do you expect me to feel sorry for you, nephew? You were given a home and a creed to follow, which is more than most half-breed Vampire spawn get. I could've had you killed at birth."

"I am no half-breed, sir. And you chose to keep me alive and in your thrall for your own selfish reasons." Christopher bowed. "Please let me know if you have a change of heart."

Not that his uncle had a heart. Christopher left and walked out into the warm sunshine of the formal gardens. He needed to breathe the clean air to get the taste of deceit out of his mouth. Surely his uncle didn't want the Vampires to rule England. Or was he simply too complacent and arrogant to believe the Vampires could succeed without him?

And then there was the matter of the Mithras Cult. His uncle was the current overlord of the English branch, and held all the power in his hands. After Christopher refused to kill Druids in cold blood, Edward had barred him from celebrating the Mithraic rites and branded him a coward. Christopher knew that if the vote went against him, his uncle wouldn't stir himself to save his life.

Laughter and the sound of music drifted out of the open windows that led into the queen's rooms. After sending up a quick prayer of forgiveness to Queen Katherine, Christopher made his way into the state apartments and toward Lady Anne Boleyn's domain. At least there he could pick up a lute, play for a while, and hopefully forget his troubles.

Chapter 5

After leaving the obliging Lady Wilkinson in the upper reaches of the ladies-in-waiting quarters, Rosalind went to find Rhys. In the immense and unfamiliar Hampton Court stable yard, it took her quite a while to locate him. She eventually found him in the tack room repairing one of the horse's bridles. He looked up briefly as she entered the room, and then returned his gaze to the bridle.

Rosalind sat opposite him and watched the intricate movement of his fingers as he sewed two of the crosspieces more tightly together. Just watching Rhys work steadied her. He was such a calm, methodical man with an undercurrent of such deep passion. After he used his dagger to cut through the thick thread, he looked at her again.

"Thank you for your patience, my lady. I was at a particularly difficult spot. Now, what can I do for you?"

"I am to stay here at Hampton Court for a while and serve the Lady Anne Boleyn."

"Aye?" Rhys rebuckled the noseband of the bridle and gazed at it critically. "Then I expect that when the carrier arrives from Wales, you'll want the rest of your belongings moved here."

"Do you think you could arrange that for me?"

Rhys stood and walked across to one of the racks, where he hung the bridle up. "Of course, my lady. I'll go back to Richmond Palace this afternoon, gather up our belongings, and bring them here. I can leave a message for the carrier with the stable boys."

"Thank you, Rhys." Rosalind stood up, her hands clasped tightly at her waist. "Do you have a moment to check on Geithin for me? I think he might have a stone in his hoof."

"Of course, my lady." Rhys's eyebrows rose, but he walked her to the narrow row of stalls until they found her horse munching contentedly on some hay. Rhys gestured for her to precede him into the stall and then locked the door behind them. They both bent down as if to examine Geithin's hooves.

"I know there's nothing wrong with Geithin, so what do you need to tell me?" Rhys asked quietly.

"Jasper was correct. Anne Boleyn is a Vampire."

Rhys hissed a curse. "She is far too close to the king. Why didn't Jasper warn us earlier?"

"That is my concern too." Rosalind sighed. "The king seems so enamored of her that I fear any word from me would enrage him. I'm already hearing stories that the king has fallen out with some of his closest allies over Lady Anne. It's as if she has bewitched him."

Rhys shifted position and felt Geithin's front right leg. "I'll contact your grandfather and ask him what we know about the Boleyn family."

"Anne and her sister lived in France for many years, so that might be why we know so little about them." Rosalind swallowed hard. "I'm not sure how well, but Christopher definitely knows Lady Anne. She seems to hold him in quite high regard."

"Lord Christopher spent most of his early life in France and Spain too, so it is possible that their acquaintance is of long standing."

Rosalind and Rhys stared at each other. "I'll have to talk to him, Rhys, and find out where he stands."

Rhys straightened and patted Geithin on the rump before helping Rosalind up. "I'll write to your grandfather today. You can deal with Lord Christopher."

"And how do you expect me to do that without giving away how much I know?"

Rhys smiled. "You'll find a way. You have the man wrapped around your little finger."

"Hardly."

Rhys's expression sobered. "If you can think of another way for us to deal with this threat, then tell me what it is. Otherwise, I suggest you use your wits and be pleasant to your betrothed."

"He'll be even more suspicious if I'm pleasant to him," Rosalind grumbled as she patted Geithin, and then left the stall. "I hate having to ask him for anything."

Rhys slapped her on the back. "You are both as stubborn as a pair of cart horses. Sometimes I think you deserve each other, and that I had a lucky escape."

Rosalind stopped walking. "Now, that is the first sensible thing you've said all day."

He looked down at her, a smile lingering on his lips. "I'm beginning to think you are right. How will you feel seeing me find another woman to adore?"

She touched his hand and closed her fingers around his. "I'll feel happy for you, once I get over being unreasonably jealous and wanting to stick my dagger in the unfortunate woman."

He kissed the top of her head. "*Cariad*, there will always be a corner of my heart dedicated to you."

"I know. It would have been much easier if I hadn't met Christopher, wouldn't it?"

"But it was always your destiny to do so. Don't you remember the prophecy?"

"Oh, the prophecy." Rosalind sighed and dutifully recited, "'The kiss of the rose is death to kin, and three will stand alone. The bonds of blood will reunite and enemies become one.' I suppose that did come true, after all. You, Elias, and Christopher supported me, and we did kill the rogue Vampire."

"Don't forget the part about your and Lord Christopher's blood bond." Rhys held open the door for her and Rosalind blinked at the sunlight. "Thanks to the prophecy, you are bound to Lord Christopher in other ways as well, aren't you?"

Rosalind made a face. "Don't remind me."

"It is quite amusing, my lady."

"For you perhaps." She sketched him a curtsy. "I must go and present myself to Lady Anne Boleyn."

Rhys paused. "Take care of yourself, and watch out for her brother, too. I have a suspicion he is dangerous."

"Don't worry. I'll keep as far away from them as I can without calling attention to myself." Rosalind picked up her skirts and started back toward the guest apartments. If she was lucky, Christopher would be dancing attendance on the Boleyns as well. She had no choice but to talk to him, but it was a risk. He already knew her far too well, and had no compunction in using all his wiles to extract information from her.

She found herself smiling at the mere thought of matching her wits against his and ruthlessly suppressed it. She would *not* let him charm or bully her. Despite his explanation about the letters, Christopher still had a lot to answer for.

Christopher sat in the window seat ostensibly strumming his lute, but actually watching who came and went from Anne Boleyn's chambers. Because of his peculiar heritage, he could sometimes sense the presence of Vampires, even the old ones. It was a bitter legacy from his mother, who'd turned Vampire during his birth and tried to turn him with her.

There were certainly more Vampires at court than there had been previously, especially around the Boleyns. Christopher wasn't sure why, but it worried him. He struck a discordant note and rearranged his fingers more gently on the fret board. When he looked up he saw Rosalind coming into the rooms. She glanced across at an oblivious Anne Boleyn and then headed straight for him.

"Christopher." She held out her hands and smiled at him.

The glory of that smile coupled with the melting softness in her fine brown eyes made him instantly suspicious. He propped the lute against the window and rose to kiss her hand. "My lady. What a pleasure it is to see you."

She simpered and looked away from him, her hand still in his. "I am to serve the Lady Anne."

Christopher squeezed her hand. "That is a great . . . honor." He didn't need to tell her that his sympathies were divided between Queen Katherine and his old friends the Boleyns. Rosalind slipped her hand through his arm and he obediently strolled beside her out into the wide hallways.

"Lady Anne said that she knew you well."

"That is true. I met all the Boleyns when I visited the French court with my uncle."

"Ah, I wondered where you had formed that acquaintance."

"I have not seen them for several years. It was quite a surprise when Lady Anne appeared to capture the king's interest."

"A surprise to many, I suspect."

He drew her out of an open doorway and into the knot garden to the south of the building. "I assume you do not approve." She glanced up at him, her gaze wary, and he smiled. "It's all right; you can still speak freely to me. I'll never betray your confidences."

"Yet you are friends with the woman who, for all intents and purposes, has usurped the queen's position."

"I must confess, my loyalties are torn. I am very fond of

Anne, but I truly hope to see Queen Katherine restored to her rightful place and the end of this dalliance of the king's." He frowned. "I'm not sure what Anne hopes to achieve. I fear she is after the crown."

"I fear that you are right." Rosalind shivered. "And yet, how can that be accomplished?"

Christopher lowered his voice. "I believe the king is well on the path to dissolving his marriage. Even though Cardinal Wolsey failed him, he is now plotting with his chief minister, Thomas Cromwell, an intelligent, well-learned man and one the queen should fear."

"And the Lady Anne is aware of this?"

"She is no fool, Rosalind. She is probably pushing the king as hard as she can."

Rosalind stopped and bent to pick a sprig of rosemary. The pungent scent reminded Christopher of his Spanish childhood.

"I hear that Lady Anne refuses to become the king's mistress as her sister did."

"From my observations as a member of the king's inner household, I believe that is true." He leaned close as if to smell the rosemary and whispered, "To the best of my knowledge, she is refusing to let him in her bed."

Rosalind arched her neck and his mouth brushed her ear, making his heart beat faster and his body react in more primitive ways. "I wish you would let me in your bed, Rosalind."

She dropped the rosemary on the ground and moved away from him. He had to wait a moment to compose himself before following her. She had the most delectable effect on his senses. He wanted to breathe in her scent, cover her naked flesh with kisses, thrust his aching prick into her warm, wet tightness . . .

He looked up to find her staring at him and he stared right back. Let her see the warmth in his eyes, the need, and the lust, whatever she wanted. He couldn't lose her again. She held his heart in her hands. "I want you, Rosalind."

She sighed. "It's never been a question of 'want,' has it, Christopher? Since our first joining on the Beltane altar, I have known we were destined to love each other. I'll always want you." He took a more confident step toward her, and she backed up two. "But we are still on different sides. How can I trust you when you are allied with the Vampires?"

He spread his hands wide. "What do you want me to do, Rosalind—walk away from every loyalty, from every pledge I've ever made? What kind of man would I be if I did that? Not the kind you should love."

"But that is what you expect me to do, isn't it?" Rosalind demanded. "How well would you love me if I was capable of giving up everything for you?" She obviously saw something in his face that made her continue. "You think that because I am a woman, I should cleave unto you and no other."

She looked away from him and picked a piece of lavender, crushed the fragrant flowers between her finger and thumb. Christopher took a deep breath.

"If I told you that I am reconsidering my current loyalties, would that help?"

"What?" Her head shot up and she blinked at him.

He caught up with her and took her arm again, continued their walk along the neat graveled path with its red rope tile border. "I am throwing myself on your mercy, Rosalind. I fear the Vampires have a sinister aim that I cannot in conscience support. And worse, they are so sure of success this time that they can afford to ignore their allies, even the Ellis family."

Rosalind stared at him openmouthed until he continued. "I have been told almost nothing. Apparently, I am suspect because of my name, and because I am allied to you."

"Who told you that?"

"Both Elias Warner and my uncle. I suspect my uncle is playing a deep game. In recent years he seemed to have lost faith in the Vampires and reckoned himself far superior, but now . . ." Christopher let that thought die. He might be suspicious of his uncle, but he still owed some loyalty to his kin. "By the way, Elias Warner sends his greetings to you."

"I'm sure he does. He must be ecstatic."

Christopher found himself smiling. "He is and that is extremely worrying."

Rosalind let out her breath. "The Druids also fear there is a plot. That is why my cousin Jasper Llewellyn sent for me."

Christopher tried to look smug. "I knew you'd come back someday. I hoped it would be because of me, but I'll accept a dire threat from the Vampire community instead."

"Unfortunately, Jasper should have reacted more quickly. If we aren't very lucky indeed, it might be too late."

"What do you mean?"

She stared at him as if he were a complete fool. "Lady Anne Boleyn, of course."

"What are you suggesting?"

"She's a Vampire, Christopher, or haven't you noticed?"

He laughed in her face and took several hasty steps away, his expression incredulous. "You believe Anne Boleyn is a Vampire? That is one of the most ridiculous things I've ever heard."

With some difficulty, Rosalind maintained her composure. "I don't think it, my lord—I *know* it."

She wrinkled her nose. "That's why Jasper asked for me. I have a better sense of smell than all the male Druid hunters. Lady Anne smells like honeysuckle."

"But how can this be? I've known Anne and her family for years."

"So I understand." Rosalind watched him carefully. "Are you sure that you suspected nothing?"

His stunned amusement turned to anger. "Are you suggesting I've known Anne was a Vampire all along?"

"It is possible, my lord. You are trained to protect your Vampire allies, aren't you?"

He marched across to her and towered over her. "On my honor, I've never sensed anything from Anne."

"I suspect your talent for recognizing Vampires is tied mainly to those of your blood."

"Are you making excuses for me now?" He glared at her. "And they aren't really of my blood, you know that."

Christopher might argue the point, and he probably always would, but the fact was that he could access the minds of his mother and her lover's blood family. In truth, his ability to detect the Spanish Vampire's thoughts had contributed to her demise.

She touched his ornately embroidered black sleeve. "Christopher, I have to be careful, you know that. We both have to be careful."

His muscles flexed beneath his sleeve. "If what you say is true—and I'm still not sure I believe it—then the king is indeed in danger."

Rosalind stiffened. "How can you not believe me? Is your loyalty to the Boleyn family greater than your loyalty to me?"

He pulled out of her grasp and turned away from her. "You don't understand. They were one of the few families that ever welcomed me, who treated me as a friend."

"I find it difficult to believe that such an alliance is more important to you than I am."

"You said it yourself, Rosalind. We both have to be careful. And as you spend every single moment telling me why we cannot be together, you are a fine one to talk." He bowed. "If you will excuse me, my lady, I believe I need to go back and speak to my uncle."

"And leave me here?"

"I fear I must. Can you not return to the Lady Anne's apartments by yourself?"

Rosalind picked up her skirts. "You are too gallant, sir. I'm quite certain that I can find my way back."

*   *   *

With some difficulty, Christopher bit back a retort and strode off toward his uncle's chamber. It was interesting that he'd learned more from Rosalind than he had from his own family. He frowned as he considered her startling statement about Anne Boleyn. But he had learned last year that Rosalind's nose didn't lie . . .

And he'd also learned something else; Rosalind wasn't as indifferent to him as she pretended to be. His future wasn't looking too promising, what with the Mithras Cult set to kill him and his current dilemma about the Vampires, but the thought of Rosalind returning his love at least gave him hope.

Christopher strode back into his uncle's presence without knocking. Edward looked up from his book, but didn't seem surprised at how quickly Christopher had returned.

"Uncle, I hear that there is indeed a plot to subjugate the king through the Lady Anne Boleyn."

"Who told you that?"

"Someone who should know."

"That was quick." His uncle smiled. "I saw you walking with the Vampire slayer."

"What she told me is irrelevant. How far are you prepared to go to support the Vampires in this venture? Do you truly wish to see the whole kingdom come under Vampire rule?"

Edward folded his hands together as if in prayer. "It has long been our family's duty to support the Vampires in their desires."

"And what exactly does that mean? I thought we were allied with the Vampires to defeat the Druids, not advance the annihilation of the human race in England!"

"Perhaps the total defeat of the Druids comes at a terrible price, nephew."

"I hope to God that it doesn't, Uncle."

His uncle's expression hardened. "I will be interested to see how you intend to stop it, Christopher, seeing as you are bound by sacred vows to destroy Druids and support the Vampires."

"You forget—I've also made sacred vows to Rosalind Llewellyn, sir."

His uncle frowned. "Are you suggesting that those vows are as important as the others you have made?"

"Of course they are. You can't have it both ways. Either I keep all my vows or none of them."

"But that is impossible."

"I know." Christopher bowed. "I wish you to understand something, sir. I will continue to protect the Vampires from the Druids. I will *not* aid them in taking over my king and my country."

Edward nodded. "Then we will be at odds, Christopher, and there will be a reckoning between us."

Christopher gazed at the man who had raised him and felt not a twinge of guilt. "I'm sorry for that, sir, but you taught me that eventually a man has to stand up for what he believes. We just don't happen to believe in the same things anymore."

His uncle stirred in his chair and his blue eyes narrowed. "You do understand that the only way out of the Mithras Cult is through your death?"

"I'm aware of that." Christopher nodded. "I'll have to take my chances with the council when they meet, won't I?"

"You think to escape your just punishment?"

Christopher smiled. "With you presiding over the court and counting the votes? No. But at least I'll have the opportunity to state my reasons for my actions, and mayhap others in the cult will understand, if not approve of my choices."

Edward's smile wasn't pleasant. "I doubt it."

There was nothing else to say, so Christopher bowed and walked out. It was apparent that his uncle was determined to support the Vampires in their quest for complete domination and Christopher was equally determined to stop him. Why had Edward had such a dramatic change of heart? He was the kind of man who would do anything in his power to preserve his own skin and perhaps his family.

Did he hope for great power in the new regime? It seemed odd, because recently, Christopher had gotten the sense that Edward despised the Vampire Council and considered himself better than his allies.

Christopher *had* to find a way to convince the other Druid slayers and members of the Mithras Cult that total submission to the Vampires' plans had never been the aim of his people. But why would they listen to him? He was not as powerful as his uncle.

He needed to find out exactly who held the Mithras Cult records, which dated back to the reign of Julius Caesar. Surely there was something in those records that detailed the cult's original purpose to kill the heretic Druids rather than advocating the destruction of their own race by the Vampires?

His thoughts turned to Marcus Flavian. He wondered whether the old bonds between them might help him in his search. It was certainly something to think on.

Chapter 6

Rosalind pretended to sneeze and hid her face in her hands. Sitting with Anne Boleyn's ladies was difficult when there were so many Vampires in such close proximity. She also sensed that in certain quarters, she wasn't welcome, which was hardly surprising considering her illustrious surname. She risked a glance at Anne Boleyn, who was flirting with some of the younger court gallants. The Vampire wasn't particularly beautiful, but she had a vivacity and charm that made men watch her and keep watching, something Rosalind had never mastered.

If she was being less than charitable, it was also possible that Lady Anne used some form of magic to enslave her followers. Vampires were able to control weaker human minds—that was, after all, how they managed to subdue their human prey long enough to feed from them. And there was a sense of something unnatural in the air, something that tugged at Rosalind's mind and made her want to fidget.

As a Druid, she was unlikely to be affected by the Vampire's compulsion, but Rosalind wished she could leave. Unfortunately, she needed to see the Lady Anne with the king, and she also wished to meet George Boleyn, Anne's handsome brother.

She heard a familiar laugh and turned to see Christopher enter the apartments with the very man she wanted. She slid out of her seat, glad that she was wearing one of her favorite gowns, with a green and gold embroidered bodice that pushed her breasts up quite alarmingly. She slipped between the merry throng until she reached Christopher's side. She gave him her most dazzling smile.

"My lord! How wonderful to see you."

At the sound of her voice, Christopher swung around, a quizzical look in his clear blue eyes. He made her an elaborate bow and kissed her hand. "My beloved." He kept hold of her hand and brought her in front of him. "Have you met Lord George Boleyn, Viscount Rochford?"

"I have not had that pleasure, my lord."

"George, this is Lady Rosalind Llewellyn, my betrothed."

Rosalind looked up into the smiling face of George Boleyn and breathed in the feral stench of fox. It took all her composure to curtsy to him and then take a step backward. Christopher retained his grip on her arm, preventing her from moving farther away.

Something unpleasant flashed in the depths of George's dark eyes. "Llewellyn, eh? A Welsh family like the Tudors, I suppose."

"Indeed, my lord." Rosalind finally found her voice. "My family has served the Tudors for generations."

"So I've heard." He winked at Christopher. "It is a good thing that this beautiful lady is betrothed to you, my old friend, or else I would be chasing after her myself."

"And then I'd have to challenge you to a duel, George, so perhaps it is best if you leave well alone."

George Boleyn burst out laughing and slapped Christopher on the back. "I see my reputation precedes me." His gaze slid over Rosalind again and she noticed that his smile hadn't reached his dark eyes. "I won't poach on a friend's property. I give you my word."

Rosalind feared her smile was turning into a snarl. It was hard to pretend to be a simpering fool for long. She pinched Christopher's wrist and he flinched.

"Lady Rosalind has a mind of her own, George. I doubt she would consider herself to be my property."

"I certainly would not!" Rosalind interjected, her patience at an end. "And I doubt any efforts to woo me away from my lord Christopher would succeed." She pinched Christopher again. "It was a pleasure to meet you, my lord."

George Boleyn inclined his head. "Indeed. I wish you well, Christopher. I suspect your marriage will be interesting."

Christopher led her away to the far corner of the room, and George went to join his sister at the center of the noisy crowd.

"Well?" Christopher demanded the moment they were alone. "What did you think?"

"He smells like a fox." Rosalind shuddered. "How fitting. He conceals his scent far better than his sister, but he obviously feels no need to cloak what he is. The Boleyns are either very arrogant or very sure of success." Rosalind licked her lips and wished for a glass of ale to take the acrid taste of the undead away. "I don't think he was particularly happy to meet me either."

Christopher let out his breath. "Do you think he knows who you are?"

"I should imagine so. Unlike his sisters, he was brought up in England. And female Vampire hunters named Llewellyn are quite rare."

"I suppose they are." Christopher stared out of the diamond-paned window and murmured, "I still can't believe they are Vampires."

Rosalind caught his hand in hers. "Christopher, you have to make a choice. You cannot allow your feelings for the Boleyns to jeopardize the life of the king. I thought the Ellis family swore to kill Druids, not aid and abet regicide."

He brought her hand to his lips and nipped her fingertips. "I'm not a fool. You don't have to lecture me on right and wrong."

"Are you sure about that?" Rosalind broke off, aware of the chill of the undead behind her. She breathed in honeysuckle and closed her mouth.

"My, my, are the lovers quarreling?" Anne Boleyn moved closer and stroked Christopher's sleeve. "But then, when passions run hot, sometimes an argument can be as welcome as rain during a thunderstorm." Her fingers lingered on Christopher's arm and Rosalind stiffened. "In the old days, we used to fight all the time, didn't we, Kit darling? But the making up was all the better, sweetened by a kiss."

Christopher smiled, but to Rosalind's relief he stepped slightly away from Lady Anne. "That was a long time ago, my lady."

"And both of us have moved on to different conquests." Anne flicked her fingers over Christopher's cheek. "Yet there is no harm in reminiscing, surely? Lady Rosalind was probably kissed at least once before you claimed her."

"Indeed." Christopher slid an arm around Rosalind's waist and drew her close to him, shielding her from Lady Anne's avid gaze. "But I'd rather be the last man a woman kisses than the first."

Anne clapped her hands. "You are such a romantic, Kit! Who would've thought it?"

There was a disturbance at the door and King Henry and his entourage swept in. Anne immediately turned away from Rosalind and Christopher and walked over to the king. She swept him a low curtsy.

"Your Majesty, I was just teasing Lord Christopher Ellis about his devotion to his betrothed."

The king smiled at Anne. "All men should be devoted to the women they love, should they not?" He beckoned to a page hovering behind him. "And bring gifts for their beloved too."

Anne gave a little shriek. "Oh, sire, you have something for me?"

Christopher leaned down and whispered in Rosalind's ear. "He does indeed have 'something' for her. He just received a packet containing many of Queen Katherine's jewels that he demanded back from her. Lady Anne will enjoy that. In truth, she was probably the one who insisted he reclaim the jewels in the first place."

Rosalind shivered as his warm breath danced over her sensitive skin. "I don't think she likes me, and I don't appreciate the way she keeps pawing you."

"Are you jealous, my love?" His soft laughter made her want to lean in to him and just surrender to his strength.

"You'd like that, wouldn't you?"

The grip around her waist tightened, and he backed them both out of the royal presence and then against the nearest wall. He lowered his head and his lips touched hers. She opened her mouth to him and his tongue tangled with hers, the delicacy of his touch sending shudders right down to her toes. He leaned in to her and deepened the kiss, the press of his body trapping her against the wall.

He tasted of exotic spices, of danger, and mostly of himself, and she craved him more than she wanted to breathe. When he raised his head, he was smiling.

"I also have a gift for you."

Rosalind gazed into his eyes. "You do?"

He removed something from the leather pouch slung around his waist and took her hand. "It's a betrothal ring." He slid a heavy gold band decorated with rubies onto her finger. "I had it made for you while you were gone."

Rosalind studied the gold band. "You were so certain I would return?"

"I knew the Llewellyns would never keep you out of a Vampire fight, and I guessed there would be more trouble at court before long." He hesitated. "I also had some forlorn hope that you might return for me."

Rosalind cupped his chin in her hand. Perhaps it was time to give him something back for his honesty. "If there were no war between our families, I would have come back to you."

His smile grew cocky. "I knew it. I am irresistible."

"And a terrible flirt."

"Perhaps." He kissed her. "I promise you, Rosalind, I will help you stop Anne from gaining power over the king. Just give me the opportunity to do it my way before you resort to killing her and her brother."

"Do you really think she will stop just because you ask her to?"

"I don't know, but at least let me try."

"But you will lay yourself open to her malice."

Christopher stepped away from her. "Why would you think that? She must know that the Ellis family is allied with the Vampires. She will not be surprised by my taking her into my confidence."

"But she also now knows you are betrothed to me, and thus you must be suspect."

He reclaimed her hand. "There is an element of risk in all of our choices, isn't there? I have to try and find out what Anne and George are up to."

Rosalind grimaced. "I suppose you do."

He looked down at her. "Aren't you pleased that we are of one mind again?"

"You haven't let me into your mind," Rosalind retorted.

"Nor have you let me into yours."

"That is hardly surprising." She changed the subject. "Do you want to talk to Jasper and Rhys about the Boleyns?"

"I suppose I should. Not that either of them will welcome my presence or my participation in their affairs."

"I'll ask Rhys to find a quiet spot for us to meet tonight," Rosalind said.

"And in the meantime, I'll go and talk to the Lady Anne."

Rosalind stroked his cheek. "You will be careful, won't you?"

"Of course I will." He kissed her forehead. "She's hardly likely to try and kill me in full view of the court."

Rosalind allowed Christopher to walk her to the entrance to the stables. She watched him go with some trepidation. Despite his confidence, Vampires were notoriously unpredictable, especially when cornered. And it was highly likely that Anne Boleyn was playing a very deep game indeed.

Chapter 7

After the king's departure, Christopher took advantage of the ebb and flow of courtiers and approached Anne Boleyn, who sat clutching the small golden cask full of Queen Katherine's jewelry as if she held the treasures of the entire kingdom.

Christopher bowed. "May I speak to you, my lady?"

"Of course, Kit." Anne patted the seat beside her.

"In private?"

Anne's pointed eyebrows rose. "I'm not sure the king would approve of that at all."

"Then perhaps you would take a turn with me around the gardens?"

Anne stood and shook out her full blue skirts. "There can be no harm in that." She placed her hand on his arm and scanned the mass of courtiers. "Unless your betrothed objects. She seemed a mite possessive for my taste."

Christopher smiled. "You did, perhaps, bait her a little."

Anne laughed. "Well, perhaps I did, but then I've always believed in living dangerously."

"So I've noticed." Christopher drew her out of the room

and into the grounds. Like an obedient flock of birds, her ladies followed along behind.

Anne threw him a sidelong glance. "And what is that supposed to mean, old friend?"

"Only that you are aiming high these days."

"And that pride comes before a fall? I've been told that many times, but I refuse to believe it."

"What makes you think you will succeed when so many have failed?"

Anne's fingernails dug into the black silk of his doublet. "You of all people should know that."

"How so?" Christopher resisted the urge to grab her wrist and pull her hand off him.

"You're an Ellis."

"I belong to that family, yes. But what does that have to do with you?"

Anne laughed softly. "Oh, Kit, you are so amusing. I know why you are here. The Vampire Council sent you to protect me, didn't they?"

Rather than look down at Anne, Christopher contemplated the hazy skyline and the spire of the local church. "Is that what they told you?"

"They didn't need to tell me. I already knew your family protected Vampires."

Christopher took a deep breath. "Until recently, I didn't even realize you were a Vampire."

"Did you not? I assumed your uncle would have told you."

Christopher had no intention of revealing his uncle's lack of faith in him. "You have been a Vampire this whole time I have known you?"

Anne patted his cheek. "Dear, sweet Kit, I have been a Vampire for the last three hundred years or so. That is why there isn't an accurate record of my birth into the Boleyn family. We manufactured something, of course, but I understand the dates were rather muddled."

"And George, too?"

"I turned George." Anne's smile turned sensual. "He has become quite important to me."

"Ah." Christopher contemplated his next move. Anne was in a remarkably confiding mood, so perhaps he should take advantage of it. "My lady, what exactly are you and the Vampire Council planning to do with the king?"

She stopped walking and faced him. "Surely you know."

"I'd rather you told me in your own words."

"Then the Council didn't send you."

"In a manner of speaking. My uncle compelled my presence here at court."

"Your uncle Edward is a cunning and devious man."

"He is, indeed." Christopher paused and made himself look into her dark eyes. If the eyes were indeed a window into a person's soul, Anne's soul appeared to be shrouded in blackness. "You still haven't told me your intentions."

Anne licked her lips, and he caught a glimpse of her fangs. "If you don't know what the Council asked of me, I'm not going to enlighten you."

"I only wished to warn you that when the Vampire Council is involved, things are not always as straightforward as they might seem."

She laughed in his face. "Are you suggesting I could get hurt, Kit?"

"I'm suggesting that you should have a care for your safety. Even here at court, Vampires are not without enemies."

Anne continued walking again, now seeking the leafy shade of the trees. Up close, Christopher could clearly see the thick coating of white leaded powder she used to protect her face and neck from the power of the sun.

"I assume you are talking about those ridiculous Druids your family hunts."

He pictured Rosalind in full fighting mode and imagined her facing Anne. "I wouldn't sound so contemptuous, my lady. They are a force to be reckoned with."

Anne lifted her chin and gave him a short curtsy. "I appreciate the warning, Kit, but nothing will stand in my way. And with you to protect me, what do I have to fear? Perhaps I will see you later." She turned on her heel and marched back toward her apartments, her entourage immediately surrounding her like a swarm protecting their queen.

"I wouldn't be so sure about that, my lady," Christopher murmured. He hadn't gained as much information as he'd wanted, but he had confirmed that Anne was up to no good and allied with the Vampire Council. He stared at the departing courtiers, a hollow feeling in his gut. It seemed he had to take a stand against his former friends, to take this information to his Druid allies and hope they would use it wisely. Even though he knew it was the right thing to do, he still hated it.

Rosalind paused to look up as an owl hooted from the top of one of the elaborately twisted brick chimneys that adorned Hampton Court. There was no sign of any other disturbance, so she continued on her way, using the outside hedge of the maze as her guide toward the apple orchard where Rhys had told her to meet him. There were no lights in the palace gardens. Most of the court was either still carousing in the great hall or abed.

She heard a blackbird's call and smiled. Rhys was ahead of her, which at least meant she was going in the right direction. She whistled back, and bent her head to avoid the low branches of the first of the apple trees. The blossoms had long gone and the hard buds of the apples now adorned every leafy branch.

"Rosalind?"

She made her way toward Rhys, who waited beside an old shack that smelled sweetly of cider and pressed apples. Beside him stood Jasper, who inclined his head a formal inch.

"Is Christopher here yet?"

"I'm right behind you, my lady." Rosalind turned as Christopher emerged from the gloom. His expression was pleasant, but his blue eyes were guarded. He stopped beside her, one hand resting on his dagger. "Master Williams, Master Llewellyn."

Rhys stuck out his hand. "It is good to see you again, my lord."

Christopher returned the handshake. "It is good to see you too, Rhys. Thank you for taking care of my lady."

Rhys snorted. "I would like to say it was a pleasure, but you know how she is."

Rosalind sighed. It seemed they were back to jesting about her again, but at least that was better than fighting. "Jasper, have you met Lord Christopher Ellis?"

"Indeed, I have."

"He will be working with us to bring down the Boleyns."

Jasper frowned. "Verily? I heard he was ordered by the Vampire Council to protect them."

"Who told you that?" Rosalind asked.

"I believe it was Elias Warner." Jasper opened his hands wide. "There is no reason for him to lie about such a thing, is there?"

Christopher took Rosalind's hand. "Elias always lies. He enjoys it. I am not in favor with the Vampire Council, nor am I in league with the Boleyns."

Jasper didn't look convinced, but at least he kept quiet. Rosalind was just about to continue when Rhys interrupted her.

"Can you prove you've not working with the Boleyns?"

Christopher let go of Rosalind's hand and squared up to Rhys. "I can give you my word that I am not."

"But why would you offer to help us bring down another Vampire?"

"For my own good reasons. Reasons that I have no intention of sharing with you."

Rosalind stepped between them and placed a hand on each of their chests. "If you intend to fight, I will work with

Jasper and ignore you both." She turned to Rhys. "*I* believe Christopher, and that is enough for me."

Rhys patted her arm. "All right, my lady."

"Thank you."

Jasper bowed. "I, however, cannot ally myself with a Druid killer. Now that you are back, Lady Rosalind, there is no longer any need for me to guard the king. However, I pledge you my support, and I will help you in any way I can before I leave."

"Thank you, Jasper." Rosalind wasn't surprised that Jasper had refused to help them. He had always struck her as a remarkably inflexible man. And perhaps it was unfair to blame him. It had taken her a long time to get used to the idea of working with one of her family's enemies. "Perhaps, before you go, you could tell us anything you know about the Boleyns' unusual habits."

Jasper hesitated. "I suspect the Lady Anne and her brother hunt for their food together at night."

"Why do you think that?"

"It is just that occasionally I get a sense that magic is being used. You know how it is possible to feel it in the air? And sometimes the Lady Anne's servants and clique seem a little dazed in the morning, as if they have slept rather more heavily than usual."

Rhys nodded. "It is certainly possible. Perhaps we should start by watching the Lady Anne at night. If we can catch her and her brother outside while they were feeding, we might be able to dispose of them without anyone knowing we were involved."

"That would be ideal," Rosalind agreed. She glanced at Christopher and saw a hint of distaste on his face. It must be hard for him to hear them discuss the death of two of his friends so casually. "Whatever we do, we must make sure we do not expose ourselves to the king's gaze."

"I agree," Christopher said. "Best to keep this as quiet as possible."

Jasper ignored Christopher and turned to Rosalind

and Rhys. "I will leave you to your plans and wish you good fortune." He bowed and disappeared back into the gloom.

Rosalind watched him leave. "I didn't really expect him to stay."

"Neither did I. We don't need him," Rhys said. "We've dealt with worse than this."

"Not much worse," Rosalind muttered. "We have two Vampires to kill this time, and because of their familial link, we'll have to try and dispose of them at the same time, or they will warn each other off."

Christopher cleared his throat. "George isn't actually her brother."

"She told you that?"

"Indeed, she said she turned him herself, which means they *are* linked by blood—"

"But not quite so closely."

Christopher took Rosalind's hand and brought it to his lips. "It makes no difference. We will succeed. We have to. Lady Anne is definitely working with the Vampire Council, and she is very confident of success."

Rosalind snatched her fingers away. "Anne has been very *confiding*, has she not?"

"You knew I was going to speak to her."

"But did you succeed in changing her mind?"

His expression sobered. "No, she seemed quite convinced she was going to succeed."

"Then we'll have to kill her, won't we?"

"You make it sound so very . . . final, Rosalind."

She met his gaze. "It has to be."

He sighed. "I suppose it does."

Before Rosalind could challenge him about his divided loyalties again, Rhys cleared his throat. "I'm going to bed. I'll see you both tomorrow night."

Christopher nodded. "That is agreeable to me."

Rhys grinned. "I thought it might be." He started back

toward the palace, leaving Rosalind staring at Christopher. He smiled at her and held out his hand.

"Shall we walk back together?"

Even though Rosalind wasn't wearing skirts, she curtsied. "That would be very pleasant, sir."

"We'll be quite safe as long as we are quiet and don't draw attention to ourselves."

She glanced up at his moonlit profile. "Well, I don't intend to make a spectacle."

His soft laughter warmed her. Sometimes, when they were alone like this, she could almost imagine a future for them together, hand in hand, mind linked to mind . . .

The scent of apple blossom drifted past her nose and she shoved Christopher to one side. "Look out!"

A dark shape dropped down out of the tree in front of her, followed by another and then another. Christopher didn't hesitate to draw his sword and line up beside her. Rosalind brandished her dagger and slowly backed away from the approaching Vampires. She couldn't smell honeysuckle or fox, so it wasn't the Boleyns.

Beside her, Christopher cursed. "Why does this happen whenever I'm with you?"

"I rather thought it was the other way around." Rosalind glanced over her shoulder, but there didn't appear to be any more Vampires behind them. "If you don't want to help me, I understand—just stay out of my way."

"Of course I'll help—I have no wish to see you skewered."

Rosalind laughed. "There are only three of them. I can take them all."

The first Vampire moved in, fangs extended, long blond hair blowing in the breeze. Rosalind waited until the female sprang and moved swiftly to her left, catching the Vampire's shoulder with a slash of her dagger. The female screamed and twisted back toward Rosalind, claws extended, fetid breath hissing out.

In her side vision, she observed the second female Vampire launch herself at Christopher. He brought his sword up and parried the blow, stopping the Vampire in midflight. She knew Christopher was an excellent fighter, but always worried whenever he engaged with the Vampires, particularly the females. With a start, she returned her attention to her own problems and recoiled as one of the female Vampire's claws caught her cheek. She pivoted and stabbed her assailant through the heart.

Before she could even kick the body away, the third of the trio was on her back. Strong bony fingers wrapped around her throat, choking the breath out of her. Rosalind staggered under the weight of the male Vampire and went down on one knee. She struggled to breathe, and everything started to go black. She brought her dagger upward and slashed at the Vampire's fingers.

With a howl of pain, the Vampire's grip loosened, and Rosalind was able to roll to one side and finish the Vampire off. As she fought to stay conscious through the muddle of blood and the smell of dying rat, she saw that Christopher's opponent was now headless and on the ground.

He ran across to her, his bloodied sword still out, his gaze intent. "Are you all right?"

She was about to answer him when his expression changed. "*Move!*"

She rolled to one side and the ground disappeared beneath her. As she fell, she saw his sword blade flash past her head and decapitate the blond female Vampire she had partially killed. When she opened her eyes she was staring up at the night sky from the bottom of the sizable ditch that edged the apple field.

"Are you injured?"

She blinked and looked up to see Christopher sliding down the bank of the ditch, his boots crunching through the dead leaves and branches. He had sheathed his sword. She hoped he'd had the good sense to make sure all the Vampires were separated from their heads.

"Rosalind!"

His impatient shout formed in her mind and lingered there. He knelt beside her and she simply stared up at him.

"You have been practicing. I can hear you in my head."

"I have indeed. It's a useful skill, is it not? To be able to communicate without words?" He closed the gap between them and kissed her forehead. "Are you sure you are all right?"

She stared into his deep blue eyes and relaxed the last of her barriers, felt him penetrate her mind with the same sense of knowing and completion as when he penetrated her body.

"I like that comparison, my love, and I hope to be inside you very soon."

Rosalind concentrated hard. *"We will have to see about that. Are all the Vampires destroyed?"*

"Aye, they are."

His mouth descended over hers and she kissed him, felt his mingled relief and pleasure build right alongside hers. She knew it wouldn't be long before they became one in all possible ways, their bodies joined skin to skin, their mouths fused . . . She slid her hand into his black hair and held him tight. After yet another close encounter with death, having Christopher in her mind and in her arms made her feel alive again. They were still linked and it felt so right she could no longer understand how they could live without each other.

He lifted his head and stared down at her, ran his thumb over her lower lip. "We are still bound together. Did you ever doubt it?"

"I wasn't sure . . ."

His eyes snapped fire. "You doubted me?"

"I doubted whether the feelings would last."

"Because we fulfilled the prophecy?"

"I thought it was a possibility." Rosalind eased out of his arms.

"Not for me. You can blame it on my Vampire family's

blood, but I regard you as my mate for all eternity. Why else do you think I'm prepared to ally myself with you?" He glared down at her. "For as long as we both live."

"You would prefer to live for all eternity?"

He took her hand and pulled her to her feet. "I would like to live beyond the current year."

"What do you mean?"

His smile wasn't convincing. "Nothing, my love. I'm sure we'll survive this."

"Christopher . . ."

He squeezed her fingers. "I'll tell you if there is need."

She took a long, slow breath both to clear her mind and to remove the taste of death an encounter with a Vampire always brought. "We have to take care of the bodies. I'll go and find Rhys—" The ground seemed to tip toward her and she felt Christopher grab her elbow and steady her.

"Your face is bleeding." He took out his kerchief and patted at the blood on her cheek. "One of the Vampires caught you with her claws."

"Yes." Rosalind stood patiently as he dabbed at the trickle of blood. "I wonder why they attacked us."

He threw the bloodied cloth onto the ground. "Mayhap to see where our loyalties lie."

"*Your* loyalties, you mean?"

"Probably." He grimaced. "And I have failed the test. Now they know I'm not averse to killing those I have sworn to protect."

"Only because they tried to kill you! You did nothing to provoke them."

"That is true, and they should be used to that by now." He looked toward the palace. "I suppose we should get back."

She sensed his ambivalence about killing Vampires resurface. He might swear on his oath that he was on her side, but old loyalties died hard and Christopher's feelings for the Vampire community were more complicated than he ever chose to admit. But he had to deal with his conscience in his own way. She'd already realized that nothing she said would make a difference.

She wiped her dagger on her ripped hose and took Christopher's proffered hand. Her cheek was throbbing and she suddenly felt tired.

"Rosalind, I can go and find Rhys for you if you wish to retire to bed."

She struggled to gather her thoughts. "No, I have to see him." She touched her cheek and winced. "Vampire claws can be infected. I'll need a special potion for this."

"I didn't know that."

Rosalind tried to smile, but it hurt too much. "It's of no matter."

He stopped suddenly and drew her against his shoulder, his voice rough, his arms wrapped around her. "Do you have any idea how much I hate to see you fight and not be able to protect you?"

She rested her forehead against his leather jerkin, glad of his support. "I'm quite capable of defending myself."

"I know that, but I still hate it."

She closed her eyes and listened to the rapid beat of his heart, the urgency of his breathing, and felt his warm strength surround her.

"Rosalind," he murmured.

"What?"

"Do you want me to carry you?"

His words forced her to pull away from him. "I'm fine. The cut is just stinging a little."

He put his arm around her shoulders. "Then let's get you straight to Rhys."

Chapter 8

Christopher winced as Rhys applied a vile-smelling green ointment to Rosalind's cheek. He hated to see her suffer, especially when every painful touch of Rhys's fingers resonated through his own mind. Luckily, Rhys had still been awake and had taken them into one of the tack rooms to clean up while he fetched his supplies. Rosalind looked exhausted, her skin pale against the angry-looking gouges, her teeth set into her lower lip as if to deny the pain. Christopher leaned forward and took her hand.

"Rhys has almost finished, love."

"Indeed, I have, my lady," Rhys said. "Come back tomorrow and I'll take another look to be sure, but I think you'll be fine."

Rosalind opened her eyes. "Thank you, Rhys." Her gaze shifted to Christopher. "And thank you for helping me with the Vampires."

"There is no need to thank me. I could hardly stand there and watch you take them all on."

"You could have."

Irritation flared in his chest. "I have allied myself with you. Don't you believe me?"

"I think *you* believe it. Whether it is that simple, I know not."

Christopher sighed. "You're right. It isn't that simple. But I intend to do my best to protect you—and save the king. Will you at least believe that?"

"Of course." Rosalind squeezed his fingers and her faint smile warmed him all the way to his heart.

Rhys stood up and began packing away the soiled rags and ointment. "Perhaps you should go to bed, my lady."

Christopher winked at Rosalind. "Rhys might insist that you are not his to order around, my love, but he seems to have some difficulty remembering it."

Rhys swung around. "I remember it. I'm just far too used to telling her what to do."

"As if you were my older brother." Rosalind allowed him to help her stand. "I suspect you'll always be like that."

Rhys chuckled and turned away, but not before Christopher had caught the hint of pain in his expression. It was hard to give up old loyalties. He, of all men, understood that.

"I suspect this Vampire attack was aimed at establishing my allegiances rather than Rosalind's."

"It's very likely," Rhys replied. "The Vampires can have no doubt where Rosalind's loyalties lie."

Even though it was true, Rhys's calm assumption that Christopher's loyalty was questionable still stung. "Lady Anne thought the Vampire Council sent me to defend her. After tonight, I wonder if she'll continue to believe it."

"It would be a good thing if she did," Rosalind said thoughtfully, her gaze moving between Rhys and Christopher. "She might share more secrets with you if she thought you were on her side."

Christopher rose. "You wish me to play both sides of this treacherous game?"

"Yes." Rosalind stood too. "We need all the help we can get. It's not as if we can just kill Anne and her brother in front of the whole court. We have to find a way to dispose of them discreetly and probably without the king's approval."

Christopher held out his hand. "We should go. Perhaps we can discuss this when you are feeling better."

Rosalind took his hand and he led her out of the stable block and back toward the Clock court, where they were both lodged. The clock struck three times, the sound echoing in the stillness. In the shadow of the archway, Rosalind stopped walking and cupped his cheek.

"I know that this is difficult for you."

He moved his head until his lips met her skin and kissed it, used the tip of his tongue to circle her palm until he felt her shiver and draw even closer. For once, he welcomed the surge of lust that shuddered through him. His need for her surpassed all other considerations about loyalty, broken promises, and the never-ending complications of his mother's Vampire legacy.

He raised his head to find Rosalind looking steadily at him, her brown eyes wide and vulnerable, and kissed her gently on the mouth. Her lips parted and he surged inside, used his tongue to lick and flick against hers in an erotic dance that simply inflamed his already starved passions.

Her fingers moved over his jerkin and he groaned as she tugged at the lacing on his undershirt and shoved her hand inside to caress his chest. His prick strained against the confines of his hose. He wanted her hand on him, her mouth . . .

Without conscious thought, he cupped her bottom and drew her up on tiptoe to fit against him. His back hit the brick wall, and he stayed there, glad of something solid behind him. She kissed him, her tongue as voracious as his, her body pressed against him from knee to shoulder. He knew he should draw back, that they were in a public place, but he couldn't seem to find the will.

"Rosalind," he murmured against her lips.

Her hand tightened in his hair and he winced. Her words echoed in his mind. *"Christopher Ellis, if you stop now, I will run you through with your own dagger."*

He wasn't sure if he was capable of stopping. His blood was on fire, and his prick begged for satisfaction. He shifted his hand and ripped at the ties on her hose. Then he slid his fingers into the glorious wet warmth between her legs. By God's teeth, she felt so delicious he almost disgraced himself and spilled his seed like an untried youth.

She made a hungry, mewling sound as he started to move. His fingers circling and sliding through her lush wet folds and the tight swollen bud at the very center of her need, he increased his tempo, slid two fingers deep, and almost groaned aloud when she tightened around him and took her pleasure. Her mind tangled with his, and her delight overflowed and enhanced the rising need within him. God, he needed her hand on him—

Before he'd even completed the thought, she untied the points of his hose and her fingers closed around his prick. He started to thrust urgently into her hand, discretion forgotten, need paramount, completion so vital that he wouldn't have been able to stop if the entire court had been watching.

His seed spilled into her hand and he kept thrusting as pleasure shuddered through him and her in an endless spiral. When he finally went quiet, his face was pressed against the crook of her neck and he was panting as if he'd run for miles.

"That was . . . not how I intended to woo you, my lady. I envisioned a bed and a long night of love play."

Rosalind disengaged her hand from his now deflated prick and smiled at him. "This was perfect."

"Not quite, as I didn't get inside you."

"Perfect for now, I meant." She rearranged her clothing, her cheeks now flushed and her eyes dreamy. He wanted to untie her hair and lay her on his bed, slowly uncover her nakedness and spend hours worshipping every inch of her skin. "I confess I was desperate to touch you."

"I'm glad to hear it, my lady." He paused and scanned her face. "I didn't hurt you, did I?"

"Not at all. In truth I feel much better than I have for months."

"You missed me, then?"

She raised her eyebrows. "Of course I did."

"Then why did you stay away for so long?" The words were out before he could stop them.

She drew away from him, her expression suddenly shuttered, her mind slamming shut against him. He felt it like a physical blow. "Because there was no reason for me to be at court."

He caught her hand. "You told me that there is always a Llewellyn at court guarding the Tudors."

"Jasper was here."

"But he doesn't have the mark of Awen, does he? And only that mark brings special access to the king."

"What do you know about it?"

She sounded defensive now, and he hated it, hated the part of himself that couldn't help but push to expose the truth, even if it hurt them both. "I know that only a few Druids are born with the mark of Awen—including you."

Her right hand went to her left wrist as if covering the evidence. "What is your point, my lord?"

"I just wondered why you felt it was all right to leave the king unprotected for so long."

"He wasn't unprotected!" She turned on her heel. "And you are being ridiculous."

"If I'm being ridiculous, why are you getting so upset?"

She swung around to glare at him. "Because you said you believed in me, and yet you are suggesting I neglected my duty to the king."

Christopher stared at her. "I do believe in you; that has nothing to do with asking why you stayed away so long."

"Mayhap I simply didn't want to deal with you. Is that what you want me to say?"

He leaned back against the wall and looked heavenward. "Of course not."

He heard her sigh. "Sometimes I don't think you know

what you want, Christopher. Sometimes I think you blame me for making your life too complicated and try to find fault simply to drive me away. Good night, my lord."

He didn't stop her leaving, knew she wouldn't listen to him if he tried. Did he truly blame her for the twists and turns of his existence? But the fact remained that she had stayed away from court—from him—and surely he had a right to wonder why.

He straightened away from the wall. Whatever Rosalind felt about him, he had an obligation to keep her safe. He watched until she entered the ladies' quarters, and then turned back to his own bed. He was on duty in the king's privy chamber in less than three hours, and he needed to rest. With his shoulder still throbbing from the Vampire's blow, and his body wanting Rosalind, he doubted his wish for peaceful slumber would be granted.

Rosalind checked to see that Christopher had left and then paused in the doorway of the ladies-in-waiting quarters. She registered the all-too-familiar aroma of wolf. Elias Warner stepped out from the shadows of the stairwell and bowed to her. He carried a candle, which illuminated his gold doublet and matching hose and his perfect face.

"Good morning, my lady."

Rosalind allowed Elias to see the silver-tipped dagger she had in her hand. "Good morning, Elias. And what exactly are you doing in the ladies' quarters at this time of night?"

"Just visiting, my lady." His smile was full of satisfaction.

"Visiting whom?"

"The Lady Anne and I are quite well acquainted."

"Is that so?" Rosalind paused, surprised and slightly suspicious that Elias had been so open. "Then perhaps you might warn her that I intend to protect the king to the best of my ability."

Elias leaned against the doorframe. "Oh, don't worry, my lady. I've already done that."

"Do you intend to kill me, then?"

He considered her, his head to one side. She couldn't help but notice two puncture marks marring the whiteness of his throat. "I would prefer it if you just went home. Strangely enough, I would hate to have to kill you."

"I cannot go home. I have a duty to protect the king from the Vampire race, even if it means I die trying."

"I know that, my lady, and I'm sorry for it."

"Don't be." Rosalind sheathed her dagger. "Why are you so devoted to Lady Anne's success? What has she promised you in return?"

Elias's smile died. "You assume that my loyalty can only be bought?"

Rosalind answered his question with one of her own. "Are you suggesting that your *emotions* are involved?"

"I'm suggesting nothing." Elias bowed. "Go home, Lady Rosalind, and you may as well take Lord Christopher Ellis with you. You cannot win this time, and you would be foolish to even try."

"But I cannot leave. You know that. And it appears that Lord Christopher has his own alliance with the Boleyn family."

"You think he would choose the Boleyns over you?"

Rosalind opened her eyes wide. "I don't know. What do you think?"

Elias stared at her for a long moment, handed her his lit candle, and then disappeared. Rosalind let out her breath. Was it possible that Elias was in love with Anne Boleyn? Or did he simply expect to gain some advantage from that relationship? Was Anne *feeding* from him to shore up her Vampire powers? Anything was possible. She'd tried to make Elias think that Christopher's loyalties were in doubt, but she wasn't sure if he believed her.

She slowly climbed the stairs toward her allotted sleeping space. With her dear friend Margaret no longer at court, she would be sharing a bed with a stranger. She imagined opening the door and finding Christopher there instead, his smile inviting, his naked body on display . . .

That was unlikely to happen until he recovered from his annoyance with her. Why couldn't he just accept her word, and not try to ferret out things that were not of his concern? Her reasons for not returning to court were hardly sinister. What did he think she'd been doing? Bedding every man she'd met? That would be quite like him.

She pushed open the door to her small room and stared at the empty bed. It seemed that she was to sleep alone. With a grateful sigh, she stripped off her torn and bloodied boy's clothing and let it fall to the floor. Her cheek still stung and she gently touched the parallel claw marks. Perhaps she should send her apologies to Lady Anne and wait until her face healed before returning. But would Lady Anne assume she was hiding?

Rosalind blew out her candle. Christopher would never understand that she'd delayed her return because she was, frankly, a coward. She'd been too afraid to face him and give in to her desire for him. It had been easier to skulk at home and let Jasper do her work for her. And she'd been right to worry. A few days in Christopher's company and she was already panting with lust, which would never do.

Chapter 9

Christopher bowed to King Henry and backed out of the royal bedchamber, George Boleyn at his side. They'd both been in attendance on the king as he dressed and readied himself for the day. The king seemed in fine spirits, his thoughts on the upcoming hunt and the beauty of the weather. There was no sign that the king had been turned yet, and for that Christopher was extremely grateful. He waited until the door shut before turning to his friend.

"Is something wrong, George? You have barely spoken a word to me all morning."

George jerked his head toward the gardens, and Christopher followed him out. Even though he'd known this confrontation would be coming, he still disliked provoking it.

It was peaceful in the gardens; the blackbirds were singing and a light breeze ruffled the treetops. In the distance Christopher could see the indistinct outline of the apple orchards. Had Rhys succeeded in getting rid of the bodies of the slain Vampires without being detected? Christopher swallowed hard. He always worried that one day he'd find a member of his mother's Vampire family at the other end of his sword and that he'd realize it too late.

"You have disappointed me, Christopher."

Christopher brought his attention back to George, who was glaring at him. "In what way?"

"Your alliance with that Druid."

"This alliance was hardly of my choosing. I was duped into fulfilling a prophecy, not only by the Druid gods but by my own uncle and the Vampire Council. And then the king betrothed us!"

"Yet you haven't broken off the betrothal."

Christopher forced himself to meet George's dark gaze. "Because my uncle decided that the connection was too useful. He expects me to give him the information I glean from Lady Rosalind."

"So you are playing a double game, then."

"I suppose I am." George didn't need to know that Christopher had no intention of telling his uncle anything at all. He rallied his forces to attack. "And what of you, George? I thought we were friends. Why didn't you tell me that you were a Vampire?"

"I wasn't one when we first met." George's expression darkened. "I did it for Anne. It is no one else's business, in any case, so why do you care? It's not as though we present a threat to you. Your family is *allied* to the Vampires."

"Which is why I thought you would have told me. Did you not think I would understand?"

"One cannot be too careful." George walked away a few paces, his hand resting on his sword hilt. In the sunlight, the blue silk of his embroidered doublet shimmered like lake water. "Last night you protected the Vampire slayer and killed some of our own."

"Would you have stood aside and watched them assault your betrothed?" Christopher held George's gaze. It was never wise to show fear to a Vampire, friend or not. "I had no choice."

"There is always a choice, Christopher."

"By all that is holy, they attacked us *both*. I had to fight or lose my head!"

George stopped pacing. "I've known you for years, and considered you my friend. But I can't allow you to interfere with Anne's plans."

"I understand."

"Then you will cease aiding the Vampire slayer?"

Christopher spread his hands wide. "I am simply trying to protect my own hide. Surely you can appreciate I am in a difficult position."

George scowled at Christopher. "How am I to know whether to treat you as a friend or as an enemy?"

Christopher bowed. "That is for you to decide. It would be easier if you and Anne set your sights lower and left the king alone."

George laughed and slapped Christopher on the back. "Anne is a very determined woman."

"What does she want, George? Really?"

"Power, my friend, power beyond your imagination. What else?"

"And you truly believe the Vampire Council will allow that? What if they are using you for their own ends?"

"They will not succeed, not if Anne and I are determined."

Christopher studied his old friend and wondered if he had ever known him at all. "I wish I had your confidence, George. In my experience, the Vampire Council will use anything and anybody to achieve their goals."

George turned back toward the palace and started walking again. "It is kind of you to try to warn me, but it makes no difference. I cannot turn back now, and neither can Anne. The king is within her grasp and nothing can stop us."

Conviction rang through George's words, and Christopher knew it was pointless to continue arguing. He could only hope George would consider his advice later and perhaps share some of Christopher's concerns with Anne.

"I cannot agree with you, George."

"Then we will be enemies?"

Christopher faced his friend. "I hope it doesn't come to that, but I can assure you, if your Vampire hordes try to kill me, or my betrothed, I will fight back."

George bowed. "I can respect you for that, even if I don't like it. But think on this, my friend: If the Vampire slayer dies, you would be a free man again. In fact, with your connivance, we could kill her for you."

Christopher almost smiled. He could no more stand back and allow Rosalind to be killed than he could stop breathing.

"I have no love for the Vampire Council and their machinations, George, so I will simply repeat what I said. Be careful."

George's smile made Christopher want to shiver. "Don't be so melodramatic. The Vampire Council is not invincible. You proved that when you had to help them dispose of that rogue Vampire last year."

"You know about that?" Christopher asked. "Then you should understand my reluctance to trust the Council at all."

George's smile died. "Don't worry about the Council. Worry about yourself, because we will not let you stand in our way."

George's bluntness made Christopher bristle, but he managed to bow and walk away. It seemed that they were indeed heading for a battle. The Boleyns were not afraid of him, or the Council, and Rosalind was definitely at risk. Christopher stared up at the red brick walls of the palace. Trying to keep everyone safe was proving harder than he anticipated.

But George seemed rather arrogant. Was that because he believed in the Vampire Council's invincibility, or because he and Anne had their own path to follow? Christopher stopped walking. He needed to find out exactly what George and Anne planned to do to the king *and* the kingdom.

At the very worst, he might have to ingratiate himself with his uncle again. He grimaced at the thought. The only other way to discover the plan was to convince one of the Boleyns that he was completely on their side.

He continued down the path. After his latest confrontation with George, he wasn't even sure it was possible, but perhaps he had planted the seeds. If George could be convinced that Christopher was more concerned about saving his own skin than about Rosalind or the Ellis family, perhaps he would reveal his true purpose.

Rosalind had suggested that he play both sides. He wondered how she would feel if he decided to take her at her word and confide in Anne. Christopher found himself smiling. Despite her outward lack of interest, he knew Rosalind wouldn't take kindly to him getting too close to any woman but her.

Ahead of him, George slowed down and veered away from the palace toward the archery court, where a group of Lady Anne's women had gathered. Christopher decided to follow. It would be a good excuse to seek out Rosalind and set her on her guard. Not that they'd parted on particularly good terms, but he was certain she would have forgiven him by now.

He reached the first group of women and spied Anne dressed in dark brown velvet and gold at the center. Elias Warner stood at her elbow and she was laughing up at George, who was whispering intently in her ear. Her gaze shifted to Christopher and her smile brightened.

"Ah, Kit! You are just in time to watch me take on your betrothed in an archery contest. We are the last two remaining archers. You will lay a wager on my winning, I hope."

Even as his heart sank, Christopher retained enough sense to bow. "You put me in a quandary, my lady. How could I choose between my two favorite women?"

Behind him, he heard a snort. He turned to find Rosalind dressed in a vibrant red gown and black hood. The rubies in the gold cross at her throat caught the sun like drops of blood. He swept her another bow. "My lady."

She ignored him and tended to her crossbow, testing the tautness of the hemp string with her gloved finger. A quiver of arrows slung over her shoulder made her look like a ferocious Amazon queen. Christopher had never seen her shoot before, but he suspected she was more than competent. Which was unfortunate, because he knew Anne considered herself an excellent shot.

He turned his back on Anne and leaned closer to Rosalind. "Did you plan this?"

She gave him an exasperated glance. "Of course not. I tried to withdraw gracefully and cede the victory to her, but she challenged me in front of everyone."

"Then take care."

"I intend to." She looked at him directly for the first time. "Will you wager on me or her?"

He smiled into her brown eyes. "You, of course. It would be unseemly to wager against my betrothed. But would you be interested in a private little side bet if you lose?"

Rosalind raised her eyebrows. "You expect me to forfeit something to *you* if I lose?"

He brought her gloved hand to his lips. "I expect nothing—and hope for everything."

"And what exactly is it you want from me?"

"If you lose?" He bit slowly down on her leather-encased thumb. "You, in my bed, naked and willing."

She smiled up at him. "Alas for you, I shall win."

"Of course, my love. Everyone knows that the Welsh are the best archers in the kingdom."

Rosalind released her hand from Christopher's firm grip and turned away. She pretended to test her bow and willed herself to stop blushing. When he looked at her like that, it was almost impossible to deny her attraction to him. His voice alone seemed designed to turn her into a quivering pool of mindless need.

"Are you ready, Lady Rosalind?" Anne Boleyn's imperious tones cut through Rosalind's bemusement.

"Yes, my lady." Rosalind turned her attention to the two large straw targets that were situated about a quarter of a furlong from where they stood. She made her way through the watching courtiers and retrieved an arrow from her quiver. Just seeing the arrow helped steady her nerves. Rhys had made it for her from supple ash wood and it was topped with soft gray feathered fletches. Christopher moved up alongside her, his keen gaze fixed on the target.

"The wind is blowing from the northeast."

"I know," Rosalind answered as she planted her feet on the line. She waited as Anne received a kiss from her brother and then a succession of well wishes from the courtiers. Rosalind knew from the snide glances cast her way that she wouldn't be popular if she won. Verily, many of those around them would expect her to deliberately lose. But she wasn't prepared to bow down to anyone, particularly a Vampire.

"Kit, dearest? Do you not wish to stand by me?" Anne asked.

Rosalind bit down on her lower lip to resist the urge to swing her bow around toward the other woman. Beside her, Christopher started to fidget.

"If you go to her, you will never see me naked in this lifetime again," Rosalind hissed.

He went still. "I'm well placed here, Lady Anne. I can see both of you remarkably well."

"Coward," Rosalind murmured.

"You told me to ingratiate myself with her," Christopher whispered back.

Rosalind chose to ignore him, and focused her energy on the target and imagined it was Anne's smiling face. She fitted her arrow into the notch of her bowstring and raised the bow to her cheek.

"Best of three, Lady Rosalind."

"Indeed, my lady."

Rosalind sighted on the target and took a deep breath. She waited for the command to shoot and then released the arrow, just avoiding the recoil of the taut string against her skin.

Two men advanced on the targets and the one on Rosalind's side held up his hand. There was a polite murmur from the watchers and some desultory clapping. Lady Anne swung around toward Rosalind. She was no longer smiling and her dark eyes glittered like burning coal.

"Well-done, Lady Rosalind. The wind appears to be in your favor."

Rosalind didn't bother to reply to such a blatant mistruth. She kept her attention on picking out another arrow and waiting for the steward to ready them for the next shot. Lady Anne resumed her place and everyone fell quiet.

The steward raised his arm, and Rosalind increased the tension of her bowstring. Just as she shot her arrow, Christopher nudged her elbow. Lady Anne clapped in delight as she was declared the winner of that round. Rosalind glared at Christopher. "What did you do that for?"

He looked down at her. "So that you don't make her look like a complete fool. Her pride will not stand for that."

"And what about *my* pride?"

He chuckled. "My lady, you will easily win the next round. You are far superior to Lady Anne at this sport."

Rosalind wanted to smile back at him, but both George and Elias were watching them closely. It would not do for anyone to think she and Christopher actually *liked* being betrothed to each other. Not that she liked him very much sometimes. They needed to maintain an air of frustration at their situation that made them seem like enemies.

The steward cleared his throat and Rosalind turned back toward the target. The fine hairs at the back of her neck stood on end and she shivered as the breeze picked up considerably. If she didn't know any better, she would think it was unnatural. She narrowed her eyes and focused all her senses on winning. A little speck of Vampire magic was not going to affect her victory.

"Do you feel that?" Christopher whispered.

"Yes, now let me concentrate." She sighted on the target and let loose her arrow, watched it penetrate the very center of the red circle. She frowned as she heard Lady Anne's whoop of victory. Rosalind waited as the two men compared the relative positions of the arrows and then called for the king's steward to come forward and decide who had won.

Lady Anne tossed her bow to Elias and went off toward the targets, her arm linked through her brother's. Rosalind followed more slowly, aware of Christopher at her side, his gaze sweeping the other courtiers, his hand resting on his sword hilt.

The steward was frowning at the two targets, which had been brought together to compare more closely. It seemed obvious to Rosalind that she had won, but no one else seemed to see it. The steward bowed to Lady Anne.

"You are the winner, my lady."

Anne smirked and cast a sidelong look at Rosalind. "Oh, dear, am I really?"

Rosalind curtsied. "If you insist, my lady." She held Anne Boleyn's gaze for as long as she could, aware of the cold, dead magic encircling their small group, and of the dazed look in the steward's eyes.

"Are you suggesting I *cheated*, Lady Rosalind?"

"Of course not." Rosalind shot a warning glance up at Christopher, who looked ready to explode in her defense. "You are obviously more skillful than I am in exploiting your advantages."

Anne stepped closer until there was no space left between her and Rosalind. She smiled to reveal the tips of her fangs. "That is true. I suggest you don't forget it."

"Oh, I won't, my lady. I'll just make sure I'm better prepared next time."

"I wish you luck." Anne's avaricious gaze roved over

Rosalind. "Now what should I take as my forfeit? That beautiful gold and ruby ring I've seen you wearing?"

"That ring was a gift from me, Lady Anne," Christopher said softly.

Anne laughed. "Then I'll not take your property, Kit. It would hardly be fair."

Christopher shrugged. "Lady Rosalind must make that decision. The ring is hers now."

Rosalind smiled sweetly at Christopher. "And I'm *so* glad to wear it. As women get older, we sometimes can become quite desperate for the joys of a husband and a family, can't we, Lady Anne?"

Anne's eyes flashed and she raised her hand. Rosalind held out the cross she wore around her neck between her finger and thumb. "If you like rubies, my lady, how about this?"

Anne licked her lips. "No, I thank you."

Rosalind leaned in to her, the cross almost touching Anne's nose. "Are you sure, my lady? It has been blessed by the Archbishop of Canterbury himself."

The magic around them wavered and died as Anne recoiled. "I'll think of something else, Lady Rosalind. Never doubt it."

"I'm sure you will, my lady." Rosalind curtsied.

Anne threw one last scathing glance at Rosalind before storming back toward the palace, proclaiming her victory to the other courtiers as she went. Rosalind let out her breath and turned to Christopher, who was still eyeing the two targets.

"You won by a handbreadth. Why couldn't anyone see it?"

"Lady Anne, or someone even more powerful than she, used Vampire magic. You felt it when the wind started to blow so suddenly." Rosalind paused to retrieve her arrow and Christopher helped her.

"Is that what it was?" He frowned at her. "How come I wasn't affected by it, then?"

"Probably because of your Vampire blood and your connection to me."

"Ah. That's right. Druids can usually shut out a Vampire's attempt to coerce them." Christopher contemplated the second arrow. "And my heritage brings me some peculiar gifts."

"I—" Rosalind's words were cut off as an arrow whipped past her face and buried itself in the target an inch from where her fingers were resting. When she opened her eyes, Christopher had set off in pursuit of the shooter, his expression savage, his long legs eating up the ground. Rosalind went to follow him and realized the arrow had gone through the sleeve of her gown and pinned her to the target. She tried not to panic as she frantically searched her hanging pocket for her dagger.

She heard the pounding of feet and harsh breathing and started sawing at the heavily embroidered hem of her sleeve. Christopher appeared beside her, his own dagger already out. "Let me help you."

It took but a moment to release her. Rosalind stared at her ruined sleeve and then at the black fletched arrow that still quivered in the center of the target. A faint trembling started in her fingers and she could do nothing to stop it. Christopher put away his dagger and gripped her shoulders, his fingers digging into her flesh.

"Are you injured?"

Numbly, Rosalind shook her head. "By the Lord's grace, I'm not." She took a few more gulps of air. "I can't decide if whoever shot that arrow wanted to kill me outright or simply scare me to death."

"I found the Lady Anne's bow and a quiver full of black-tipped arrows on the ground but no sign of the shooter." Christopher's expression darkened. "Did you see anyone?"

Rosalind put away her dagger and took Christopher's proffered arm. "No, I didn't, but the last person I saw with the bow was Elias Warner."

"Perhaps it is time we paid him a visit, then."

Rosalind matched her steps to his. "Perhaps it is."

Chapter 10

"I have no idea what you are talking about, Lady Rosalind." Elias looked from Christopher to Rosalind, his expression as pure as fresh-fallen snow. "Why would I shoot an arrow at you?"

"Because you wish me dead?" Rosalind answered. They'd found Elias strolling back to the palace and had persuaded him to stay out in the gardens with them.

A hint of some emotion passed across Elias's normally inscrutable face. "There are many Vampires who wish you dead."

"That's true, but most of them aren't offering their blood to the Lady Anne."

Beside Rosalind, Christopher stiffened. "You're *feeding* her?"

Elias raised his eyebrows. "That is no business of yours. I've known Lady Anne for hundreds of years. What we do together is entirely up to us."

"Does she feed from her 'brother,' as well?"

Anger glimmered in Elias's silver eyes. "Of course not. He is far too young and weak to sustain her needs."

"Yet she seems very close to him."

Elias looked away from Rosalind, and one of his hands clenched into a fist. "Be that as it may, I did not try to kill you."

"Well, someone did." Rosalind watched him closely. "And as you were the last person seen holding Lady Anne's bow, it might have been you."

Elias interrupted her. "I am not stupid enough to try and murder you in public. I might have aided Lady Anne's victory with a little magic, but that was the extent of my influence. If you wish, I will inquire as to who it might have been. Will that make you leave me alone?"

Rosalind glanced at Christopher. "That would be most generous of you."

Elias bowed and they watched him stride away. Christopher took Rosalind's hand. "That was odd. Elias seemed quite unlike himself."

"He did, didn't he?" Rosalind followed Elias's progress until he entered the courtyard. "I wonder what is going on. He sounded almost jealous of George Boleyn." She frowned. "Sharing blood with another Vampire indicates a deep bond, doesn't it?"

"Indeed. It is normally done only by mated couples. But on occasion, when a Vampire needs to increase his strength or abilities, he can drink the blood of an older Vampire and take on new powers."

"Which is probably why Anne Boleyn likes to drink from Elias rather than George. She needs all the power she can get to keep the king under her thumb. But why would Elias agree to it?"

"Mayhap he is in love with Anne." Christopher heaved a deep sigh. "I know all too well how it can crush a man's spirit when the lady he loves doesn't return his feelings."

Rosalind pinched his sleeve. "*You* should consider a career as a traveling player."

He covered her hand with his own. "And you should get yourself to bed. You've had a shock."

"I have, indeed, but we still don't know who shot that

arrow." She looked up at him. "We are playing a dangerous game, aren't we?"

"Yes, and I don't like it at all." He patted her hand. "I also have come to the conclusion that if we wish to stop this murderous entertainment, I need to ingratiate myself with the Boleyns."

"I already suggested that."

"I know, but I'd hoped to avoid it. Duplicity is not my strong suit and, as you know to your cost, I am sometimes honest to a fault. It would be so much easier if the Boleyns were not so well protected by the other Vampires and the king himself." Christopher stared off into space. "I suppose I should also go and speak to my uncle . . ."

"Don't do that unless you have to. He strikes me as a very evil man."

"My uncle? He has a very low opinion of you, too." Christopher frowned. "Despite my best efforts, I suspect I will never be free of his influence."

Rosalind found herself patting his sleeve. "He is but a mortal man."

Christopher gazed at her as if she had said something profound. "He is, isn't he? I wonder whether that is why . . ." His voice trailed off and he blinked at her.

"Why what?"

He started walking, his strides so long she almost had to skip to keep up with him. "We have to assume that Elias is very firmly in the Boleyn camp and perhaps has high hopes of Anne elevating him to great power ahead of George."

Rosalind accepted his abrupt change of subject with as much grace as she could muster. "That sounds fair, although I suspect George will have something to say about that."

Christopher held the door open for her. "I should imagine he will. He has never enjoyed being second best. Elias had better watch out. I'll ask Rhys to keep a close eye on Elias while I watch George and you watch Lady Anne."

Rosalind shivered as she pictured Anne's malevolent stare. "I hate being near her. Her scent makes me gag."

"I'll try and win her favor again and maybe that will give you an excuse to keep away. She'll assume you are jealous."

Rosalind snorted. "As if I would be envious of her for any reason."

"That sarcastic tone is perfect, my love," Christopher said gravely. "Maybe we should manufacture a quarrel between us in front of the Boleyns to convince Anne that we are at odds."

Rosalind glared up at him. "We never need to *manufacture* our quarrels. They seem to arise quite naturally. And I am *not* jealous of Anne. She had her chance with you and she gave you up."

"And now you have me. Speaking of which, when do I get my prize?"

"Your prize, sir?"

"You lost the contest, therefore I win." He winked. "I'm anticipating you—naked and under me in my bed."

Rosalind swept him a deep curtsy. "Alas, my lord, I was distracted and we failed to shake hands on the bet." She met his gaze. "And, as an honorable man, you *know* I won."

His smile died. "Rosalind . . ."

"It is barely midday, sir." Rosalind brought her hand to her forehead. "I am going to lie on my bed because I am still shaking from my close encounter with death."

"I could keep you company, hold you in my arms, whisper sweet nothings in your ear."

Her whole body softened and yearned toward him. "But you wouldn't stop there, would you?"

He regarded her seriously, his blue eyes intent, his far-too-kissable mouth a scant inch away from hers. "Probably not." He sighed and bent to kiss her cheek. "Go to bed, my love. I'll talk to Rhys and see you later."

"Thank you," she whispered.

His smile was soft and for her alone. "You will make it up to me, I trust."

She held his gaze and bit down on her lip. "I might."

He groaned and moved away from her. "You are a

temptress sent by the devil. Now go to bed before I put you over my shoulder and carry you up there myself and be damned to what everyone thinks."

She blew him a kiss and ran up the two flights of stairs to her solitary dormer room. She locked the door behind her and leaned against it. The shock she'd held at bay since the arrow had almost killed her shuddered through her and she barely made it onto the bed.

Suddenly, she wished Christopher was there, his arms wrapped around her, his mind supporting and completing hers. But as they both knew, there were eyes everywhere at court. If he'd followed her up the stairs, someone would've seen him and the gossip about them would start afresh. She couldn't afford to give Anne Boleyn the opportunity to denounce her to the king for having loose morals.

Rosalind closed her eyes. The king. She needed to warn him again about the dangers surrounding him. She doubted he would believe her if she named her suspects, and it was vital for her to remain at court. So she would continue to fight on alone. Desperation flooded through her. When would this end? Not for the first time in her life, she doubted her ability to stop the Vampire threat.

She took several deep, steadying breaths. She wasn't quite alone. She had Christopher and Rhys at her side. Her grandfather had trusted her to save the Tudors once and she had succeeded then. She could *not* let him down.

Christopher waited until Rosalind was out of sight before returning to the Clock court, his smile dying, his thoughts focused on his uncle Edward. Edward had been frail ever since a fever had left him bedridden for months the previous winter. Was it really worth fighting him on every issue when he would soon be gone?

Christopher hesitated by the archway. Mayhap that brush with his own mortality explained Edward's sudden reawakening of interest in the Vampire cause. Did he hope for something more than an increase in power? Christopher shook his head. If so, Edward had miscalculated, because it didn't appear that the Vampires needed the help of the Ellis family at all. Yet his uncle seemed so confident . . .

It made no sense at all. Christopher glanced back at the ladies' quarters and imagined Rosalind in bed. He wanted to be with her so badly his prick was permanently hard. With all the discipline he could muster, he focused on something to help him solve at least one of his problems. In the distance, he spotted Sir Marcus Flavian practicing swordplay with one of his men. He reckoned that was as good a place to start as any.

Christopher threaded his way through groups of men practicing fighting skills. In the distance he could hear the sound of horses being galloped along the jousting course and the smack and splinter of lances meeting. The smell of wet, rusting chain mail blended with the searing heat from the armorer's braziers as the man repaired a broken sword.

When Christopher approached, Sir Marcus glanced up at him before returning his keen gaze to his opponent, but his words were for Christopher.

"What do you want, my lord?"

"Just to speak with you, but there is no hurry. Pray continue." Christopher was quite content to stand and admire Marcus's skill with the sword. If they ever came to blows, which seemed likely, it was good to have some knowledge of an opponent's capability. And, even though they had once trained together, Christopher was eager to see what new tricks Marcus had learned.

Marcus was of wider build than Christopher but slightly shorter. What he lacked in reach, he made up for in sheer brute strength. Christopher knew that Marcus's forebears were a mixture of Romano British and Viking, which accounted both for his size and his warlike nature.

It took Marcus only another ten punishing blows to have his opponent on the ground and offering up his surrender. Christopher nodded as Marcus took off his helm to reveal his damp blond hair and strode toward him.

"You still fight well, I see."

Marcus sheathed his sword, the metal grating against his scabbard. He waved the other men away and set his helm on the bench with a thump. "What do you want, Ellis?"

"To ask you something."

"About your impending death? I've already offered to be your executioner when the time comes."

"Marcus—"

Marcus swung around and shoved his finger in Christopher's face. "I cannot believe that you, an *Ellis*, have betrayed your own kind."

A sense of weariness enveloped Christopher. He was so tired of being judged and condemned. "You know me, Marcus. Do you think I willingly betrayed anyone?"

"It seems you are not the man I once knew." His ex-friend's gray eyes were as cold and inflexible as the armor he wore.

"I did what I had to do."

"That's no excuse."

Christopher grabbed Marcus's arm. "I *said* I did what I had to do. I didn't say I liked doing it. I was betrayed by those who should've had my best interests at heart, and now I am trapped within a web of lies and blood oaths and promises that would defeat any man."

"This is scarcely of interest to me."

"It should be. One day you might find yourself in the same position." Marcus cursed and tried to shrug out of Christopher's hold, but Christopher held on. "For God's sake, listen to me. I cannot allow my uncle to win."

Marcus frowned. "Your uncle is the head of the cult. His word is law."

"And that is the problem." Christopher let go of Marcus and stepped back. "Ask my uncle what his plans are for those who worship Mithras, and then come and talk to me. I can only hope it won't be too late."

"To save your puny neck?" Marcus sneered.

Christopher stared at him. "No, to save this country from being ruled by Vampires."

"What?"

"You heard me. The Cult of Mithras has been enlisted to protect the Vampires not so they can live beside us in peace but so they can conquer the entire human race. Ask my uncle, and then decide whether I am simply a coward trying to save his own skin."

Marcus's gaze lingered on Christopher's face. "I'll do that, and then I will come and find you and beat you to a pulp."

"You can certainly try." Christopher walked away toward the stables to find Rhys. He wondered how his uncle would deal with Marcus's questions and what the result would be. He knew Marcus to be a rigidly proper man who would never countenance Vampire domination. Christopher exhaled. Perhaps he wouldn't have to see his uncle face-to-face after all. Marcus might do his work for him.

When Rosalind came back into the royal apartments that evening, she winced at the noise. A band of musicians occupied one corner of the room and Anne and the king, accompanied by their courtiers, were engaged in a rowdy country dance around the chamber. The king's cheeks were red with exertion and he was laughing uproariously. Anne was more contained, but her dark eyes glinted brightly and her hand gripped the king's large one so tightly her knuckles gleamed white.

Rosalind edged backward until she reached the far corner of the room and found a seat. She pressed her hand to her aching forehead and wished she'd stayed in bed after all. Opposite her, surrounded by many beautiful women, sat a laughing George Boleyn. Rosalind remembered the days she'd spent with Queen Katherine; the pious simplicity of her court and the ready warmth the queen had always shown Rosalind.

"Lady Rosalind, come and dance."

She jerked her head up and saw Christopher standing in front of her, his hand imperiously stretched out toward her. "I'd rather not, my lord."

He frowned and raised his voice. "Why not, my lady? Are you determined to spoil my pleasure?"

Behind Christopher, somebody laughed and Rosalind realized they had already excited some interest. "I am not disposed to dance, my lord. I have a headache."

"Nonsense!"

Before she could protest, he grabbed her hand and yanked her to her feet. She pulled back against him, and he glared at her. "Are you determined to resist me, my lady?"

"Are you mad?" she hissed.

He leaned in close and whispered, "No, we're fighting, remember?"

"Oh, for goodness' sake!" Rosalind pulled her hand free and said loudly, "I do not appreciate being made into a spectacle, my lord. Please excuse me."

She flounced away from him in the direction of George Boleyn, and stopped right in front of the Vampire to make sure she had his attention. Christopher grabbed her shoulder and spun her around to face him.

"I do not appreciate being left standing by myself like a fool!"

"Then go and find some other poor woman to pester."

Christopher looked sulky. "But you are my betrothed."

Rosalind moved close to him and spoke so that only he and George Boleyn could hear her clearly. "And I'm tired of pretending to be happy about that."

"You think I feel any differently? Your family is my enemy."

"Then why don't you petition the king for your release? He's standing right over there." Rosalind curtsied and rushed out of the room. Surely that should be enough to convince the Boleyns that she and Christopher were not happy with their lot? And it freed her from another excruciating evening with Anne and the other Vampires. Rosalind gathered up her skirts and gave a little skip. After seeing Rhys, she could return to her bed with a clear conscience and leave Christopher to loudly proclaim his grievances to a no doubt very sympathetic George Boleyn.

Christopher scowled after Rosalind and then glanced down at George Boleyn. "I suppose you heard all that."

George smiled. "I told you your betrothal to that woman would be bad for you."

"I've tried to behave well with her, but . . ." Christopher sat down heavily next to George. "She is quite difficult."

"Difficult? I'd suggest impossible." George nudged Christopher in the ribs. "My offer still stands. Let her go out and fight without you, and she'll be dead within a week."

"She is stronger than you think."

"So I've heard, but despite her overinflated reputation, she is but a woman." George yawned and got to his feet as the music came to a crashing finale. "I suppose I'd better ask one of these oh, so willing ladies to dance. Why don't you do the same?" He beckoned to his sister, who had just finished dancing with the king. "In fact, why don't you dance with Anne? The king won't complain because he holds you in high regard, and I'm sure she'll be more than willing to commiserate with you over your betrothed's bad temper."

Christopher remained seated. It would not do to appear too eager to go along with George's plans. "Why this sudden change of heart, George? A few hours ago you were threatening to kill me."

"I talked to Anne. She believes you are still bound to our cause and working to protect us. She believes your relationship with the Llewellyn bitch gives you the perfect disguise."

Christopher forced a smile. "Anne is a wise woman."

"Then you will no doubt seek her counsel about your love life."

"Do you need counseling, Kit?" Christopher rose as Anne swept toward him, her eyebrows raised as she caught the end of George's comment. The heavy necklace of pearls and rubies that hung around her long, elegant neck was one Christopher remembered Queen Katherine wearing. "Where is the lovely Lady Rosalind?"

George chuckled. "Crying into her pillow, I should imagine. It seems she doesn't take well to being ordered about."

"What woman does?" Anne took Christopher's hand. "Have you quarreled?"

"We always quarrel." Christopher didn't even have to pretend to be irritated. It was true. "Lady Rosalind has a mind of her own."

"Another excellent quality in a woman, but I can understand that it might exasperate you." Anne drew him into the dance and took his other hand. "A man wishes to be superior in his own household."

"Pretty words, but do you not wish to rule the king?"

She lowered her eyes demurely. "Of course not. He is my sovereign, and he has my complete allegiance."

"And if he made you his queen?"

She caught his gaze and he found he couldn't look away. "He *will* make me his queen, and then we will rule this country together."

Her quiet certainty impressed him, and her eyes were so beguiling that he felt as if he were falling into a deep, dark pool. Her smile widened and she squeezed his hands. "We are alike in so many ways, Kit. Both forced to survive alone, both prepared to take risks to get what we truly desire."

"Are we?" His skeptical words sounded hollow to his own ears, his desire to believe in her strengthening with every quickening breath. His heart was beating fast in his chest. He wanted to pick her up and protect her from any man who ever threatened her.

"We know each other so well, my old friend. Why should we be at odds?"

He licked his lips as Anne continued to study him, and

remembered how it felt to kiss her, to take her in his arms and hold her tight. "We . . . should not be enemies."

Her smile was both tender and inviting. "You see how easy it is for us to agree? We *should* be working together to defeat our enemies. With you by my side, I'm certain I could accomplish all my desires, and yours."

He shivered as her fingers trailed over his jaw.

"Kit, are you well?" Her teasing voice brought him back to the present, and the fact that he was staring at her like a callow youth, as if she held the key to all knowledge. He blinked hard and tore his gaze away from hers. He had to keep a clear head. Sympathizing with the Boleyns again was not part of his plan. He pictured Rosalind in his mind and immediately felt better.

Anne released his hand and curtsied. "I must go and attend to the king. He doesn't like to see me talking to any man but him."

Christopher nodded and walked away to the farthest corner of the room. He felt as if he were waking from a dream. Had Anne affected him in some way? He couldn't quite remember what he'd said to her, or what she had replied. All he knew was that for one moment he had wanted desperately to believe in her. Christopher shoved a hand through his hair and escaped into the wide hallways of the palace. He would do well to remember his own advice. Anyone connected to the Vampire Council was a threat and was to be avoided at all costs.

Chapter 11

"Did I tell you that according to your grandfather, there is no true record of Lady Anne's birth?" Rhys asked as he slid his dagger into its sheath and buckled his belt around his waist. "It seems a false document was produced to satisfy the gossip, but the dates don't agree. Most people think it's because Lady Anne doesn't wish the king to know her true age, but we know better."

"Indeed, we do." Rosalind checked that her sword scabbard was securely fastened to her belt and bent to slide another dagger into the back of her soft leather boots. She watched Rhys pull on his thick leather jerkin and settle it across his muscled shoulders. "Have you noticed any pattern to the Boleyns' nighttime activities yet?"

"Not really." As he stretched, Rhys tugged her braided hair and she scowled at him. He stared over her shoulder into the stable yard. "Is Lord Christopher coming with us tonight?"

"I know not. Gossip says he spends his evenings cavorting with the Lady Anne and the days toad-eating her brother."

Rhys considered her, his hazel eyes amused. "You know why he is doing that."

"He *says* it is to gain more information for us, but I'm beginning to doubt him. He's completely ignored me for the last two weeks and he goes off by himself when we patrol at night." Rosalind bit down on her lip. "He seems enamored of Lady Anne."

"Are you jealous, *cariad*?"

Rosalind turned away from him to button her jerkin. "It's not that. It's more the way he looks at her, as if he can't look away, as if she has him in her power."

"Do you think she has bewitched him?"

"I suppose it is possible. I assumed his Vampire blood would protect him from her magic, but obviously I was wrong. Mayhap it has the opposite effect and he is more vulnerable."

Rhys grimaced. "That would be a disaster for us all."

"Indeed, but as Christopher is avoiding me, I doubt he will want to hear anything I have to say on the matter. You know how he is."

"Oh, I know. He's likely to take offense. But it will have to be done, Rosalind. We cannot allow him to bring us all down."

"I know. I'm just trying to find the right moment."

Rhys raised an eyebrow. "Of course, it may be he has simply fallen out of love with you, and into love with Anne."

"Rhys!" Rosalind glared at him. "What a horrible thing to say."

He shrugged, making his leather jerkin creak. "You're the one who is letting it happen."

She put her hands on her hips and faced him. "We agreed that I would stay away from him. We quarreled publicly so that he could ingratiate himself with the Boleyns."

Rhys strolled toward the stable door. "Rosalind, you have only to snap your fingers and that man will come running back to you. You know it."

"I'm not so sure anymore."

Rhys stared at her. "This isn't like you, my lady. Are you giving up?"

She raised her chin at him. "I've never had to fight for a man, and I'm not sure if I want to start now."

He grabbed her hand and pulled her hard against his chest. "Excellent. Then kiss me and get him out of your head for good."

She tried to push away from him, all too aware of his familiar scent and the comfort she would undoubtedly find in his arms. "I can't do that."

He feathered his lips across hers. "Are you sure?"

"She's sure, Williams. Now let her go before I have to teach you to mind your manners yet again."

Rosalind turned her head to find Christopher leaning against the doorway, his expression particularly unfriendly and his hand on the hilt of his sword. She deliberately stroked Rhys's cheek and smiled up at him.

Rhys grabbed her by the elbows and firmly set her away from him. "Oh no, my lady, don't involve me in your games anymore."

Christopher advanced upon them and Rosalind pretended to be busy checking her weapons. His boots nudged hers. "We've had this discussion before. If you want to be kissed, ask me."

She slowly raised her head. "I don't like the taste of honeysuckle. It makes me gag." Rosalind turned on her heel and strode out into the grounds, Rhys behind her. Christopher remained where she'd left him. It wouldn't take him long if he wanted to catch up with her, so she lengthened her stride and hoped for the best.

Rhys beckoned her toward the blind side of a wall of the south-facing tower, where a set of steps had been cut into the red brick.

"We need to go up on the roof."

"Do we have to?" Rosalind shaded her eyes and looked upward into the gloom of the starless night. She sensed Christopher was right behind her now, but he didn't say a word.

"Aye. I couldn't work out how the Boleyns were leaving the palace without being detected, until I realized they were traversing the rooftops."

"Clever," Rosalind replied. "Then I suppose we have to climb up."

"I'll go first. I'll wait for you at the top." Rhys started to climb, his booted feet scrabbling for purchase on the small steps. Rosalind waited until he was past the first-floor windows before she started her ascent. She didn't wait to see if Christopher was following her. She could already feel his gaze between her shoulder blades like the point of a dagger.

It seemed to take forever to reach the rooftops. Fortunately, it was neither raining nor windy, hazards that would probably make the steps unclimbable. Rosalind was breathing hard by the time she vaulted over the low ornamental crenellation set around the edge of the roof space. She spotted Rhys to her left, concealed behind a series of massive chimney pots.

Rhys was dwarfed by the towering brick spiral chimney, which was over twice his height. Cardinal Wolsey had spared no expense fitting out his palace with more chimneys than any other grand house in England. They peppered the roof of Hampton Court in groups of four or more and dominated the skyline for miles.

Rosalind jumped as Christopher pushed past her and headed for Rhys.

"Do you know where they emerge?" Christopher asked. Dressed in his favorite black, he almost disappeared in the shadows thrown by the chimney stacks.

Rhys pointed toward the western corner of the building. "Over there. Directly above the royal apartments. They're not usually alone either."

"I wouldn't expect them to be." Christopher unsheathed his dagger. "Shall we go?"

Rosalind stared after him. It seemed that Christopher didn't wish to talk to her at all, and that was most unlike him. Normally if she displeased him, he was all too happy to tell her about it.

She followed after the men, using the base of the chimney stacks as support against the slope of the pitched roofs. Above them, an owl hooted and was answered by its mate. Rhys stopped moving and held up his hand.

"Someone is coming." His whisper barely carried on the still night air.

Rosalind inhaled the faint scent of strawberries mixed with horse. "At least two Vampires, one male, one female, but not the ones we seek."

"They are probably a scouting party, making sure it is safe for the Boleyns to come up," Rhys murmured. "Perhaps we should wait a while and see what they do." He gestured to a narrow gap between two of the chimneys and they followed him over.

"Agreed," Christopher answered Rhys and took up a position in front of Rosalind that completely obscured her view.

She shoved at his leather-clad shoulder, but he refused to move. She punched him again and he deigned to look down at her. "What do you want, my lady?"

She glared at him. "How do you expect me to fight when you are blocking my dagger hand?"

He raised his eyebrows. "Then why don't you move?"

"Because—"

"Shh." Rhys motioned them to silence and Rosalind took a step back until she was clear of Christopher's bulk. She immediately missed the warmth of his body and his own particular male scent of spices and oranges.

Ahead of them there was a soft curse, and the sound of a tile clattering off the roof. Rosalind adjusted her grip on her dagger and peered into the darkness. The smell of Vampire was stronger now. She stayed still, trying to identify each particular scent so that she knew how many opponents they should expect to have to fight.

She held up four fingers to Rhys and Christopher, who

both nodded. There was still no sign of the Boleyns. Rosa-lind held her breath as the first pair of Vampires crept past their hiding place, seemingly unaware of potential ambush. The scudding clouds cleared from in front of the moon and Rosalind tensed. There were at least two more Vampires coming up on them.

Rhys touched her shoulder and they all moved out and onward across the roof. She glanced both ahead of her and behind her, aware that the first couple of Vampires might double back and attempt to trap them. In the moonlight, Christopher's expression remained shuttered, his move-ments those of a man blindly following orders rather than avidly leading the hunt.

Rosalind frowned as she caught a hint of orange blos-som coming off Christopher. That was odd; had he simply doused himself in too much perfume? Before she could fin-ish the thought, Rhys hissed out a warning, and they were suddenly surrounded. Four Vampires approached them from two sides, trying to force them back into the corner of the roof.

Rosalind readied her silver-tipped dagger and ran at the smallest of the four Vampires, a female with long brown hair and what would have been a sweet face apart from the fangs and the bloodlust burning in her eyes. Rosalind grabbed the woman's arm and tried to force her to her knees. She was rewarded by a kick to her thigh that almost brought her down instead.

Ignoring the pain, Rosalind changed her grip on the Vampire's forearm and shoved hard, hoping to catch the female off guard. She succeeded in getting the Vampire off-balance, and followed up her small advantage by stabbing the creature in the neck. There was a gurgling sound fol-lowed by a screech and the Vampire's fist connected with Rosalind's head.

Rosalind let herself fall and brought her opponent down with her. She twisted her head to avoid the snapping fangs and plunged her dagger upward, slitting the Vampire's throat, the flood of cold, lifeless blood making her gag and curse as it covered her chest. She shoved the still-writhing body off her and looked for Rhys and Christopher.

Rhys had already dispatched one of the males and was busy with the other female. Christopher was fighting a white-haired Vampire and although he appeared to be winning, his movements lacked clarity, and seemed almost unnatural, as if he had to force himself to fight.

Rosalind had little time to wonder about him as she struggled to her feet and used her sword to separate the Vampire's head from her body. She took two steadying breaths and resisted the temptation to swipe at the Vampire blood that trickled down the inside of her jerkin.

Christopher's opponent hit the ground and his sword slashed down in a graceful arc to finish the kill. Rhys was smiling as he detached the fallen Vampire's head from its body and wiped off his sword. His smile died when he spotted Rosalind leaning up against the chimney stack.

"Is that your blood?"

Rosalind grimaced. "No, but I can't wait to get it off me." She swallowed hard, her senses still clogged with the Vampire's overpowering sweet strawberry smell, her mind drowning in the coldness and bleakness of death. She shivered. She hated this, the reality of the kill, the way the undead stained her thoughts.

Christopher approached, his quick glance taking in Rosalind's state. She reached for him in her mind and felt a quickening of feral interest, a hunger that seemed attuned to the Vampire's blood. With a shudder, she slammed her senses shut against him. He went still and looked at her as if he had never seen her before.

With a shake of his head, he sheathed his sword and looked at Rhys. "Should we expect any more?"

Rosalind stared at him. "Aren't you going to ask me if I am unhurt?"

He glanced over his shoulder at her, his expression guarded. "I—"

Rosalind ducked as another Vampire jumped down from the top of one of the chimney stacks. Christopher shoved her behind him. Before she could summon the energy to either object or fight, Rhys was on the woman, his sword out, his dagger in the other hand. The female laughed and stepped backward as if inviting Rhys to follow her.

She leaped up onto one of the chimneys and then onto another. Rhys and Christopher followed her, Rosalind a distant third. Rhys cursed and tried to scale one of the stacks, his fingers scraping along the brick edge, but he wasn't tall enough to reach. Christopher might have achieved it, but he was already running ahead, trying to cut off the Vampire.

From what Rosalind could see, the female had long black hair and was quite young. She jumped gracefully from chimney to chimney until she finally descended at the far side of the building. Rhys continued to advance, and so did Christopher, all of them now perilously close to the edge of the roof. The Vampire laughed again and jumped onto the small crenellated wall.

In front of her, Rosalind heard Christopher's breath hiss out on a curse. As Rhys stepped forward to swing his sword at the Vampire, Christopher brought his blade up and deflected the blow. The sound of clashing metal rang loudly in the silence.

"Christopher, no!" Rosalind started forward, desperate to reach the two men and the laughing blue-eyed woman. With another impulsive motion, Christopher threw himself toward the Vampire, who promptly disappeared.

Rosalind fought back a scream as Christopher continued onward, his hand outstretched, his boots losing purchase on the slate tiles.

As he pitched forward, Rhys caught Christopher's jerkin and hauled him back onto the roof. Christopher landed with a thump on his stomach, his breath huffing out like he'd been winded. Rosalind stared at his prostrate form and slowly backed away from him. He'd deliberately prevented Rhys from killing the Vampire.

She couldn't bear to see his face.

With a choked sound, Rosalind turned and ran back across the roof, her mind in chaos, the image of Christopher lunging at the female Vampire replaying itself endlessly in her mind. She reached her room without incident and locked the door. What on earth had happened to him? Had he truly forsaken her and thrown in his lot with Anne Boleyn and the Vampires?

He'd even seemed disinclined to fight. From that brief glimpse inside his mind, she'd known something was very wrong, that his dormant Vampire senses seemed to have emerged and multiplied. Even when he looked at her, it was as if he was reluctant to meet her gaze.

Rosalind continued to fight tears as she stripped off her ruined clothing and scrubbed herself free of the Vampire's bloodied scent. She pulled on her night robe, and went to the window to stare down into the courtyard below. It was stuffy under the eaves of the great house and she opened the window.

It was partly her fault. If she'd been more aware, the last Vampire would never have been able to sneak up on them like that. She should have cleared the stench of Vampire from her senses more quickly. But would it really have made any difference? She doubted she would ever be able to clear the pain of Christopher's betrayal.

Christopher winced as Rhys kicked him hard in the ribs.

"What in God's teeth were you doing, Ellis?"

Christopher rolled over and found Rhys standing over him, his sword pointed at Christopher's throat, his scowl ferocious. He swallowed hard. "I'm not sure."

Rhys gestured for him to rise, and Christopher got slowly to his feet, aware that every bone in his body was aching from the impact of the cold tile and stonework. "Thank you. You saved my life even though I put you in danger."

Rhys snorted and sheathed his sword. "Save your explanations for Lady Rosalind. What I want to know is who that Vampire was. She looked exactly like you."

Christopher closed his eyes and tried to picture the moment when he'd recognized her, when he'd known at some bone-deep level that he could not allow the female to be killed. Was it before or after she'd smiled at him, or when her mind had briefly touched his? Or when her fresh orange-blossom scent had engulfed him and made him forget everything but reaching out to her? He was no longer sure. All he knew was that he had to protect her.

With all the sincerity he could muster, he met Rhys's hard gaze and offered him half the truth. "I have no idea who she is, but perhaps her looking like me did make me hesitate."

"You did not hesitate, my lord. You saved her from my sword, then pursued her like a stallion after a mare. If I hadn't caught you, you would have plummeted to your death!"

"I know, and I'm grateful for your charity."

Rhys sighed. "If you'd seen Lady Rosalind's face a moment ago, you might consider falling to your death a kinder fate than the one she has in store for you."

Christopher swung around, but there was no sign of Rosalind. "Where is she?"

"She ran away."

"*Rosalind* did?"

Rhys's smile was sarcastic. "Aye, my lord. Perhaps seeing you throw yourself at another woman *upset* her."

Christopher scowled through the pit of anxiety growing in his gut. "Yet it is all right for her to throw herself at you."

"I kissed *her*, Ellis, and she let me because you have been ignoring her." Rhys cast him a sidelong glance. "And you are a fine one to talk. You've collected quite a harem, haven't you?"

"I'm doing the job that both you and Rosalind asked me

to do." Christopher spoke through his gritted teeth. "It's not easy, you know."

They started walking back toward the stairs, both knowing that the Boleyns were hardly likely to show themselves now. Christopher couldn't help but glance back at the place where the Vampire had disappeared. Would he ever see her again? Somehow he suspected he might, and then what in God's teeth was he going to tell Rosalind? She, at least, deserved to know what he suspected.

He paused to allow Rhys to descend first, aware somewhere in his mind of Rosalind's distress, even though she was trying to keep him out. Surely Rosalind could not really believe he cared for Anne, for any other woman.

Inside him, emotions shifted, blurred, and fought for dominance. Pain engulfed his thoughts and Christopher clutched a hand into his windblown hair. He had to talk to Rosalind. He had to convince her that he hadn't changed his allegiances. But had he? A tide of blood-tinged blackness threatened to overwhelm him. By all that was holy, he was drowning in slick, wet redness . . .

Without allowing himself to think any further, he concentrated on Rosalind and making his way to her. Rhys would think him a fool, but Christopher would not allow anyone to stand in his way.

His sense of Rosalind grew stronger. He pictured her in her room, looking out of the window into the Clock courtyard below. Christopher kept skirting the edges of the rooftops until he sensed the window he was looking for. He took off his cloak and his bulky leather jerkin and prayed that his shoulders would fit. For the second time that night, he launched himself off the roof, and in through what he hoped was the safe haven of Rosalind's window.

Chapter 12

Rosalind gasped as a pair of booted feet came through her window followed by the rest of a man's muscular body. Even when she realized it was Christopher, she still backed away and greeted him with the point of her dagger. He closed the window with a bang and advanced toward her, his damp black shirt open at the neck to display the curve of his throat. His hair was disheveled and his eyes a dark, impenetrable blue.

She lifted her chin. "Get out."

"I need to talk to you."

"And I told you to get out!"

"Not until I've had my say."

Rage boiled in her chest and she marched right up to him and slapped his cheek. "I have nothing to say to you. Go back to your Vampire kin."

He grabbed her dagger hand and knocked the blade free. "Not until we've discussed this."

She tried to kick his shins, realized it would hurt her bare feet more than it would him, but did it anyway. "What is there to discuss? Unless you wish to free me from my betrothal. *That* I will discuss."

His hands slid up her arms and cupped her shoulders, his fingers warm and hard against her skin. "Rosalind, we will remain betrothed until we are married."

"Or until one of your Vampire lovers has me murdered."

"I do not *have* any Vampire lovers."

She glared at him. "I don't believe you. Who was that woman?"

A muscle twitched in his cheek. "I'm not sure. Her appearance surprised me just as much as it did you."

"I doubt that."

"Rosalind." There was a hint of impatience in his tone now. "Why are you being so difficult? You agreed to the plan. In truth, you persuaded *me* into it."

"That woman wasn't part of any plan I agreed to—unless you are foolish enough to suggest that was Lady Anne in disguise and you *had* to save her."

Christopher raised his eyebrows. "You are jealous?"

"Mayhap you play your part too well."

"And you do not? I haven't noticed you sighing after me, my lady. You seem quite happy to make merry with all the other courtiers."

Rosalind looked away from him. At some level she knew he had good reason to be annoyed by her reaction to his conduct with Anne Boleyn. But she sensed he was deliberately avoiding her questions about the woman he'd been prepared to leap off a building for. Something was wrong with him and she needed to determine exactly what it was.

His tone softened. "By the saints, I want no other woman but you."

She shoved him away. "You lie."

"I speak the truth." His shoulders bowed as if he carried a heavy load. "If you don't believe me, share my thoughts."

Rosalind closed her eyes, relaxed her own barriers, and tentatively allowed her mind to blend with Christopher's. She saw his truth there, but not only that. There were shadows where once there was light, the taint of Vampire magic where there had once been a strong defensive wall. Christopher was hiding things from her, but were they *his* secrets, or those he held for someone else? Anne's unmistakable influence pervaded Christopher's mind like mold on cheese.

Rosalind fought back a gasp and cupped his bearded cheek, where the heat from her slap still lingered. What in God's name was she to do? Was Christopher even aware of what was happening to him? She had to find a way to reach him and reestablish the connection between them. But at what risk to herself? By opening up to Christopher again, would she make herself vulnerable to Anne?

"Rosalind? What in God's name is the matter? You look as if you have seen the devil himself."

She opened her eyes and stared at Christopher, who sounded as uneasy as she felt. Whether or not he knew it yet, and she suspected that in some part of his mind he did, he had been bewitched. She rose onto her toes and kissed him full on the mouth, felt his instant response in both his mind and body. Would this help? Would joining with him allow her to strengthen his mind, perhaps without him even realizing it?

He returned the kiss, his mouth softening under hers, his arms locking around her with a ferocity that surprised her. "I thought you were going to kill me." He murmured the words against her lips.

She sunk her teeth into his lower lip until he yelped. "There are many ways to kill a man, my lord."

"Is that so?" He kissed her hard until she almost forgot how to breathe. "That sounds like a contest no man could resist."

He allowed her to back him up to the bed and push him down. She followed him, one hand twisted in his thick black hair, the other tugging at the ties of his shirt. She didn't feel like being kind. Whatever Christopher believed, this was a battle she intended to win.

He groaned as she knelt over him and pulled his shirt over his head. She bent and licked his tight nipple, caught it between her teeth until he bucked and reached for her. She slapped his hands away and knelt up to attack the points of his hose. He was already hard and ready, his shaft pressing against the supple buckskin, as if eager for her attention. She rubbed her palm over his groin and felt his prick jerk in response.

"Rosalind, by all the saints—be careful."

She ignored his hoarse plea, and focused her attention on uncovering his thick length, her need for him as sharp as a blade. She had to have him inside her again, had to make him think and dream only of her, and not of Anne Boleyn, *never* Anne Boleyn. She grasped the base of his cock and guided him inside, gasped at the heat and thickness of him, at the sense that he would never fit inside unless she surrendered to him completely.

He watched her through lowered eyes, his hands fisted on the bedcovers, his breathing as ragged as her own. Rosalind took her hand off his shaft and brought herself completely over him. She remained still, waited for her body to accept him, to surround him, to cherish every pulsing inch of him.

He licked his lips and his fingertips grazed her thigh. "Let me touch you."

She glared down at him. "You may not."

"How do you intend to stop me?"

She made as if to climb off him, and his hand fell back on the bed. "All right, I'll be still."

"You had better be, or I'll tie you to the bed."

His heated gaze met hers. "As if I'd let you."

"You'd let me." She sank back down on his prick, and he gasped. Rosalind sought his mind, found him wide-open to her. The intensity of his desire burned so brightly she could almost taste it. As she settled into a rhythm over him, she made him experience each deliberate rock of her hips, each tightening of her inner muscles on his shaft. He started to move under her, his hips arching, his booted feet planted on the bedcovers.

She didn't allow herself to think, just encouraged the flames to consume her, to send her to heights she could never scale without this particular man. And, as she consumed him, so she burned herself, discovered needs that only he could meet, and that only fanned the flames higher. Her religion had taught her well. Fire didn't just destroy; it purified and encouraged new growth.

"Rosalind . . . I need . . ." Christopher's face contorted as his shaft thickened and began to pulse, until the heat of his seed filled her. She took her own pleasure and fell forward onto his chest as her legs trembled and gave out on her.

Before she could recover her breath, he rolled her onto her back and stared down at her, his blue eyes glinting. "We're not done, my lady. You may have noticed, I'm not quite dead yet."

Christopher stared down at Rosalind's swollen mouth and flushed cheeks. Having her again was like coming home. She made him burn so brightly. He disposed of her nightgown and studied her luscious breasts and pale skin, the bruises and scars from her many encounters with the Vampires. She stirred uneasily beneath him, her dark hair spread out over the pillows like a rippling waterfall. He dropped a kiss on her flat belly and she shivered.

He stripped off the rest of his clothes as quickly as he could. Somewhere in his mind, fear lingered. She might desert him like a malicious fey from a fairy story, leave him forever bereft and unable to exist without her. He returned to the bed and grasped one of her wrists. "Must I tie you to the bed, my lady, so that I can take my pleasure without fear of being stabbed, or bitten, or scratched?"

"You enjoy most of those things."

"True, but the thought of you spread out like a feast is certainly appealing." He kissed the inside of her wrist, used his tongue to trace the pale blue lines under her skin to the crook of her elbow. She moaned and he leaned over her, bringing both her wrists over her head. "Perhaps this will suffice for now."

His mouth settled over her nipple and he drew strongly on her until she arched up off the bed like a bow. He kissed her other nipple until she was panting and then moved lower, paused at her stomach to delve his tongue into her navel. She gasped his name and he released her hands, settled himself between her legs and used his mouth and tongue and fingers to bring her close to another climax. Close but not quite enough to take her over.

He raised himself up on his elbows to look at her. "Do you like this, my lady? Do you like my mouth on you?"

She didn't reply, and Christopher used the tip of his finger to circle the tight swollen bud that guarded the entrance to her body. "You don't? I can stop if you wish." He smiled at her again, his finger poised over her wet heat, where he could clearly feel the throb that echoed the frantic beat of her heart.

"You know I like this, you are just being . . ."

He bent his head and blew on her flesh, noticed the faint abrasions on her skin from the roughness of his beard. "Being what?"

"Your usual arrogant self."

He crawled up her body until he straddled her. "I am arrogant?" His prick was hard again now, and more than ready for her. "I thought the idea was to try and swive each other to death."

"Christopher Ellis!" She gasped, but in her mind he felt the jump of excitement his words had produced.

He grinned at her. "Have you something you want to say to me?" He edged closer, his knees at her shoulder level now, his shaft arching away from his belly and angling toward her as if seeking the delights of her tongue. "If not, I have much better use for your mouth."

He wrapped one hand around his aching shaft and rubbed the wet tip against her lips. "Take me inside. Make me hard for you."

He felt her hesitation, aware that he was taking a risk. Rosalind never liked being ordered around and he would be placing his most prized asset in a very vulnerable position.

"Why should I, when you deny me release?"

"An excellent point, my love, but one that can easily be remedied." He reversed his position, until his head was now over her quim, and his shaft was perilously close to her mouth. In his mind, he sent her a graphic picture of what they could both now do.

"Oh," she whispered, her breath dancing over his aching flesh. "I didn't realize that was possible."

Christopher ducked his head and licked her quim, almost came when he felt her mouth close over the crown of his prick and give him a hard suck. Then all was confusion bound with lust, and the glorious sounds of sucking and licking and, God, he had to have her now, or he would explode in her mouth. He reached down to disengage his cock and had to grit his teeth when she only reluctantly released him.

It took him only a moment to swing around, rearrange her legs over his elbows, and plunge deep inside her welcoming heat. She gasped his name, her fingernails digging into his shoulders, her heels thumping on his buttocks as if trying to force him even deeper. He closed his eyes as his cock was squeezed and squeezed until he feared a glorious, painful death was indeed going to be his just reward.

She came again and he gritted his teeth against the overwhelming sensations of her mind and her body convulsing both around him and within him. But beneath her pleasure, he sensed her fear for him, and her determination to do—what exactly? His body kept moving even as his mind recoiled from the stray thought that he was being manipulated.

He kissed her throat and felt the sudden urge to sink his teeth into her skin and mark her, *bite* her. Dark pleasure shuddered through him and blackness scalded his thoughts, turning lust into something else, into the desire to drink from her until she was just an empty shell. Anne's laughter echoed in his head, urging him on.

He wrenched his mouth away and reared over her, his hands planted on either side of her head. She reached for him, her concern pushing at the darkness that had engulfed him.

"Christopher, look at me. Let me help you. Let me in."

He was panting like a hunted animal, his gaze fixed on hers. Light flooded through his thoughts, her light, her love, and he collapsed back over her, his hips still thrusting. All he wanted was to couple with his mate and spill his seed.

Sensation gathered at the base of his spine, and in his tight balls, and he knew he was about to gain his release. He kept thrusting, half aware of Rosalind's cries and totally enmeshed in her mind. He gave her all his emotions, felt them returned, cleansed and enhanced, and then climaxed deep inside her. He groaned, feeling every pulse of his shaft and the warm, wet yielding heat around him.

He rolled onto his back and drew her with him. His eyes were starting to close when she nudged him in the ribs.

"We have something to discuss."

Christopher grimaced. "Can't we just enjoy the moment?"

She nudged him again. "Tell me who that Vampire was."

"For the love of God, Rosalind, I told you. I don't know her."

"Then why did you save her from Rhys's blade?"

"I can't explain it, but for a moment I forgot she was a Vampire, and I simply reacted—I thought she was about to go over the edge."

Rosalind came up on one elbow to peer down into his face. "I don't believe you."

He moved away from her and sat up. "What do you want me to say? You've obviously made up your mind that I am busy cavorting with as many Vampire lovers as I can bed at once."

With an impatient sound, Rosalind pushed her tangled hair back over her shoulder. "That's not what I think. I thought we agreed to be honest with each other."

"I am trying to be honest. I've never seen that particular Vampire before."

"Yet you were willing to risk death for her."

"I know, but I—I don't know *why*."

Rosalind studied him so closely he wanted to fidget. "Did you get a sense of her in your mind?"

"Yes, if you must know, I did."

"She looked like you."

Even though he knew she wouldn't believe him, he shrugged as if he didn't care.

"Be careful who you bed, Christopher. Mayhap, after your mother abandoned you, she made herself a new family of Vampires," Rosalind went on. "That girl could be your sister." She turned her back on him and climbed out of the bed.

Christopher blinked at her. "What are you doing?"

"Getting dressed, as you should be."

"But we haven't finished."

She swung around to look at him, her gaze steady, her eyes sad. "We've finished." She started to pick up his clothes and throw them to him. "You must go."

"Rosalind, whatever you are thinking, it is nonsense."

"It is not." She clutched his shirt to her breasts. "You need to protect yourself better, my lord."

"From you?"

"Mayhap, but also from your Vampire allies."

He held out his hand for his shirt and then pulled it over his head. "Is this because you are jealous of that girl?" He flinched as she threw him his left boot, which landed perilously close to his groin.

"I am not jealous. I am merely concerned that you do not betray us to the Vampires."

"Why would I do that? You know I have no desire to

see the Vampires rule this kingdom." He pulled on his hose and boots.

She sighed and touched his cheek. "Promise me you will work on your defenses."

He caught her fingers beneath his own. "Are you seriously suggesting my loyalty to you is in doubt?"

"I'm not suggesting anything." She took a deep breath. "I'm telling you that we can no longer fight together."

"What? Is this because of what happened with that female Vampire? You must know it was an aberration. I would never betray you."

"Not willingly." Rosalind turned her back on him and drew a thick shawl around her shoulders, her mind shut against his again. "As I said, look inward and work on protecting yourself."

He pushed down his instinctive desire to argue as the full enormity of the problem hit him. "You don't trust me?"

She looked back over her shoulder at him. "I . . ."

Anger laced with confusion shuddered through him. She couldn't abandon him, not now, not when he could still smell and taste their lovemaking, feel her warmth in his body and his mind. "You can't hide all your thoughts from me. You fear I'm not strong enough to resist Anne. You believe I'm becoming more like the Vampires you hunt and kill. Is that what you saw in my mind?"

She finally looked at him. "I saw Anne's influence spreading like a disease."

"And you think it will *help* to shut me out?"

"No." Distress flared in her deep brown eyes. "I just know that I cannot trust you to fight by my side."

"Yet you can trust me in your bed."

"I can *reach* you in my bed. I can connect with your mind and—"

He dropped his hand. "And heal me? Is that why you let me lie with you, so that you could 'heal' me? I thought you wanted me!"

"I do, but . . ."

He walked across to the window and flung it wide, his male pride wounded. "Perhaps we should make a bargain, then. I'll keep out of your way in a fight, and in return you can open your legs for me whenever I want you."

"That is unfair." Rosalind's cheeks flushed with color.

"And is it fair of you to treat me like this? I'm risking my life by staying close to the Boleyns—by doing what *you asked me to do*—and in return you treat me like the enemy!"

She crossed the small space and touched his sleeve. "You are not thinking rationally."

He pulled out of her grasp. "I agree there is nothing *rational* about this, my lady. You forsake me when I need you most and expect me to be happy?"

She bit down on her lip. "When you calm down, you'll realize this is best. I just want you to go away and think about it."

"Stop treating me like a child or an invalid!" He wished she would argue back; her attempts to placate him fueled something dark and aggressive in his mind. "I'll not leave until you've agreed to my bargain. My absence in battle in exchange for my presence in your bed." He needed her, even if she didn't need him, but he was damned if he was going to tell her that.

Rosalind studied him for a long moment. "All right."

"As gracious in defeat as ever." He managed to bow. "Take care of yourself when you're fighting the Vampires. I'm sure Rhys will do a fine job of protecting you." Before she could reply, he pulled himself up and out of the window and back onto the roof. Beneath his shirt, his heart was thumping as if he'd had to run for his life. Rosalind didn't trust him, and the Boleyns didn't really trust him either. In his mind, he detected the faintest hint of malicious laughter. He was back where he'd been for most of his life— alone, under suspicion, and determined not to let anyone see that it bothered him.

With a groan he sank down to the rooftop and dropped his face into his hands. His night had been filled with the most extreme of emotions, from the terror of the female Vampire almost falling, to the delights of Rosalind's bed, and then back again to the fear of losing her. Was she right? Had Anne Boleyn contaminated his thoughts?

He shuddered as he pictured Anne's face. Had she been in that bed with him? Interfering in the most precious and intimate moments of his life? Christopher cursed. He knew it was true. He'd felt her influence, *her* bloodlust, not his, *never* his.

A pair of familiar bare feet appeared in his vision, but he refused to look up. He heard Rosalind sigh and crouch down in front of him; her hands came to rest on the barrier of his knees. Her scent, *their* scent invaded his senses, made him want to reach for her and never let her go.

"It isn't like before, Christopher. You are no longer alone and I am no longer capable of deserting you. I know what you are doing is necessary, and dangerous. We just need to be careful. You do understand that, don't you?" He continued to squeeze his eyes shut, as if he were a child and thought to make himself invisible. She stroked his hair, her thumb tracing the ridge of his ear. "I'm worried about you."

He had nothing to say to that, nothing she wanted to hear anyway. She tugged at his hands and he let her pull them away from his eyes. In the moonlight, she was so beautiful, her mouth swollen from his kisses, her cheeks reddened from the rasp of his beard.

She took his face between her hands. "I still love you."

He stared into her eyes, saw the truth of it there, and wondered why he still felt so desperate. It was as if something within him was trying to make him doubt her . . . Anne's face flitted through his thoughts, her expression triumphant.

He took a deep breath. "And I love you. But I'm not safe anymore, am I? So why would you believe anything I say?" He looked down at her feet.

"I do believe you, but we can no longer fight together. I'm too afraid you might end up killing me."

"I could never do that!"

"Not knowingly, but what if Anne *is* controlling your thoughts?"

He met her worried gaze. "I will keep her out. I swear to you."

At that moment, it was all he could give her. She leaned in to him and rested her forehead against his. "Good night, Christopher."

He managed a nod and she got off her knees and disappeared back over the edge of the parapet. Her white nightgown stuck to her damp skin, and he could see the curve of her breasts and buttocks, her glorious unbound hair falling to her waist.

Christopher waited until he heard her window shut and closed his eyes. Anne was there waiting for him, ready to taint his memories of their lovemaking and turn them into something he should be ashamed of. He pictured the wall he'd learned to construct so painstakingly in his mind and found it riddled with holes.

With a sigh, he got to his feet and made his way back down to the ground and then across the deserted inner courtyard to his bedchamber. There was no sign of his manservant, Roper, so he stripped off his bloodstained leather jerkin and let it fall to the floor.

"Did you enjoy your tryst, Kit?"

He stiffened and brought his dagger hand up as the scent of honeysuckle filled his small room. Anne appeared in front of him, her hair loose down her back, her body swathed in a floor-length robe. She circled him, one long fingernail scraping against the skin of his bearded jaw.

"What are you doing here, Anne?"

Anne pouted. "George and I were all ready to go out and hunt for food when you and those Vampire slayers spoiled our fun. I thought you were supposed to be loyal to me, Kit."

Christopher met her gaze. "I am loyal to you. My uncle insists I occasionally consort with the Druids to allay their suspicions."

"And when you say 'consort,' you mean bed?"

"I bed only one of them, my lady."

"Ah, yes, the Lady Rosalind." Anne inhaled. "I can smell her on you."

He shrugged and hoped desperately that he could keep the ragged ends of his mind closed to her. He felt far too vulnerable to deal with Anne now. "It keeps the lady content."

He winced as her fingernails dug into his skin. "But I do not like it, Kit."

With a soft curse, he grabbed her wrist and pulled her hand away. "Then take the matter up with my uncle. I am a mere puppet in his hands—you know that." He couldn't keep the bitterness out of his voice and hoped she heard it.

She turned his hand over and, while her tongue licked a wet, hot circle, she grazed his palm with the tip of her fangs. "It is a shame you are not a full Vampire, Kit. I would enjoy having you in my bed."

Christopher closed his eyes as Anne flooded his mind with salacious images of them entwined on her sheets. He couldn't push her out, realized the full extent of his contamination with every labored breath and the sick excitement twisting through his gut, his prick, his balls . . . He couldn't even call on Rosalind to help him—exposing her to Anne would surely cause a disaster.

With all the strength he could muster, he set Anne away from him and folded his arms across his chest. "Don't forget, I am allied with a Druid, which would not suit your tastes at all."

Anne laughed. "It is indeed a shame, my old friend." Her smile disappeared and Christopher found himself slammed to the floor. "Do not swive her. I command it. I will know if you do, and punish you accordingly."

He could barely breathe, let alone speak, as invisible

hands wrapped around his throat. His vision blurred and he raised a hand in a last appeal, but Anne had gone. He collapsed forward, gulping down air, and concentrated on regaining control of his shaking limbs.

After a long while, he managed to strip off his clothes and climb into bed. He looked up at the ceiling and turned his thoughts inward. Rosalind was right to be worried. He could now see that Anne's influence permeated his every action. He could not allow her that power over him. He needed to patch up his defenses fast, even if that meant asking Rhys for help.

He blinked hard in the darkness. No Vampire would ever control his destiny again.

Chapter 13

"I want to talk to you, Ellis."

Christopher looked up from the lute he was re-stringing and found Sir Marcus Flavian towering over him. He fought down a spark of hope, knowing it was far too early to count on Marcus for anything. With elaborate slowness he tightened the new lute string and retuned the instrument before setting it to one side.

Marcus turned on his heel and headed for the great hall, which was usually deserted in the early part of the day. As he bowed and left Anne's presence, Christopher received a careless wave of her hand. Her black gaze followed him, and he felt a slight pressure in his head, as if she wanted him to be aware of her ability to inhabit his mind at will.

In the last three weeks, with Rhys's quiet help, he'd become quite skilled at blocking Anne from the most vulnerable parts of his mind. He'd learned to maintain a delicate balance between shutting Anne out completely, and letting her think she was still influencing him. Rhys had taught him how to protect his most exposed senses and rebury his Vampire instincts. To Christopher's relief, Rhys had proved an excellent instructor. But it was still a struggle, one he always feared he might lose.

Each time they met in the stables, Rhys brought him up-to-date about his and Rosalind's various scraps with the Vampires. Fights Christopher was no longer involved in, a fact that burned like a smoldering coal in his gut. He trusted Rhys to defend Rosalind with his life, but it still wasn't good enough. He hated not being there for her, hated seeing the bruises she tried to hide from him when he joined her in bed, hated himself for still needing to join his body and mind to hers to shore up his tattered defenses. Having Rosalind kept Anne out, but it was a dangerous balance to maintain and one that risked his life if Anne became aware of it. But if he didn't have that release, that sense of coming home, he feared he would run mad.

Marcus halted by one of the bare trestle tables and sat down, and Christopher took the bench opposite him. Apart from a lone scavenging dog and a couple of servants freshening the rushes, there was no one within hearing distance.

Christopher raised an eyebrow. "Well?"

Marcus stared down at the scarred oak table. "Your uncle . . ."

"My uncle, what?"

"Is not himself."

"In what way?"

Marcus's forthright gaze met Christopher's. "He seems to believe that the only way forward for the Mithras Cult is to obey all the dictates of the Vampire Council."

Christopher relaxed a little. "I told you so."

"Aye, and I didn't believe you." Marcus grimaced. "His commitment to this course seems quite . . . irrational."

"Is that so? And what do you intend to do about it?"

"I suggested it was time he called the cult members together to share his thoughts on the matter."

"That is an excellent idea."

"I'm not sure about that, and I doubt he'll listen to me. His power is absolute."

Christopher frowned. "There must have been other instances when the cult leadership was challenged, Marcus. What do the records say? Surely there is a way for a madman to be deposed."

"You believe your uncle is mad?"

"I'm not certain. What do you think?"

"I *think* I should speak to old Brother Samuel at Westminster Abbey. He holds the records of the cult in trust." Marcus sat back and eyed Christopher. "This doesn't mean that you are absolved of your crimes."

"I never assumed that it did. Verily, the thought never occurred to me."

"Liar," growled Marcus.

Christopher smiled. "While you are looking at those records, I'd appreciate a look too."

"You believe there is a way to challenge your death sentence?"

Christopher stood up. "A man can dream, can't he?"

Marcus's skeptical expression didn't alter. "In any struggle, dreamers are always the first to die."

"I disagree. Hope is a precious thing." Christopher bowed. "Will you tell me if the cult members are summoned? I would like to attend such a meeting."

"Your uncle will not welcome your presence."

"Then we won't tell him I'll be there, will we?"

Marcus nodded. "If it happens, I'll send you word."

"I appreciate it."

Christopher walked away whistling. The first inkling of a way out of at least one of his problems had emerged in the unlikely persona of the unsmiling, unhelpful Marcus Flavian. If he could rid the Mithras Cult of his uncle's malign influence, that would be something. It didn't quite solve the problem of his impending death, but it was a start.

He was still smiling as he rounded a corner and walked straight into Rosalind. Her breath hissed out as he caught her by the elbows and steadied her. She was dressed in his favorite colors of dark red with black velvet sleeves. After a quick look around, he drew her closer into the shadows of the wall.

"Are you all right?" His gaze sharpened as he noticed how stiffly she held herself. "Are you injured?"

"I fell from a tree last night."

"And?"

"I bruised my ribs."

He briefly closed his eyes. "Rosalind, if you will not let me help you, please, send for Jasper. You and Rhys cannot fight them all."

"We have to." She swallowed hard and straightened away from him. "They don't want to kill us yet. They're toying with us, like cats playing with a terrified, wounded mouse. I assume they're waiting for the Boleyns to come and finish us off personally."

"Rosalind"—he heard the anguish and frustration in his own voice—"let me fight with you. I've rebuilt my defenses. I swear to you that I—"

She placed her fingers over his lips. "No, we can manage. Please don't put yourself in danger."

He kissed her fingers and held on to them. "I feel like a coward, hiding behind his woman's skirts."

"You are fighting your own battles, and they are equally important." She glanced over his shoulder. "I have to go. The king wishes to talk to me."

"And what exactly are you going to tell him?"

Her shoulders bowed. "Nothing to implicate the Boleyns. So far I have no evidence that will convince him, or bring him out of the spell Anne has put him under."

"We have to find something. We cannot go on like this." He released her hands and she was gone, leaving him facing the stone wall, a dull ache in his heart that never seemed to lift. Furtive meetings, rushed lovemaking, and the threat of death hanging over them both. Defying Anne took so much of his strength, it couldn't go on for much longer. But how in God's name were they going to bring it to a close without one of them dying?

* * *

After her unexpected meeting with Christopher, Rosalind made her way to the king's privy chamber. She kept her head down to avoid looking at any of the other courtiers. It seemed there were Vampires everywhere these days, their scent overwhelming her, tormenting her every night with dreams of being drowned in their blood.

"Good morning, Lady Rosalind."

"Good morning, Sir Henry."

Sir Henry Norris bowed to her and then opened the door into the king's inner sanctum. Rosalind moved past him and then came to an abrupt halt as she saw George Boleyn laughing with the king. She forced a smile and dropped into a low curtsy. "Good morning, Your Majesty, Lord Rochford."

"Ah, Lady Rosalind." King Henry beckoned her to rise. "And how are you this fine morning?"

"I'm well, sire." She looked pointedly at George Boleyn. "I understood that you wished to speak to me, Your Majesty—in private."

"I can see that I am not wanted here, sire. I will await your presence in the outer room." George bowed to the king and then half turned to Rosalind. "Good morning, my lady."

Rosalind let out her breath as George stalked out of the room and banged the door behind him. She looked back at the king, who was watching her intently.

"You do not like Lord Rochford?"

"I hardly know him, sire."

The king crossed over to the fireplace and took his seat. "Yet he seems to know you quite well. In fact, he was just talking about your betrothal."

"Lord Rochford was?"

"Aye, he suggested that his friend Lord Christopher Ellis wished to end the arrangement."

"Is that so, sire? I wonder why Lord Christopher did not tell you so himself."

"Perhaps he thought Lord Rochford was higher in my favor."

Rosalind had nothing to say to that. She simply stood and waited as the king continued to study her. Had Christopher really asked to end their betrothal and, if so, why hadn't he spoken to her about it? Unease gathered in her stomach and she swallowed hard. Would it be better for her to agree, and at least free Christopher from this impossible situation? Was that what he was trying to do for her?

"I'm not sure what to say, Your Majesty. As you know, my family and the Ellises have long been enemies."

"Yet you managed to ally with Lord Christopher for long enough to kill that Spanish Vampire." King Henry shifted in his seat. "*And* you should remember, young lady, that I abhor family enmity and would consider your marriage a step in the direction of peace."

Rosalind met his hard gaze. "I am your willing subject to command, sire. I will abide by any decision you make."

"As is right and proper." The king nodded. "I shall consider the matter further." He lowered his voice. "Now tell me if you have any more news about this latest Vampire threat."

Rosalind tried not to look away. "There is definitely a threat, sire. You should be on your guard."

"A threat from whom?"

"I cannot be specific, sire. There are more Vampires at court than there used to be, and your life is in danger." Rosalind paused. Was there anything she could say that might hint that the danger was closer than he could possibly imagine?

"What exactly are you suggesting, my lady?"

"Your Majesty, you are the most intelligent man in the whole of Europe. I need hardly explain anything to you. Your natural shrewdness and devout faith will protect you from harm."

The king rested his bearded chin on his hand. "You are reminding me again not to trust anyone, aren't you?"

Rosalind curtsied. "Yes, sire. Not even your closest friends."

"Or family? Or . . . lovers?"

"Anyone, sire. You hold great power in your hands, and there are many who would like to rob you of it."

"That I understand." King Henry nodded slowly. "I will be on my guard. I trust you will inform me if you discover exactly who it is who wishes to kill me."

Rosalind hesitated. "Sire, there are many ways for the Vampires to defeat you. They may not seek your death, but rather to control you and, through you, rule the country."

"I would be alive and yet in thrall to the Vampires?" The king shuddered. "That is sacrilege."

"It is a possibility, sire. Do not assume an assassin would come to kill you. Think about how close people are allowed to get to your royal person."

The king's fat fingers went to his throat. "The Vampire would suck my blood, make me one of them?"

"They might, sire." Rosalind held his gaze. "I hope to prevent it."

King Henry made the sign of the cross over his heart. "A fate worse than death, to live in thrall to another's commands. I shall be wary, my lady. Do not worry."

"Thank you, sire. And I will do my best to make sure that nothing happens to you either."

The king nodded and waved his hand for her to leave, his expression dark, his hand already reaching for the prayer book beside him. She hoped she'd said enough to keep him on his guard. Hopefully, his suspicious nature would keep him alive despite anything Anne Boleyn could do with her magic. It was lucky for all concerned that Anne had refused to join the king in his bed or else all would be over.

As she passed through the outer chambers, Rosalind smiled at Sir Henry and ignored George Boleyn, who sat glowering in the window seat. It was becoming harder and harder to pretend that all was well, when her body ached from the ceaseless fighting at night, and her mind was saturated by Vampire scents. She wanted Christopher by her side. She needed him, but she couldn't have him. With all the courage she could muster, Rosalind picked up her skirts and headed back to serve Anne Boleyn.

Christopher paused in the passageway that led between the Lady Anne's apartments and the servants' route to the stables. Ahead of him he could hear Anne's high-pitched voice engaged in an argument with a man who was definitely not the king. He kept close to the shadows of the wall and moved nearer.

"Elias, you are being ridiculous," Anne hissed. "Of course nothing is wrong."

"Then why do you allow that youngling, that underaged Vampire, to share your bed instead of me?"

"Oh, for goodness' sake! I've told you. George amuses me."

"He does more than that."

There was an impatient rustle of skirts. "He is just entertaining me while I wait for the king to fulfill his promise. When I am queen, you can take your rightful place at my side."

"Are you sure about that, Anne? Or do you intend to elevate George rather than me?"

Christopher held his breath.

"Darling, we have known each other for centuries." Anne's voice was purring now as if she was intent on kissing her way around Elias's objections. "You mean more to me than any other man of my acquaintance."

"Anne . . ." Elias went quiet and Christopher tried not to think about how Anne had stopped his words. After a long while, Elias said, "You had better not be lying to me, my lady, or I'll take great pleasure in breaking your pretty little neck."

Anne laughed. "And I promise that when I am done

with George, you may have the pleasure of killing him for me."

Christopher stayed still as Anne's light footsteps faded away. He waited for another minute or two and then moved forward—straight into Elias Warner, who barred his way.

"What do you want, Lord Christopher?"

"I'm merely on my way to the stables."

"And heard far more than you should."

"Do you intend to kill me for it? Come, it's not as if I didn't know that you and the Lady Anne are . . . What exactly are you to her, Elias? Her supper?" Christopher groaned as Elias shoved him against the stone wall and grabbed him by the throat. "What's wrong? Did I hit a nerve?"

Elias's fangs emerged and glinted in the feeble light. "You—you know nothing."

Christopher held his gaze. "I know that she is a lying bitch. You know it too. You just don't want to admit it."

Elias's eyes glowed an unearthly red, and then he calmed, abruptly releasing Christopher. "Do not speak of my lady like that."

Christopher rearranged the collar of his shirt. "When you realize that she is just using you, come and talk to me."

Elias's eyebrows went up. "I thought you were loyal to Lady Anne."

Christopher deftly ignored the question. "George Boleyn hates you, and I know him well enough to realize he will never relinquish his hold on Anne to you."

"He will be easy to kill," Elias retorted.

"Not if Anne has drained you of all your powers to serve herself. What if that is her plan, to weaken you while she feeds George Boleyn?"

"She is not feeding him. I would've seen the marks."

"It depends where she allows him to feed from her, doesn't it? Some places are far more intimate than others." Christopher watched anger stir on Elias's normally bland face. "I'll bid you good day." He started off down the passageway toward the stables.

"Wait," Elias called to him.

Christopher half turned. "What?"

"You have always been one of George's closest friends. Do you swear she is feeding him?"

"So George told me. He tends to be indiscreet when in his cups."

Elias took a long, unsteady breath. "Then I am indeed compromised."

Christopher continued on his way. If they could persuade Elias onto their side, they might stand a chance against Anne. Elias of all people must know her secrets, her fears, her deepest desires. And knowing those things would make it much easier to plan her doom.

He found himself smiling as he emerged into the busy activity of the immense stable yard. The pleasant weather meant the smell of horse dung and wet straw was noticeably absent, for which he was very grateful. As Christopher walked along the row of stalls, Rhys called his name.

Christopher entered the open door of the stall and saw Rhys had just finished grooming Rosalind's horse. He was tying off the neat braids in the horse's mane with needle and thread. A large bruise on his cheek marred the paleness of his skin and his left wrist was tightly bound. Like Rosalind, he bore the scars of his debilitating fights with the Vampires.

"How are you today, sir?"

Christopher regarded the man whom he now sometimes considered less of a rival and more of a friend. "I'm worried about Rosalind."

Rhys bit through the thread before stowing the needle and thread in his leather pouch. "So am I."

Christopher sat himself down on the upturned feed bucket. "I asked if she would consider recalling Jasper Llewellyn to court to help her, but she refused."

"She doesn't wish to ask for help from her family. She thinks it makes her look weak."

"I offered my services as well, but she didn't seem to think that was a good idea either."

Rhys's smile was strained. "And she is right. You know that."

"But I've made great strides in my efforts to guard my mind. Anne Boleyn is no longer influencing me as much as she thinks. You know that."

"But if you start fighting with us again, the Vampires will no longer trust you at all, and we can't afford to lose that link."

"Then what are we to do? Neither of you can go on for much longer without being seriously hurt."

"We'll do what we must, sir. We have no choice." Rhys patted the horse and gathered up his equipment. His hazel eyes met Christopher's. "There's another reason you should keep away from the Vampires."

"What?"

"That female—the one who looks like you?" Rhys looked uncomfortable. "She asks me about you."

"Asks *you*?"

"Aye."

"Since when do you speak with Vampires? Why haven't you killed her?"

Rhys's pale skin colored. "She is proving very hard to catch." He shoved a hand through his thick auburn hair. "I haven't mentioned it to Rosalind."

"Probably best not to." Christopher regarded Rhys closely. "And what exactly does the female say?"

"She wants to know where you are, and what your name is."

Christopher struggled to conceal his surge of interest. "What do you tell her?"

"Nothing. But I thought you should know." Rhys fingered his dagger. "I should probably kill her before she comes after you."

"No, don't do that." The words were out before Christopher had time to think. "But don't talk to her either."

Rhys made a face. "She makes it very difficult for me not to. She seems as curious about you as you are about her."

"I'm not curious."

Rhys threw him a skeptical glance.

Christopher took a deep breath and voiced the suspicion he and Rosalind had shared. "I fear my mother may have had children with her lover after he turned her."

"It's possible." Rhys nodded. "And that makes things even more complicated, doesn't it?"

"I'm not sure. All I know is that I can't imagine being able to kill her."

Rhys slapped him on the back. "If it comes to that, I'll do it for you."

Chapter 14

"Let me come with you," Rosalind said urgently. She saw the refusal form on Christopher's face before he voiced it. "Why can't I come?"

"Because neither Marcus nor the monk who holds the Mithras Cult records for safekeeping will want to speak to me if I turn up with a Druid."

Rosalind sighed. "I suppose not." She glanced around the cold, deserted storage room. "I should go back. I might have been missed."

Christopher took a firmer grip on her hand and pulled her toward the large fire screens that had been abandoned in the corner of the room until they should be needed again in the winter. He stepped between the screens and into the small, dark, intimate space behind them, drawing Rosalind with him.

"Christopher." Rosalind stopped talking as his fingers shaped her cheek and traveled in a slow caress around her face, tracing her nose, her mouth, her brow, and her chin. She couldn't help but simply enjoy his touch.

His lips followed the path of his fingers, his mouth as delicate as a feather. She shivered as his hand slid under the veil of her hood and he stroked her hairline and down her spine.

"Rosalind," he whispered against her mouth, "bide a moment and kiss me."

She opened her mouth to him and he took possession of it, his tongue flicking against hers, his breath also hers now, and so precious that she wanted to stay entwined with him forever. His fingers continued to tease down the back of her neck as if he were playing a lute and was intent on drawing the sweetest sound from her. The kiss went on and on and he made no effort to deepen it. His hands didn't stray from her head. Hers did. She brought her hands up to his shoulders and simply held on as he continued to kiss her cares away.

She knew he needed to give her this solace, this support, when he couldn't protect her in any other way. And she gave it back to him, aware of the daily battle he raged against Anne Boleyn's malign influence. Aware too, of his struggle to remain true to her and subvert that part of his Vampire nature Anne had deliberately tried to rouse and manipulate.

With a soft sound, Rosalind stood on tiptoe and tried to fit herself against Christopher's muscular form. She wished she had her boy's clothes on. Her heavy silken skirts, stiff embroidered bodice, and petticoats kept her too far away from him. She yearned to feel his skin close to hers, close enough to touch, and lick, and nip.

Soft laughter echoed in her mind. "*Rosalind, with such indecent thoughts, you will unman me.*"

She sent him an even more salacious image, her mouth moving over his muscular chest, down past his flat belly, and beyond to claim him . . . He groaned, but he didn't stop kissing her.

"*I cannot make love to you here. Rhys says you—*"

She drew her mouth away from his. "You are asking *Rhys* whether you should bed me now?"

"No, I just don't want to hurt you."

"It's been *days* since we last shared a bed." Goodness, was that her voice trembling like an untried girl's?

He winced and covered her mouth with his fingers. "I know how long it has been. Trust me on that."

She arched away from him. "Then when?" She hated the thought that she sounded like a shrew or a nag. "We need each other. Or at least, I need you."

His eyes flashed a brilliant blue. "I want you. Don't ever doubt that. But I also want you well enough to fight the Vampires."

"I'm perfectly well, and verily, the Vampires seem less willing to fight at the moment. I'm not sure if they are scared, or if they are planning something worse."

"I'd suspect the latter." Christopher's expression hardened. "Anne grows more confident every day, and the king is closer to destroying the Church in his mad pursuit of her."

Rosalind frowned. "Which is why you need to go and investigate the records of the Mithras Cult."

"Do you think I am derelict in my duty to you? I can only assure you that I'm not. My uncle is involved in this business. If I can find a way to get rid of him, I can perhaps bring down the Vampire Council and the Boleyns at the same time."

Rosalind studied his face. She doubted that was the whole story, but she had sense enough not to tell him so. She had just made up her mind to press him further when she heard voices coming down the hallway.

"Kit, darling, is that you?"

Beside Rosalind, Christopher tensed. "It's Anne. Stay here, and I'll go out to her."

Rosalind bit back a hasty retort. She'd much rather they faced the would-be queen together and killed her once and for all.

She grabbed for Christopher's sleeve. "There is no one about. We could kill her right now."

He pulled out of her grasp. "She is never alone," Christopher hissed. "George is probably right behind her. Stay here." Through a gap in one of the folding screens Rosalind watched as Christopher headed to the entrance of the room and bowed to the approaching figure.

"Lady Anne."

Anne raised her chin and stared at Christopher. "What are you doing here all alone, sweet Kit?"

"I thought I saw a friend of mine heading for the stables, but I must have taken a wrong turn."

Anne sniffed. "You're lying. You're still following that Llewellyn wench around, aren't you?"

Christopher managed a shrug. "I have to keep an eye on her, you must understand that." Another voice echoed down the long corridor and Christopher stiffened. So much for their opportunity to kill her. He recognized the exquisitely polite tones of Elias Warner. All too aware of his bloodthirsty betrothed behind the screens, Christopher approached Anne with a smile.

"Lady Anne, perhaps we should go back," Christopher said diplomatically. "The king will miss you."

"Who cares about the king?" Anne snapped.

Christopher paused. "Surely his majesty is key to your continuing success, my lady? Without his favor we are all but nothing."

"The king and the Vampire Council think they own me!"

"But you can hardly expect to succeed without their help."

"Ha!" Anne sounded as if her patience was at an end. She paced the floor in front of Christopher, her hands fisted in the skirts of her burgundy red gown. "I hate the king fondling and groping me, promising me so much and then making me wait. By human standards, I'm getting old. If he doesn't marry me soon, I'll never be able to give him the son he wants."

"But you're immortal," Christopher said carefully, trying to ignore Anne's unsubtle demands on his mind and senses to agree with her. "You have all the time in the world to conceive a child."

"You know nothing—"

"Lady Anne?" Christopher cleared his throat. "Perhaps you might consider being more discreet. This discussion should hardly be held in public."

"I suppose you are right." Anne's hands closed into fists and her dark bloodlust surged through Christopher. "Sometimes I'd like to destroy them all." She half smiled at Christopher. "Although the king has his uses, of course."

"As do Elias and my uncle."

Anne waved a dismissive hand. "As do many slaves." She grabbed his arm. "Are you going to run back and tell tales to your uncle? He'll never move against me. he has far too much to gain."

"In what way?"

Anne's smile faded. "He will not aid you. His dislike for you is well known, which is why you are far better off throwing in your lot with me, dear Kit." She stroked his cheek. "I understand you and want the best for you. Remember that."

Christopher found himself nodding and she released him.

"You are right. I really should be getting back now." She curtsied to Christopher and then paused. "I was merely expressing my understandable frustration in these constant delays to my plans to someone I can trust." Her black gaze swept over Christopher and he felt a dark compulsion tug at his senses. "I *can* trust you, can't I?"

He bowed. "Of course you can, my lady."

Anne nodded and waved a careless dismissal. "Then good evening to you, Kit, and we will speak no more of this."

Christopher waited until Anne had disappeared completely before walking back to the screens where Rosalind had concealed herself. She emerged to join him, Elias

Warner at her side. Christopher could only wonder at what point the Vampire had appeared there and how much he had overheard, as his expression revealed nothing.

"Well, that was certainly enlightening," Rosalind whispered.

Elias turned suddenly and punched his fist through one of the screens. "I knew it. Anne is going to betray both me and the Council."

"With the help of my uncle, so it would seem," Christopher added.

Elias shoved the broken screen to one side and swung around to glare at Rosalind and Christopher. "This cannot be allowed to happen. I have invested far too much of my personal worth, my reputation, my future . . ."

"And don't forget your blood." Christopher watched Elias closely. "Blood that the Lady Anne passed on to her paramour, George Boleyn."

Elias stopped pacing. "The Council will never believe the Boleyns are working against them."

"Perhaps they aren't. Perhaps they are only trying to shut you out and not the Council."

"That would be . . ." Elias's breath hissed out in a curse. "I will have to speak to the Council."

Rosalind patted Elias's gold-clad shoulder, her tone both encouraging and conciliatory. "You should. Find out if Anne and George have undermined your position. I wouldn't be surprised if they have."

Elias met her gaze and then Christopher's. "If I discover I have been betrayed—"

Christopher held up his hand. "You will tell us, and we will work together to destroy the Boleyns. I give you my word on that."

Elias nodded and then disappeared, his expression lethal. Christopher let out his breath. "I have never seen our dispassionate friend so angry. This could work out to our advantage, love."

"If Elias is willing to disobey the Vampire Council *and* deceive his longtime lover."

Christopher smiled and bent to kiss her nose. "He has been set aside for a younger rival. That is a very strong motivator indeed."

"I hope so." She kissed him back and he longed to stay right there and woo her into temporary pliant submission. With a rueful smile, he set her away from him.

"I have to meet Marcus."

"And I intend to go to bed—that is, if Rhys doesn't send for me . . ." She leaned in to him and he saw her exhaustion, the hollows in her cheeks and the wary mistrust now ever present in her brown eyes.

Despite himself, he kissed her again. "When I pass through the stables, I'll tell Rhys to leave you be. I doubt the Boleyns will be abroad tonight. So take your rest and dream of me."

"I'll try." She managed a small smile. "Be careful, Christopher."

"Of course." He blew her a kiss and headed out to find his horse and Marcus Flavian. Worry churned in his gut as he contemplated the tangled path ahead of him. There was nothing he could do except hope and pray that out of the darkness would come a solution that would save those he loved—even if he couldn't find a way to save himself.

Despite the darkened streets, Christopher could easily spot their destination. The hulking outline of Westminster Abbey was ablaze with lights, the scent of incense and burning wax hovering over the giant structure like a permanent, mystical cloud. Marcus gestured at one of the narrow side alleys.

"We'll go around the back and enter through the cloisters. I've already alerted Brother Samuel that we are coming."

Christopher dismounted and, finding no willing urchin in sight ready to hold his horse, loosely tied the reins to the nearest tree. Marcus did the same and they set off into the darkness, the towering stone walls of the abbey on their right. A lantern burned over an arch-shaped oak door set into the thick outer walls, and Marcus rapped on the door.

It was opened by a young monk dressed in the traditional black garb of the Benedictine order. His cowl was lowered and, in the flickering light, his pale scalp gleamed like a plucked goose. Christopher shuddered at the sight of it, and thanked God he had never been called to the Church.

Marcus inclined his head. "Brother Samuel is expecting us."

Christopher concealed a smile. That was Marcus, abrupt to the point of rudeness. Had he ever questioned his allegiances, or wondered at the dictates of the cult's leader before? Christopher was still surprised that Marcus had decided to go this far and investigate.

The young monk bowed. "Brother Samuel is awaiting you in the north cloister. I will take you to him."

"Thank you," Christopher said, which earned him a shy smile from the boy and a disapproving glance from Marcus. They followed the monk through the eastern side of the cloister, which at this time of the night was deserted. The scent of overcooked cabbage and the murmur of voices drifted across from the dining room. Underfoot was the far pleasanter aroma of freshly laid rushes.

The northern side of the cloister was split into smaller carrels to allow several monks to study and work at the same time. In the farthest corner, a single candle on a high desk illuminated the shape of another black-robed figure.

"Brother Samuel is over there."

The young monk disappeared in the direction of the dining room, and Marcus took off his hat and strode forward, his boots loud on the uneven stone floor. Christopher followed along behind, his gaze fixed on the elderly man perched on a high stool behind the desk.

"Sir Marcus. And how are you this fine evening?"

"I'm well, Brother Samuel." Marcus shifted his stance and glanced back at Christopher. "May I introduce Lord Christopher Ellis?"

Brother Samuel observed Christopher closely, his round face a study in concentration, his blue eyes narrowed. "Ah, I've heard a lot about you."

Christopher bowed. "I dread to think from whom."

A smile flickered on the elderly monk's face. "Your uncle said you had a tendency to levity."

"And he would be right about that, at least." Christopher moved closer so that he stood next to Marcus. "Did Marcus tell you what he was looking for?"

Brother Samuel sighed. "Indeed, he did."

"You disapprove?"

"I am not here to judge the actions of the cult's members, only to provide a safe place for the records to be stored and the promise of secrecy for all eternity."

Marcus leaned close. "Did you find anything?"

Brother Samuel indicated three rolls of parchment and a leather-bound book. "I found several instances of the cult leader being challenged."

"Successfully?"

"In some cases, yes, in others, no." Brother Samuel slid down from his stool. He was surprisingly short, his bald head level with Christopher's chest. "I'm going to have my dinner. Please treat the documents respectfully and do not remove anything, or else I will send someone to kill you."

Marcus nodded his thanks and took the monk's stool while Christopher stood behind him. With great care, Marcus unrolled the first scroll and immediately frowned.

"What language is this?"

"It's a form of clerical Latin."

Marcus squinted at the closely written lines. "I suppose it is. Can you read it?"

Christopher was already scanning the intricate script. "It's about a challenge made to the leadership in 1098. A successful challenge, when the leader of the Mithras Cult was convicted of taking bribes from various members to procure their advancement over others."

"How was the challenge brought?"

Christopher stopped reading. "This scroll doesn't say. Perhaps it will become clearer when we read the others."

For a while they worked in silence, carefully unrolling the scrolls and then reading the pages Brother Simon had marked in the leather book. Eventually Marcus rubbed his eyes and stared at Christopher.

"It seems quite straightforward. Any member can step forward and cite his grievances, then ask the assembly to vote on the fitness of the leader to address his concerns. If the assembly agrees that there is just cause, a vote can be taken of the entire membership to relieve the leader of his responsibilities."

"Aye, it *sounds* straightforward. But who would be willing to stand up to my uncle?" Christopher frowned at Marcus. "And don't ask me to do it. I'm not considered a full member of the cult, and I'll be too busy defending myself against the charges laid against *me* to worry about the rest of you."

"Then I suppose I'll have to do it." Marcus looked resigned as he rolled up one of the scrolls. "But there is that other option."

Christopher's attention had wandered back to the open book, where another page had been marked with a note that bore his name. "What option?"

"Single combat between the challenger and the leader."

"I suppose you'd prefer that to standing up like a lawyer and being reasonable," Christopher said. "But I hardly think my uncle will accept your challenge."

"If he likes, he can choose a champion. Yes, the challenge may be the better solution. If he's dead, there is no possibility of him trying to organize another revolt to reclaim his position."

Marcus sounded so remarkably matter-of-fact that Christopher wanted to smile. He turned the pages to the slip of parchment and started to read.

Marcus slammed the book shut. "That's enough for tonight."

"But I haven't finished." Christopher only just managed to sound civil. "We agreed that I was to be given the opportunity to consult the records too."

"You've consulted them. You know what we have to do to rid the cult of your uncle and return us to our original mission of killing Druids."

"But that doesn't really help me, does it?"

"I thought you said you didn't expect to avoid your fate."

Christopher glared at him. "I said I was prepared to die for what I believe in."

"And as you won't renounce your vows to that Llewellyn wench, you'll die." Marcus picked up the heavy book as if it weighed nothing and balanced it on his palm. "There's nothing here that will help you."

"You don't know that." Christopher held out his hand. "Give me back the book."

"Gentlemen!" Christopher spun around to see Brother Samuel waddling toward them, his expression agitated, his face flushed. "Do not draw attention to yourselves! You are not even supposed to be here at this time of night."

Marcus bowed and put the book back on the desk. "I apologize, Brother Samuel. We will take our leave of you." He jerked his head in the direction of the door. "Come on, Ellis. Thank you for your help, Brother."

Christopher added his thanks and was about to follow Marcus when Brother Samuel tugged on his sleeve. "You should come back and see me alone."

"You would permit that?"

Brother Samuel's gaze turned hard. "I confess to having some unworthy thoughts about your uncle. I would be willing to help you."

"Perhaps I might come back at the same time tomorrow night?"

"Oh, no," Brother Samuel whispered. "You must wait at least a fortnight until I'm able to arrange to see you like this again. I'll send you word at court."

"Thank you." Christopher nodded. "Your help might prove invaluable."

Marcus beckoned impatiently, and Christopher hurried to catch up with him, his thoughts in disarray. If his uncle was brought down, would he stand a better chance of surviving? The answer was probably no, but he couldn't deny the faint hope in his heart.

As he mounted his horse, his thoughts turned to Rosalind. She wouldn't appreciate him keeping this matter from her, but it seemed it was his nature to want to protect her. If she knew, she'd want to help and he couldn't allow that, didn't want her anywhere near the Mithras Cult or his uncle. So he would shoulder this burden alone, honor all his vows as best he could, and pray she would never have to know about it at all.

Chapter 15

Rosalind looked up as Christopher appeared in the doorway of Anne Boleyn's apartments. It was early evening and the ladies were waiting for the king and his courtiers to join them for the night's entertainment. The windows were open to dispel the stuffiness of built-up heat and a slight breeze blew in from the gardens. When Christopher spotted Rosalind, he turned away with a disdainful glare and focused his considerable charms on Anne. Rosalind sighed and picked up the book she had been reading. The only time he truly smiled at her these days was when he was in her bed.

And he was hardly ever there . . . The script on the page turned into a meaningless jumble as a wave of heated longing washed over her. Rosalind brought her hand to her brow and fought a sudden dizziness. Anne's loud laugh echoed through her head and Rosalind set her teeth. She hoped to God that Anne wasn't trying to use magic against her.

"Oh, Kit." Anne laughed again. "You are *so* wicked."

Rosalind told herself not to look over at the handsome pair, but it proved impossible. Christopher wore dark blue and black with a silver embroidered ruff. Around his neck hung a heavy chain, embellished with blue sapphires that matched his eyes. He was on one knee, laughing up at Anne as he kissed her fingertips.

Rosalind's own fingers twitched and she wished she had her dagger handy. Jealousy was indeed an unpleasant emotion. It made her feel far guiltier about what Rhys had gone though when she'd met Christopher. Perhaps it would be better if she simply retired to bed. At least then she wouldn't have to watch Christopher make a fool of her.

She placed the book of psalms on the table and rose to her feet. Unfortunately, the movement caught Anne's eye, and she glanced across the room at Rosalind.

"Are you planning on leaving, Lady Rosalind?"

Rosalind curtsied. "I'm not feeling very well, Lady Anne. Pray excuse me."

"I'm afraid I can't do that." Anne glanced down at Christopher. "We need you for the game I'm planning to play when the king arrives."

Even as she sensed danger, Rosalind tried to be pleasant. "I hardly think I will be missed, my lady."

Anne pouted. "You will stay."

Rosalind had to bite her tongue against a desire to blurt out that Anne had no power to tell her what to do at all. Unfortunately, queen or not, Anne already had all the trappings of royalty, and Rosalind could not afford to defy her publicly.

"As you wish, my lady."

Christopher stood as the king entered and bowed low, his expression so pleasant and amiable that Rosalind wanted to shake him. She'd learned at an early age to hide her Druid roots, but Christopher had perfected the art of presenting himself to the world as a whole new creature. Would such a master dissembler ever relax his guard enough to truly be himself? She was immediately ashamed of that disloyal thought. He was himself with her. She at least knew that.

Anne clapped her hands. "Sire, I have thought of an excellent game for us to play."

"You have, my dear?" The king smiled benevolently down at Anne. "Then let us play."

"It's quite simple, Your Majesty. The gentlemen will hide, and we ladies will try to find you."

King Henry laughed. "I like the sound of that! How long will you give us to conceal ourselves?"

Anne looked thoughtful. "We will count to three hundred, but you must not leave this building or go up the stairs."

"Agreed." The king turned to his male attendants and commanded, "We will all play."

Rosalind swallowed down a wave of nausea and tried to concentrate on the glittering crowd of courtiers. It was just the sort of game the king loved—slightly risqué, and an opportunity for him to get the Lady Anne alone, if but for a moment. From the whispers of the other women, it seemed that they also valued an opportunity to hunt down a man of their choosing. From the speculative glances being cast Christopher's way, she began to wonder how many of them would be looking for her betrothed. She realized she had no choice but to play along.

She obediently stood with the other women as they chanted the numbers up to three hundred. When she opened her eyes, she had to hold on to the nearest solid object to prevent herself from falling. Rhys was always nagging her to eat more. Perhaps he had a point. She spied a flagon of sweet red wine on the table and helped herself to a goblet. At least she felt warm now and ready to find her "beloved."

Anne's receiving room was already deserted. Rosalind could hear the shrieks and giggles of the other women as they sought their prey. Of course, she did have an unfair advantage in finding Christopher, which she would be more than happy to exploit if it shortened the time of the stupid game.

She located Christopher in her head, pictured him in his dark blue doublet and silver chain. Not wishing to appear too confident, she slowly made her way through the suite of rooms, avoiding anything that looked man-shaped, intent on the rear of the building where she expected to find Christopher.

Couples were already huddled together in various alcoves and behind tapestries. Giggles and sighs penetrated the silence and Rosalind found herself reluctantly smiling. She noticed the king had yet to be found by the Lady Anne, and was beginning to look annoyed.

A hand grabbed her arm, and she was spun around to face George Boleyn.

"Are you looking for me, fair lady?"

"Of course not." She tried to pull out of his grasp, but he refused to let go. "I will leave that to your wife!"

At her reference to Lady Jane, his unwanted and apparently unloved wife, George's expression darkened. "She will not be my wife for much longer."

"You can't really expect Anne to marry you. Everyone thinks you are her brother."

He smiled. "By the time Anne has enslaved the king and the Vampires are in control of this land, no one will dare question us."

"She will never marry you when she has Elias."

George shoved her back against the nearest wall. "You know nothing, Vampire slayer!"

"I know that Elias is powerful, and that you should watch yourself." Rosalind managed to disengage herself from George's grip and stepped around him. She reached into her hanging pocket. "Now leave me be. I have a real man to find."

George lunged for her, but Rosalind let him see the dagger concealed in her left hand. He backed off with a polite smile that did nothing to ease either Rosalind's anger at being caught off guard or her sense of danger.

She moved more quickly now, all too aware of the scents of the Vampires around her, both male and female. The light diminished as she stumbled down a shallow step and through an arch-shaped door that led toward the kitchens and washhouse. Her hand brushed against the stone wall and she went still as she heard an all-too-familiar voice.

"Oh, Kit."

In the gloom ahead of her, she could just make out a couple, the woman's dark head turned upward toward the man, his mouth coming down to cover hers . . .

Despite the fury threatening to explode though her chest, Rosalind kept walking until she stood right next to Anne and Christopher. She cleared her throat.

"I believe the king is waiting for you, my lady. Was it your intention to find and kiss every man in the game?"

Anne turned around, a victorious smile on her red lips. "Verily, I wanted to kiss only this man."

"No, you only wanted to let me see you kissing him, which is a different matter entirely."

Anne laughed. "You believe what you want to believe, my dear. Perhaps you aren't the right woman for him, after all."

"Are you suggesting you'd give up the king for my betrothed? You're not that dim-witted."

Anne's eyes glowed red and her fangs snapped toward Rosalind's throat. "Do not speak to me like that."

"Or what?" Rosalind brought her dagger hand up. "I'll fight you, Vampire. Just give me an opportunity."

Anne tossed her head, making the fine jewelry around her neck rattle. "I have no time for this. You'll be dead soon enough, Vampire slayer, and then I'll have your beloved Kit all to myself."

"Unless I kill him first."

"Now that I would like to see." Anne laughed and headed back toward the main corridor, her wine-colored skirts gathered in her hands.

Rosalind turned to glare at Christopher, who had remained leaning against the wall. She poked him hard in the ribs and he looked at her innocently. "What?"

"You were kissing Anne Boleyn."

He rubbed his fingers against his lips and over his tight beard. "I suppose I was."

Rosalind stared at him, her hands on her hips. She realized she was shaking and thumped him on the chest again. "She's lucky I didn't have my sword with me. I would've enjoyed skewering you both."

He caught her flailing fist within his grasp. "What else was I to do? She had me pinned against the wall like a butterfly. I could hardly shove her out of the way, could I?"

His reasonable tone made Rosalind even angrier. "You could have made some polite excuse. You could've set her aside—"

"Not if I wished her to believe I am still hers to command." His smile was as bitter as she hoped the taste of Anne had been. "I hate this." He glared back at her. "And I hate the doubt I see on your face even more."

She stared at him and felt his tangled misery, his certainty that she was about to walk away from him and not look back. Instead, she squared up to him, stood on her toes, and kissed his mouth until she erased Anne's scent and all she could taste was him. He didn't stop her, accepted the kiss as the gift it was, and returned it in full measure.

His arms closed around her hips and drew her even closer. She grabbed for his shoulders as he pivoted and lifted her higher until her back was against the wall. With a soft groan he dropped his head and nuzzled her breasts, his hands delving beneath the voluminous velvet of her skirts, seeking her nakedness.

"I want you, Rosalind. I need—"

"But what about the Lady Anne?"

"I'll keep her out of my thoughts. I swear it."

She kissed the side of his neck, his ear—any part of

him she could reach, as they fought to bare enough skin to come together. Need roared through her and she heard herself whimpering as he finally guided her down over him and she felt his thick length, his heat, his gasp of achievement as he slid home.

Too quick, too fast, too urgent, but it had to be enough. Caught between the wall and the hard thrust of Christopher's hips, Rosalind's pleasure grew until she could no longer contain it. She sent it out to him, felt him join her in a fiery climax that left her sagging and helpless against his strength.

Their harsh breathing sounded loud in the small space as he carefully lowered her to the ground and wrapped her in his arms. She pressed her face into his chest and felt the cold metal chain against her cheek.

"If I hadn't found you, would you be like this with her?" she whispered.

Beneath her hands, Christopher went still. "Rosalind, I knew you'd find me. By all the saints, I was counting on it."

Rosalind closed her eyes as her strength deserted her and an absurd desire to cry filled her thoughts. "I'm so tired, Christopher."

He put a finger under her chin so that he could see her face. His gaze was full of concern. "I've never heard you complain or admit to any weakness before."

"I'm not complaining now. I'm just telling you the truth." Her voice trembled and she struggled to correct it. "I fear I am not as strong as I thought. My body seems to be rebelling against me and I cannot see a way for us to defeat the Vampires."

He brushed her hair away from her face. "It's hardly surprising, love, when you've been caught in a fight for weeks on end. Anyone would feel the same. I'd feel it myself."

"But you'd never admit it."

"I thought I just did." His smile was sweet and full of love. "You can go home, Rosalind. Leave me and Rhys to finish this business."

"I cannot. I am a Llewellyn. We never give up. We'll die trying."

Christopher rested his brow against hers. "There has to be something . . . there just has to be."

They stayed like that for a long moment and then Christopher raised his head. "Why don't you go to bed, my lady? I'll make your excuses to Anne and the king. We have to keep you well."

"Rhys says I just need to eat more regularly, but my appetite seems to have disappeared."

"You should eat." Christopher took her hand and led her toward the lighted hallway. A male shadow blocked the exit and Christopher tensed.

"I beg your pardon," Elias Warner said. "Am I interrupting something?"

"Not at all, Elias. How can we help you?" Christopher put his dagger away and tried to look benign.

"I . . ." Elias hesitated and glanced behind him. Christopher turned back toward the room they'd just vacated.

Elias followed them, his expression grim, his mouth set in a hard line. "I have spoken to the Council. They are confident the Boleyns intend to honor their alliance."

Christopher guided Rosalind to a stool and made certain she sat down. "Do you believe that?"

"No. I know Anne better than any other Vampire still living, and that includes George and the Council. I no longer believe she wishes to subjugate the king and the nation to the Vampire cause at all."

"I agree with you."

Elias raised his eyebrows. "You do?"

"I've only known her in this life, but she has always struck me as a woman of enormous ambition."

"Aye." Elias paused. "If she can get what she wants out of the king, without being beholden to the Council, I suspect she will do so."

"But what does she want?" Rosalind asked. "Is it not enough to be queen of the Vampires?"

"I'm not so certain," said Christopher. "I think Elias is right, and that she would be far happier to rule by herself than if the Vampire Council kept interfering and trying to govern for her. She must realize that, once they get her to turn the king, she is unnecessary. One tantrum from her and they'll get rid of her in a second."

Elias nodded. "But at the moment, Anne controls the king, and she'll be even more confident when she is his queen."

Christopher glanced at Rosalind, who looked as desperate as he felt. "Then what can we do? If you insist on betraying Anne to the Vampire Council, and they believe you, they'll force her to turn the king immediately and then kill her."

Elias grimaced. "I know."

"We can't let her turn the king," Rosalind said urgently. "We have been trying to dispose of the Boleyns for weeks. So far it has proved impossible to tempt them away from the court and out into the night without them being surrounded by a band of guards."

"They'll be hard to kill," Elias said absently. "Anne is almost as old as I am, and nearly as dangerous."

"More so, I fear."

Elias's half smile made Christopher shudder. "I can be dangerous when crossed, my lord."

"I'm sure of it," Christopher replied. "So what can we do?" With an apologetic glance at Rosalind he continued. "The Druids are not strong enough to destroy all the Vampires who have gathered at court to protect the Boleyns. There seems to be an endless supply of them. A simple execution is impossible."

Elias sighed. "I cannot fathom why she hasn't simply turned the king. Surely she has had the opportunity."

"She must want something more from him," Rosalind said. "What can it be?"

Elias sank down onto one of the stools. "Mayhap she thinks it safer to turn him when she is indeed the queen.

As his legal wife, it would be far harder to get rid of her." Elias rubbed a hand over his face. "She can't just want to be queen. There must be something she believes he can give her that no one else can."

Christopher patted Elias on the shoulder. "Let's think on it. Perhaps together we can come up with a solution."

Elias stood, his expression grim. "The king is almost ready to set the kingdom on its head and divorce Queen Katherine. Our time is running out."

Chapter 16

Christopher looked up from his frowning contemplation of Anne Boleyn and her brother to find his uncle standing in front of him. He stood up and said, "Good morning, sir. Is there something I can do for you?"

"Indeed, there is." Edward gestured awkwardly with his hand. "Will you walk with me?"

Christopher waited as his uncle slowly turned around, his long body bent over his cane, his shoulders hunched with the effort of keeping his balance. Despite the heat, he wore a heavy gray cloak lined with fur, which seemed to weigh him down even further. Christopher almost felt sorry for the man, but not sorry enough to offer his help, which he knew would be spurned. They paced side by side down the long stone hallway away from the chatter of the other courtiers.

"How can I be of assistance, Uncle Edward?"

His uncle's cane tapped out a hollow sound on the stone flagstones. "First let me say I am pleased with your care of the Boleyns." Satisfaction tinged his uncle's dry voice. "It's remarkable how a threat to a man's existence can make him review his more foolish decisions and repent."

Christopher swallowed down all the comments that rose to his lips and kept smiling.

"I've also heard you have severed your ties with the Llewellyn wench, which pleases me even more."

"Yet I'm still betrothed to her. I notice you've made no effort to get me out of that."

"When Anne and the Vampire Council take power, Rosalind Llewellyn will die—as will all her Druid kin. You can be sure of that. There is no point in upsetting the king unnecessarily by killing her now."

Christopher snorted. "You mean upsetting him more than turning him into a Vampire might?"

His uncle glanced up at him, his blue eyes frosty, his pursed lips the same color as his gaze. "I see you still haven't learned to respect your elders."

"That's not quite true. I respect your wiles for using the Vampire Council and the Boleyns to further your own ambition."

Edward halted. "What do you mean by that?"

"Lady Anne told me all about how you and she were plotting together." Christopher forced himself to meet his uncle's penetrating gaze. "Have a care, Uncle. Whatever she has promised you, she has probably promised the same to George, Elias Warner, and every other member of the Vampire Council."

"Give me leave to doubt that. Lady Anne certainly has a talent for taking what she wants. But you must admit that the bargain we have between us is unique. I can offer her as much as she can offer me."

Christopher tried desperately to think what that could mean. If he tried to pretend he knew, it was highly likely he would rouse his uncle's suspicions. It was no doubt more prudent to withdraw with the knowledge that his uncle was indeed in league with Anne and work on finding out exactly how on another occasion. But then he'd never been a prudent man.

"Of course you are important to her success, sir."

"Indeed. I can bring many advantages to her side."

Christopher stopped walking. "Such as the Mithras Cult."

"Exactly." Uncle Edward smiled. "Which brings me to what I wanted to say to you. You will present yourself at the crypt chapel of Saint Bethesda in Cheapside tomorrow night at nine to answer for your crimes against your fellow members."

Christopher masked his surprise. He hadn't expected to be invited to the meeting that would decide whether he should go to trial.

Edward patted Christopher's black sleeve with his gloved hand. "I will, of course, take into account your current change of heart, although I fear the other members of my council will not consider that penance enough for your crimes."

"Well, thank you for that reassurance, Uncle. I'll be there."

Christopher bowed and headed toward Anne's apartments, his mind in a whirl. His uncle was indeed in league with Anne Boleyn. It also explained why the Mithras Cult had been ordered to follow only the dictates of the Vampires. But exactly what had Anne offered Edward in return for his support?

Christopher turned to watch his uncle's stumbling gait, and remembered his ill health. Could it be that Anne had promised to turn Edward into a Vampire, thus giving him immortality and immunity from death?

Christopher let out a curse. It might well be that simple. It would be like his uncle to put his own skin ahead even of his devotion to the Mithras Cult. He and Anne Boleyn were very alike indeed.

"Rhys, I told you, Christopher said he would get away if he could. Lady Anne watches him closely, you know that."

Rhys's face took on a mulish expression that Rosalind

knew all too well. "He needs to be here. How can we discuss how we mean to go forward if he fails to make an appearance?"

"You can't have it both ways, Rhys. We told him to keep away from us."

It was after midnight and, even though she was dressed in her boy's garb, Rosalind was cold sitting on the palace rooftop. She drew her cloak more firmly around herself and studied Rhys, who sat opposite her. His long legs were drawn up to his chin, his arms wrapped around them. His hazel gaze seemed far away.

"Is something wrong, Rhys?"

He jumped as if she had poked him. "No, my lady. I'm just thinking through what you've told me."

"And?"

"I have no idea what a Vampire wants," he said flatly. "Especially one like Anne Boleyn, who already has more than any other woman in the kingdom."

"Do you think she wants to rule in the king's stead?"

"How could she do that? She's a woman."

Rosalind frowned at him. "Maybe she intends to make history. Women are quite capable of ruling, Rhys."

"As if I didn't already know that." Rhys ran a hand through his thick pelt of red hair. "Let us suppose Anne wants to rule the kingdom; why not turn the king now, or simply kill him?"

"Because she has to be legally married to him to gain his powers in this mortal world?"

"Aye, that's a possibility, and might explain both the delay and the king's current good health." Rhys glanced over at the waning moonlight. "And how is your health, my lady? Are you still puking?"

"Yes." Rosalind made a face at him. "I am beginning to wonder if Anne Boleyn is having me poisoned."

"She's certainly capable of it, and poison is a woman's weapon."

"Not one that I would choose. I'd much rather use my dagger."

Rhys chuckled. "Perhaps you should find a wisewoman and ask her about your sickness."

"I might do that if it gets any worse. I hate being sick."

There was a scraping sound on the edge of the parapet and Christopher's gloved hands appeared. He levered himself up over the crenellations and onto the flat roof.

"Good evening, Rhys."

" 'Evening, my lord."

Christopher smiled at Rosalind and she suddenly felt warm. "And how are you this fine night, my lady?"

"I'm quite well, sir." Rosalind shifted over to allow Christopher to sit on the stone ledge beside her. "You managed to evade the Boleyns, then?"

"They were entertaining the king, so I was able to slip out." Christopher hugged Rosalind and then looked expectantly at Rhys. "Have you come up with any ideas to bring down the cursed Boleyns?"

Rhys cleared his throat. "No, but I know it's simple enough; we just have to discover what Anne wants more than anything else in the world."

"And yet she already appears to have everything, including the prospect of lording it over a whole nation full of Vampires." Christopher groaned and rubbed his bearded chin.

Rosalind stared at Rhys and then at Christopher. "I wonder . . ."

Both of them turned to her. "What?"

Rosalind stood and started pacing the small space. "If Anne believed she could rule the country in her own right, would she do it?"

"She'd probably love to, but no one would accept a female ruler, not the king's privy council, parliament, or the Vampire Council," Christopher said.

"That's what Rhys said, and it reminded me of something I heard Anne say, that she wanted to marry the king so that she could give him the heir he desires. What if she gave King Henry an heir and then killed the king? She could rule through her son."

Christopher looked thoughtful. "What would stop her from simply doing away with the king and choosing another Vampire to create an heir?"

A familiar voice broke into the conversation. "Because Vampires, especially those who are older and more powerful, tend to be unable to have young."

Rosalind turned to face Elias, who had appeared on the roof behind her. "Is that so?"

He floated down to stand beside her. He wore a dull brown silk doublet that blended into the darkness. "Most Vampires make their 'children' by turning other humans. It has proved difficult for Vampires to breed amongst ourselves." He nodded at Rosalind. "Your theory is an interesting one. At her age, Anne might believe she needs a lusty human male to provide the 'new blood' necessary to create a child. She may indeed be pinning her hopes on the king."

"Which would explain why she hasn't turned him yet."

"Indeed." Elias took a seat beside Rhys. "I'm not sure if that really helps us or not."

Rosalind crouched in front of him. "It might help us. What if we could guarantee that Anne would give the king an heir?"

"What madness is this?" Christopher asked.

Rosalind sought his gaze. "We do not have the time or the resources to stop Anne becoming queen. It is a near certainty. But what if we offer her a bargain? One that means she will be assured of giving the king an heir? If we promise her that, maybe in exchange we can make her promise not to turn the king."

Rhys interrupted. "But what if we help her get with child, and then she turns on us and kills the king anyway?"

"We'll make the bargain a sacred one. If she tries to break it, we will expose her dark secrets to the king."

Rosalind looked hopefully at all the men and saw only their doubts. "We have to do *something*. If we bind her with sacred vows, even for a little while, it gives us more time to work out how to disentangle the king from her magic and make sure he realizes what he is really facing."

"But how can we ensure she has a child?" Christopher asked.

Rosalind smiled. "Rhys and I will take the matter up with our Druid priests and Elders. Remember, the Vampires and Druids share a common ancestry, and fertility rites are a foundation of our beliefs."

Christopher had the grace to blush as if he too remembered their heated encounter on the Beltane altar the previous year. "It sounds preposterous, but I cannot think of anything else, so you might as well try."

"Thank you, Christopher." Rosalind looked at Rhys and Elias. "Are you both in agreement too?"

"Aye," Rhys said. "I'll come with you to the stone circle tomorrow night."

Elias stood up more slowly, his thoughtful gaze fixed on Rosalind. "I will see if I can find out anything that supports your theory, my lady." He hesitated. "It does make a certain sense. I have never succeeded in producing a child, and George is so new that any child of his would be an easy kill for most Vampires."

Rosalind took his hand and he looked startled. "Be careful, Elias."

He brought her fingers to his lips and kissed them, his breath as cold as the grave. "I will be, my lady."

Elias disappeared and Rosalind turned to face Christopher, who was still frowning. "Don't feel sorry for him, Rosalind, or he'll start thinking about making you his life mate again."

"But I do feel sorry for him. He obviously cares for Anne far more than he is prepared to admit."

"Are you suggesting that Vampires can have feelings? I thought they were all soulless monsters."

Rosalind held Christopher's gaze. "I was wrong about that."

"And I was wrong about the Druids." Christopher nodded at Rhys. "Some of you are quite pleasant."

Rosalind raised her eyes heavenward. Sometimes, Christopher's tendency to jest when things became serious was quite irritating. "Rhys and I will confer with the Elders tomorrow night."

Christopher headed back toward the edge of the roof, his black silk doublet glinting with silver threads in the moonlight. "Why would they agree? Surely they will not allow their ancient knowledge to be used to help a Vampire?"

Rhys moved closer to Rosalind. "They helped you, didn't they?"

"Well, they allowed me to survive the stone circle twice, so I suppose that's true, but surely that was different. That was because of the prophecy."

"The Druid race will always do what it must to survive."

Rhys sounded harsh and Rosalind understood why. Their race was dying out. She could only hope that the threat of the Vampires taking over the whole country would sway the Elders' decision in their favor.

Rosalind caught Christopher's hand. "We will do our best. How did it go with your friend Marcus?"

"Not terribly well. Marcus was quite happy to accept my assistance in deposing my uncle, but rather unwilling to help me help myself."

Rosalind frowned. "Why do you need his help?"

He opened his mouth and then shut it again. "I must learn to keep a still tongue in my head when I am around you. You make me far too confiding."

"What is going on? Are you in danger?"

He glanced down at her, his ready smile bittersweet. "I'm in no more danger than a year ago, so don't fret." He kissed her hand and gave it back to her.

She tossed her head. "Either tell me the truth or don't. I care not."

He cupped her cheek. "I cannot tell you. That's the truth. There—will that do?"

She stamped her foot. "Christopher, you promised to be honest with me."

"And I'm trying to be. I'm also trying not to betray others who are involved. I owe them my silence. Can't you see that?"

"I suppose I have no choice in the matter."

He chucked her under the chin. "Don't pout, love. It is most unbecoming."

She scowled at him instead. "Is that better?"

"Infinitely."

Rhys cleared his throat. "Have you lovebirds finished?"

"We have, indeed." Christopher bowed and walked away, leaving Rosalind staring at his back.

"Verily, I'm worried that Christopher is not telling me the whole truth."

"About what?"

"About the Mithras Cult. Why is it so important for him to deal with his uncle and the cult when we need all his attention here with us?"

"I have no idea."

"And that is why I'm worried."

Rhys folded his arms across his chest. "What do you expect me to do about it?"

"Watch out for him. Tell me if you hear any gossip."

"While I'm also watching out for the Vampires?" Rhys sighed. "Is there anything else? Would you like me to lie down on the ground so that you can walk all over me properly?"

Rosalind bit her lip. "I'm sorry. I didn't mean it like that."

He turned his back on her.

"What is it, Rhys?"

He slowly turned around. "It's just that I seem far too willing to care about women who will never come to care for me."

"Is there someone else?" Rosalind found it surprisingly

hard to ask the question without making it sound like an accusation. "Are you in love with another woman?"

"I am . . . a fool." He headed off toward the stairs. "A fool who needs to seek his bed and stop talking."

Rosalind followed along more slowly. Had Rhys really met another woman? She'd hardly think he had time, what with all the fighting they had been doing recently. She took a deep breath of the cool air and savored the silence. It was a victory of sorts. In one night, she'd managed to make both Christopher and Rhys stop talking and walk away from her.

Chapter 17

Rhys grabbed hold of Rosalind's hand and helped her through a tangle of dead branches and dried-out sage bushes. The waterfall that guarded the secret valley was almost silent now, its sound and flow reduced to a small trickle of brackish water that crept through the rocks rather than cascaded.

The ancient stone circle at the bottom of the valley looked the same, rising from the ground as if it had grown there as naturally as the wilderness that surrounded it. Rosalind pressed her hand to the nearest upright dark blue stone and felt an immediate pulse of energy. The sun was setting behind the trees, leaving the circle bathed in a warm welcoming glow.

"Are we expected, Rhys?"

"I prayed for help, so I assume someone will come." Rhys's reply was unhurried, his calm gaze fixed on the inner circle of stones where the altar lay. "If we wait in the center and make an offering, I'm sure they'll find us."

Rosalind walked slowly through the outer circle and onward, her mind recalling the last time she was here, when the powerful Spanish Vampire had almost succeeded in killing her, the king, *and* the men she loved. With a shiver, she drew her cloak around her and pushed the memories away.

Rhys drew a leather pouch from his jerkin pocket and crouched down in front of the altar where a flat piece of scorched rock gave evidence of other sacrificial fires. He cleared a space in the dirt and laid out narrow strips of bark and twigs.

"Willow to ask for the gift of sight, birch to protect us against the Vampire evil, and oak for fertility and luck," Rhys murmured. On top of the small pile he added some sage leaves. "That should do it."

Rosalind watched as he struck a flint to produce a spark, slowly blew on a wisp of grass until it glowed red, and then built up the fire until it was capable of devouring his piled-up twigs.

Sweet-smelling smoke rose from the small fire. Rosalind closed her eyes and breathed in deeply. The herbs cleansed her thoughts and reduced her anxiety. She felt far more ready to face whatever was coming. Beside her, Rhys took a hasty breath and went still.

She opened her eyes to see three figures emerging from between the stones. Two elderly men and one woman, all dressed in simple white robes. Rosalind quickly knelt down beside Rhys.

The woman spoke first. Her pure white hair was long and unbound, yet her face looked remarkably young. She smiled at Rosalind and Rhys. "I am the Lady Alys. We have come at your request. Why do you seek our help?"

Rosalind looked at Rhys, whose gaze urged her to speak for them. "Our request is unusual in that it might appear to help our enemies."

"Indeed?" The woman beckoned Rosalind to her feet. "Tell us more."

Rosalind took a deep, steadying breath, and relayed everything she could think of about Anne Boleyn, the king, and the Vampires. When she ran out of things to say, she stepped back, and Rhys took her hand in a comforting clasp.

"Your request is indeed unusual." The woman glanced at her companions, who had remained silent. "We shall deliberate."

With that, the three figures seemed to dissolve into the smoke. Rosalind rubbed her eyes, unsure if she had really seen such a thing. Were not the Druid Elders mortal? Or was it that being within the stone circle gave them a measure of power unheard of in the human world?

"Are we supposed to wait?"

"I assume so." Rhys sat down on the ground and crossed his legs. He patted the space next to him. "We might as well. It's not as if we have anything else to do."

Christopher studied the thick door that led into the crypt of Saint Bethesda's chapel. A faint light shone from under it, so he knew he was in the right place, and he was certainly expected. He'd come unarmed, knowing that weapons were forbidden to all, also knowing that the chances of his life ending abruptly and painfully were quite high.

With a quick prayer to God and every saint he could think of, he knocked on the door. It was opened by Marcus Flavian, who acknowledged him with a curt nod.

"You are unarmed?"

"Yes, Marcus. You can check if you like."

"No matter. If you try anything, I'll kill you with my bare hands."

"I assumed you would." Christopher followed Marcus into the main body of the crypt and came to a halt. Candles illuminated the mosaic-tiled floor and the old oak benches that smelled of incense and damp. Twelve men, the minimum required for a meeting such as this, were gathered in the small space. His uncle sat in the center dressed in his ceremonial red robe, looking rather like an emperor about to dispense justice.

Christopher bowed, but he didn't say anything. If they expected him to beg and plead for his life, they would be disappointed.

His uncle cleared his throat. "Christopher Ellis, you have been summoned before your peers to answer charges of breaking your vows."

"In what way?"

"You have allied yourself with a Druid."

There was some whispering amongst the hooded men. It reverberated through the walls and floor of the echoing crypt.

"At *your* command. Is not your word law, as leader of the Mithras Cult? If I had disobeyed you, wouldn't I be in the same position I am now?"

"We are not here to debate my leadership or answer your questions. We are here to determine whether you should be tried for breaking your vows."

Christopher made sure he looked at all the faces. "Am I not allowed to defend myself?"

"If the brethren decide that you must answer to the entire Mithraic court, you will have a chance to defend yourself then."

"Freely?"

His uncle's smile was chilling, his satisfied expression indicating that the babblings of an already condemned man wouldn't hold much weight with any court. "As freely as you wish." He turned to the rows of silent men. "I would ask you to vote. All those who believe Lord Christopher Ellis should be tried for treason to our cause, please raise your hand."

There wasn't a single member who was willing to go against his uncle and not send Christopher to trial. Not that he'd expected anyone to stand up for him. He glanced over at Marcus Flavian, who had also voted against him. He could only hope that by the time they decided to try him properly the leadership would have changed for the better. Or that he would've received fresh information from Brother Samuel that he could use to set himself free.

Uncle Edward cleared his throat. "It is unanimous. Christopher Ellis, you will stand trial."

"And when will that be?"

"As soon as I can arrange it. We need to call out the entire membership."

As Christopher stepped out of the center of the circle, Marcus pushed past him.

"By your leave, sir. There is another matter I should like to discuss."

Christopher stiffened as his uncle glared down at Marcus. Trust Marcus to seize an opportunity and use the meeting for his own benefit.

"Sir Marcus Flavian?"

"I would also like to address the entire membership."

"For what purpose?"

Marcus sucked in a visible breath. "To challenge your leadership of the Mithras Cult."

Silence greeted his remark, a silence that seemed to grow bigger and fill the small space until there was no air left.

"You have no right!"

"Verily, I do, sir. According to the records, which I have consulted, there is a formal process for these occasions when the leader is challenged. As an honorable member of the cult, I am allowed to express my grievances and request your response in front of the entire membership. If we do not find your answers satisfactory, we can vote to replace you as leader."

Edward stood up, his face white with fury, his hands braced on the arms of his chair. Christopher backed away toward the door. He didn't want his uncle thinking he had anything to do with this. Marcus stood his ground, his stance wide and his expression a study in polite defiance.

"I will consult the records myself, Sir Marcus. If I find

that you are correct, of course, I will follow the correct procedure."

"Thank you." Marcus hesitated.

"What is it now?" Edward snapped.

"If we are gathering the membership to sit in judgment on Ellis, I ask that I may address the question of your leadership at the same time."

"Don't you wish to gather your evidence first?"

Marcus smiled for the first time, his gaze fixed on Edward. "I have my evidence."

Edward sat back down again with a thump. "You should take care, Marcus Flavian. Some members of the cult might not like you challenging their leader."

"Is that a threat, sir?"

"Not at all. Merely a warning. I am quite confident that my leadership will survive your attempt to overthrow it."

Marcus bowed. "I'll bid you good night, sir."

Christopher was out of the door before Marcus even finished speaking. He had no wish to talk to his uncle, who would be furious beyond measure at this turn of events. Especially now, when Edward believed he was so close to getting what he wanted through Anne Boleyn.

With a soft whistle, Christopher mounted his horse and headed back for Hampton Court. He still wasn't a free man, but at least he'd witnessed his uncle's shock at finding his leadership under fire. And as matters stood, he needed every scrap of good news he could get. As he walked his horse back out onto the main thoroughfare, he had the most peculiar sensation that he was being watched. The sensation persisted as he kicked the horse into a canter, and it followed him all the way back to Hampton Court.

Rosalind yawned and quickly covered her mouth. She had no idea what the time was, but from the grayness now edging out the black, she suspected it was almost dawn. Even though Rhys's shoulder had proved a comfortable place to lay her head, the rest of her was cramped from sitting in the same position for so long.

"Should we go, Rhys?"

He stirred beside her, and she moved away from him to allow him to stretch. "Perhaps we should."

Rosalind stood and took a moment to straighten her legs before offering Rhys a hand. He grinned at her as she pulled him up. "Thank you, my lady."

She turned to answer him, and went still as the three Druid Elders appeared behind him. Rhys spun around too, his grin slowly fading to be replaced by a look of reverence.

The woman called Alys slowly inclined her head. "We have deliberated and we are in agreement."

Rosalind realized she had been holding her breath. It seemed presumptuous to ask what the decision was, but she couldn't help looking hopeful.

"We will help you defeat Anne Boleyn and the Vampire Council. Our duty is to our race and yours is to safeguard the king."

"Thank you," Rosalind whispered. "We are humbled by the honor you do us."

"We will provide you with a fertility charm that the Lady Anne Boleyn must wear about her person. We will also make her a potion that she will need to drink every day until she conceives."

The woman waved her hand over the stone altar, and a small blackish item appeared. Rosalind stepped closer to examine it. It was the size and shape of an acorn, which Rosalind already knew was a symbol of fruitfulness, and made of something that resembled wood.

"This charm is carved from ancient bog oak, which is one of the most potent fertility charms known to us."

Rosalind picked up the charm and held it in the palm of her hand so that Rhys could examine it. It was almost weightless. "I will take great care of it, my lady."

"I'm sure you will. But while it is in your keeping, do

not allow it to touch your skin. You have no need of its powers."

Rhys offered his kerchief, and Rosalind wrapped up the acorn charm and stowed it in her leather pouch.

Rhys cleared his throat. "My lady, how shall we obtain the potion?"

"I will send a wisewoman to you. She will prepare the potion and give you all the necessary instructions on its use."

"Thank you, Lady Alys," Rosalind said. There was a singsong tone to the woman's voice that reminded Rosalind of home. "We will do our best to protect our kin and destroy this Vampire."

"You must succeed. We are all counting on you."

The woman and the men faded back into the shadows of the stones and Rosalind was left with Rhys. She patted her leather purse and managed to smile at him. "Let's hope that this is the key to bringing down the Boleyns."

Rhys smiled back. "Well, if it isn't, we won't have much time to worry about it. I imagine if Anne and the Vampire Council succeed, we'll be quite high on their list of people to dispose of." He turned and headed back the way they had come. "Now we'd better get back, or you'll be missed."

Rosalind followed more slowly, her mind in a whirl as she tried to work out what they should do next. They had to wait for the wisewoman to make the potion for them, but apart from that . . . Rosalind clutched her stomach and ran toward the nearest clump of bushes. By the time Rhys came back to find her, she had already stopped retching and knelt on the ground struggling to breathe normally.

"Are you all right, *cariad*?" Rhys's hand landed on her shoulder.

Rosalind wiped her mouth on her sleeve and got to her feet. "I'm fine now."

Rhys cast her a quick glance and then wrapped his arm around her shoulder. "When we meet the wisewoman, you will consult with her as well. Promise me."

She leaned in to him, suddenly glad of his warmth and solid strength. "Don't worry. I will."

It was, perhaps, unfortunate that the first person they met as they approached the darkened stables was Christopher. He waited for them to reach him, his hands on his hips, his expression unamused.

"You look like lovers returning from a tumble in the hay."

Rhys didn't release her. "My lady was unwell and, as you weren't available, I was merely seeing to her safety."

"Well, I'm here now, so you can unhand her."

"She'll probably swoon if I do." There was an edge to Rhys's voice that made Rosalind feel tired.

"Not if I am holding her," Christopher snapped.

She managed to push herself away from Rhys and lean up against the corner of the stable block. "There is no need for either of you to take me anywhere. I am perfectly well." They both stared at her, their expressions equally skeptical. "For goodness' sake! I have already promised to consult with a healer. What else do you want?"

"For you to go to bed." Rhys glanced around the still-quiet space. "The grooms and stable hands will be up soon. The king is going hunting."

Christopher held out his hand. "I'll take you."

"You are not meant to be seen with me, especially near my bedchamber."

Christopher's hand dropped to his side. "Sometimes I want to pick you up, throw you over my shoulder, and damn all this pretense."

"We might soon have a solution to that."

"What?"

Rosalind managed to edge past him toward the path. "Why don't you tell him, Rhys, while I put *myself* to bed?"

Christopher stared at Rhys, who was faintly smiling. "What happened?"

"The Druid Elders agreed to help us. They gave us an acorn charm that is full of fertility magic. If Anne wears it close to her skin, she will conceive an heir for the king."

Christopher let out his breath. "Do you think it will work?"

Rhys raised his eyebrows. "Of course I do. A wise-woman will visit us to give us a potion Lady Anne will need to drink as well."

"Do you think it will be enough to tempt Anne into a temporary alliance with us?"

"I don't know, but it's the only thing we have left to try, isn't it?" Rhys nodded. "Good night, my lord."

Christopher watched Rhys leave, and stared out into the night sky, searching for answers that weren't there. A shadow appeared on his left, and he reacted instinctively, his sword blade flashing in the moonlight. He looked up at the high wall that surrounded the stable yard.

A figure dressed in black boy's clothes perched on the top of the wall, long hair loose in the breeze, blue eyes spar-kling. The scent of orange blossom drifted over Christopher. His gut tightened as he recognized the Vampire female he believed was his kin. Rhys and Rosalind were instantly for-gotten. Had the Vampire followed him to the earlier meet-ing as well? Had she overheard their discussion?

"What do you want?" Christopher asked, his sword at the ready, just in case she did the unthinkable and sprang for him.

"I was just seeing you home safely, my lord." Her voice was sweet and breathy with a hint of a Spanish accent.

"Who are you?"

"Don't you know?" Her blue eyes widened.

"I know very little about Vampires."

She pouted. "But you should know me!"

"Why?"

She sighed and looked reproachful. "Didn't Rhys tell you?"

Christopher tried to concentrate his thoughts. The fact

that Rhys had continued to chat with one of his enemies was a conversation for another, less dangerous time.

"What do you want from me?" Christopher demanded.

She raised her chin at him in a manner strangely reminiscent of Rosalind. "To tell you my name, which is Olivia, and to ask for yours."

He stared at her for a long moment. "I'm Christopher."

Her smile was slow and beautiful. "I thought so."

She disappeared before he could ask her what that meant, and he was left staring at the wall.

Chapter 18

"You are most heartily welcome, Mistress Hopkins." The elderly woman wore the simple garb of a countrywoman, her patterned skirts arranged decorously around her ankles, and her gray hair covered by a cream cap. There was nothing of the magical about Mistress Hopkins, just an air of calm good sense that made Rosalind feel comfortable with her.

"Thank you, my lady. I am glad to be of help." Mistress Hopkins's smile included Rhys, who leaned against the door of the abandoned shack to prevent anyone else from bursting in and finding them there.

Mistress Hopkins took the cloth from the large wicker basket she held and placed it on the floor. "I have here all the ingredients for the potion, and I have written out the instructions. I suggest you do not give the Lady Anne the recipe. It would be better for all of us if she doesn't know exactly what is in it and has to rely on you, or someone of our faith, to make it for her."

"That's a good point," Rosalind said. "We need all the advantages we can get against her."

Mistress Hopkins looked perturbed. "From what I've

heard of the woman, she dabbles in just enough magic to make herself dangerous."

Rhys peered into the basket. "She's dangerous, all right. What exactly goes into the potion?"

"It is a distillation of oak and willow bark, which promote healing, birth, and fertility." As she spoke, Mistress Hopkins laid out a series of sealed jars on the folded cloth. "This is mistletoe cut by one of our priests from an oak tree using a golden scythe on the sixth day of the moon, and this is vervain, which is said to unlock the womb."

"These things promote fertility?"

"Aye—if Lady Anne wears the acorn charm as well, she could become pregnant within one moon cycle." Mistress Hopkins drew a piece of parchment from the basket. "And here is a prayer to recite before drinking the potion."

"I suppose we'll have to give that to Anne," Rosalind said reluctantly.

"You will, but because she is using our magic, she will not be able to change the spell and use it on anyone else for her own evil gain."

Rosalind smiled for the first time. "That is excellent news."

Mistress Hopkins patted Rosalind's knee. "And there is another thing you might suggest to the lady. She should pluck a new heartsease flower every day and study it. If the face of the flower has five lines to the right, that means prosperity and fertility. She must take the flower and keep it under her pillow that night."

Rhys straightened and peered through the cracks of the boarded-up window. "I'm not sure if we want to help her quite that much, but thank you, mistress. Is there anything else we need to know?"

Mistress Hopkins started to repack the basket, her movements steady and assured. "If the lady refuses your bargain, you must bring everything back to the stone circle, especially the acorn charm."

"Oh, we will. We certainly don't want Anne stealing Druid magic in the hope of using it against us."

Mistress Hopkins showed Rosalind a small bottle containing the made-up potion. "You—or someone you trust—can make up more from the ingredients I have put in the basket. If you run out of anything just let me know." She hesitated. "There is one other thing about the potion we hope will benefit us, and help to defeat Lady Anne."

"What is that?" Rosalind bent to help Mistress Hopkins with the basket.

"Although vervain *is* a powerful fertility herb, it also thins the blood and will weaken her Vampire powers. Lady Anne will need to feed far more often just to maintain her strength, which has to be a good thing."

Rosalind took Mistress Hopkins's hand and squeezed it. "Thank you."

"This woman, or any Vampire, cannot be allowed to rule this country. We are all glad to help."

Rhys fixed his gaze on Rosalind and she tried to ignore him. "Is there a way for us to contact you, Mistress Hopkins?"

"Ask for my husband, Thomas. He works in the smithy here at Hampton Court. He'll pass on any message. We live quite nearby."

Rhys cleared his throat. "I'll escort you back to your husband, Mistress Hopkins, *after* Lady Rosalind has had a word with you, *alone*."

Rosalind scowled at Rhys as he went out whistling and slammed the rickety door behind him.

"What is it, my dear?"

Rosalind brought her gaze back to the serene face of Mistress Hopkins. "I've not been well."

"In what way?"

"I've been puking and feeling dizzy. I fear Anne Boleyn is poisoning me."

Mistress Hopkins beckoned to Rosalind. "Come here and let me look at you."

It proved impossible to ignore that tone. It reminded Rosalind too much of her mother. She waited patiently while Mistress Hopkins looked in her mouth, studied her eyes and then her skin.

"I don't think it is poison. That would leave its mark on you all too obviously." Mistress Hopkins sat back. "How is your appetite?"

"Sometimes I feel so hungry I want to eat all day, and other times I want nothing."

"When did you last have your courses?"

Rosalind stared at Mistress Hopkins. "What does that have to do with my stomach?"

"When, my lady?"

Rosalind tried to think. "I'm not sure. In truth, I've never been very regular . . ."

Mistress Hopkins drew a delicate breath. "Is it possible you might be breeding?"

Rosalind just stared at her, her tongue seemingly stuck to the roof of her mouth. "I . . ."

"Is it possible?"

Rosalind's fingers flew to her cheek. "Oh, my goodness. Don't tell anyone!"

"I would never break your confidence, but"—Mistress Hopkins nodded toward the door—"if you are with child, you should at least tell the father so that he can marry you as soon as possible."

"Rhys isn't the father," Rosalind muttered. "It is my betrothed."

Mistress Hopkins stood up and smoothed down her skirts. "That would be Lord Christopher Ellis, then. The Druid slayer."

Rosalind bit down hard on her lip.

"Don't cry, my lady. There are ways to stop—"

"I could never do that. Please, don't even suggest it."

Mistress Hopkins sighed. "Then I wish you well. Your life will not be easy, and your child will be unwelcome to many."

Rosalind couldn't even begin to contemplate that horrible truth. She simply nodded at Mistress Hopkins and sat down suddenly again. She felt a hand smoothing her hair.

"My lady, make sure to eat regularly, even if it is only a piece of dried bread or a handful of fruit. Ginger is excellent to help with the nausea as well. And keep away from that fertility charm. You don't want to produce a litter of children."

"Thank you," Rosalind whispered.

"I wish no harm on you, my dear. A child is a precious thing, regardless of its parentage."

Rosalind remained where she was until she heard Mistress Hopkins open the creaking door and call to Rhys. She waited until their voices faded down the path, but found she was still unable to get up. Little by little her breathing evened out and her dizziness lessened. She had to be strong now. She stared down at her clenched fingers, caught the flash of the ruby Christopher had given her. There was no way she could let on to either Rhys or Christopher that she was with child. Both of them would insist she leave court, and she had no intention of doing that until Anne Boleyn was well and truly beaten.

But what of the child? Mistress Hopkins had tried to conceal her distaste at the thought of a babe with such mixed bloodlines, but many would share her prejudice. Both she and Christopher knew what it was like not to fit in, and to be different. Would their child feel the same?

Rosalind placed her hand over her still-flat stomach and took another deep breath. It didn't matter. She would love and protect this babe with her life. She hoped only that when she *did* tell Christopher, he would feel the same. And she would have to tell him at some point, even she knew that.

She raised her head and wiped her eyes. She would carry on for as long as she was able. Her mother had never believed a woman needed to mollycoddle herself when pregnant and Rosalind didn't believe it either.

She heard Rhys whistle, and picked up the heavy basket,

ready to greet him when he opened the door and asked his pointed questions as to her health.

Later that evening, after Rhys had deposited the contents of the basket in a safe place, Rosalind met him back at the ruined shack. Christopher and Elias were already there, the three men making the cramped space even smaller. Rosalind offered them all a smile and sat down on the nearest stool.

She let Rhys tell Christopher and Elias what had transpired with the wisewoman, saw their faces light up with a suggestion of hope for the first time in a long while. While Rhys talked, Christopher glanced at her more than once. She strove to present him with her most serene face and as open a mind as she could manage under the circumstances.

Elias listened intently, wincing as Rhys mentioned the effects of vervain on a Vampire's blood as if he understood the necessity of using it, but still found it painful to hear.

Rhys stopped talking and looked at Rosalind. "Is there anything you would like to add, my lady?"

"No, I think you covered everything admirably," Rosalind said. "Do you wish to say something, Elias?"

"I have confirmed that Anne has never succeeded in bearing a child. I thought as much, but it never hurts to check." Elias met Rosalind's gaze. "I also learned that she has been actively seeking ways to make herself more fertile." He sat back. "It would seem that your chances of persuading her to accept your bargain—if at least for a while—are high."

"Oh, do you think so, Elias?" Rosalind asked. "You know her better than any of us."

His silver-gray gaze rested on her for a long moment. "If you present the offer to her in the right way, she will certainly consider it. Why wouldn't she? The power to thumb her nose at the Vampire Council and rule all of England and Wales through her son? I would take the chance."

Christopher stood up and paced the small space. "How are we going to present this 'opportunity' to Anne?" He pointed at Elias. "If you or I do it, she'll know we've changed sides and we'll lose that advantage. She already hates Rosalind, and Rhys isn't powerful enough to handle her by himself."

Rhys snorted. "I am, my lord. I'm quite happy to volunteer to be the bearer of this particular piece of bad news."

Rosalind took a deep breath. "You're not strong enough, Rhys. I'll come with you. We'll do it together."

Christopher strode over and glared down at her. "You will not go near that woman."

Rosalind stood up and shoved at his chest until he backed up. "I will do what needs to be done. I'm no coward."

"By all that's holy, Rosalind—"

Elias interrupted Christopher. "Lady Rosalind is right, my lord. She is the only one Anne will listen to. Anne won't be able to ignore the opportunity to meet her deadliest foe face-to-face and mayhap kill her."

"Thank you, Elias. At least you are making sense," Rosalind said, ignoring Christopher, who was still glowering at her. "Do you think you could arrange for Anne and me to meet somewhere without George and the rest of the court?"

"And me," Rhys said. His expression was stubborn enough that she knew he wouldn't let her go alone.

"I can probably do that," Elias murmured.

Christopher gave a short laugh. "What a pity you haven't been on our side from the start, Elias. We could've finished Anne off weeks ago."

Elias pointedly ignored Christopher and focused his attention on Rosalind. "As you know, the Lady Anne professes to have Lutheran leanings and thus avoids attending services at the king's chapel. Of course, she is simply avoiding the Mass because she doesn't like to take the Host, but the king tolerates it, because he is growing disenchanted with the Church as well. I might be able to arrange a meeting after one of the Lutheran services."

"That is an excellent idea, Elias." Rosalind smiled at him and he almost smiled back. "We are so grateful for your help. It cannot be easy to plot against a woman you care about."

Elias stiffened. "I do not 'care' for her, my lady. I merely wished to use her to gain power."

Rosalind chose not to argue. "And what of your standing with the Vampire Council? Are you in danger?"

"If Anne takes power and ignores the Council, they'll remember that I warned them, so I foresee no problems in my future."

"Unless our plan fails," Christopher muttered.

Elias turned his cold, charming smile on Christopher. "If we fail, we will all be executed, and then we'll have nothing to worry about."

"And Anne doesn't deserve you, anyway," Rosalind added. "How any woman could prefer that puffed-up peacock George Boleyn astonishes me."

"You are too kind." Elias bowed.

Christopher shot Rosalind another glare, but at least Elias looked less strained and more his usual self-contained self. She'd never considered he might have feelings.

"Then we are agreed. Rhys and I will offer the bargain to Anne Boleyn."

Christopher let out his breath. "And I'll keep George away."

"And I will ensure that your meeting with the Lady Anne is uninterrupted," Elias added.

Rhys sat back down. "Now all we have to do is work out how best to approach a poisonous snake."

By the end of the conversation, Rosalind was sure that she and Rhys would at least be heard. Knowing Anne Boleyn's temper, there was still a risk of them being killed, but they had to try.

Christopher joined her on the short walk through the

walled kitchen garden back to the palace. He gradually slowed his pace until Rhys had disappeared from sight. Rosalind glanced up at him.

"We should not be seen together, especially in the dead of night."

"Agreed."

They continued to stroll, and Rosalind allowed him to hold her hand. "Do you think Anne will agree to leave the king alone?"

"If we can give her what she really craves." Christopher looked down at her. "I'm still not convinced that we have it right."

"But what else is there?"

He sighed, the sound soft in the darkness. "I know not. If it doesn't work, we are going to be in worse danger than we already are."

"And probably dead." Rosalind squeezed his hand. "Don't forget that."

Christopher stopped walking and swung around to face her. "What are you hiding from me?"

How typical of him to just throw such a provocative remark in her face. Rosalind tried not to look guilty. "Whatever do you mean? I thought you were the master of deceit."

His mouth thinned. "I've told you everything I can, which is more than I can say for you."

"Christopher, you have told me nothing. You have closed so much of your mind off from me that sometimes I feel as if I barely know you at all."

"You *know* me."

"Then why can't you tell me what is really going on with the Mithras Cult?"

"Because it is not your concern."

Rosalind started walking again. "Yet it takes up a considerable amount of your time and energy."

He caught her by the elbow and held on. "Are you suggesting I neglect you?"

She gazed into his narrowed blue eyes, felt the banked frustration of his gaze. "You are certainly distracted."

"You are trying to distract me by quarreling now, aren't you?" He let go of her arm. "You have no intention of answering my questions at all."

"I'll answer you when you answer me."

"Don't be childish, Rosalind."

Verily, she felt like stamping her foot like a child and maybe screaming at him, but then it felt as if her emotions were hardly her own anymore. She took a deep, steadying breath. Was he right? In trying to protect her own secrets, was she simply lashing out at him? No, he was definitely trying to conceal something from her.

"This is getting us nowhere," she snapped.

"Agreed." He sounded as angry as she felt.

"Then perhaps we should simply part until both of us are in a better mood."

He cupped her cheek. "Rosalind, please . . . tell me what is wrong. Are you ill? Rhys said you consulted the wisewoman today."

"Rhys worries over me like a mother hen, you know that." She felt steadier now, the lies slipping past her tongue far too easily. "If I was truly sick, he would tie me up and send me back to Wales without a thought."

"I suppose that is true." Christopher leaned in to kiss her forehead. "I'm worried about you."

"And I'm worried about you."

His smile was strained. "I can take care of myself, Rosalind."

"As can I," she retorted.

"I know that," he said softly. "But you are my heart. You are the reason I exist. If something were to happen to you, I would no longer wish to live."

Rosalind felt as if he had just driven a knife into her

soul. How could she not tell him about the babe? What if the worst did happen and one of them didn't survive Anne Boleyn's wrath?

"Christopher—"

His fingers covered her lips and he whispered, "There is someone watching us."

Rosalind carefully inhaled. For some reason, breeding had only enhanced her sense of smell, especially when it came to detecting Vampires. "I sense a fox."

"George?"

"Yes."

"I hope he does not recognize you dressed as a boy, but we should put some distance between us." He paused. "Or should we have a quarrel in case he has already worked out who we are?"

Rosalind bit down on her lip. "I don't want to fight with you anymore, Christopher."

He contemplated her for a long moment, and she eventually dropped her gaze to his booted feet. His tone became formal. "If there was anything you could do to help me in my struggle with the Mithras Cult, I would ask it of you. I would hope you would do the same." He inclined his head. "I'll waylay George so that you can escape. Good night, my lady."

He bowed and left her standing there, her heart too full of contradictions to do anything to make things better. And what could she do? She couldn't tell him about the child, and thus she had to deal with her own guilt—and his mistrust. And he might claim that the Mithras Cult had nothing to do with her, but she sensed otherwise. Recently, there was a sense of desperate purpose behind his more lighthearted remarks that made her very suspicious.

Rosalind continued on her way to bed. What would happen to them? Keeping secrets from each other was hardly a promising sign for their future together. It made her dislike herself. She opened the door at the bottom of the stairs that led up to her bedchamber and slowly ascended. Whatever happened, she had a Vampire to vanquish. All of her other problems would simply have to wait their turn.

After making sure that a drunken George Boleyn reached his quarters safely, Christopher returned to the stable yard. As he saddled his horse, he prayed that Rhys wouldn't see him leaving and tell Rosalind. She was already far too suspicious. And, of course, he'd neglected to mention that Brother Samuel had summoned him to come to Westminster Abbey cloisters at two that very morning.

Christopher drew the hood of his cloak over his head to conceal his features and led his horse out under the archway that guarded the entrance to Hampton Court. Once outside the grounds, he mounted and started his journey back to the center of London.

At this time of night, the roads weren't crowded with courtiers, the king's messengers, or the poor traveling to see the king eat his dinner and receive the scraps from his table. Christopher urged his horse into a canter and leaned forward in the saddle. He hated not being able to tell Rosalind the truth, but he couldn't admit his life was in danger. She'd want to help him, and he would never let her near the likes of Marcus Flavian and the more extreme elements of the Mithras Cult.

Dust thrown up by his horse's feet made him cough and he sat back a little, easing the horse into a slow trot. Eventually, the black outline of the city and the glinting shine of the Thames came into view. He slowed even further to ford the river, which was at low tide, and was then swallowed up into the narrow lanes and leaning buildings of the city. The stench of rotting refuse and the rats scurrying out from under his horse's hooves made him want to retch. He much preferred the countryside, could never imagine why anyone would want to live in such a rabbit warren as this.

Westminster Abbey was still lit, a warm beacon within such a seething mass of humanity. Christopher tied up his horse in the same place, and knocked on the arched door. No one answered him, and he knocked again, this time more loudly. He stepped back, one hand instinctively going to his sword hilt. A faint scraping sound drew his attention back to the door, which opened to reveal the face of the young Benedictine monk who had admitted him and Marcus on their previous visit.

"Good evening," Christopher murmured. "Brother Samuel is expecting me."

Confusion flickered in the monk's eyes. "But I thought I'd already admitted you—"

Christopher pushed past the startled monk and headed as swiftly as he could toward the cloisters. A light burned in the far corner of the north cloister and he went toward it, almost at a run.

Brother Samuel was slumped over his desk, one hand stretched out as if pleading for help, a dark red pool of blood around his head. Christopher drew his sword, but there was no one there. He unconsciously licked his lips as the scent of the rapidly cooling blood reached him and despised himself for it.

"Brother Samuel!" The young monk's anguished cry cut through the stifling silence.

"Quiet." Christopher reached out a hand and slapped it over the monk's mouth. "Calm yourself, Brother. We don't want to rouse the whole monastery." He could feel the monk shivering through his fingers. "Let me at least see if he is alive before you panic."

Christopher released the monk and cautiously stepped forward into the candlelight that focused the eye all too clearly on the ghastly scene. It appeared that Brother Samuel's throat had been slashed. Christopher circled him and noticed a scrap of yellow parchment still clenched in the dead monk's fingers. With all the care he could muster, he extracted the parchment and smoothed it out.

In the poor light, he could hardly make out the closely written script. He squinted hard at it and made out the word

"Vampire," but couldn't calm his breathing sufficiently to make any sense of it. He folded the scrap in two and stuffed it into his leather pouch while he continued to study Brother Samuel. There were no other signs of a struggle. It appeared that whoever had killed the monk had simply walked up behind him, cut his throat, and walked away.

But who would do that, and why? Christopher stared into the blackness of the cloisters as if the answer would magically appear. Next to him, the young monk was praying, the sound soothing and rhythmic. The ancient words calmed Christopher so that he could at least think.

"What is your name, Brother?"

"It is Cedric, sir, Brother Cedric."

"I do not know where your allegiances lie, Brother Cedric, but you need to make a choice. You must either alert your brethren to what we have discovered, or go back to bed and wait for him to be found like this in the morning."

Brother Cedric drew a shuddering breath. "I am Brother Samuel's successor as keeper of the Mithras Cult records. I must preserve them at all costs, though it means abandoning my poor master's body. I will not betray your presence here."

"I thank you for that," said Christopher, and grasped his hand. "I need to know what was on that parchment. Can you search the records and let me know what is missing? It might be important."

Brother Cedric grimaced. "It was obviously important enough to kill for. I will do my best to help you bring the killer to justice."

"The man you admitted earlier, the one you thought was me—did you get a clear look at his face?"

"No, sir. His face was concealed by his cloak and he didn't speak a word. I was a fool. I just assumed it was you, and I didn't question him."

Christopher patted the distraught monk's shoulder. "A perfectly natural mistake. Do not blame yourself."

They walked back through the deserted cloisters to the

doorway, and Christopher put away his sword and bowed formally. "Brother Cedric, I'm sorry for your loss."

"You'll find the killer, won't you?"

"I will, and I'll let you know when I do."

"Thank you, sir." Brother Cedric made the sign of the cross. "God be with you on your quest. Brother Samuel did not deserve to die in this way. He was a good and faithful servant both to God and to the Mithras Cult."

"Amen to that. I'm sorry to have brought such trouble on you."

Brother Cedric managed a smile. "I knew the risks when I agreed to become Brother Samuel's apprentice."

Christopher opened the door. "Be careful all the same, Brother Cedric. I doubt the killer will return, but please, be on your guard."

"Indeed I will, sir. Good night."

As Christopher mounted his horse, he considered the young monk's remarkable composure. He felt no such certainty that Brother Samuel's murderer would be found, mainly because he had absolutely no idea where to start looking for the villain. The possibilities were far too wide.

He threaded his way back through the narrow streets toward the Thames, his thoughts in chaos. What had Brother Samuel wanted to show him, and who on earth had decided the information was too dangerous for him to see? His faint hopes of finding a way out of his vows to the Mithras Cult had taken a death blow. His very survival was in doubt.

For a moment, Christopher stared into the murky depths of the river and considered fleeing. But there was still a Vampire to deal with, and a betrothal to put an end to. He couldn't leave quite yet.

Chapter 19

"Good luck," Elias murmured.

Rosalind glanced up at Rhys as the door closed behind them with an almost silent click. Elias had hidden them in a secret room off the chamber where the Lady Anne was listening to a sermon from her chaplain, William Parker. Through the thick paneled walls, his voice sounded like the drone of a wasp, his actual words incomprehensible.

Rosalind fingered the dagger in her hanging pocket and swallowed hard. Rhys was a study in silent concentration, his expression calm, his hazel gaze fixed on the small peephole that allowed them to see into the other room. Elias had shown them how to work the latch that opened the door into Anne's room and left them to ponder their mission.

After what seemed like hours in the small stuffy chamber that resembled nothing more than a glorified linen closet, Rhys held up a finger and moved away from the peephole. Rosalind crowded close behind him.

"She is alone and Elias promised he would keep her that way for as long as we need," Rhys whispered.

"Then we might as well get on with it," Rosalind said,

surprised at how calm she sounded. Rhys nodded and gave his attention to the complexities of the latch. The panel swung silently open and they stepped out just as Anne Boleyn looked up in surprise. She still held her prayer book, and calmly placed it on the table at her side.

Rosalind held up her hand. "Please don't call for help. We just want to talk to you." She hated having to sound so amenable, but they'd all agreed it was the only way to approach Anne.

Anne drew herself up to her full height and smiled, her fangs elongating. "I don't need help. I can rip out your throats in less time than it takes to scream."

"That is true," Rosalind answered. "But wouldn't you like to hear what we have to say first? We have a bargain to offer you."

Anne strolled closer. "What could you possibly offer me? I have everything a woman wants and more." She fixed her gaze on Rhys and licked her lips.

"Everything?" Rosalind moved in front of Rhys, giving him the opportunity to palm his dagger. "I agree that you have succeeded magnificently, but how safe are you? Isn't there anything else you desire?"

Anne tossed her head. "The king has already agreed to get rid of his old Spanish wife and marry me. I will be queen of this land."

"And as queen, your duty will be to give the king what he wants most in life—an heir."

Anne's triumphant expression disappeared and her black eyes narrowed. "So?"

Rhys spoke for the first time. "With all due respect, my lady, you are a Vampire of great age, and we all know that it isn't easy for Vampires to breed."

"How dare you presume that you know anything about me at all?"

"As your enemies, it is in our best interests to discover your weaknesses."

"The king is young and healthy. He will get me with

child within a month." Anne snapped her fingers in Rosalind's face.

"Getting you with child is not the issue, is it? Queen Katherine's womb quickened many times with the king's seed, but only the princess Mary survived."

"That is because she was married to him under false pretenses and against the holy dictates of the Church." Anne resumed her seat and smiled up at them as if she didn't have a care in the world.

"You may choose to gamble on that, but we are offering you the certainty of a living, breathing child," Rosalind answered.

"And why would you do that?"

"Because you can do something for us in return."

Anne stared at Rosalind for a long moment. "This is preposterous. Why should I even listen to you, let alone trust you?"

"You don't need to trust us. All you have to do is agree to our bargain. We will give you what you want, and you will give us the same."

"And what exactly *do* you want, Lady Rosalind?" Anne's foot beat a rapid tattoo against the leg of her chair.

"In return for offering you the means to give the king an heir, you will not turn the king into a Vampire or allow the Vampire Council to subjugate the rest of the population."

"What the Vampire Council intends to do is scarcely my concern, is it?"

Rosalind affected surprise. "You intend to rule with the Vampire Council dictating your every command? They are extremely unlikely to allow you, a mere woman, to actually govern the kingdom."

Anne stopped fidgeting. "I will be queen."

Rosalind stepped forward. "But once you have turned the king, you become expendable. What is to stop the Council from killing you and ruling the kingdom themselves? If you hold on to the king with your own powers, and give him a son, the Council will not be able to undermine you, and you won't be dependent on them at all. Everyone in the nation will be subservient to you."

Anne raised her eyebrows. "And for helping me to achieve all this, all you want is for the king to remain human?"

"It is enough for us," Rhys replied quietly. "A life for a life. A human male to give you as many children as you wish. Surely that is fair?"

"How could you possibly help me conceive a child? Not that I'm saying I want one."

Rosalind tried not to let her impatience show. "Druids and Vampires share a common ancestry. Our Elders have given us fertility magic to ensure you breed."

"Druid magic?" Anne stood up, her color high, her hands clasped tightly together as she paced the strip of carpet that covered the wooden floor. "I would be a fool to take it. You mean to try to poison me, no doubt."

Rosalind glanced at Rhys and they both bowed. "Mayhap you could think about it, my lady. The magic is strongest when the new moon appears, which will be in three days' time. You could give us your answer by then."

As Anne flicked a hand in dismissal and continued to pace, they backed toward the door and finally escaped. Rosalind let out her breath.

"Well, at least she heard us out and didn't kill us."

"Aye." Rhys's answering grin was full of relief as they headed out into the warm sunshine. "Let's find Lord Ellis and tell him the good news."

Christopher dismounted from his horse and turned to see his manservant, Roper, bearing down on him, his expression as disapproving as ever.

"What is it, Roper?" Christopher asked as he loosened the girth and gathered the reins in his hand.

"Message for you, my lord." Roper extended his grimy hand to reveal a piece of parchment sealed with red wax in the shape of a bull's head.

"Thank you, Roper. Who delivered the note to you?"

Roper sniffed. "It was that big man, the one who likes to frown at everyone. Sir Marcus Flavian, I think."

"Ah." Christopher stopped to look at Roper. "Do you have a family, Roper?"

"Not really, sir."

"Nobody you intend to spend your old age with?"

"Not apart from you, sir." Roper looked suspicious. "Why are you asking me these things? Are you planning on turning me off to starve?"

"Not at all, Roper. I'm just trying to ascertain how content you are in my service."

He had no intention of telling Roper that in reality he was thinking about his own death and what would happen to his faithful, if gloomy, manservant. Perhaps he could ask Elias or his uncle to find Roper a new position. Christopher sighed. It was the only option. Roper would hardly take advice from two Druids like Rhys and Rosalind.

"I'm expecting Master Warner to meet me here. If you see him, will you send him to the stables?"

"Aye, if I must." Roper grunted, folded his arms, and leaned back against the wall, a piece of straw dangling from his pudgy lower lip.

Christopher walked his horse through into the main stable yard and handed him over to one of the palace grooms. He strolled around to the rear of the stables, where he was assured of more privacy. With that taken care of, his focus shifted to the note Roper had given him. He used the tip of his dagger to break through the thick seal. The only words were a date and time a week hence. There was no signature to what he knew was his death warrant.

With a soft curse, Christopher folded up the letter and stared out over the pristine pastureland. Heat shimmered in the air, turning the distant cornfields into golden, swaying motion. A warm breeze brought the scents of summer toward him and he breathed them in. He sat on one of the straw bales and contemplated the beauty around him.

Despondency settled low in his gut and for the first time he allowed himself to face the real possibility of his death. The scrap of parchment he'd retrieved from Brother Samuel's hand had given him no real clue as to what the monk had wanted to tell him. He fumbled with the catch of his leather pouch and tried to stuff the letter from the Mithras Cult inside.

A shadow fell over him and he looked up to see Elias Warner bending to pick something up.

"Is this yours, my lord?" Elias held up the piece of bloodied parchment that had somehow fallen out of Christopher's pouch. "It smells of death."

Christopher recognized the paper and went to snatch it back. Elias held on to it, his expression curious. "What exactly do I have here that is so important?" He bent his head to examine the tiny script. "This is part of an ancient text. Why is it in your possession?"

Christopher squinted up at Elias, who was standing with his back to the sun. He couldn't tell Rhys or Rosalind about his maneuverings with the Mithras Cult, but it was time to confide in someone.

"I ripped it from a dead man's fingers."

"A man you killed?"

"No, a monk I suspect was murdered because of me."

"Ah." Elias contemplated the crumpled scrap. "That makes things a lot more complicated. Where is the rest of this?"

"Not where it is supposed to be."

"You stole it?"

Christopher scowled at Elias. "Why do you always assume the worst of me? I didn't take it. It was already gone. All that was left was this piece."

"Which I assume is not much help to you."

"Exactly." Christopher contemplated the scenery for another long moment. "Elias, if things should become . . . complicated . . . would you be prepared to aid me?"

"In what way?"

"Would you make sure that Rosalind and Rhys stay alive?"

There was such a long silence that Christopher was forced to turn and look at Elias.

"Do you fear that Anne will kill you, then?"

Christopher forced a laugh. "Not Anne."

"Then who?"

"The Mithras Cult. I'm sure you know of them."

"I assume they do not approve of your alliance with Lady Rosalind."

"They do not."

"And even a man of your great wit and charm cannot change their minds?"

"Not with my uncle heading the prosecution."

"But I heard his leadership was challenged." Elias frowned. "Verily, I assumed it was your doing."

Christopher shrugged. "I had a hand in it, but it is Marcus Flavian who is challenging him, not me. Since I refused to kill Druids indiscriminately, I no longer have full voting rights."

"Yet they can use the full force of their law against you."

"Indeed, my uncle is a very clever man."

Elias sat back. "This document, what were you hoping it would tell you?"

"I'm not sure." Christopher's shoulders slumped. "Something to help me defend myself against the court in some way."

Elias stood up and smiled. "In the event of your death, I will make sure that Master Williams and Lady Rosalind are safe. If necessary, I will forcibly remove them from the court."

Christopher rose and held out his hand, which Elias took. "I appreciate that. I know it cannot sit well to protect Vampire slayers."

"I have developed a strange fondness for both of them." For a moment, Elias looked quite human. "It is most worrisome." He glanced over Christopher's shoulder. "Ah, I see Lady Rosalind and her faithful groom approaching now."

"Don't say anything to her about what I have asked."

Elias raised an eyebrow. "But surely she should know to come to me if any ill befalls you?"

Christopher forced a smile for the rapidly approaching pair. Rosalind was wearing a new gown of dark green and brown that made her skin glow. "She doesn't know about the threat to my life."

"How is that possible?"

"Because I haven't mentioned it to her."

Elias slowly shook his head. "You are a fool, my lord."

"A fool who doesn't have time to discuss his failings at this precise moment."

Elias nodded. "All right, my lord. I'll keep this to myself."

"Thank you." Christopher raised his hand in greeting to Rosalind and Rhys. "How went your meeting with the Lady Anne?"

Rhys grinned. "Well, we're both still here, aren't we?"

"Did she accept?"

"Not exactly," Rosalind said. "We gave her three days to think it over."

"Three days?"

"The charm will work best on the night of the new moon, which is in three days' time." Rosalind smiled at Christopher and he drank in the sight of her warm brown eyes and her luscious red mouth. "I think she will agree."

"I'm not so sure," said Rhys. "But then I'm not a female."

Christopher took Rosalind's hand and kissed it. "Let's hope that Rosalind is right. We could do with some good news." Only three days before the potential fate of the nation might be decided. Only seven days left for him to live. At least he would get to see the downfall of the Boleyns. That would count for something. He realized he was still holding Rosalind's hand and squeezed it tight.

Rosalind looked up at him. "Are you all right, Christopher?"

"I am very well, my lady." He released her and turned back to Elias, who was watching Rosalind intently, a frown marring his usually unlined brow. "Perhaps, Elias, you could use your influence with Anne to sway her toward our cause."

"Time has proved that I have very little influence with her." Elias's smile grew. "But if I stoke the flames correctly in George's presence, his refusal to take the proposal seriously might push Anne the other way. And I would quite enjoy seeing George in a rage."

Christopher smiled as Elias took his leave. He could only hope that Elias would keep his promise to look after Rosalind and Rhys. It was strange that in his whole life, the three people he trusted most were a Vampire and two Druids. It was too late for him to get to know his half sister, far too late . . .

He realized Rosalind was talking to him, and tried to listen. Her hope for the future was both balm and poison to his spirit. He so wanted to share her optimism, but with a death sentence hanging over him, he couldn't quite enjoy the moment. Finally she gave him a poke and said, "Do you still not approve?"

"Of what?" he asked.

Rosalind rolled her eyes. "Have you been listening to me at all?"

"I've been trying to."

Behind her, Rhys made a noise, and Rosalind rounded sharply on him. "Are you laughing at me as well?"

Rhys bowed. "Not at all, my lady. I just wanted to remind you that you are performing in the king's masque at dinner, and you are supposed to go and rehearse."

After another suspicious glare at them both, Rosalind curtsied and departed, her head held high, her skirts in her hand as she picked her way back over the field.

Rhys's lazy grin disappeared to reveal the strong man beneath. "Now, my lord, let us have the truth between us. It is whispered in the stables that you have been involved in a murder."

"Is that so?" Christopher raised his eyebrows.

"A monk who was believed to be connected to the Mithras Cult was found murdered in the cloisters of Westminster Abbey."

"And why should that have anything to do with me?"

Rhys stepped closer. "Because I saw you leave the palace late last night, and I waited for you to return. By my reckoning you had plenty of time to get to London, kill the monk, and get back."

"What if I was out visiting someone else?"

"Like who? You have no interest in any other woman but Rosalind, and your half sister spent most of the night bothering me with her questions about you."

Christopher grasped at the opportunity to distract Rhys with all the fervor of a starving dog. "She told you I am related to her?"

"It's quite obvious, Ellis. She looks just like you, and she told me she favors her mother."

"Does Rosalind know about these cozy little chats you're having with a Vampire?"

"This does not concern her."

"Verily? Is not your attachment to my half sister a form of revenge on both of us?"

Rhys's mouth tightened. "There is no 'attachment.' She is just an annoying little girl."

Christopher headed back toward the stables. "I'm not sure I believe you."

Rhys followed him, his pale skin flushed, his fists clenched. "Don't walk away from me. I haven't received a single answer from you about that monk's death."

Christopher stopped and pointed his finger in Rhys's face. "I didn't kill that monk. Are you satisfied?"

"Not really." Rhys considered him. "Perhaps I should mention it to Rosalind after all."

"You do that and I'll mention your increasing interest in my sister."

Rhys met Christopher's gaze and neither of them moved. "It seems that we are at an impasse."

"And let's keep it that way. Good day to you, Williams."

"Good day to you, sir."

Christopher strode off toward the palace, leaving Rhys behind. With a disgusted sound, Christopher raised his eyes to the heavens. Why was everything becoming so complicated? He had far too many secrets to guard, both his own and other people's. All he wanted to do was survive long enough to see that Rosalind was safe.

He rounded another corner and a hand reached out and grabbed him. Even as he went for his dagger, he relaxed as he was pulled hard up against Rosalind. She looped her arms around his neck, her brown eyes serious, her lips formed into a tempting pout. When she kissed him, he opened his mouth and touched his tongue to hers, took her love and gave it back to her.

The kiss went on and on. He had no idea how to end it—didn't want it to end, because every breath he took, even those he shared with Rosalind, brought him closer and closer to death. Eventually she drew back, her cheeks flushed.

"I love you, Christopher."

"And I love you."

Her smile faltered and she kissed him once more before sliding out from his grasp and disappearing into the shadows. He touched his mouth and tasted her sweet scent, glad that she had caught him and reminded him of their bond. He frowned as another thought struck him. Rosalind had almost sounded apologetic, as if she too was keeping secrets from him . . . He smacked his hand flat against the brick wall. He was a fine one to talk.

Chapter 20

Rosalind waved frantically at Rhys as he walked his horse into the stable yard.

"Rhys, where have you been?"

Rhys dismounted. He was wearing a hat, but his color was high and his pale skin was starting to burn in the heat of the midday sun. "I've been to London to pick up a letter from your grandfather. What has put you into such a dither?"

Rosalind grabbed his leather jerkin. "The Lady Anne has sent for us."

Under her hand, Rhys went still. "That is indeed good news. When does she want to see us?"

The clock behind Rosalind started to strike twelve, the sound booming and rebounding around the enclosed walls of the courtyard. "Now."

Rhys beckoned one of the stable hands and gave a few crisp instructions about his horse. He handed both the reins and a farthing over to the boy. Rosalind stared pointedly at Rhys's unruly hair and dusty clothing and he shrugged. "If she wants to see us now, the Lady Anne will have to take me as she finds me."

Rosalind guided him back through the intricate passageways and hallways of the massive palace until they arrived at the same room where they had met Anne before.

"I told Christopher where we would be, and he has promised to look out for our return," Rosalind said.

Rhys nodded and took a moment to smooth down his auburn hair and pat his leather jerkin. He smiled at her. "Are you ready, *cariad*?"

"As ready as I can be," Rosalind answered and knocked on the door. Anne's faint voice bade them enter, and after a last long, reassuring look at each other, Rosalind opened the door.

Anne sat in an ornate gilded chair in the center of the well-shaded paneled room. She was dressed in black velvet with slashes of red in the lining and cuffs of her sleeves. Her hood was also black, which emphasized her small scarlet-painted mouth and pale skin, and made her eyes look darker and more fathomless. Rosalind and Rhys bowed, but neither of them spoke.

Anne stirred in her seat. "I have decided to hear more about your offer."

Rosalind tried to look calm. "There is not much more to tell you, my lady. We offer you our Druid magic in exchange for your promise not to turn the king or aid the Vampire Council."

"You do realize that if you aid me in obtaining a son, the struggle between us will not be over? And, that with my son beside me, I can rule for eternity?"

"We understand that risk."

"Because you believe you will eventually find a way to stop that from happening."

Rosalind nodded. "Of course we do, my lady."

Anne's fingers drummed on the arm of her chair. "Then why help me in the first place?"

"Because we are not strong enough to prevent your marriage to the king. Right now our concern is to protect the king's continued good health. It is our sacred duty."

Anne considered her. "At least you are honest about it."

"There is little to be gained from dissembling."

"And if I refuse your bargain?"

"We will continue to try to kill you, and eventually we will succeed. Or, the king will grow tired of you because you cannot provide him with an heir, and our task will prove even easier."

Anne looked down at her hands. "I could simply turn the king into my Vampire slave."

"If that were your only aim, you would already have done it. A woman of your abilities must want more. You could rule the entire kingdom."

There was a long silence. All Rosalind could hear was Rhys's steady breathing behind her and the quick thump of her own heart.

"I want the king's child."

Rosalind let out a breath she hadn't realized she'd been holding. "Then let us help you."

Anne rose and walked over to the empty ash-blackened fireplace. "Tell me exactly what the Druid magic promises me."

"A successful quickening of your womb within six moon cycles of wearing the charm and taking the potion."

"And a living child who will inherit the kingdom?"

"That is what we were told by our Druid Elders, my lady, and they cannot lie when delivering sacred news." Rosalind tried to keep the tremors out of her voice.

Anne swung around and held out her hand. "Give me the potion."

"When you agree not to turn the king into a Vampire."

"Yes, yes." Anne beckoned impatiently. "Or aid the Vampire Council in their efforts to turn the whole nation. I understand."

"But do you agree?"

Anne straightened. "I do."

Rhys stepped forward to stand beside Rosalind. "Then first we must say the oath that binds us to this bargain."

"What oath?" Anne's suspicious gaze flashed between Rosalind and Rhys.

Rosalind took Rhys's hand and held out hers to Anne. "My lady?"

With an impatient gesture, Anne reached for Rosalind's and Rhys's hands. Rosalind repressed a shudder at the Vampire's closeness. Anne's grip was birdlike, her skin cold and lifeless, her honeysuckle scent overwhelming.

Rhys cleared his throat. "If we break faith with one another, may the green earth gape and swallow us. May the gray sea burst loose and overwhelm us. May the sky of stars fall and crush the life out of us forever."

Power from Rhys surged through Rosalind's fingers and onward to Anne Boleyn. All three of them gasped as their hearts beat together and their blood flowed through all of them, as if they had been welded together into a burning ring of molten metal.

Anne ripped her hands free and stepped backward. Color infused her face, turned her eyes red, and elongated her fangs. She looked what she was now, a powerful Vampire hiding within the shell of a beautiful woman. Rosalind itched to draw her dagger and simply kill the Vampire, but she had to see this through. Her loyalty to the king must supersede her own desires, and she too was now bound by the dictates of the sacred oath.

Rhys squeezed her hand and let it go. He turned to Anne and bowed. "Do not break the vow you have made to us to save the king, my lady, or you will suffer the consequences."

Anne licked her lips. "I will keep my vow if you keep yours. Now give me the potion!"

Even though her hands were still shaking, Rosalind opened her hanging pocket and slowly took out the securely wrapped charm, the small bottle of potion, and the parchment containing the prayer. She crossed to the sturdy oak table and unwrapped the charm, taking care not to touch it. Despite her best efforts, she felt the tug of her own fertility, the surge of life within her womb.

"You must wear this charm close to your skin at all times."

Anne peered at the small acorn-shaped trinket and shuddered. "It is ugly."

"It is one of the most powerful fertility charms in the world."

"I suppose I'll have to bear it." Anne grimaced. "At least it is small and can easily be hidden about my person. Now what about this potion?"

Rosalind handed her the small clay bottle. "On the days when you do not bleed, you must take three drops of this potion on your tongue every morning before you break your fast and then say the prayer."

Anne snatched the parchment out of Rosalind's hand and began to read it out loud.

> *"Brighid bhoidheach, Goddess bright*
> *Lend me your power for this night*
> *With the essence of spirit, fire of Ruis,*
> *bend the laws of the universe to my plight*
>
> *By unicorn horn and chaste, sweet child awaken*
> *Hear Brighid's call.*
> *bán Gèadh quicken my womb*
> *Give the unborn child flight*
>
> *Air, Fire, Earth, and Water*
> *Witness my prayer and come to my aid*
> *As the adder overtakes the stag,*
> *so too shall we prevail.*
>
> *As I will it, so mote it be."*

Rosalind closed her eyes as the words drifted over her. She had a strange desire to rip the parchment out of Anne's hands and stop her using such sacred words simply for her own ambition rather than from a true desire for a child. She waited, hands fisted at her sides, as Anne gathered together the items and stuffed them into her hanging pocket.

"If the potion doesn't take effect immediately, how will I get more?"

Rhys bowed. "If you need more, my lady, send for me in the stables. My name is Rhys Williams. I will make sure you are provided for."

"I'm sure you will, Master Williams." Anne's bright gaze swept over Rhys. "You seem to be a man of your word." She glanced slyly at Rosalind. "Mayhap you will find some consolation close at hand when Kit Ellis repudiates your hand in marriage after all."

"I'm sure I will, my lady." Rosalind inclined her head. "I would wish you success, but I hardly think you would believe me."

"Indeed, I would not." Anne settled herself back into her chair again. "I want you to know that if I die because of this accursed agreement, I have made arrangements with the Vampire Council to have the king and both of you killed instantly."

"I expected no less, my lady."

Rosalind and Rhys turned to go. There was nothing left to say. Either their plan would work and the king would be safe—at least for a while—or it wouldn't, and they would be dead and beyond anyone's help but God's.

Christopher had managed to avoid George and his other friends and find something to do in the stables until his fellow conspirators returned. Now he watched Rhys and Rosalind approach and tried to judge the success of their mission from their expressions.

Rhys saw him and jerked his head in the direction of Geithin's stall. Christopher put back the piece of tack he'd been pretending to mend and walked casually along the line of stalls until he reached the one he wanted. Christopher entered and drew the door shut behind him. Geithin munched placidly on his hay, undisturbed by all his visitors. Rosalind leaned against the wall; her color was disturbingly pale, but at least Rhys was smiling.

"Did Lady Anne take the bait?" Christopher asked.

"She did," Rhys said. "But not without making it quite plain that if she believes we have betrayed her, then we and the king will die."

Christopher glanced at Rosalind, who had closed her eyes. "That was to be expected." He moved around Geithin's hindquarters and touched her shoulder. "Are you well, my lady?"

Rosalind shivered. "As well as can be expected, having given an ancient Vampire the means to procreate."

"We all agreed that there was nothing else we could do."

"I know, but I still wanted to reach for my dagger and just end her life once and for all."

Christopher bent to kiss her cheek. "Such a bloodthirsty wench. Sometimes I fear for my chances in our marriage bed."

Rosalind shrugged away from his touch. "According to the Lady Anne, we will never be married. Once she has secured her position, she intends to keep you dancing attendance on her."

"As if I would let her." Christopher scoffed. "I'm betrothed to you and we *will* be married." Saying it didn't make him feel any better, but he couldn't allow Rosalind to lose confidence in him now.

To his dismay, the glance she threw at him was skeptical to say the least. He caught her hand. "We will be married, Rosalind. I swear it."

Rhys moved toward the door. "I'm going to the Druid circle to give thanks for the success of our mission. Are you coming, my lady?"

Rosalind gently pulled free of Christopher's grasp. "I have to go, Christopher. Keep watch on the Lady Anne and George while we are gone."

Christopher bowed extravagantly. "Yes, my lady. Of course, my lady."

She followed Rhys out, which left him in the stall staring at her horse. If she *was* married to him, would it make her future better or worse? As a titled gentleman, he had land, an income, and a house to bestow on her, but would she want such things? Wouldn't she just want to forget all about him and go back to Wales with Rhys?

Christopher patted Geithin's rump and slowly withdrew from the stall. The notion of marrying Rosalind was now lodged firmly in his head, but how in God's name was he going to achieve his aim? He had no powerful friends at court, and no clergy among his relations. He stopped to stare at the bright sunlight creeping through the narrow diamond-paned windows. And recalled that he knew a very upstanding monk at Westminster Abbey.

It was late when Rosalind finally managed to get to bed. She'd prayed with Rhys at the stone circle, but no one had come, so eventually they'd left and made their way back to Hampton Court. Then she'd had to change her dress and endure an afternoon of watching the king frolic with Anne and her ladies. Lady Anne seemed to be glowing, her smile triumphant, her attitude that of a reigning queen.

Rosalind made herself dance and smile, but she wasn't exactly enjoying herself. Christopher was also there, dazzling in black and gold, but as he avoided her at all costs, she gained no comfort from him at all. It was a struggle simply to find the energy to sit there, let alone pretend that everything was well.

Pride kept her chained to her seat. She had no intention of allowing Anne to think that she had been defeated by their bargain. But by the time she endured the evening banquet and entertainment, she was more than willing to seek her bed. As she reached the top of the stairs, she tripped over the hem of her ornate silver and red gown and had to grab on to the wall. The weight of her embroidered skirts felt like fifty pounds of lead.

She fell into her room and let out a breath, tensed when she sensed another presence beside her. In the darkness,

Christopher touched her cheek and then her shoulder. She stood still and let him, her energy too drained to manage the simplest of tasks. He knelt at her feet, and helped her out of her jeweled slippers, his fingers warm as he unrolled her stockings, his touch so careful that she wanted to weep.

He kissed her foot and slowly got to his feet, his mouth a tantalizing inch away from hers. His tongue flicked out and feathered along the seam of her lips and she parted them with a gasp. His kiss remained light, as if he sensed her exhaustion, as if he wanted to give to her rather than take or demand.

While he kissed her, his hands continued their work of releasing her from her gown and bodice. Her heavy skirts fell to the floor, followed by her petticoats and bodice. He bent his head and unlaced her stays, licked a warm trail of kisses between her breasts. Her hand slid into his hair and she traced the fine bones of his scalp.

She shivered as his mouth moved over the linen of her shift and came to rest on her nipple. A pang of near pain shot through her as he suckled, and she tightened her grip in his hair and heard him groan deep in his throat. His scent entwined with hers, and she breathed in the musk of his need, felt the softening of her limbs and her center. She reached out with her other hand and grabbed his shoulder, found only the shocking allure of bare skin and continued her exploration to find him already naked.

He drew her backward toward the bed and sat her on the edge, his touch so sure and so safe that she wanted to melt into him, to lie back and let him take her wherever he wanted to. He crouched in front of her, a mere shadow in the intimate darkness, and spread her knees. She moaned as his mouth followed a path up the inside of her thigh, the rasp of his beard an added layer of sensation that sent her desire spiraling.

He reached her core and licked a slow, lascivious line over her already willing and wanton flesh, then deepened his invasion with his mouth, his fingers, and his teeth, until she was writhing beneath him. He licked her again and thrust three fingers deep inside her. She took her pleasure from him in long, shuddering gasps, drinking in the sensation, drowning in the desire he created in her.

With a rough sound he joined her on the bed, his thighs spreading hers wide, his wet, hard prick seeking her, entering her, possessing her. She welcomed him, lay pliant beneath him, simply enjoyed his body joined to hers in this most intimate of embraces. When he finally started to move, he was slow and languorous, as if he too wanted to make each moment last forever.

She wrapped her arms and legs around him and held him tightly within the cradle of her body, felt his muscles flex and release with each thrust, each tremor as he fought to keep the pace slow and even. His mouth sought hers, his tongue thrusting into her mouth in the same rhythm as his prick, giving her no escape—not that she wanted to escape him at all.

Eventually, he lost his smooth rhythm and started to move faster, to demand more, to push her to limits she had never explored before. She climaxed for him and then again as he continued to thrust into her, his buttocks flexing and driving into her until he spilled his seed in a hot flowing rush that shook her to the core.

After a long while, he kissed her and rolled away to the side of the bed. She heard him putting on his clothes and pulled the covers over herself. He left as silently as he'd arrived, leaving her lying awake, her body satiated but her mind in turmoil.

Rosalind opened her eyes and stared up at the ceiling. Despite the intensity of his lovemaking, Christopher hadn't shared his thoughts with her at all. But she'd understood him all too well. He didn't need the words when they both knew he was saying good-bye.

Chapter 21

Christopher contemplated his second-to-last day on earth with a sense of resignation. He'd not had word from Brother Cedric and could only hope that he had not met a similar fate to his master's. Despite his concern, Christopher reckoned the worst thing he could do was storm into Westminster Abbey and start demanding things.

With a sigh, Christopher returned his attention to the Mass. But within moments, his gaze had wandered upward to the gold hammer-beam roof and the silver painted stars on the dark blue background. He'd already met with his confessor and been absolved of his sins. His will was written and in the hands of his lawyer. There was nothing else he could do to safeguard his immortal soul and, apparently, very little he could do for Rosalind, unless he found a way to marry her.

As he genuflected and left his pew, Christopher found himself walking beside George Boleyn, who looked extremely unhappy. Christopher risked a smile.

"Is everything all right, George?"

George scowled, his dark eyes flashing. "Everything is just fine."

"I understand that the king has found the means to annul his marriage with Queen Katherine. Surely that is a great thing for your family. There is nothing to stop your advancement now."

George grabbed Christopher's arm and drew him out of the stream of exiting courtiers and into the shadows at the back of the chapel. "It is a great thing for my sister. Yet she seems to have already forgotten those who have helped her achieve her aims."

"Surely not, George. She holds you in the highest esteem."

"You would think so, wouldn't you? Especially after all I've done for her." George lowered his voice to a virulent hiss. "I even became a Vampire for her! And that is not as pleasant an existence as she promised it would be."

Christopher clasped George's shoulder. "I'm sure once Anne marries the king, she will remember what she owes you. How could she not?"

George made a disparaging sound and started walking toward a small door concealed in the stairwell. Christopher followed him. He had the notion that in the mood George was in, he might be heading straight for Anne. Christopher was very curious to see Anne's demeanor now that she was in possession of both the king's promise to marry her and the Druid fertility magic.

"Anne has gotten above herself. She claims she needs nobody's help and owes no one any favors."

"Really? That does sound a little harsh."

George flung open another door and kept walking through a series of small rooms that Christopher had never entered before. The strong smell of Anne's favorite perfume wafted toward him, and he realized he had entered her bedchamber.

Anne was sitting with her feet up before the fireplace. She wore a long robe and her black hair hung down her back to her waist. Christopher halted and let George march forward to confront her.

"I hear that you have made a deal with the devil, sister mine."

"Which particular deal do you mean?" Anne turned to gaze at George. "I have made so many."

"The one with the Druid scum." George pointed his finger in Christopher's direction. "The one with *his* bitch of a betrothed."

"Oh, are you here too, Kit?" Anne smiled and put down her goblet. She looked as satisfied as a cat that had cornered a large mouse. "Did Lady Rosalind tell you what she has done?"

"Tell me what?" Christopher quickly shut down his thoughts. Let Anne delve into his mind at will. She would find nothing but puzzled innocence to worry her there.

Anne languidly waved her hand and rose to her feet. "Rosalind Llewellyn and her handsome accomplice—Rhys something—came to see me."

"Williams? He is nothing but her servant."

Anne wagged her finger. "Don't try to deceive me, Kit darling. I know that you have successfully blocked my attempts to bewitch you to my cause, and Elias told me long ago that you are linked to the Druid with blood." She slowly licked her lips. "I, of all people, know that is a bond that can never be broken."

George blocked her path. "Yet you seem to have forgotten about your bond with me!"

Anne wrinkled her nose. "You are becoming a nuisance, George. If you cannot be quiet, I will kill you."

"I am your lover, not your slave. Just because you have finally let the king into your bed—"

George didn't finish his sentence as Anne reached out, grabbed him by the throat, and shook him like a rat. "You are what I choose to make you." She pushed him away and he reeled on his feet. "Now get out. I will deal with you later. I need to talk to Kit."

George threw her a vicious glare and left, one hand still

protecting his throat. In the sudden silence, Christopher concentrated on gathering his defenses.

"Now, where were we?" Anne said. "Ah, yes. We were discussing your connection with the Vampire slayer."

"We are still connected, that is true. It's the reason why my uncle hasn't broken the betrothal. You know that."

"I know it is much more." Anne moved closer, and Christopher forced himself to meet her black gaze without showing any fear. "And yet you have feigned dislike."

"We've already discussed this. I have done what is necessary to protect myself and those I care about."

"You care about her."

Christopher smiled. Verily he had nothing to lose at this point. If Anne wanted to hasten his death by a day, it hardly mattered.

"Yes, I care for her. How could I not? She is the bravest woman I have ever met."

A flash of anger lit Anne's eyes. "Braver than I, dearest Kit?"

"Much braver, my lady."

"You truly believe that?" Anne paced a hasty circle around the room, her hands locked together at her waist. "Yet she toys with your affections."

"She has the right. By consorting with you, I have not exactly shown myself to be loyal to her, have I?"

"That is not what I meant, Kit." Anne faced him, her expression concerned. "You know of the bargain she and her Druid brethren offered me?"

"I know of it."

"And you were not surprised by her vast knowledge of Druid fertility magic?"

"Why would I be?"

Anne sighed. "Oh, Kit, I hardly know how to tell you this."

"Tell me what?"

"That Rosalind Llewellyn has deceived you."

Christopher tried to keep his face blank. "Do you really think I am going to believe your lies?"

Anne clasped her hands to her bosom. "You can believe what you want, Kit. I just hate to see you stand by a woman who has betrayed you in the most elemental way."

Christopher didn't ask for an explanation. But he readied himself, sure she was going to provide him with one whether he wanted it or not.

Anne stared at him, a challenge in her eyes. "You do not care?"

Christopher held out his hands, palms up. "I do not have time for your insinuations. Either tell me what you want to say, or give me leave to go."

Anne drew a quick breath. "I heard this from Elias Warner, a man I trust implicitly. He journeyed into Wales last year after Rosalind Llewellyn left court."

"He didn't mention it to me."

"He has some fondness for you; perhaps he didn't wish to be the bearer of such bad news."

"A position you are quite willing to assume in his stead."

Anne drew herself up. "I, at least, remember that we were once friends. And friends do not deceive each other."

"Pretty words, Anne, but we both know they mean nothing coming from you."

Anger glittered in Anne's eyes and Christopher reeled under the dark threat of her magic.

"Very well, then. Did you not wonder why your betrothed stayed away from court for so long?"

"She had her reasons."

"Indeed, she did." Anne watched him narrowly. "She was busy giving birth to your child."

Christopher fought back his instant denial, even as his mind furiously counted the long months of Rosalind's absence. "Why would she do that?"

"Why do you think? Your child is unusual, to say the least." She kept watching him. "*You* are unusual. Would not the Druids be *interested* in such a child?"

"What are you suggesting, Anne?" Christopher was proud of the calmness of his tone.

"I'm not suggesting anything. But you must be wondering why your intended left Wales without her babe."

"In truth, I would commend her for keeping any child away from this viper's nest of a court."

"Oh, Kit, your loyalty does you credit, but do you really think your child is safe with Rosalind's monster of a grandfather and his Druid priests?"

"There is no child," Christopher managed to force out.

"Ask your betrothed what the Druids plan to sacrifice this next Samhain night."

"That is a ridiculous accusation."

"Are you sure about that?" Anne shook her head. "You of all people know how it feels to be abandoned to your fate by your mother. Are you certain that Rosalind Llewellyn would not do the same to her child—out of duty, or love, for her Druid religion?"

"Have you finished?"

Anne's smile was triumphant. "I believe I have."

"Then I will bid you good day." Christopher bowed and headed for the door. He kept walking until he found himself in a part of the palace he didn't recognize. His breathing was so ragged that he had to stop, had to sit down, had to . . . He rested his forehead against the stone wall and closed his eyes.

No.

Rosalind would never do that to him. It was disloyal of him even to think it. She *loved* him; he knew it. She wouldn't . . . but she had been defensive when he'd asked her about her long absence from court, and recently she'd been keeping secrets from him. Had Elias told her that he knew about her child, and had she feared Christopher would find out?

As his stomach churned, Christopher struggled to take a deep, calming breath. He had to believe this was simply Anne's last attempt to pit him against Rosalind. Logic and common sense demanded it. But there was still a part of him that wanted to weep. Rosalind had told him once that Druids didn't practice human sacrifice anymore. Could she really have lied to him? Or mayhap she had no idea what her grandfather planned to do with the babe. A sudden coldness gripped him. Speculation was useless. He had to find Rosalind. Now.

Rosalind sat in the royal apartments and tried to concentrate on the embroidered slippers she was making for her grandfather's birthday. It was hard not to think about what Anne might be doing with the potion, and how successful it could be. Rumors were already flying that Anne had succumbed to the king's desires on the previous night. Rosalind hated the idea of giving Anne anything she wanted, but the practical, pragmatic side of her realized there was no other option.

"Lady Rosalind?"

She looked up to find Christopher in front of her. Her tentative, welcoming smile died as she contemplated the iciness of his blue gaze. "My lord?"

He bowed stiffly. "I wish to speak to you in private."

Rosalind ignored the whispering from the other ladies and put down her sewing. Christopher didn't bother to wait for her and was already disappearing through the door. Rosalind picked up her brown satin skirts and followed him out of the sunny room and into the darker recesses of the attached kitchens.

Christopher stopped by one of the large sweet-smelling storerooms that held preserving jars filled with last year's summer fruit and flung open the door.

Rosalind followed him in. "Christopher, whatever is the matter?"

He stared down at the mud floor. "There is something I need to ask you."

"Then ask."

He still wouldn't look at her. "I know I shouldn't even have listened to her, but she was determined to tell me, and as Elias already knows . . ."

"Elias knows what? I have no idea what you are talking about." Rosalind hoped she didn't sound as defensive as she feared. Had he somehow guessed her secret? That might explain his anger. "If you wish to accuse me of something, please go ahead. I'm listening."

He cursed softly and stared into her eyes. "Tell me about my child, Rosalind."

She took a step back and flattened her hand over her stomach. "Why on earth would you ask me that?"

"Answer the question!"

Fright mingled with guilt gave her voice the snap she needed. "I need not answer you when you bark out commands to me as if I'm your dog!"

He took a menacing step closer. "Tell me."

Rosalind swallowed hard. How had he guessed, when she had scarcely acknowledged the pregnancy to herself? And why was he shaking with anger? "I . . ."

"Why so reluctant to answer, my love? Aren't you supposed to be pleased and eager to share the news of our little bastard? Most women want children, don't they? Even my mother, I suppose, 'wanted' me—to use me as a bloody bargaining counter in her game of deceit."

The venom in Christopher's voice made Rosalind bite her lip.

"I am not like your mother."

"Is that so? Because your reluctance to tell me about the babe makes me wonder if it's even mine. Did you take a lover while you were so conveniently missing from my side?"

"Of course not!"

"Then why didn't you tell me?"

Even as hurt shuddered through her, she met his disbelieving gaze. "I had my reasons."

His mouth twisted. "I'm sure you did."

Desperately Rosalind tried to reach through his blistering scorn. "I *wanted*—"

He cut her off with a decisive gesture. "Yet what *I* want seems to be completely irrelevant to you, does it not?"

Rosalind faced him then, her fists at her sides, her heart banging in her chest. "What exactly has Elias said? Or is there someone else involved? You said 'she'—would that be the Lady Anne Boleyn? She scarcely has my best interests at heart."

"Just answer me." He lifted her chin with two hard fingers. "Did I get you with child?"

She had to fight to think up a reply that wouldn't inflame his anger, but it was impossible. Rage flooded through her. Whatever Anne had said had tainted his view of their offspring. Would she be the only person glad to hold such a babe in her arms?

This wasn't the way she would have chosen to deliver such important news, but she couldn't lie to his face. "Yes. But as it seems obvious that the thought of me having your child is abhorrent to you, mayhap I did the right thing to conceal my condition."

His face contorted and he recoiled from her. "By all the saints, Rosalind," he whispered. "What have you done?"

She stepped out of his reach as dread curdled her stomach. "Nothing that need concern you. I promise you will never have to see the child." It took all her strength to run from him then. She expected him to call her back, to demand that she face him and explain herself. But he didn't come after her. He didn't do anything to stop her walking away from him at all.

Rosalind kept running until she reached her bed, and flung herself down on it. She tried to think through the waves of anguish flooding through her. Christopher didn't want this child—their child. Could he not face the idea of being a father to a babe whose kin were at one another's throats? She'd thought better of him, thought he of all people would understand.

She rolled onto her back and pressed a hand to her stomach. Tears slid down her cheeks as she murmured a protective prayer over her child. What had provoked such an outburst from Christopher? And what on earth had Anne Boleyn said to stir the pot? The thought of Anne knowing anything about their child was terrifying.

Rosalind only became aware that something was not right when it was too late. Christopher's palm was over her mouth and her hands were tied together. She tried to kick out at him, but only succeeded in hurting her bare feet on his hard thigh. When he gagged her and slung her over his shoulder, she could do nothing but endure the jolting down the stairs and pray she wouldn't puke.

It was now dark outside, so she must have slept a little. Christopher wrapped her in his cloak and took her down to the silent stables. He paused long enough to show her a trussed-up Rhys in the corner of her horse's stall being guarded by Christopher's manservant. With the assistance of his servant, Christopher mounted his horse and tucked her in front of him. There was no possibility of escape, so she endured the ride in seething silence, imagining all the possible ways she could hurt him when he finally released her.

But would he release her? The possibility of being tossed into the River Thames haunted her. Surely he wouldn't do that? She started to struggle against the stifling folds of the cloak, but he simply tightened his grip and kept her secured.

She could smell the river now, the unpleasant odor of dead fish and other even less agreeable refuse. Christopher halted the horse and got down, easily supporting her with one hand as he gained the ground. To her annoyance, before she could contemplate her escape, he immediately picked her up again, and walked forward into the foggy gloom. He paused to kick open an old oak door and she found herself inside a small church.

Christopher's boots echoed as he marched up the center aisle. Rosalind could see nothing but the dirty red and brown tiled floor and the glow of candlelight before the painted rood screen.

"Good evening, Father."

A quivery voice answered him. "Good evening, my son. Is this the lady?"

"Indeed it is, Father."

Rosalind gulped as she was righted in one smooth motion and placed on her bare feet. She swayed, and Christopher wrapped his arm around her shoulders.

The priest eyed Rosalind, his kind face full of worry. "I cannot marry you if she is gagged, my son. She must consent."

"As I told you, Father, she is a little simple in the head. She does want to marry me. Don't you, my darling?"

Before Rosalind could shake her head, Christopher bent down to whisper in her ear, "Defy me and Rhys dies."

She stared into his eyes and saw no hint of the man she loved, only a calm, cold desire to achieve his aim. He even forced his mind into hers so that she could gauge the sincerity of his deadly intentions.

Was this a nightmare? The sensation of the cold tiles beneath her feet assured her that she was indeed awake, and in some discomfort. Had Christopher been possessed by Anne Boleyn completely? But then why marry her? Surely Anne would have ordered him to kill her?

Christopher took off the gag, and Rosalind moistened her dry lips. "Why are you doing this?"

"To protect what is mine."

"But why now?"

"Because this is how I wish it."

Rosalind studied his all-too-familiar face for a long wrenching moment. "If you do this, if you force this wedding on me, I do not wish to see you ever again."

"Have no fear of that," he bit out. "Then you agree to the marriage?"

She thought of the babe, *his* babe that grew within her womb. Their child did not deserve to be born a bastard. Whatever was wrong between them, surely all she needed was time to solve it. And if he was indeed bewitched, she could deal with that as well. She took a deep breath. "I will agree—for Rhys's sake."

In the silent, sacred space his laughter was shocking. "Not for the sake of the child?"

She ignored him and turned to face the priest, felt Christopher's dagger bite into the ropes around her wrists and free her. He took her left hand and she stared straight ahead, not willing to look at him, not willing to acknowledge him until she'd made her stilted replies, heard his, and become his wife.

They didn't speak on the way back to Hampton Court, and Rosalind was glad of it. Misery engulfed her and she was no longer sure she had made the right decision. As Christopher left her at the bottom of the stairs and stalked away without a word, Rosalind finally allowed herself to cry.

Chapter 22

His last day on earth, and he was not only a married man, but apparently a father as well. Christopher groaned and closed his eyes. He had to face Rhys now instead of cravenly skulking off to bed to drown his sorrows in a bottle of fine Rhenish wine.

But if Christopher wanted to make sure he was given access to his own child, Rhys would have to be dealt with. Rosalind he couldn't even bear to think about. He knew in his soul that she couldn't have countenanced her own child's sacrifice, but the rest of it ... How could she abandon a babe like that? Christopher groaned. Maybe it was more common than he thought, or maybe he just attracted coldhearted women who wanted to rip out his soul.

His conscience whispered a protest. Rosalind wasn't like that. She didn't have a dishonest bone in her body. If she'd wished to betray him, she would've done so to his face and told him about it too, not by deceit. But she hadn't denied the existence of his child ... had, in truth, confirmed his suspicions quite readily.

He entered the stables and gestured for Roper to leave him with Rhys in the deserted tack room. Kneeling beside

Rhys, he sawed through the ropes that bound him and removed the gag from his mouth. Before he could retreat to a safe distance, Rhys was on him, his dagger to Christopher's throat, his knee lodged on Christopher's chest.

"What in God's name is going on, Ellis? Have you run mad?"

"If you'll get off me, I'll tell you."

With a contemptuous shove, Rhys let him go and stood up, his color high and his hazel eyes radiating fury.

"What do you want to know, Williams?"

"I would've thought that was obvious. Why in God's name did you set your servant on me and kidnap Rosalind?"

Christopher met his gaze. "You are an excellent liar, Rhys, but not that good."

"I am not lying."

"Are you trying to tell me that Rosalind, who trusts you with everything, didn't tell you about the child?"

For a moment, Rhys looked completely baffled. "What child?"

"The babe she delivered while she was in Wales. *My* child, I assume, unless she is a whore as well as a witch."

"Shut your filthy mouth!" Rhys demanded. "Has that Anne Boleyn finally turned you into her creature?"

"No child of mine will be murdered for the sake of your bloody religion."

Rhys set his jaw. "Ellis, I fear you have lost your mind. There is no child—"

Christopher grabbed Rhys by the throat. "Just tell me exactly where her grandfather lives so that I can get the babe before it is too late." Rhys tried to pull out of his grasp, but Christopher tightened his grip. "Tell me."

Rhys stopped struggling and spoke slowly. "There. Is. No. Child. Whoever told you that was lying."

"Then Rosalind is a liar, for she said so herself."

"She could not have said that, unless . . ."

Christopher shook him hard. "Unless what?"

"I need to speak to Rosalind, but I swear to you by the

bloody cross of our Lord Jesus Christ there was no child born while we were away from court."

Christopher released Rhys and turned away, almost too sick at heart to respond. "Who am I to believe? You, or the woman who told me to my face she had betrayed me?"

Rhys made a disgusted sound. "It seems your loyalty is a fragile thing, my lord, easily broken when poison is whispered in your ear."

"That isn't true. I went to Rosalind, asked her for the truth. She denied nothing." Christopher realized he was shouting and fought to control his voice. "She admitted there was a child."

"Then you must have asked the wrong question."

"What in God's name is that supposed to mean?"

"Nothing to you," Rhys sneered. "You've already condemned her, haven't you?"

"I've *married* her. Rosalind is my wife and subject to my rule."

Rhys was breathing as hard as he was, and their gazes locked, their weapons at the ready for the vicious brawl they both circled closer and closer to starting.

"I need to speak to my lady," Rhys said through gritted teeth.

"Obviously. But remember she is my wife now, so she cannot leave court without my permission. In truth, she can do *nothing* without my permission. Remind her of that, won't you?"

Rhys stuck his finger in Christopher's face. "You are behaving like a fool. Rosalind will never forgive you for this. Never."

Christopher grabbed Rhys by his jerkin and shoved him against the wall. "That is none of your concern. Rosalind has no choice. She is my wife. She must cleave to me until death."

Rhys shot him a dark look. "Aye, and if I have anything to do with it—that can be speedily arranged."

Christopher started to laugh. "Don't worry, Rhys. It al-

ready has. You'll have to stand in line with everyone else."
He let go of Rhys and held up his hands. "Try and kill me, if
you like. I'd almost prefer a bloody fight to the death with
you than the alternatives."

Rhys put his dagger away. "I refuse to give you the satisfaction. If anyone ends your life, it should be Rosalind. I'll
be quite happy to watch."

Rhys stormed out, slamming the door behind him, and
Christopher stared out of the grimy window. Rhys had
made him feel like a fool and stirred all the latent doubts
he'd buried in order to achieve his aim of forcing Rosalind
to marry him. His emotions threatened to boil over again
and he shoved them down. He needed to be calm.

He had to revise his will before nightfall. He guessed
Rosalind would not want a penny from him, but at least he
had safeguarded his child. He would use all his recently ac-
quired wealth and status to make sure his child was taken
from the Druids and . . . sent where? Who would want such
a child, tainted by both Druid and Vampire blood?

He would.

But he wouldn't be there, would he? And yet he'd always sworn to do better than his parents had, to love his
children and protect them from all harm. How ironic that
his father had died protecting him, and he was about to do
the same whilst safeguarding the future of his own child.
What a twisted legacy to pass on to a mere babe.

Christopher swallowed down a huge swirl of pain. He was
also set on taking his child from its mother. How would the
babe feel about that? But Rosalind's choice had made anything else impossible. So the child would have neither parent
in his life. Surely that had to be better than ending up as a pawn
in the bloody war between the Ellises and the Llewellyns.

With that thought firmly in mind, Christopher left the
stables and went to find his confessor to set about rewriting
his will.

*   *   *

Rosalind woke up to the now-familiar sensation of her stomach grumbling. She cautiously sat up, and then had to make a dash for the basin by the window. By the time she crawled back into bed and contemplated the bright sunshine pouring in through her diamond-paned window, she was definitely awake.

She glanced down at her left hand and saw the plain gold band Christopher had shoved on her marriage finger at the end of the short wedding ceremony. With a shudder, she took the ring off and slid it under her pillow. Not that it would do much good. It was impossible to avoid the fact that she was now Christopher's lawfully wedded wife.

Her stomach heaved again, and she picked up one of the pieces of bread she'd taken from the previous day's meal, and broke off a small piece. It seemed to take forever to chew the dried bread and force it down with a sip of ale. But she'd discovered it was well worth the effort to appease her belly. She chewed more bread and gradually felt better.

Nothing made sense anymore. Christopher's behavior was incomprehensible. The man who'd coerced her into marrying him last night was not the Christopher she thought she knew at all. What had happened to alter his feelings for her? It *had* to have something to do with the Boleyns. Only Anne had the power to seriously disrupt Christopher's peace of mind.

Sure now that her stomach would keep its peace, Rosalind got out of bed and dressed in her favorite gown. She might not understand what Christopher had done, she might want to lie in her bed and weep for everything she had lost, but she still had to make sure Rhys was unharmed.

She paused at the door and looked back at her rumpled bedclothes, remembered Christopher lying there with her, and swallowed back tears. What was her grandfather going to say when he found out she was actually married to a Druid slayer? Would he cast her out as Christopher had predicted long ago? Rosalind gripped the doorframe. Was that it? Did Christopher want her alone, abandoned, and totally dependent on him?

Rosalind shook her head. She would never ask him for anything ever again. If her grandfather no longer wanted her, she would find another life and another way to protect her child, the perfidious Lord Christopher Ellis be damned.

When she reached the Clock courtyard, she saw Rhys coming toward her, his expression grim. When he reached her, he bowed and spoke in a low voice.

"Is it true? Did Lord Christopher *marry* you last night?"

"He did." Rosalind started toward the great hall to find some food. "I had no choice in the matter."

"Because he had me trussed up like a sacrificial lamb to command your obedience. I'm sorry."

They continued to the great hall in silence. Rhys held the door open and followed her inside. "Sit down, my lady. I'll find you something to break your fast."

Rosalind was happy enough to let him serve her. The smell of food still occasionally turned her stomach and vast quantities of it were the worst. Rhys returned bearing a small jug of ale and a platter filled with food.

"Here you are, my lady."

Rosalind took a piece of coarse bread and dipped it in the honey oozing from the piece of honeycomb on the side of the pewter plate.

"You are still not eating well," Rhys commented.

"That is because I'm still puking." Rosalind concentrated on the sweetness of the honey and not the effort it took to force the food down.

"Ah." Rhys stared at her for so long that she began to wonder what was wrong.

"Do I have honey on my chin?"

"No."

"Then why are you staring?"

"Because now it all makes sense." Rhys slapped his thigh. "I am a dolt not to have realized it sooner. You *are* breeding."

"So?" Rosalind raised her eyebrows at him.

"That explains it."

"Explains what?"

"Some of Lord Christopher Ellis's outlandish behavior."

"I do not want to talk about him."

Rhys's understanding gaze met hers. "Did you tell him you were carrying his child?"

She bit down hard on her lip and tasted honey. "He already knew, and he was disgusted."

"He *thought* he knew."

"What on earth does that mean?"

Rhys stood up. "He has some ridiculous notion that you have already had the child. He has been seriously misled."

"Already had the child? Why in God's name would he think that?"

"Because that's what Anne Boleyn told him, of course."

"And he believes *her* instead of me?"

"Rosalind, you as much as told him she was right. He believed *you*, not her."

Rosalind stood too. "He told me that Elias knew as well. This makes no sense—"

"Good morning, Lady Rosalind, Master Williams." Elias Warner's cool voice cut through her fierce contemplation of Rhys. "Are you both well?" He glanced at Rosalind. "Have you seen Lord Christopher this morning?"

"I have not, Master Warner, and I hope never to see him again for the rest of my days."

Elias's expression registered mild alarm. "Are you sure about that? Because I have heard the strangest rumor."

Rosalind narrowed her eyes. "And what would that be?"

Elias bowed. "That congratulations are in order."

"Because I've been forced to marry that loathsome Druid killer?" Rosalind hissed.

Elias looked pained. "Forced is *such* a harsh word. I'm sure his intentions were good. With his trial scheduled for tonight, he had to consider his mortality, set his affairs in order, and so forth."

Rosalind grabbed Elias's gold-embroidered sleeve. "What do you mean? What trial?"

"He didn't mention it to you? That seems rather odd."

"What trial, Elias?"

Elias gently detached Rosalind's fingers from his arm. "Your husband is being tried by his peers in the Mithras Cult this evening."

"For what crime?" Rhys asked.

"For consorting with a known Vampire slayer. Let's hope that the rumors of your wedding don't reach the ears of anyone in the cult, or Lord Christopher will not be given the luxury of a trial. They'll simply behead him."

Rosalind sat down with a thump. Christopher's problems seemed to magnify with every breath she took. What on earth was going on inside his head?

"Why didn't he tell me?"

Elias exchanged a glance with Rhys. "Perhaps he didn't wish to worry you, my lady."

"Worry me? Did he perchance think I wouldn't notice if they killed him tonight? Did he seriously believe that forcing me to marry him would make everything all right?"

Her voice had risen to a screech and others in the hall were starting to look over at them. Not that she cared. Her fingers curled into claws. She wished Christopher was beside her right now so that she could share her thoughts about liars and cheaters and deceivers . . .

"Where is this meeting being held?"

"I have no idea, my lady. Lord Christopher did not confide the details in me. That is why I am seeking him."

"Yet he *did* confide in you. At least he did that."

"This is scarcely a time for recriminations, my lady," Elias murmured. "I *am* trying to help."

"Christopher is a fool," Rosalind retorted. "He doesn't deserve any help. He has misjudged me, made assumptions about my character, forced me into a marriage for reasons that I cannot even begin to fathom, and—"

Rhys touched her shoulder. "And we will still try to save him."

"I will not," Rosalind snapped and folded her arms tightly across her chest.

Rhys ignored Rosalind and addressed Elias. "We have to find out where that meeting is being held. There is . . . someone I know who might be able to help."

"Indeed?" Elias looked intrigued. "Someone who might be able to accompany me when I attempt to waylay Lord Christopher and prevent his death? I can scarcely expect you or Lady Rosalind to step into that particular nest of adders."

Rhys wouldn't even look at Rosalind. "Aye. She is one of your kind. She will not fear the Mithras Cult. I will bring her to you this evening at the stables."

Elias bowed. "That will suit me well."

Rosalind touched his arm. "Why are you doing this, Elias? Surely your alliance with us ended when you did your part to stop the Lady Anne?"

"We haven't stopped her quite yet, have we?" Elias asked. "And, to be honest, I have a great deal of respect for Lord Christopher. He has led a difficult life, and yet he has tried to hold to all his vows."

Rosalind had no answer to that. She obviously wasn't feeling quite as charitable about Christopher as Elias and Rhys were. Elias turned to leave, and she remembered something else.

"Elias, did you know that I am breeding?"

He shrugged gracefully. "I sensed the change in you; the pulse of his blood became yours. Vampires are sensitive to such things."

"Did you tell Christopher?"

"No. Did he say I did?"

Rosalind paused to think. "He said that you knew. But it was someone else who told him."

Elias frowned. "Who else?"

"He didn't say, but I'm sure it was Lady Anne. She must have used your name to convince him that she was right."

"It sounds rather like something Lady Anne would do, and she might have sensed the change in you herself," Elias murmured. "Perhaps you should ask Lord Christopher to explain himself."

"If he lives long enough," Rosalind muttered. "And if I don't kill him first myself."

Elias departed, and Rhys looked as if he were trying to slip away unnoticed as well. Rosalind cleared her throat. "Rhys? Who exactly are you going to send to aid Elias?" He turned back, but he wouldn't meet her eyes. "Rhys . . ."

He sighed. "That girl we met on the rooftops that night."

"You mean that *Vampire* we *fought*."

"She is a Vampire, that is true, but she holds Christopher's interests close to her heart." Rhys paused. "She is Christopher's half sister. She will want to help him, and I suspect she knows more of his doings than anyone."

"Because she follows him about?"

"Aye. She is very interested in him."

Rosalind studied Rhys's familiar face for a long moment, but he gave nothing else away. Why did everyone keep secrets from her? It seemed that no one needed her help, and that suited her perfectly.

She nodded. "Then go and find her. I hope to God that none of you is killed trying to save that worthless Druid slayer."

"Rosalind, Christopher isn't . . ."

"We can't choose whom we love, Rhys. I've found that out for myself, but I don't have to stand by and watch him destroy himself."

Rhys started to say something, and then kissed her hand and left. Rosalind stared down into the rushes that covered the floor until she could breathe more easily. Her life felt like a series of terrible knots in a skein of silk and she had no idea how to untangle even one of them.

Chapter 23

In the semidarkness of the hazy summer evening, Christopher walked slowly down to the stables and took the time to appreciate his surroundings, to smell the flowers and to be thankful he was still alive. Every sensation seemed clearer and more distinct, as if his mind was desperately trying to catalogue everything he would soon lose.

He mounted his horse and said good-bye to Roper, who muttered a begrudging reply. He hoped his manservant would be pleased with the bequest he had left him in his will. He doubted anything would really make Roper happy, but he had done his best to safeguard the man's future.

It seemed to take no time at all to reach the crypt of St. Bethesda's Church. He vaguely wondered how all the members of the Mithras Cult would fit in such a small space. But he didn't have to worry about that. All he had to do was comport himself well enough to die with dignity. He took another deep breath and began to pray. He prayed for Rosalind and their child, for Rhys and Elias, for the king and for all those who had touched his complicated but mercifully short life.

The last of the sunlight disappeared behind the church

and he was plunged into darkness. It seemed a fitting moment to open the door into the crypt and face his destiny. As Christopher stepped inside, the blaze of candlelight momentarily blinded him. Someone touched his arm and he turned to find Sir Marcus Flavian at his elbow.

"Good evening, Lord Christopher."

"Good evening, Sir Marcus." Marcus looked far too jovial for such a solemn occasion. But then he was probably busy anticipating his rise to power and the fall of Christopher's uncle.

"Are you ready, my lord?"

Christopher shrugged. "I suppose there is no other answer but yes, is there?"

Marcus's smile set all Christopher's nerves bristling, but he didn't let the other man see it. Marcus guided him through the twisting passages until they were deep inside the crypt. Christopher sensed the weight of the church pressing down on them like a living thing. Eventually, Marcus stopped and placed his hand on a stone tablet carved like a bull's head set in the wall. With a grinding noise, the stonework slid to one side to reveal another darker passageway.

"After you, my lord."

Christopher had little choice but to comply. For all he knew, Marcus might have decided to lead him to his death without a trial at all. As the tunnel narrowed even further, he put his hand out to help him feel the way forward and encountered rough-hewn stone. A light glimmered in the distance, and he made his uncertain way toward it.

He emerged into a small circular space lit by a single burning torch. Ahead of him was an arched door adorned with symbols of the Mithras Cult. He recognized the horns of the bull; Sol Invictus, the sun god; and Mithras rising from the rock. The door was edged with red to represent the spilled blood of sacrifice. Christopher swallowed hard.

Marcus slipped past and opened one of the double doors. He peered inside. "It seems they are ready for us."

"Oh, good," Christopher said.

Marcus only bowed and gestured for Christopher to come forward. It felt as though he had stepped into a vast open space, which was much bigger than he had anticipated. The room was circular and lined with tiers of stone seating rather like a Roman arena. Nearly every seat was occupied by a brown-robed, hooded figure. Christopher estimated there were at least two hundred men there, all ready to pass judgment on him.

At the opposite end of the room sat his uncle, dressed in his red ceremonial robes and bull headdress. He was surrounded by the twelve members of his council. Christopher walked down the steps into the center of the circle, Marcus at his side.

"I bring the accused, Lord Christopher Ellis, to you, Pater Heliodromus," Marcus said, his voice echoing around the space.

Edward rose and spread his arms wide. "We ask you, Great God Mithras, Slayer of the Bull, lord of all the ages, to part the mists and let your glory shine through. In your wisdom, show us what fate you desire for this miscreant."

Christopher wanted to smile at that. Mithras had better agree with his uncle, or there would surely be hell to pay. The other members of the cult stood too and echoed his uncle's prayer. Marcus said nothing, but Christopher could feel the tension vibrating through him as they waited.

When the others sat down, Marcus stepped forward. "Pater Heliodromus, I wish to speak."

Edward frowned. "You will have your turn, Marcus Flavian. That has already been agreed."

Marcus took another deliberate step. "I want my turn now, *before* Lord Christopher's trial."

"What is this nonsense?"

"I am challenging your rule. I do not think you fit to preside over the trial of your own nephew."

A buzz of excited whispering circled the room, and Christopher tensed. What game was Marcus playing? And if his uncle was deposed before his trial started, would he get a better hearing or a worse one?

Edward bent to speak to his council and then straightened. "There is no precedent for what you suggest. We will proceed as planned."

"Mayhap we might vote on it first?" Marcus glanced at the packed crowds. "Surely there are enough members here to decide. Who here thinks it well to consider the leadership of the cult first?"

To Christopher's unbelieving gaze, about half the hooded figures raised their right hands and their voices to agree with Marcus. Had his uncle really alienated so many of the cult with his authoritarian dictates about bowing down to Vampire law? It seemed as if he had.

The council conferred again, and Edward got back up. "Very well. We will vote on my leadership first." He nodded at Christopher. "You may stand down until I call you again."

Christopher was quite happy to back away from the center of the circle and sit. Marcus seemed unperturbed, his head held high, his gaze unwavering.

"In pursuit of my claim, I do not wish to put the full membership to a vote, Pater Heliodromus. I wish to challenge you to combat to the death."

The murmurings in the hall grew louder, and Christopher frowned. Surely Marcus had enough support to carry the vote against Edward without invoking that clause? Did he truly believe the only good enemy was a dead enemy?

Edward made a calming gesture to the other members. "We must consult the records about such an audacious challenge."

"There is precedent." Marcus strolled close to the hooded monk who sat guarding the stack of leather-bound books on the low table. Christopher recognized the young but determined face of Brother Cedric. "Show them the documents Brother Samuel found."

There was another lengthy silence while Brother Cedric

showed the council the required passages, and they conferred again. Christopher found himself tapping his foot and almost groaned at his own stupidity. Was he so eager to die that he couldn't wait to see what happened to his uncle first?

Finally Edward addressed the crowd once more. "There are indeed other instances of the leader being challenged to fight rather than be voted out. But when the leader is as old and frail as I am, he may choose a champion to represent him in this fight."

Marcus bowed. "I understand."

Christopher tensed as his uncle's gaze traveled around the hall and finally settled on him. "I choose Lord Christopher Ellis as my champion."

Marcus smiled and Christopher rose slowly to his feet. "If I am not considered worthy to be a cult member, how can I be worthy to fight for you?"

"Perhaps it is a way for you to redeem yourself in Mithras's eyes and find your path to redemption." Christopher couldn't think of anything to say to that and Edward continued. "While the hall is prepared for combat, you may go and arm yourself and say your last prayers."

At Marcus's signal, two men came up behind Christopher and grabbed his arms. His question remained unanswered as he was led away to the back of the hall and thrown into a small room. The door was then locked behind him. A pile of weapons was neatly stacked on the table. It seemed one way or another, he was destined to die that night. Someone had made very sure of that indeed.

"I thought you didn't care what happened to him?" Rhys said as he checked his weapons and peered through the darkness for a glimpse of Elias.

"I don't," Rosalind said. "I only came out to make sure that you are not going to take any foolish risks."

Rhys raised an eyebrow. "I'm no fool, my lady. Walking into a meeting of the full Mithras Cult isn't my idea of bravery at all. It reeks of stupidity. I'm quite happy to let Elias do it."

"And that *other* Vampire."

"That Vampire is called Olivia, and she is now your kin, seeing as you are married to her half brother."

Rosalind huffed. "Some kin are better not acknowledged."

"How so, my lady?"

Rosalind twirled around and saw the dark-haired Vampire sitting on the wall behind her. The Vampire jumped down to the ground and walked up to Rosalind. She smelled of orange blossom. Rosalind tried not to breathe in the familiar scent as a swarm of good and bad memories of Christopher assaulted her. The Vampire seemed to have no such qualms in daintily inhaling.

"You smell like my brother. Is it true that you are his wife?"

"It's true." Rosalind reckoned the Vampire was about her age of twenty or so, but it was hard to tell with Vampires sometimes. "Are you really his half sister?"

"I am." The Vampire sank into a curtsy. "My name is Olivia Del Alonso."

Reluctantly, Rosalind studied the other woman. She was the image of Christopher, her eyes that same startling blue, her long braided hair the black of a crow's wing.

"I know that you cannot like me, but I promise I won't hurt you. You are family now, like Christopher."

"I suppose I should be grateful for that," Rosalind said. "And in return, I will try not to kill you."

Olivia smiled. "You are a very famous hunter, my lady. Rhys has told me tales of your exploits together."

"Has he?" Rosalind glanced across at Rhys, but his attention was fixed on Olivia's face. "Are you really going to help Christopher tonight?"

"Of course. He does not deserve to die." Indignation flushed Olivia's cheeks. "You must feel the same."

Rosalind kept her lips pressed firmly together in the semblance of a smile. She didn't know how she felt about Christopher at this moment. She was still far too angry to allow herself to be reasonable or forgiving.

Elias appeared and greeted Rhys and Rosalind; then his keen gaze shifted to the young Vampire in front of him. "Olivia, we haven't met, but I understand you might be able to help us."

"I shall do my best, Master Warner." Olivia looked serious. "I believe I know where the Mithras Cult holds its meetings."

"Then we had best go and do what we can to save Lord Christopher before it is too late."

Elias turned to Rosalind and kissed her hand. "Don't worry, my lady. I'm sure we will all survive this."

"You can only do your best, Elias. I thank you for even trying." It was hard to get the words out, but it was the best Rosalind could manage. She would never beg for anyone's favor again.

To her surprise, Elias kept hold of her hand. "Despite his faults, your husband is a good man. A man I am proud to consider my friend. If he has hurt you in any way, I am sure there is an explanation for it."

Rosalind stared at Elias, hardly able to believe that the Vampire was able to show far more compassion and understanding for her human husband than she was able to do.

Elias placed his hand on Olivia's throat and they both disappeared, leaving Rosalind staring at Rhys. She rubbed hastily at her eyes. Rhys made a comforting sound and drew her into his arms.

"It's all right, *cariad*. They'll all be safe."

"But I told you I didn't care, and by all that is holy, I do!"

Rhys kissed the top of her head. "You didn't need to tell me anything. I know you love Christopher. Why else would you feel such anger for him if you didn't?"

Rosalind couldn't answer him, but at least it gave her hope. She raised her head. "While they are busy trying to save Christopher, perhaps we should meet later and hunt down the Boleyns and their allies?"

Rhys frowned and let his gaze travel down to her stomach. "Are you sure you want to do that?"

Rosalind stamped her foot. "This is exactly why I didn't want you and Christopher to know I was breeding. I *knew* you wouldn't let me fight." She raised her chin. "I want to fight. I need to do something. If you refuse to accompany me, I'll just go out by myself."

Rhys grunted something uncomplimentary in Welsh. "All right, I'll come with you."

Rosalind managed a smile. "Thank you, my friend."

"Just don't expect me to explain why I let you hunt Vampires to his lordship when he returns."

His quiet confidence helped to settle her nerves more than he would ever know. "But, luckily, you are no longer responsible for my behavior, Rhys. My husband is."

"Exactly, and if he were here now, he'd probably put you over his knee."

"But he is not, so for once I shall do as I please." She reached for his hand. "Let's hunt. One last time."

Rhys nodded, his gaze full of understanding that made tears prick at the back of her eyes. "I've already said I'd come with you. I'll meet you back here at midnight."

Marcus unlocked the door and entered the small room where Christopher was reluctantly residing. He looked remarkably pleased with himself.

"Ellis, we need to compare weapons and make sure we are evenly matched."

Christopher laid his sword and dagger on the table. "Shouldn't someone impartial do that?"

Marcus shrugged. "They are all busy and they trust me."

"Which is rather foolish of them." Christopher contemplated the other man. "Did you plan this together, you and my uncle?"

"Plan what, Ellis?"

"This plot to annihilate me at all costs?"

"I have always believed in making certain my enemies perish."

"And I am your enemy?"

"You betrayed your brethren with that Vampire slayer."

Christopher shook his head. "Then your clumsy attempts to persuade me to betray my uncle were simply to lure me to my death?"

Marcus looked unrepentant. "In truth, I care not how I achieve my aim of ruling the cult and bringing it back to its true purpose: killing Druids, not kissing the Vampire Council's feet. You, my friend, are expendable."

"Did you know my uncle would choose me to fight for him?"

"I didn't, but I hoped he would. I believe at this point he is probably keener to see me die than you."

"And even if I kill you in combat, he can still dispose of me at my trial. How convenient."

Marcus smiled. "It seems you cannot win, Ellis, so let's make a bargain. Let me defeat you, and I promise I'll kill your uncle as soon as I am leader of the cult."

Christopher sat down on the only bench and gazed up at Marcus. "And if I'm dead, how am I supposed to know if you keep your word? Do you think I am a fool?"

Something shifted in Marcus's gaze and Christopher straightened. "It was you who killed Brother Samuel, wasn't it? To stop him from giving me the information that might've helped get me out of this trial."

"I killed him, yes, but I didn't get the information. Something, or someone, had already ripped out the page."

"So you murdered Brother Samuel, an old, frail, innocent monk, to make sure he couldn't tell me what it said."

"I told you, I am a careful man."

The door opened and Edward appeared. Marcus ignored the older man and walked past him. "Think on my offer, and let me know what you wish to do."

Edward frowned. "What did he want?"

"To compare weapons." Christopher picked up his dagger and examined it closely. "So I am to be your champion, Uncle."

"It seemed fitting, nephew. It gives you a chance to leave this world defending your true beliefs."

"You mean defending *your* beliefs. Lies I no longer accept."

Edward sat down and faced Christopher. "I cannot allow Marcus Flavian to take over now. I have come too close to achieving my desires."

"Again, it is all about what you want, isn't it? Not what is meet for the cult. Why do you think so many of the brethren voted against you? They do not want this alliance with the Vampires any more than I do. Can't you see that?"

"You do not understand. If we ally with the Vampires, we will be safe."

Christopher laughed. "You mean when the Vampire Council and Lady Anne Boleyn take over the whole kingdom? That will never happen. Lady Anne cares only about herself. She has no intention of sharing power with the Council, let alone with you."

"You lie."

"Why would I lie, especially now, when my life can be measured in scant moments rather than in years? Anne told me so herself. She has already made a bargain with the Druids. Our enemy has become her ally. I'll swear on it."

Edward visibly paled. "She has not! She promised me that if I brought the Mithras Cult to her aid, she would give me immortal life."

Ah, so *that* was it. Anne had offered a dying man a new version of salvation. One that meant he sacrificed his immortal soul, but gained power and an endless lifetime to use it.

"She will not be helping you now. She has become so arrogant that she believes she can rule the king and the country alone." Christopher walked up to his uncle. "So it seems your plans are doomed to failure."

"Not if you defeat Marcus Flavian."

"Why should I want to do that?"

"So that I can retain my power over the cult!"

"And what good does that do me? You're still going to ensure my death by trial." Christopher strode across to the door and banged on it. "No, I think I'll go with Marcus Flavian's suggestion, and let him kill me, so that he can depose you and have you quietly murdered afterward."

Edward gaped at him as if he couldn't catch his breath. The door swung open, and Christopher helped Edward up and guided him firmly through it. "Now, if you would leave me alone to say my last prayers, I would be most grateful."

He slammed the door himself, and walked back into the center of the room. He went down on his knees and stared at the stone cross carved into a niche on the wall opposite him. What a way to end his life, caught between the ambitious jaws of other men. He wanted to laugh and smash his fists against the stone just to feel something except this spreading numbness and sense of unreality.

Something shimmered and danced before his eyes and he struggled to his feet. Elias appeared in front of him, followed by the female Vampire Olivia, who held her finger to her lips. She went to the door and waved her hand over it before returning to Elias's side.

"No one will get in for a little while, Master Warner."

"Thank you, my lady." Elias smiled at Christopher. "My lord, are you well? You look a little shaken."

"As would you if you'd been put in an impossible situation."

"How so?" Elias asked as calmly as if Christopher were pondering which doublet to wear.

"My uncle has been challenged as cult leader by Sir Marcus Flavian, and has chosen me to be his champion in the fight to the death."

Elias frowned. "But aren't you supposed to be facing a trial?"

"*That* will only happen if I defeat Marcus." Christopher

let out a laugh. "Then my uncle can try me for my crimes and get a second chance to kill me."

"I did not know Marcus Flavian intended to overthrow your uncle."

"Marcus doesn't like my uncle's servility to the Vampire Council. He feels the cult has strayed from its old Druid-killing ways."

Olivia had taken the seat beside Christopher and now she poked him. "Marcus Flavian is a bad man."

"I know that, but so is my uncle, and both of them are determined to kill me."

Elias held up his hand. "This makes things a little more complicated, but the good news is Lady Olivia found some information that will preclude your trial. That is why we are here."

Christopher looked at Olivia in astonishment. "Was it you who stopped Marcus from stealing the parchment from Brother Samuel?"

Olivia bit her lip. "I managed only to get the document. I got there an instant too late to stop him from killing the old man. I am sorry about that."

Briefly Christopher met her familiar blue gaze. It was like looking in the mirror. "You did your best. I appreciate it, but how can this information help me?"

Olivia handed him a rolled-up piece of parchment. "It clearly states that no man of impure blood can *ever* be enrolled in the Mithras Cult." She glanced at Elias. "I know nothing about this Cult. I took the parchment because I knew the murderer wanted it. I didn't realize the information was important until Master Warner explained it to me."

"It means that because I have Vampire blood, I should never have been allowed into the cult in the first place. My uncle surely knew that, and yet he allowed me to join to bend me to his will."

"So if you show this parchment to the jury, they cannot convict you. They have no jurisdiction over you, as you are not purebred."

Christopher stowed the parchment inside his doublet and heaved a sigh before looking up at his two rescuers. "Thank you. An hour ago I would've assumed this would clear my name, and I would be free. But now . . ."

"You have to fight Marcus and beat him, and then face down your uncle," Elias said firmly.

"Is that all?" Christopher said and rose to his feet. "Then I suppose I'd better get on with it."

"I will find a way to help you," Olivia said.

Christopher turned to her and kissed her gently on the forehead. "Do not put yourself in any danger for me. I know neither of you can be comfortable in a church. I want you to survive this. Do you understand?"

"I'm a Vampire, brother. Of course I will survive."

Christopher shook Elias's hand. "I owe you so much."

Elias met his gaze head-on. "I have come to value your . . . humanity, my lord, and your friendship." Elias sounded faintly puzzled by his own admission, and Christopher fought an unexpected smile. "I do not wish to see you die quite yet."

"Then I will do my best not to."

Christopher drew in a big gulp of air. He felt as if nothing else could hurt him. His destiny was in the hands of God and his Vampire allies. All he could do was fight to stay alive, and suddenly he wanted to live. His child needed him. The force of it, the pure joy of it slammed through him, making him aware that while there was still a sliver of a chance to keep him alive, he would never ever give up.

Chapter 24

Christopher buckled on his sword and slid his dagger into its sheath. Elias and Olivia had disappeared, leaving him alone to contemplate his opponent. Marcus was a ferocious fighter, but at least Christopher knew him well. Like any man, Marcus had his weaknesses, and Christopher intended to exploit them all. Of course, Marcus knew his weaknesses too, but then he had a Vampire on his side.

Marcus barged back into the room, his head high, confidence brimming from every rippling muscle. "Are you ready, Ellis?"

"I'm ready," Christopher replied.

Marcus gave him a sidelong glance. "And are you prepared to die easily? If you agree, I'll make it as painless as possible."

Christopher inclined his head an inch. "That is very generous of you, but I do not care to die on the off chance that you might keep your promise and kill my uncle. You haven't proved very trustworthy, have you?"

A dull red flush crept up Marcus's thick neck and his face darkened. "You are a fool, Ellis. I'll enjoy dismembering you even more now. I'll show no mercy, even if you beg."

Christopher ignored him and marched forward into the circular space that would serve as their battlefield. His feet sank into sawdust and sand. Someone had obviously decided that covering up the flagstones would make cleaning up the blood much easier. He wondered if it was his uncle. He was such a conscientious man.

Marcus drew up beside him, his sword already out of its scabbard. Edward, now robed in his full regalia, the bull's-head mask pulled down low over his forehead, stood and held up his hands.

"Oh, Great God Mithras. Send your favor onto one of these men. Prove the righteousness of my cause!"

There was some muttering at such a one-sided prayer, but it soon subsided. Marcus stepped back a sword's length and bowed to Christopher. "May the best man win."

Christopher bowed as well. "I will, because unlike you and my uncle, I have right on my side, not the lust for personal power."

Marcus grunted and lunged at Christopher, his right arm swinging wide like a man scything a field of corn. Christopher easily avoided the heavy-handed blow, and struck back, his sword glancing off the leather of Marcus's jerkin. Marcus parried again, and this time Christopher caught the edge of the blow on the side of his sword. He felt the dull ache of it reverberate up his arm.

He stepped back and studied his opponent's wild blond hair and narrowed eyes. Marcus looked like the Viking berserkers he was descended from. But men in the grip of bloodlust could make mistakes and commit acts of pure folly. That was why they rarely survived for long. And Marcus had no idea how much sword practice Christopher had put in killing Vampires over the past year.

Christopher settled back to play the dangerous game of taunting a berserker, to force him into an error, to make his temper boil over and forget reason.

For a little while, there was nothing in Christopher's world but the grunts of effort Marcus made and his answering parries, the slide of their feet in the sand and the collective reaction of their audience. Blood trickled down Christopher's left arm from one of Marcus's lucky thrusts, but he didn't have time to staunch the flow.

Marcus advanced again and Christopher braced himself for another brutal attack. His breath hissed out, and Marcus caught him off-balance, his sword raised at an awkward angle, his feet struggling to maintain his stance. The shock of the blow made him bite his tongue, but he still pushed back, the tip of his blade nicking the underside of Marcus's arm and drawing a sudden flash of red.

"Christopher, call his blood to you."

For a second, Christopher almost faltered, until he realized it was Olivia speaking to him in his head. He backed off and circled his opponent again, using the small reprieve to formulate his reply.

"I don't know how to do that."

"I know. If you want to win, let me do it through you. This man does not deserve to live."

Christopher ducked to avoid a blow that would've separated his head from his body and managed to shove Marcus back again. He was aware that his strength was waning, while Marcus seemed unstoppable.

"Christopher. Let me help you!"

Was it honorable to accept her help? He was no longer sure if he cared. Marcus had killed an innocent monk and deserved a long sojourn in hell. He opened his mind to Olivia and allowed her dark magic to sweep through him and outward. In an instant, Marcus's expression changed as the cut on his upper arm began to bleed profusely.

Marcus shifted his bloody grip on his sword and groaned.

Christopher pressed his advantage, swung his blade hard and fast at Marcus's chest, saw the man's slow reaction and met, not the answering bite of a sword, but cloth, and skin, and finally jarring bone. He pulled back and watched Marcus fall to his knees, blood pouring now from the dual wounds, his eyes wide and stunned, and his sword falling from his hand into the sand of the arena.

Finally, Marcus toppled forward and went still. Christopher dropped to one knee and pushed him onto his back. He checked the man's lifeless eyes and felt for his heart, which was mercifully stilled. Christopher stood and sheathed his sword, then walked forward to the Mithras Cult council. He managed to bow.

"I have won, Pater Heliodromus. You are safe."

Edward bowed back, his expression triumphant. "We thank you. Please take a moment to clean yourself up for your trial."

Christopher nodded at the council and retreated to the same room where they had confined him earlier. After a little while, a man brought him a bowl of water, some coarse soap, and a rag. Christopher remained sitting on the bench, his hands clasped around the hilt of his bloodied sword and his mind in turmoil.

He sensed a presence in the room and inhaled the now-familiar scent of orange blossom. Olivia crouched down by his side, her nostrils flaring as she breathed in the smell of his and Marcus's blood. Christopher leaned his sword against the bench, got to his feet, and started to wash his hands. He wondered if this was how Judas Iscariot had felt after he had betrayed his friend and savior.

"You did not betray anyone, Christopher. Marcus wanted to kill you and you were defending yourself."

Startled, Christopher glanced up at Olivia, who held the washcloth out to him. He'd forgotten he'd given her access to his thoughts. He tried to shut the link down as quickly as possible before she settled in.

"I should have defeated him honorably."

Olivia sniffed. "You did. I hardly had to do anything to make matters worse. He was already bleeding to death when you struck that second blow."

Christopher wanted to believe that quite desperately. But he'd done what was necessary. Perhaps it was wrong to cavil at the means of achieving it. He let out a slow breath as the scent of blood mingled with lye soap caught in his throat. Still too close to the link with Olivia, the blood enticed him and made him hunger for more . . .

He shook off the sensation and concentrated on cleaning his skin. Olivia prodded his shoulder and he hissed out a curse. "You are still bleeding. Let me see."

"If you promise you'll not suck me dry."

She made a face at him and helped him out of his heavy jerkin and pulled up his sleeve. She untied the laces of his black undershirt to reveal his shoulder and the top of his arm. "You'll need to bind this."

He handed her his dagger, watching in some bemusement while she ripped off a strip of fabric from the hem of his undershirt and made a competent job of washing and binding his wounded left arm.

Just as he was about to commend her skill, she put her finger, stained with his blood, into her mouth. He caught her wrist. "I didn't give you leave to feast on my blood. What are you doing?"

"I'm just making sure I have your taste fresh in my mind. I know we are kin, but if anything goes wrong, this will help me find you more quickly."

He grunted. "What else can go wrong?"

"Nothing, I am sure. Now you just need to deal with your uncle. Let's hope that his gratitude for your saving his life will make him more amenable."

Christopher struggled to assemble his thoughts through the tug of pain that throbbed through his upper arm. "I don't know about that. He hates me."

Olivia stared at him. "But he is your kin."

"And I am contaminated with Vampire blood."

She rose to her feet and patted his good shoulder. "I am glad that you are who you are. I am proud to call you kin."

He managed to smile back, and then she suddenly disappeared, leaving the bloodied cloth she'd been holding to flutter to the ground. The door opened and his uncle appeared. Christopher stayed where he was and started to clean Marcus's blood off his sword.

Edward studied him for a long moment. "I'd rather hoped you would not survive."

"Thank you."

Edward sighed. "Because now I have to preside over your trial . . . and execution."

"How terrible for you."

"There is no need for levity, nephew. You are accused of the most heinous of crimes. I cannot be seen to be lenient toward you simply because you are my nephew and you just saved my life."

Christopher retied the loose neck of his black undershirt and grabbed for his heavy leather jerkin. It was an effort to get it on when his left shoulder hurt like the devil. "Shall we not compromise?"

"How so?"

"Just let me go free. I promise never to darken the doors of the Mithras Cult again."

"That will not suffice, Christopher."

"Are you sure about that? Because otherwise I must go into court and defend myself to the best of my ability, and you might not like the results."

Edward's smile was chilling. "You will not prevail, nephew. Whatever puny arguments you advance, you *will* die. Resign yourself to your fate, and I will make sure your death is quick and merciful."

Christopher got to his feet and steadied himself against the comforting bulk of the table. "Then let us go ahead."

He followed his uncle out into the main chamber for the third and hopefully final appearance before the cult. He had no idea what time it was in the outside world, and whether he had managed to live another day or was still trapped in the last disastrous one. It didn't matter now. He had one last chance to change his future, and he had to make it pay off.

*   *   *

As the clock struck twelve, Rosalind changed into her boy's clothes and headed down to the stable yard to meet Rhys. He was already there, his usually calm face drawn and tense.

"Has there been any word of Olivia and Elias?" Rosalind asked him.

"None," Rhys replied. "I am starting to worry."

Silently Rosalind considered Rhys. Surely they should know something by now. She tightened her grip on her dagger. Christopher couldn't be dead. She would know. It would feel as if she had lost half her soul.

"Elias and Olivia will come back, I'm sure of it. They are immortal, after all." But Christopher isn't, she didn't have to add. She started to walk out toward the apple orchard to begin her usual patrol.

Rhys fell into step beside her. "I'm sorry, *cariad*."

She wouldn't look at him, but she did manage to frame a reply. "There is nothing to be sorry about. Christopher is already dead to me. What he did to me—"

Rhys stopped walking and gripped her shoulder. "You have a right to be angry, Rosalind, but—"

"But what? Christopher has treated me abysmally, and I could not force my way into a meeting of the very men who want to kill me in order to save him from himself! Perhaps if he had told me what was going on, we might not have reached this point."

"Men think differently about these things. Perhaps he thought he was protecting you."

"That would indeed be quite like him." Rosalind stared out into the darkness, her senses kicking up as she smelled Vampire. "But he promised me the truth."

"And he told you many times that he had also made vows to protect others."

"Oh, for goodness' sake, Rhys. Why are you defending him?"

"Because you cannot, and I think it is tearing you apart," he said softly.

Tears blurred her vision, and she angrily pushed them away. "Don't say that. Don't make me want to give in to these feelings again."

"Sometimes we have to give in, Rosalind. It's called loving someone else more than we love ourselves. I had to give you up. I thought I'd never survive it, but I did."

"Then you should understand why I am giving Christopher Ellis up, for good this time."

He chuckled. "You can't. That's the problem. He is part of you. If you could forget him, you would've done it a long time ago. As you told me, Rosalind, we can't choose who we love. And now you are married to him, for better or worse."

Rosalind drew her dagger as the smell of Vampire grew stronger. "I have no time for this now, Rhys. There are Vampires about."

He tensed as a lone figure broke through the trees and strolled toward them, his hands raised in the air. To Rosalind, the young man smelled like a vole, an earthy feral scent that curdled her stomach.

"What do you want?" Rosalind asked, her dagger on display, even if his wasn't.

"I have a message for you." The man bowed. "Your presence is required at the Druid stone circle."

"Why would a Vampire be entrusted with such a message?" Rhys said.

"I know not. I was simply told to tell you Master Warner needs your help, and that if you wish to save him, you should go to the circle."

"Told by whom?"

"Lord George Boleyn, Viscount Rochford."

Rosalind and Rhys exchanged a glance before bidding the Vampire a curt good-bye. Rhys waited until the man had disappeared into the trees before turning to Rosalind.

"Do you think it is a trap?"

"I'm sure it is, but if Elias is in danger, we cannot leave him there with George."

Rhys made a face. "Are you sure about that?"

"Elias has been more than helpful to us."

"For his own good reasons."

"That is true. But I believe he has come to think of us as his friends and, as his friends, we are going to help him."

Rhys sighed. "I knew you were going to say that. But how did Elias end up with George if he was supposed to be saving Lord Christopher?"

"That is another good question." Rosalind started to walk back toward the stables, her stomach churning. "Perhaps when we save Elias, he will be able to give us some answers."

Christopher waited in the center of the newly cleaned circle as his uncle and the council filed in. Since defeating Marcus, he'd lost all sense of fear and was filled with a calm certainty that his cause was right and that the Mithras Cult members would have to recognize it.

Edward stood and held his hands upward. "By the power vested in me by the holy God Mithras, I call this court to order. Before us stands a man accused of the most hideous crime of aiding and abetting our enemies, the Druids."

A low rumbling filled the space, but Christopher didn't let it worry him.

His uncle continued. "The keeper of the Mithras Cult records will defend us, while the accused has decided to defend himself. Brother Cedric, please read out the charge."

Brother Cedric stood and cast an apologetic glance at Christopher before clearing his throat. "Lord Christopher Ellis is charged with allying himself to Lady Rosalind Llewellyn, a member of one of the highest-ranking Druid families in the kingdom. Can you deny that association, Lord Christopher?"

"I cannot. The king forced me to become betrothed to Lady Rosalind, and all my efforts to break that betrothal have been fruitless. What is curious is that my family has made no such efforts to change the king's mind."

Brother Cedric frowned. "Are you suggesting that this association was somehow sanctioned by the cult, Lord Christopher?"

Christopher met his uncle's furious gaze. "Indeed I am. Ask my uncle."

"I am not on trial, here," Edward snapped. "I do not need to answer to anyone."

"The facts are the facts. This 'association' began when you commanded me to swive Rosalind Llewellyn, and despite being stripped of full membership and banned from our sacred ceremonies, I did your bidding. Surely I am to be commended rather than condemned?"

Christopher walked over to Brother Cedric. "You must have a record of my name being struck from the rolls about six years ago. Would you like to confirm that for the council?"

Brother Cedric cleared his throat and read from the book of minutes. "Written this fifth day of November, fifteen hundred and twenty-five. For his refusal to perform his duties, from this day forth, Christopher Ellis will no longer be considered a full member of the cult. Signed by the current Pater Heliodromus."

Christopher nodded as Brother Cedric passed the book up to the council. "As you see, I am not a full member of the Mithras Cult and thus subject to your harshest rules."

Brother Cedric put the book down. "He does have a valid point, Pater Heliodromus."

Edward glared at Christopher. "He is still bound by the sacred vows he took. Nothing can overthrow those."

"Nothing, Uncle?" Christopher returned Edward's stare with good measure. "If you refuse to acknowledge my truth, I have more evidence to share with you." He had no regrets now. He'd given his uncle the opportunity to step down gracefully and set him free, but he'd chosen not to. Now he had no compunction in bringing his uncle down with him.

Christopher withdrew the much-folded piece of parchment that Olivia had given him from his pocket. He carefully spread it out. "This parchment also comes from the archives. It states that only those who are *pure of blood* may be inducted into the Mithras Cult. Is that not so?"

As he passed the parchment to Brother Cedric for verification, he saw the first faint flash of alarm on his uncle's face. "What relevance does this have to the charges?"

"All the relevance in the world, seeing as you perjured yourself to induct me into the cult."

A gasp ran around the assembled members, followed by a buzz of conversation that refused to die away.

"What are you suggesting?"

"That I am not pure-blooded." Christopher let his gaze rove over the assembled members. "Most of you already suspected that. Rumors about my 'mixed' blood have circulated for years, and they are indeed true."

Edward stood up. "You have no proof of such a thing."

"Actually, I do." Christopher snapped his fingers, and Olivia materialized beside him. Her likeness to him was unmistakable, her features set in the same uncompromising lines as he suspected his were. "May I introduce my half sister? As you might have noticed, she is a Vampire."

Shouts and shocked cries rained down from the benches and Edward struggled to restore order, his face white, his voice ineffectual.

Christopher turned to the monk. "Brother Cedric? Do you believe I have just cause to nullify this trial?"

"I do, my lord. You are unfit to even stand in front of this court." Brother Cedric raised his voice. "All those in favor of calling a mistrial say 'Aye.'" The resounding roar of agreement made both him and Christopher wince.

Edward tried to shout above the racket. "You may not make this decision. That is up to the council after you have voted!"

A chorus of boos greeted his words, and shouts of "Vampire lover" and "betrayer." Edward sat back down, his face ashen and his hands shaking.

Brother Cedric nudged Christopher. "May I suggest you leave rather quickly, my lord? I do not think the membership are very pleased to have you or your sister in their midst. I would rather they expended their anger on your uncle rather than on yourself. I doubt he will survive this added blow to his authority."

Christopher shook Brother Cedric's hand. "Thank you, Brother."

"Thank you for finding Brother Samuel's killer and bringing him to justice. Now go, and let your uncle deal with the turmoil he has created."

Christopher started for the door, but Olivia tugged urgently on his sleeve. "This way," she said. "We must hurry." When he turned to her, she touched his throat, and everything blurred into a seamless motion that made him want to puke. He landed in soft grass and stayed down until the dizziness abated. He needed time to reflect on what had just happened and craved his bed like his next breath.

Olivia crouched down beside him, her face full of concern. "Christopher? Are you all right? We have to help Elias. He is in danger."

Christopher raised his head and met her worried blue gaze. He felt as weak as a newborn lamb, but he had to help Elias. He owed the man his life. He struggled to his feet and let Olivia steady him.

"Where is he?"

"At the Druid stone circle. I cannot go there alone." She shivered. "I'm not sure how Elias got in there, or why he would choose such a place."

"I can take you." Christopher recognized the oak trees rimming the edge of the valley that concealed the stone circle. "Follow me."

Chapter 25

Rosalind and Rhys tied up their horses and crept down the hillside toward the stone circle. Although it was dark, the moon was bright, and it was possible to see quite clearly. Rhys led the way, his bigger body making a path for Rosalind through the dry long grass and trailing branches.

"There are numerous Vampires around the boundary of the stone circle," Rosalind whispered. "They probably can't get inside, but they are waiting for us."

"How many?" Rhys murmured.

"At least a dozen, I think, and all quite young by their scent. Not the Boleyns either."

"Of course not. They prefer to get others to do their dirty work. Let's split up and take as many as we can from either side."

Rosalind nodded, and crept toward the right of the circle. She spotted the first Vampire, his back to her as he looked down on the dull upright stones. It took but a moment to creep up behind the young man and stab him through the heart, not much longer for her to decapitate him.

She kept moving, her senses alert as she tried to pinpoint her next victim. Something smelling of daisies crashed into her from the side and Rosalind went down, grabbing at the Vampire's arm and deflecting the death blow to her heart. She shoved her other hand into the Vampire's long hair and, as they rolled down the incline, she wrenched back the female's head to expose her throat and slashed at it.

By the time they reached the bottom of the slope, she was straddling the Vampire, and was busy avoiding the woman's snapping fangs. Behind her, she heard a commotion and caught the scent of fresh blood. She tried not to let it distract her. If another assailant came up on her now, there was little she could do about it.

With all her strength, she shoved the Vampire's head to one side, heard the cracking of bone, and saw the life leave the female's eyes. Breathing heavily, Rosalind stabbed the creature through the heart and then used her sword to lop off the head. The scent of orange blossom surrounded her and she looked up to see Olivia in front of her.

"Get away from me, Vampire," Rosalind hissed. "I am not in the mood to be merciful."

"Neither are we."

Rosalind blinked as Christopher appeared behind Olivia, wiping his bloodied dagger on his buckskin-clad thigh. Seeing them side by side left Rosalind in no doubt of their close relationship. "What are you doing here?"

"The same as you, I suspect. Trying to save Elias."

Rosalind got to her feet and brushed at her knees. She couldn't look at Christopher and prayed he wouldn't touch her. At this precise moment, she wasn't quite sure if she would stab him or kiss him. It was probably best to follow his lead and deal with the current problem rather than give in to the seething current of her emotions.

"All we know is that George has him, and that we were to meet in the stone circle."

"*George*?" Christopher asked. "Not Anne? Why in God's name would George venture into a Druid stone circle?"

"Mayhap George did it to taunt us. The circle isn't as

dangerous or difficult to enter between festivals." Rosalind kept her gaze on Olivia, who was staring back at her. "George is a fool. Anne would never provoke a Vampire of Elias's age."

"We all know that," Christopher muttered. "Now, how are we going to get Elias out of his clutches?"

Rosalind gathered her strength and looked at him. "*You* don't need to do anything, my lord. Rhys and I will take care of it."

She gasped as Christopher grabbed hold of her leather jerkin and yanked her up so that they were nose to nose. He looked as if he had gone through hell, his blue eyes ravaged, his mouth a hard line. "Rosalind, I know you think you hate me, but please, let us put aside our feelings for the moment and concentrate on saving Elias."

She glared into his narrowed eyes. "We do not need you. Go away and take your little sister with you."

Christopher dropped her so abruptly she stumbled backward. He spoke to someone behind him. "Oh, there you are. Mayhap you can talk some sense into my lady. What can Olivia and I do to help?"

Rhys strode forward, sheathing his sword, his face breaking into a smile when he saw Christopher and Olivia. "My lord, my lady, you survived!"

Christopher thumped Rhys on the shoulder. "I'll tell you about it later. Now, how can we save Elias?"

Rosalind turned away from them all, and pretended to watch the trees for Vampires. The injustice of it burned in her gut. It seemed everyone had forgotten what Christopher had done, except her. Mayhap they could rescue Elias without her help as well. She started back up the hill, and Rhys blocked her path.

"Where are you going, my lady?"

She wouldn't look at him. "You have this all well in hand, Rhys. You scarcely need my help."

"What?" He held out his hand. "I need you to go into the stone circle with me."

"Why not take Lord Christopher? I'm sure he'll be far more useful than I will ever be."

Rhys's sigh of exasperation made her want to bolt, but suddenly a black leather doublet loomed out of the darkness. She inhaled the scent of blood, Christopher's and someone else's. He had been injured. Even through both their efforts to protect their minds, she could feel his pain.

"My lady, please." Christopher spoke softly. "I realize you are upset, but surely Elias deserves our help."

"Upset? Why on earth would you think that, my lord?"

A muscle tightened in his jaw but, for once, he didn't answer her. He just kept staring until she wanted to squirm like a worm on a hook.

She bit down on her lower lip and turned her gaze away, refused the subtle plea emanating from his mind as well. He tried to take her hand, and she snatched it back. She turned to Rhys instead.

"All right. I will help. Tell me what you want me to do."

Rhys exhaled and put his arm around her shoulders. "Just come with me into the inner circle. We'll do our best to bargain with George while Olivia and Christopher see off any Vampires who threaten us."

"How can we trust them to kill their own kind?" Her words sounded cold even to her own ears, and Christopher cursed under his breath. "My lord has not proven very reliable in such circumstances before."

Christopher swung around, his expression lethal. "Rosalind!" The anger in his voice made her glad. He *should* feel hurt, feel shame, feel as bereft and betrayed as she did.

"Not now, my lord." Rhys shoved Christopher away, and stood between them, one hand on Rosalind's shoulder. "Let's concentrate on getting Elias, shall we, and leave the rest for later?"

Rosalind shrugged off his hand and started toward the circle, Rhys just behind her. She didn't look to see what Christopher and his half sister were doing. She couldn't bear to.

Multiple scents drifted over her, and she spun around to warn her companions just before half a dozen Vampires exploded from the trees. It was all chaos then, a matter of stabbing and hacking, of avoiding snapping fangs and claw-like fingernails—of merely surviving. She found herself fighting back-to-back with Christopher, both of them moving away from the main fight, surrounded by four Vampires intent on killing them.

She fought on until her arm was like lead, and there was only one opponent left attacking Christopher. His face was pale, and he looked exhausted. Suddenly he stumbled and left himself open to a killing blow. Without thinking, she lunged forward to save him, and met the force of the blade with her own. Christopher went down as the Vampire's lifeless corpse fell beside him.

In the sudden deathly quiet, Rosalind waited for Christopher to rise, but he didn't. After a quick glance around, she crouched down and crawled over the Vampire's body to where Christopher lay. He was on his left side and was cursing like a fiend. She stood and used the toe of her boot to roll him onto his back.

He gasped and grabbed at his left shoulder, his face in the moonlight now a sickly green. Rosalind felt a flutter of fear at his condition. She wanted to take him in her arms and hold him. How could she be so pathetic? She swallowed down her concern. "Can you get up?"

He set his jaw. "I'm fine. I just—need a moment. Go back—to whatever you were doing."

She didn't waste another second on him, but turned on her heel and strode back toward Rhys. Christopher caught up to her, but she ignored the heaviness of his breathing and the fresh undercurrent of pain radiating from him.

"You were going to leave me there?"

She kept her gaze on Rhys. "You said you were fine, and you definitely don't need me for anything really, do you?"

He groaned. "Are you going to take these little jabs at

me all night? I'm already bleeding enough. Can't you see that?"

She forced herself to face him and smile. "No. Now leave me alone."

He grabbed her arm. "You are still my wife, and I swear by all that is holy that there will be a reckoning between us."

"So you say. But we both know that your word is worthless, don't we?"

All the good humor was stripped from his expression to reveal the hard steel of the man beneath. "Rosalind, I've escaped death twice tonight, and for what? To face you in this humor?"

"I do not know, my lord. I am simply trying to save my friend. A man who has been more loyal and honest than you have ever been."

"I can see it is pointless trying to reason with you," Christopher snarled. "Perhaps you will be more amenable after we have sorted out this muddle."

"I doubt it."

He bared his teeth in a humorless smile. "Then I'll have to find a way to persuade you to listen to me, won't I, *wife*?"

"You can certainly try, but you promised never to bother me again if I agreed to this sham of a marriage."

"You have that wrong, my lady. You told *me* you never wanted to see me again. I certainly didn't agree to that."

Rhys cleared his throat. "Lady Rosalind? Are you ready to come with me to the stone circle?"

"Indeed, I am, Rhys." Rosalind moved sharply away from Christopher. Verily, at that moment, to avoid Christopher's furious, heated gaze, she would have braved Anne Boleyn's private chambers.

"We need to determine what George wants," Rhys said. "I've asked Olivia to seek out Lady Anne, and make her aware of what her brother is doing."

"You are trying to make things *worse*?" Christopher asked.

"No, I don't think Anne has orchestrated this, do you? She cannot want us to die. We are bound to her by oath *and* she cannot get the potion if she kills us."

"That is true," Rosalind said, nodding. "Perhaps she will be able to stop George."

"Let's hope someone can stop him. He is an arrogant fool." Rhys took her hand and walked through into the inner circle. Rosalind shivered as her gods took note of her presence, and she sensed their alarm and concern.

"How did George get in here?" she whispered to Rhys.

"Elias has been here before, remember? Perhaps that's why the gods let them through."

Rosalind spotted two figures by the central altar and took a deep breath. "I see them."

"So do I. Let's approach with great caution."

George leaned against the stone altar where Elias lay. George glowed vividly like a bird in full plumage in red satin with gold embroidery. Elias's face was as pale as his gray silk doublet. A thin trickle of blood from a puncture wound on Elias's throat marked a winding passage down the stone to the ground. Elias's eyes were closed, but at least he was breathing.

"Ah, I see your rescuers have arrived," George said. "I hoped you would be killed trying to get to me, but it seems you survived despite the odds."

Rosalind met his gaze. "What do you want, George?"

Anger flickered in George's dark eyes. "To make my 'sister' suffer."

"And what does that have to do with us?"

"You have conspired with her to ruin me. You have made sure that Anne has turned against me, and so you will all suffer."

"We have done nothing. If Anne no longer treats you with the respect you deserve, you should take the matter up with her. We are merely a small irritant, and far beneath your notice."

George pointed a shaking finger at Rosalind. "No! It all

went wrong when you turned up. It must be your fault. She made a bargain with you, a filthy Druid, a Vampire slayer!"

"She used us as she used you, can you not see that?" Rosalind felt pressure in her mind, though whether it was from Christopher or the magic of the circle she wasn't sure. But it was definitely a warning. "Perhaps we could help you defeat her. Wouldn't that be better?"

"You think I'd trust a Druid?" George sneered.

On the altar, Elias stirred and Rhys sidled closer to him, his dagger at the ready. Rosalind stepped nearer to George to mask Rhys's movement. "Please, my lord, we wish you no harm."

George's laughter was wild and edged with fear. "Liar. You all lie to me. Do you think I'm dim-witted?" He lunged for Rosalind and she let him catch her and pin her against his chest. She gagged as his foxlike stench surrounded her. Rhys moved too and his knife blade flashed out, freeing Elias's bounds.

She is coming! Christopher's blunt warning screamed in Rosalind's head, and she looked up to see Anne Boleyn and Christopher entering the stone circle. Anne had a knife to Christopher's throat, but he looked as calm as Rosalind.

"Well, isn't this nice," George sneered. "My 'sister' and one of her paramours have joined us. Have you come to watch them die, Anne?" He preened like a peacock. "I lured them all here, even the mighty Elias Warner, the man you consider more worthy than me. I'm quite happy to kill them all if it makes you look at me again."

While George was distracted, Rosalind glanced at Rhys, who nodded. She elbowed George in the stomach, ignored the burning heat of his blade as it skimmed over her throat, and rolled neatly out of his way. Elias sat up and Rhys tossed him his dagger.

Anne moved past Christopher and confronted George, her black velvet skirts sweeping over the cracked stone floor, her ruby necklace shining more brightly than Elias's spilled blood.

"You are such a fool, George. You aren't strong enough to kill them, and I'm certainly not going to help you." She nodded disdainfully at Rosalind and Rhys. "If I destroy these two, my bargain with the Druids will be void, and I cannot afford to do that. And, despite his betrayal, I need Elias too. He is so powerful he can work with the Vampire Council to make things more favorable for me."

George hissed and pointed his dagger at her throat. Anne laughed, the sound grating. "You don't have the courage to kill me. I *made* you."

"I've had enough of this." Elias got down from the altar, his normally silver eyes glowing red. He stalked up to George and glared at him. George fell to the ground, his fingers clawing frantically at his throat as if someone was squeezing the life out of him.

Anne held up her hand. "Stop it, Elias."

"He tried to kill me."

"If you let him live, I'll leave you alone. I won't betray you to the Vampire Council and I'll reinstate you as my premier adviser."

Elias looked unconvinced. "Why do you want him?"

"Because his death at this particular time would cause me difficulties with the king. I need him to live and play the part of my devoted brother."

Elias waved his hand, and George fell forward gasping and wheezing. "I accept your terms, my lady."

Anne kicked George in the ribs. "If you wish to survive, you will continue to serve me as my 'brother' and you will be grateful for my mercy for the rest of your pitiful existence. Do you understand?"

George gave a muffled sob. Anne snapped her fingers and he disappeared.

Rosalind was aware of Rhys coming to stand by her right shoulder and Christopher to her left, both of them protecting her. Anne swung around to stare at them, and the men tensed.

Her black gaze flitted over Rosalind. "I want to kill you

so badly, but I can't. One day, however, I *will* find a way to have you murdered. Don't ever doubt it."

Anne came closer until she was eye to eye with Christopher. "You have betrayed me, Kit. I gave you every chance. I told you how she concealed your own child from you. Yet here you are, still at her side. You chose her over me."

"I love her, my lady."

"Ha!" Disgust rang through Anne's voice as she brought her hand up to cup Christopher's chin. "What a terrible shame you have no claim on me at all. Because unlike her, *you*, my dear friend, *can* be punished."

With one savage motion, Anne angled Christopher's neck and her fangs flashed out.

"No!" Rosalind screamed and yanked Christopher away, but not before his blood spurted out and he crumpled to the ground. Anne disappeared, Christopher's blood still smeared on her laughing mouth.

Chapter 26

Rosalind sank to her knees in front of Christopher and desperately tried to staunch the flow of blood. Rhys and Elias joined her and lifted Christopher to lie on the sacred altar. Rosalind stared wildly at Rhys. "What can we do? I can't stop the bleeding!"

Rhys handed her his kerchief, and she pressed it to Christopher's torn throat, watched it instantly redden.

"We can pray to the gods to help us save him, my lady."

"There must be something else! How far away are we from Mistress Hopkins or a surgeon?"

"Too far, even if we could move him." Rhys grimaced and glanced down at Christopher's pale face. "Pray for him, Rosalind. That's the only thing we can do for him now."

"That isn't good enough!" She was aware that she was shouting, but she didn't seem able to stop. Elias touched her shoulder.

"I could turn him into a Vampire," Elias said quietly. "If he loses all his blood, I could at least do that for him."

Rosalind stared at Elias, who held her gaze and allowed her to see the sincerity of his offer in his silver eyes. Would Christopher want that? Traitorous thoughts slid into her mind. If he was truly a full Vampire, at least he would know who he was and have a family and a half sister ... but he wouldn't want her and their child, would he? And he would be turning into her worst nightmare.

"Rosalind, no! How can you even consider such a thing?" Rhys said urgently. "You will be denying his soul eternal rest!"

Rosalind stared at Rhys's anguished face. "But I cannot bear to watch him die. Surely he deserves another chance?"

"A chance to become a blood-sucking monster?"

"Not all Vampires are monsters, Rhys. Even I have realized that." With trembling bloodied fingers, she pushed back a lock of Christopher's dark hair and took a long shuddering breath. She loved him. It seemed she had no choice.

"If that is the only way left to save him, Elias, then do it."

As if her words had been a channel to the world beyond, a bright light enveloped the stones, and the white-haired Druid Elder, Lady Alys, stepped through the upright stones behind the altar. Elias covered his eyes and backed away, leaving Rhys and Rosalind huddled over Christopher.

Lady Alys smiled at Rosalind. "You have made a brave, loving choice, my daughter. Your sacrifice is deemed worthy of the gods. Now step away from your mate and let me attend to him."

When Rhys grabbed Rosalind firmly by the shoulders and pulled her against his chest, a sob tore from her throat. The female Druid laid her hand on the ragged gash on Christopher's throat, and her lips moved in silent prayer. Power flooded the small space, vibrating through Rosalind's heart and heating her very bones.

Rhys shuddered too, his grip on her tightening until it hurt.

On the altar, Christopher groaned and tried to sit up. The Druid Elder placed her hand on his chest and held him down. "Do not be so eager, my friend. You need to heal."

Rhys let go of Rosalind, and she realized she was crying. "Thank you, my Lady Alys."

The Druid smiled. "Despite his ancestry, this male has already shown himself to be worthy of our help and of you." Her gaze drifted over them. "As have you all. Even you, Elias Warner." Elias rose to his feet, a wary look in his eyes. The Druid smiled. "Do not fear me. I wish you no harm, Vampire."

Elias slowly nodded. "Thank you."

Wiping away her tears, Rosalind approached Christopher, who was trying to lever himself up on one elbow. "It seems you have survived again," she said. "Fortune does favor fools."

His grin was full of pain. "Aye."

Rosalind spun around to confront the Druid. "Anne Boleyn deserves to die for this! I don't care about our bargain. I cannot *bear* to see her sit on the throne with her son to succeed her!"

The Druid's laughter was sweet, melodious, and so unexpected that it stopped Rosalind's anger. "Anne Boleyn will not sit on the throne for long. In five of your years, she will no longer exist."

"How can that be?" Rosalind asked. "Haven't we given her *everything* she needs to survive?"

"Some people are never satisfied, and Anne Boleyn is one of them. When she fails to give the king the son he desires, she becomes desperate enough to break her bargain with us, and so brings about her own downfall."

Rhys cleared his throat. "But, my lady, with all due respect, your magic promised her a son."

The Druid shook her head. "No, our magic promised her a child who would inherit the throne."

"I do not understand," Rosalind whispered.

"The fertility spell will work, but Anne will bear only one living child to the king, a girl who will be named Elizabeth."

"But a woman cannot rule this kingdom."

"Not yet. But by the time Elizabeth is a young woman, she *will* reign, and reign for many glorious years."

"Without her mother by her side."

"Indeed. Her mother and George Boleyn will be executed for adultery, incest, and high treason. Between us and the Vampire Council, who will also be out for vengeance on Anne, we will make sure the king has all this information at hand. Elizabeth will never know her mother or her mother's true ambitions for her."

"I wish I could feel sorry for Anne, but I don't," Rosalind replied.

As Christopher listened to the incredible conversation, he struggled to sit up and swing his legs over the side of the altar, which was now streaked with both his and Elias's blood. As he watched, the blood seemed to sink into the stone and disappear. Gingerly, he felt his neck and found no sign of the open wound he'd feared, only smooth skin. His left arm appeared to have been healed as well.

Rosalind looked shaken and angry, yet she was still determined to go after Anne for his sake. That warmed him, made him want to stumble over to her and wrap her in his arms. He doubted she'd let him touch her yet, though; soothing Rosalind's ruffled feathers might take the rest of his life. He let that astounding thought sink in. He *had* a life to lead. He was finally free and he intended to make the most of it.

Rosalind finally glanced in his direction and frowned. "The lady told you to stay where you were."

"I am staying here. I'm just sitting up."

He looked at Lady Alys and bowed as best he could. "Thank you for saving my life."

"You deserve to be saved. You have taken great risks for our race, a race you were brought up to hate and fear."

"I have done what I have out of love, my lady," Christopher replied. "Lady Rosalind knows that."

"And you will continue to protect her?"

Christopher placed his bloodied hand on his heart. "For the rest of my life."

The Druid nodded and opened her arms wide. "My blessings on you all." Light streamed from her fingertips and she was devoured by it until nothing remained but shining dust motes.

Elias strolled over to Christopher and stood contemplating the stone altar. Christopher frowned at him. "Elias, I can sense you in my head."

Elias touched the side of his face where a purpled, bloody bruise flowered. "George caught me unawares and hit me on the head. As I lost consciousness, I managed to direct our journey here, but that was all I could do to help."

"Elias, do you not wish to discuss our new bond?"

Elias sighed. "If I must. Perhaps it is because our blood flowed together over this sacred stone." He glanced dubiously at the ancient inscriptions. "Maybe it will wear off."

"If it does not, then we are almost family, Elias," Christopher said.

Elias met his gaze. "It would seem so, and for me that is indeed a gift, as I have no one else left."

Christopher held out his hand. "Thank you for your help."

"Nay, I must thank you all. I never expected you to rush to save me."

Rosalind came forward and kissed Elias on the cheek. "Of course we came. We care for you."

While Rosalind was close, Christopher reached for her hand and caught it within his. He waited as Rhys obligingly led Elias a little away from them. "Am I forgiven, then?"

She looked down at their clasped hands. "No, you are not."

"Even though I nearly died three times in one night, and you even agreed to let Elias turn me into a Vampire if I would only live?"

"You heard that?"

"It was the very last thing I heard, and you were extremely brave even to consider it."

She colored. "It was nothing."

"It was everything, love. You chose to give me up to my Vampire family, knowing it might mean the end of everything we had together. You chose to protect me."

"I—I preferred that you survived."

"Why did you want me to survive?" he asked gently.

"Because . . ."

She still wouldn't look at him, and it irked him greatly. "Rosalind?"

She raised her gaze to his, and her eyes were full of tears. "Because even when I want to hate you, it appears that I cannot. Are you satisfied now?"

He hid a smile. "Completely, love." He squeezed her fingers. "If you will allow me to explain my actions, surely you'll understand why I did what seemed necessary to protect you."

"Ah, it was all about protecting me, and not about your foolish notions of male superiority?"

Christopher closed his eyes for a brief moment. "Rosalind, I'm tired, and I don't want to argue with you, but there is one thing I must know. Where is our babe?"

She laughed. "Where do you think—in a chest in my room?"

"Rosalind . . ."

"Oh, for goodness' sake." She grabbed his hand and placed it over her belly.

He gulped in some much-needed air. "What? Not back in Wales?"

"Christopher, I am but a month or two increasing."

He sagged against her shoulder. "I thought you'd already had the child."

"When I was in Wales?"

"Aye. Anne said— Well, she told me that you'd had my babe and hidden it away from me." He didn't dare tell her the horrific thing Anne had suggested she'd done with the child. He'd save that confession for another day, preferably one when there were no weapons at hand.

Rosalind pulled away from Christopher. "Why didn't you ask me?"

"I did. You seemed to confirm it. You said that what you chose to do with your child was none of my business."

She sighed. "And I thought you knew I was breeding and didn't want the child. I was so terribly hurt. And I was afraid you would send me away from the fight."

He paused to think about that, and then resolutely met her gaze. "And I probably would have."

There was another long silence and then he took her hand again. "We have been at cross-purposes, have we not?"

"I suppose we have, but that does not explain our *wedding*."

Christopher brought her hand to his lips and kissed it. "Love, we have the rest of our lives to argue about that, *and* for you to prove what a worthless knave I truly am. Can we not let it be for now? I would dearly love to hold you." She remained stiff, her gaze directed away from him, and he kissed her fingers again. "Please, Rosalind."

With a muffled cry, she flung herself into his arms and he held her tight, his soul rejoicing at this new start, this fresh opportunity to finally live his life with the woman he loved. He cupped her chin and brought her mouth up to meet his and kissed her with everything he was. She kissed him back, gave him her mind too, her lips fierce and hot and desperate.

He drew back and gazed at her. "I do want this babe, Rosalind. I want our child to know he was created out of love, and that no matter how complicated his bloodlines, he is ours to cherish and protect." He brushed the lush curve of her lower lip with his thumb. "Who better to raise an unusual child than two misfits like us?"

"There is that." Rosalind swallowed hard, her eyes bright with unshed tears. "You assume it will be a boy, then."

He grabbed her hand and held it against his chest. "It has to be a boy. I cannot imagine dealing with a little girl like you, my love. My heart would surely fail."

She smiled at him and everything in his life suddenly made sense. She was *his* future as well as the future mother of his child. What more could any man want?

Rhys cleared his throat and Christopher reluctantly drew back. "What is it?"

"Elias and I believe it will be safer to remove yourselves from court while Anne lives out the rest of her days."

"And how do you propose we do that?"

Elias stepped forward. "You have not yet visited the property the king has gifted you to go with your elevation into the peerage. I suggest you take Lady Rosalind there immediately."

Abruptly, Rosalind straightened away from Christopher. "We are not running away, Elias. If Anne wants to fight, we'll fight her."

Christopher wrapped his arm around her waist and drew her back against him. "No, we will not."

She turned to stare at him, her brown eyes wide and anguished. "Why not?"

"Because you were right. I cannot risk our child."

She pushed him away. "You cannot order me around like that!"

"You are my wife. You promised to obey me, remember?"

"But I didn't mean it!"

Rhys touched her elbow. "Rosalind, stop thinking about what you want and consider the babe. Elias pointed out that your child will be of interest to both the Druids and the Vampires."

Rosalind wrenched herself out of Christopher's embrace and walked away from them, her arms wrapped around her waist. "I will not let anyone take my child."

Christopher wanted to smile at the heat in her voice. She would make a ferociously protective mother, and he was glad of that. "Then you must listen to reason. I'm not suggesting you leave court by yourself. I will be with you." He grimaced. "I'm not going to be very welcome around here either. We will keep the child safe together."

"But where?" She stared at him. "Where will such a child be safe?"

"That is what I was going to tell you, my lady," Elias interrupted. "The estate that the king has bestowed on Lord Christopher has a most interesting feature."

"What do you mean?"

Elias smiled. "The manor house at Avebury is set within an ancient stone circle, which will offer you protection against the Vampires. That is why I suggest you and Lord Christopher leave for there immediately."

Rosalind locked gazes with Christopher. "Is this what you truly want to do?"

He nodded.

"Not fight on?"

"No, love."

She swallowed hard and her shoulders sagged. "Then for the sake of the babe, I agree."

Christopher went toward her and wrapped her in his arms. "You will never regret this, my lady. For as long as I draw breath on this earth, I will keep you and the babe safe."

"I know that, although I am quite capable of seeing to that task myself." She relaxed against him for the first time, and he gladly held her close. He kissed her forehead, her cheek, her ear, any part of her he could reach, and she sniffed. "I still haven't forgiven you, though."

He thought his heart would overflow at her querulous tone. "Of course not."

"And I still want an explanation."

"Once we are safely away, you shall have all the explanations your heart desires, and a proper wedding if you require one."

Christopher looked up at Rhys and Elias. "Do you really think we should leave now?"

Both men nodded and Rhys spoke. "As soon as you can pack your bags, my lord. All is ready for you at the manor. Elias has made sure of that. In truth, he 'helped' the king pick this particular property for you."

"You will stay here and weather the storm?"

Rhys glanced at Elias. "We will. I will write to you regularly and keep you informed."

Christopher nodded. "And will you send Olivia my thanks, Rhys?"

Something like regret flickered in Rhys's eyes. "Of course, my lord."

Christopher managed a smile. "Then all is well." He looked down at the top of Rosalind's head and kissed it. "It's not the end of the world, love. I'm sure the Llewellyns will be back to save the king another day."

Rosalind gazed at him and then at Rhys and Elias, her head held high like a queen. "The Llewellyns will *never* leave the monarch unprotected against the Vampire threat."

Christopher took her hand and urged her toward the exit. "Let's go and pack, and we can be on our way as soon as we have the king's permission to leave."

Rosalind paused. "And what exactly do we tell the king?"

"That he is safe for now, but that he should remain ever vigilant."

Rosalind sighed. "What on earth will happen next?"

Christopher found himself grinning down at her. "That remains to be seen, my love, but I can guarantee the Vampires will be busy plotting again."

"But we will have five years of peace." She leaned her head against his shoulder. "At least we will have that."

And many more years, if Christopher had his way. With all the time he intended to spend pleasuring Rosalind in bed, he hoped they'd have more than one child to worry about and distract their mother. And if the king ever did call on Rosalind again, he'd be right by her side in the midst of any fight. He took her hand and led her up the slope of the valley.

It was time to enjoy this respite while Anne Boleyn destroyed herself and not worry about whatever came next. The mere thought of having his own home, and his wife and child in it, made him swallow down the most unmanly desire to cry.

Rosalind looked up at him and caressed his cheek. At least she understood him. Perhaps he should simply enjoy the freedom to *live* in peace with the woman he loved. Dubiously, he studied his bloodthirsty wife. It would be hard to convince Rosalind to give up her weapons, but he was a very persuasive man, and it would certainly be fun trying.

Turn the page for a special preview of

Mark of the Rose

Coming in August 2011 from Signet Eclipse.

Avebury Manor, England, 1537

"Rhys! Where are you?"
Rhys Williams stirred and half opened his eyes.
Bemused, he stared up at the leafy fronds of the willow
tree above his head and blinked at the brightness of the sun
slanting through the green darkness. His tangled dreams
of a black-haired Vampire faded as he registered the impatient tone of his best friend and fellow Vampire slayer,
Rosalind Llewellyn.

No, not Llewellyn anymore—Ellis. Even after all these
years, her married name still sat uneasily on his tongue.

"Rhys!"

He sat up, knowing that if he didn't attend to her, she'd
come and find him, and in her current condition, that might
be unwise. Her husband would not thank Rhys for exposing his precious wife to the blistering summer heat. Rhys
left the blanket on the ground, pushed aside the heavy cur-
tain of hanging branches and headed back toward the tall,
elegant manor house, where Rosalind awaited him.

Despite his best efforts, his heart still beat harder when
he saw her. Seven years had passed since she'd married the
Druid slayer, and yet she seemed content to bear Christo-

pher's children and love him despite being disowned by her family. Rhys envied their happiness, and still occasionally wished he had succeeded in gaining her love for himself.

Rosalind shaded her eyes and smiled up at him. "Were you asleep?"

"Aye."

She tucked her hand into the crook of his elbow and walked with him toward the kitchens. "Is your arm still giving you pain?"

"None at all. Because of your excellent care, I am more than ready to leave and go back to my duties."

Rosalind shivered. "Promise me to be more careful, Rhys. When you first arrived here, I thought you were going to lose that arm."

He patted her hand. "I'll be careful. It's not every day a man walks into a Vampire ambush."

She sighed. "I fear you are taking too many risks."

"You don't need to worry about me, Rosalind. I'm more than capable of dealing with a few Vampires."

"So I've heard. Your reputation as a slayer these days far exceeds my own."

He held open the door that led into the back wing of the house. "Unlike you, I have nothing else to do with my time."

"You could come and visit us more often."

"I'm not supposed to visit you at all. Your grandfather has expressly forbidden it. I come when I can and I am very grateful for the care you have given me."

Rosalind bit her lip and turned away from him. "I wish I could fight with you again. I'd keep you safe."

Rhys opened the door into the large homely kitchen and waited for Rosalind to walk past him. The smell of baking bread made his mouth water. "I don't think Christopher would let you fight with me."

"I surely would not." A dark-haired man with startling blue eyes looked up from his perusal of the documents spread out on the table. His narrowed gaze passed over

Rhys and came to rest on Rosalind. "Not while you are carrying our child, my love."

Rosalind sniffed and went to sit beside her husband. Rhys followed more slowly and took the bench seat on the opposite side of the oak table. His attention was caught by the king's royal seal.

"What have we here?"

Christopher grinned at him. "We have finally been rewarded by King Henry for our part in the downfall of Anne Boleyn." Christopher pushed a parchment adorned with numerous seals and signatures over to Rhys. "You will enjoy this." He pretended to preen. "I have been made an earl."

"Congratulations, my lord." Rhys couldn't help liking Christopher despite himself. The man was not only a worthy opponent on the battlefield but he had a good heart and all the skills of a diplomat, when he chose to use them.

Christopher handed him another document. "And you, my friend, have been created a baronet."

"A what?" Rhys grabbed hold of the thick parchment and began to struggle his way through the complex Latin phrases. Christopher pointed at a section halfway down the page, and Rhys read his own name. He looked up at Christopher. "What exactly does that mean?"

"It means that you are now *Sir* Rhys Williams, and you have a title to pass down to your children."

Rhys grimaced. "An English title."

"An English title bestowed upon you by a Welsh king. I do not believe it would be wise to refuse such an honor," Christopher said gently.

Rhys stared at his elaborately inscribed name. "It doesn't sit well with me. My country has been destroyed by the English monarchy. What will they think of me at home if I come back with a title?"

"If they have any sense, they will welcome your elevation."

"I suppose I have no choice but to accept this honor and

make the best of it." Rhys sat back and contemplated his hosts. "Was that why you called me, Rosalind?"

She frowned at him. "That isn't enough for you?" She shared a quick glance with Christopher. "Unfortunately, the other news isn't so good. We had a letter from Elias Warner."

"He's still at court, I presume." Rhys said.

While Anne Boleyn was alive, Rhys had visited the court infrequently, knowing Anne would exact vengeance on all those she believed had tricked her into giving up her quest to turn the king into a Vampire.

"Elias is still there, looking out for the interests of the Vampire Council."

"And why did he write to you?"

Rosalind handed him Elias's letter. "He is concerned that there is a plot afoot to destroy Queen Jane." Rosalind's hand went to her own rounded belly. "All is not well with her and he fears she will not live long enough to deliver the king's child."

"If she is ill, there need be no plot nor Vampire at fault." But in truth an uneasy feeling stirred in Rhys's gut.

"You may be right, but we must investigate. He asks us to return to court and help discover what ails the queen."

Christopher stirred and put his hand over Rosalind's. "Rosalind and I can't leave the protection of the manor house and the stone circle. We have to think of the babe, and Nicholas, of course—he needs to be protected at all times, Rhys. You know that. And while Rosalind is breeding, I am the only person who can take on that responsibility."

Rhys let out a frustrated breath. Rosalind and Christopher's son, Nicholas, was now six and a delightfully normal child—apart from his abilities to sense the undead and communicate his thoughts directly to his parents. Despite their attempts to conceal his interesting powers, both the Druids and the Vampires were aware of him, and that was not good. Only the protection of the stone circle that surrounded the village and the manor house kept the Vampires at bay. Leaving Nicholas without the protection of at least one strong slayer could be disastrous.

Rhys straightened his spine. "So you think I should go and represent us all. But I'm not a Llewellyn. I have no special access to the king or the queen. Would not your cousin Jasper be the better choice?"

Rosalind produced another letter and showed it to Rhys. "Jasper has been wounded and has returned to Pembrokeshire."

"Then who, in God's name, is guarding the king?"

"His sister, Verity. She wrote to me to explain what had happened to Jasper and to ask for my help."

"Little Verity Llewellyn?" Rhys shook his head. "What does she know about fighting Vampires? The last I heard of her she was getting married."

"She is a widow and has come to court to serve the king and queen. She felt it was her duty."

Rhys snatched the letter out of Rosalind's hand and read it impatiently. "She should've stayed home, minding her own business. How does she think she can help? She has no training, and no ability to fight."

He pictured Verity in his mind, her sweet face, her long blond hair and shy smile. They'd shared a childhood in the rambling Welsh manor house of Sir John Llewellyn, along with Rosalind and her siblings. The thought of Verity running into even the most inept of Vampires made his blood run cold. He placed the letter on the table and smoothed it out with his fingers.

"It seems as if I have no choice. Someone has to stop Verity Llewellyn from doing something foolish."

Rosalind gave him a relieved smile. "I'm so glad you've decided to go. Verity will definitely need your help."

Rhys shoved a hand through his damp auburn hair and groaned. "I just hope I am not so busy acting as her nursemaid that I have no time to deal with this problem with the queen."

Christopher gathered up the documents and separated

them into two piles. "I'm sure you'll do fine, Sir Rhys. With your new status you will be able to mingle more freely with the gentlemen of the court, and Verity is already established as one of the queen's ladies."

Rhys studied Verity's neat handwriting. She'd written in Welsh, which was as good as code, as most Englishmen couldn't understand it. He tried to remember how long it had been since he had seen her, how long since he'd returned to the only home he'd ever known.

"How old *is* Verity now?"

Rosalind looked up at him. "She is of a similar age to me, I believe—about five and twenty."

"And she hasn't married again?"

"Not all women wish to be married, Rhys. Maybe she loved her first husband so desperately, she has sworn never to have another."

"And maybe she is just contrary, like most of the Llewellyn women," Christopher murmured, then grunted as his wife elbowed him in the ribs. "I'm certain she will be glad to see you, Rhys, and more than willing to learn anything you can teach her. I imagine she only means to remain at court until Jasper is recovered."

Rhys nodded and took the papers Christopher had given him to take back to his bedchamber to study them further. He went up the worn staircase to his rooms deep in thought. If Elias was worried enough to contact the Druids, things must have been dire indeed. The thought of Verity being alone at court surrounded by such evil made Rhys shudder.

He surveyed his meager possessions and packed them into his saddlebags. In his career as a Vampire slayer he'd learned not to become attached to possessions or to people. Apart from Rosalind, and where had that led him? He thrust that thought away and flexed his left arm. His wound had healed well and it was time for him to leave.

Rhys started cleaning his weapons and stowing them away in his pack. If he was lucky, he might be able to persuade Verity to go home straightaway and then deal quickly with the situation himself. He smiled as he gathered his daggers up to take to the smithy for sharpening. Knowing how sweet and malleable Verity was, he didn't anticipate much of a problem.

Richmond Palace

Rhys tugged irritably at the stiff linen shirt Rosalind had insisted on making him to go with his new doublet and hose. Despite his birth, he was far more accustomed to playing the servant than the master, and he felt decidedly out of place. It was already hot in the packed outer court of the king's audience chamber, where he waited with all the other hopeful petitioners to be seen by his monarch. Christopher had instructed him to present his new papers to the king's official and wait to be escorted into the royal presence.

"Sir Rhys Williams?"

"Aye." He looked up at the man dressed in black who had called out his name, and with some difficulty, pushed his way through the crowded room.

"The king will see you now."

Rhys managed a grateful smile and followed the court official past the guards and into the relative quiet of the king's presence chamber. Of course, the king was never alone, being constantly attended to by the gentlemen of his bedchamber and members of his Privy Council, but at least Rhys could breathe more freely.

"Ah, Sir Rhys. It is a pleasure to welcome you back to court."

"Your Majesty does me great honor." Rhys stepped forward and knelt at the king's feet. Rubies glinted on the king's leather shoes.

"You may rise, Sir Rhys."

Rhys stood and fixed his gaze on the king's massive chest. It was only the second time he'd been this close to King Henry, and he felt the power and authority that radiated from him.

"I have received a letter from Lord Christopher Ellis recommending you to my service, Sir Rhys."

"I would be honored to serve you in whatever capacity you require, Your Majesty." Rhys hated the obsequiousness in his voice, but what else could he do? In order to save the king from the Vampire threat, he needed to be as close to him as the Vampires.

"My chamberlain will find you a suitable position."

"Thank you, sire." Rhys bowed low again and backed away as the next petitioner was announced. He would not share Elias Warner's concerns with the king until he had spoken both to the Vampire and to Verity Llewellyn. There might be nothing amiss at all.

One of the king's gentlemen touched his shoulder when he reached the door. "Sir Rhys, you may lodge in the east tower with the other single gentlemen. Send your servant with your bags to Master Hugh Fraser and he will assist you."

"Thank you." Rhys found himself smiling as he walked away. He hadn't brought a servant with him, only his horse, Artio, so he supposed he would be unloading and taking his own bags to Master Fraser. He paused and beckoned to one of the pages who was passing through the hall.

"Where are the queen and her ladies, boy?"

"They are in the pleasure gardens, sir."

Rhys was already familiar with the layout of the palace, so he had no difficulty finding his way to the gardens. His thoughts turned to the last time he had been at court, and to beautiful Olivia Del Alonso, Christopher's half sister. He had never spoken of her with Christopher but often wondered what had become of her. Was she still at court and would she remember him? He wasn't sure if he wanted to see her or not. She'd seemed so young for a Vampire and so ... unspoiled. Seven years might have changed her into a hardened killer who would be happy to suck him dry. One never knew with Vampires.

He shaded his eyes against the bright sunlight and

searched until he found a cluster of well-dressed ladies sitting in the shade of some oak trees.

Queen Jane was easy enough to spot. She sat in the center of her ladies and wore a gray silk gown stitched with pearls, which matched those on her gable headdress. Rhys had no memory of meeting Jane Seymour before she had married the king, but even he could see that she looked pale and tired.

He approached the group, and waited until one of the ladies drew the queen's attention in his direction. When she gestured for him to approach, he moved closer and went down on one knee.

"I apologize for disturbing you, Your Majesty. I am Sir Rhys Williams. I wished to make myself known to you, and to a distant cousin of mine whom I believe is among your ladies."

The queen's smile was small but polite. "It is a pleasure to meet you, Sir Rhys. Which one of my ladies is your kinswoman?"

Rhys smiled back. "I wish it were all of them, Your Majesty, but I seek Lady Verity Llewellyn."

"Lucky Verity," someone whispered as Rhys tried not to react to the wave of feminine interest surrounding him.

"I am here, Your Grace."

Rhys looked up as a woman stepped out from the shadows and came toward him. Her long blond hair was contained by a French hood, and her wary blue gaze was fixed squarely on his face. She was taller than Rosalind and her figure was more rounded, but she had the same remarkable grace.

Queen Jane waved Rhys to his feet. "Mayhap you would wish to speak to your cousin in private, Sir Rhys. You may walk with her in the gardens, but make sure you bring her back before we retire inside."

Rhys bowed low. "Thank you, Your Majesty." He offered his arm to Verity. "My lady?"

Anticipation shuddered through Verity as she rested her

fingers on the silk sleeve of Rhys's brown doublet. He led her back toward the main path that ran around the edge of the garden. She'd almost not recognized him. In the ten years since they'd last met, his skinny frame had filled out and he seemed at ease with both his height and his body. There was an air of command about him now and an edge of hardness to his mouth.

His silk doublet was modestly adorned with black embroidery and cut to flatter his broad shoulders. Unlike some of the gentlemen at court he needed no padding to exaggerate the curve of his calves or to plump out his chest. A workmanlike sword rode on his hip and she guessed that like most Vampire slayers, he had a silver-tipped dagger or two concealed about his person as well.

"It is a pleasure to see you again, my lady."

His soft Welsh accent warmed her. He reminded her of home and safety, of the innocent girl she had been before her marriage. It made her want to fling herself into his arms and beg for his help. But it would not be wise to allow him to think she was weak. She still had no idea why he was here, or what he wanted from her.

"It is a pleasure to see you again, too—is it Sir Rhys now?"

"I have lately been made a baronet."

"How exciting. When did you return to court?"

"I returned this morning." He hesitated and looked down at her, his hazel eyes careful. "I am here on a matter of great importance to us both."

Verity felt a flush come over her face. She attempted a flirtatious laugh and flattened her hand over her jeweled bodice. "I hope you are not an emissary from my grandfather. I have told him a thousand times that I have no wish to entertain any more suitors."

"Of course not. I would never even think—" Rhys's stunned expression and stuttering denial made Verity want to kick him.

"Oh. Of course you have not. I was only teasing." She

squeezed his arm and felt the muscles tense beneath the fine fabric. "Why would you ever think of me in those terms? You only had eyes for my cousin Rosalind."

A flush darkened Rhys's pale skin and he looked away from her. "Your cousin Rosalind is very happily married to another man."

"She married an Ellis. How could she be happy?"

"Trust me, she is."

"You have seen her since her marriage?"

He paused and then glanced around to check that they were alone. Shade from the elm trees that grew along the side of the path put his face into half shadow. "That is why I am here. Rosalind asked me to come and assist you."

"She received my letter?" At his nod she continued. "Why couldn't she come herself? Did her husband forbid her?"

"He most certainly did."

"And you allowed him to treat her like that?"

"Rosalind is an extremely bloodthirsty woman, but even she wouldn't consider herself capable of fighting Vampires in the seventh month of her pregnancy."

"Oh"—Verity stared at him—"I can see that might be a hindrance."

Rhys nodded. "Which is why she sent me. I understand your brother Jasper has been injured and that you have gallantly offered to take his place guarding the king and queen. You need no longer worry about that."

Something about the way he spoke to her—kind but dismissive—made her feel small and unnecessary. She raised her chin so that she could look into his eyes and found her attention wandering to the dark auburn of his hair and the way the sunlight brought out the copper and crimson in it.

She forced herself to focus and struggled to appear confident. "There is always supposed to be a member of the Llewellyn family guarding the king and queen. It is our duty."

"I know that." He hesitated. "But some of the Llewellyn

family have trained their whole lives to protect the monarchy."

"And some of them have not." She paused. "Like me, you mean."

"I'm sure your intentions are good, Verity, but in all conscience, I can hardly allow you to risk your life in the service of the Tudors when you have no real notion of what you are doing." He patted her cheek. "It is not a simple task. I trained with Rosalind for years before she became such an accomplished Vampire slayer."

Anger gathered like a fist in Verity's chest. As a child she'd idolized Rhys, had built silly fantasies around how he would marry her one day and they would live happily ever after. Even when she'd realized he was smitten with Rosalind, she thought given the chance she could change his mind. If only she'd really known what an arrogant, patronizing man he would turn out to be, she would have saved herself hours of useless daydreaming.

"I am a Llewellyn. You are not," she said as icily as she could. "As a Druid, your duty is to me and my family."

His brows drew together and he looked genuinely puzzled. "And I am offering to do my duty."

"And dismissing my help."

All traces of amiability disappeared from his face, and she could see the hard strength and purpose beneath the charm. When had he become such an inflexible man? What had changed him?

"My lady, I do not need your help."

"Are you quite sure about that? As a Llewellyn, I have access to the king and the queen that you will *never* have. You need me more than you realize, Sir Rhys." She glared at him. "In fact, perhaps you are the one who is superfluous here and should leave."

Before he could reply, Verity deliberately looked past him toward the queen's party and bobbed a curtsy. "I have to go in now. The queen is retiring. It was a pleasure to see you again, cousin, and I wish you Godspeed on your journey home."

She whisked past him and headed for the safety of the queen's ladies. Indignation filled her thoughts. How dared he presume that she was useless? He hadn't seen her for ten years and his immediate assumption was that because she was female she would only hinder his cause? Had he ever thought that about Rosalind? Somehow she doubted it. Verity wanted to smack his patronizing face but contented herself with walking away from him as if he had never existed.

Rhys remained rooted to the spot and watched Verity chatter to her companions as she walked into the palace. In the sunlight her hair held every color from white to brown gilded with gold like a ripening field of wheat. He wanted to go after her and demand she listen to him but he suspected her answer would have been the same.

He cursed under his breath and headed back to the stables, where he had left his horse and his bags. Unfortunately, some of what Verity had said was true. He did need her cooperation if he truly wanted to solve this mystery of what was wrong with the queen.

It never paid to underestimate a woman, especially a Llewellyn, but he feared he had already fallen into that trap. Christopher would have been amused, but Rhys should've known better. Now he would have to charm his way back into her good graces.

He threw a coin to the stable boy who had been watching his possessions and picked up his bags. Not that charming Verity Llewellyn would be a hardship. She was as beautiful as he had remembered—and he'd always enjoyed a challenge.

ABOUT THE AUTHOR

Kate Pearce was born into a large family of girls in England, and spent much of her childhood living very happily in a dreamworld. Despite being told that she really needed to "get with the program," she graduated from the University College of Wales with an honors degree in history. A move to the U.S. finally allowed her to fulfill her dreams and sit down and write that novel. Along with being a voracious reader, Kate loves trail riding with her family in the regional parks of Northern California. Kate is a member of RWA and is published by NAL, Kensington Aphrodisia, Ellora's Cave, Cleis Press, and Virgin Black Lace/Cheek.

Also Available from

KATE PEARCE

Kiss of the Rose
The Tudor Vampire Chronicles

Desperate to defeat King Richard III and gain the crown,
Henry Tudor made a pact with the Druids binding him
and his heirs to the Druids' struggle against vampires.
Ever since, the Llewellyns, a vampire-slaying family, have
been in the king's employ. Now Henry VIII reigns, and
his father's bargain has been almost forgotten—until
bloodless corpses turn up in the king's bedchamber. To
save the king, vampire hunter Rosalind Llewellyn must
form an uneasy alliance with Druid slayer Sir Christopher
Ellis. But soon, Rosalind must face an unthinkable truth:
that her sworn enemy may be her soulmate.

**Available wherever books are sold or
at penguin.com**